Praise for *My Sister's Grave*

"One of the best books I'll read this year."
—Lisa Gardner, bestselling author of *Touch & Go*

"Dugoni does a superior job of positioning [the plot elements] for maximum impact, especially in a climactic scene set in an abandoned mine during a blizzard."
—*Publishers Weekly*

"Yes, a conspiracy is revealed, but it's an unexpected one, as moving as it is startling . . . The ending is violent, suspenseful, even touching. A nice surprise for thriller fans."
—*Booklist*

"Combines the best of a police procedural with a legal thriller, and the end result is outstanding . . . Dugoni continues to deliver emotional and gut-wrenching, character-driven suspense stories that will resonate with any fan of the thriller genre."
—*Library Journal*, starred review

"Well-written and its classic premise is sure to absorb legal-thriller fans . . . The characters are richly detailed and true to life, and the ending is sure to please fans."
—*Kirkus Reviews*

HER
FINAL
BREATH

HER FINAL BREATH

ROBERT DUGONI

THOMAS & MERCER

Published by Thomas & Mercer, Seattle

www.apub.com

Amazon, the Amazon logo, and Thomas & Mercer are trademarks of Amazon.com, Inc., or its affiliates.

ISBN-13: 9781503945029
ISBN-10: 1503945022

Cover design by David Drummond

Printed in the United States of America

To every man and woman who wears a uniform, carries a badge, and spends their days and nights working in the criminal justice system to keep the rest of us safe. We are often too quick to criticize and too slow to say thank you.

When it comes to psychopaths, there is no medication. There is no treatment. There is no cure. There are only prisons.

—Jeni Gregory, PhD, LICSW, CCM, CCTP

CHAPTER 1

Tracy Crosswhite watched the minivan pull into the parking lot, noting a car seat strapped into the backseat and a yellow "Child On Board" placard dangling in the window. The woman who got out wore a black ballistic vest, blue jeans, and a Seattle Mariners baseball cap.

"Detective Crosswhite?"

Tracy shook the woman's hand and noticed that it felt small and soft. "Just Tracy. You're Officer Pryor."

"Katie. I really appreciate this. I'm sorry to take up your time after hours."

"Not a problem. Teaching helps keep me sharp. Do you have glasses and ear protection?"

"Not my own."

Tracy hadn't thought it likely Pryor would have her own gear. "Let's get you fitted then."

She led Pryor into the squat concrete building, the office of the Seattle Police Athletic Association. Like most shooting ranges, it was remote, at the end of a narrow drive in an industrial area twenty minutes south of downtown Seattle.

The man behind the counter greeted Tracy by her first name, and Tracy made the introduction. "Katie, this this Lazar Orlovic. She'll need eye and ear protection, and we'll need a target, a couple boxes of ammo, and a roll of tape."

"Training for the qualification test? Coming up in what, a couple weeks?" Lazar smiled at Pryor. "You're in good hands." He pulled boxes of ammunition and protective glasses off shelves and hooks behind the counter. "We keep trying to get Tracy to make it official and come down here full-time to train the newbies. What do you say, Tracy?"

"Same as always, Lazar. I'll come when people stop killing each other."

"Right, and when farts stop smelling." Lazar looked around the counter. "I'll have to get the tape from the back."

When Lazar was gone, Pryor asked, "Why do we need tape?"

"To cover the holes in your target."

"I've never seen that done before."

"You've never shot as much as you're about to."

Lazar returned and handed Tracy a roll of blue tape. She thanked him and led Pryor back outside. "Follow me," she said and slid into the cab of her 1973 F-150 Ford truck. She'd sold her Subaru after returning from Cedar Grove. She could have afforded something new, but the older-model truck fit her. The engine took a few minutes to warm, especially on cold mornings, and the body had a few nicks and dents, but overall it didn't look half-bad for its age. Besides, the truck reminded Tracy of the truck her father drove to their shooting competitions when she and her sister, Sarah, were kids.

Two hundred yards down cracked pavement filled with potholes, Tracy parked near the entrance to the Seattle Police Combat Range. She got out to the familiar pop-pop sound of discharging guns and the barking of large dogs. She had no idea what brain trust had decided to put the SPD K-9 kennel adjacent to the shooting range, but she felt bad for the dogs, and anyone who had to spend more than a minute in the kennel listening to them.

The range was accessed through a gate in an eight-foot cyclone fence with a single strand of razor wire strung across the top. Tracy blew warm air into her fists while waiting for Pryor. The weather forecast was typical for a March evening, cold with a light drizzle. Perfect for training purposes.

"How should we start?" Pryor asked.

"You shoot. I watch," Tracy said.

Fifteen plywood shooting stations, or "points," stood twenty-five yards from a metal overhang cantilevering over a sloped hillside littered with spent bullets. Tracy chose the station farthest to the left, closest to the kennel but away from the two men shooting on the right side of the range. She spoke over the barking and the reverberating bursts from the shooters' guns. "We'll start with the failure drill, three yards from the target, three seconds to fire four shots. Two rounds to the body, two rounds to the head."

"Got it," Pryor said.

They clipped the target—a caricature of a "bad guy" with bulging hairy arms and a menacing face—to a piece of pressboard and set it up beneath the overhang. Then they paced back three yards to a mark on the ground. Tracy said, "Low ready."

Pryor unholstered her Glock, pointed the barrel at the ground, and assumed a blade stance, legs shoulder-width apart, left foot slightly forward of the right. Tracy nudged the inside of Pryor's left foot an inch to give her a wider stance.

"Go," Tracy said.

Pryor raised her weapon and fired three shots. As Tracy expected, Pryor flinched with each discharge, which caused the barrel to shift, ever so slightly, off target. She saw it a lot with newbies, especially the female recruits.

"Ready," Tracy said.

Pryor slipped her ear protection off her left ear. "Aren't you—?"

"Low ready," she repeated.

Pryor readjusted the ear protection and retook her stance.

"Go."

Pryor shot again.

"Ready," Tracy said. "Go." And Pryor shot a third time.

She had Pryor repeat the process until she'd emptied the magazine. When Pryor lowered her gun, she was winded from the adrenaline rush.

"Your arms and shoulders getting tired?" Tracy asked.

"A little bit."

"And yet you're shooting better."

"I am," Pryor said, looking at the target through her yellow-tinted glasses.

"I can train you to shoot *better*," Tracy said. "I can't train you to shoot. You have to get past the violence when you discharge your weapon. You're anticipating the noise and the recoil, which causes you to flinch, and that throws your shot off. The only way to get over it is to shoot, a lot. How frequently are you coming to the range?"

"I'm trying to get down here when I can," Pryor said, "but it's hard. I have two little girls at home."

"What does your husband do?"

"He works for a construction company."

"Does he want you to keep your job?"

"Of course. We need the money."

"Then he needs to watch your daughters so you can practice." Tracy showed Pryor her right thumb. "Do you know what that callus is from?"

"Shooting."

"Loading my magazine. I'm here twice a week, rain or shine, night and day. The only way to get better at shooting is to shoot. You fail to qualify and you can't work. They put you in a remedial training program. You carry a stigma. You're a woman, Katie. You don't need any other reason for them to think you're incompetent."

Pryor needed to hear it. Her husband really needed to hear it.

"Now, are you willing to work at this?"

Pryor pulled out her cell phone from the back pocket of her jeans. "Let me call home."

As Pryor stepped away to make the call, Tracy started to reload her magazine. One of the men who'd been shooting at the opposite end of the range approached. "You ladies come down to take out some pent-up female aggression?" Johnny Nolasco was captain of the Violent Crimes Section, Tracy's boss. He was also an ass.

"Just doing a little shooting, Captain."

"Qualifying test coming up," Nolasco said. Despite the cold weather, he wore a skintight short-sleeve shirt, putting the barbed-wire tattoo on his right biceps on full display. "Should we make it interesting?"

Tracy's qualifying target from her graduation from the police academy had replaced Nolasco's target in the trophy case at the entrance to the school. In the intervening twenty years, no one had achieved a higher qualifying score, and Nolasco's ego had never recovered. "I'm good," she said, continuing to reload.

"Not that good," Nolasco said, looking Pryor up and down before leaving.

Pryor ended her phone conversation and stepped back to Tracy. "Who was that?"

"The reason you need to pass your qualifying test."

———

Darkness set in, along with a layer of marine fog that colored the stanchion lights a sickly yellow and reduced visibility. Tracy encouraged Pryor to ignore the elements and focus on subtle shooting techniques, like how to properly use her gun sight. "If you can shoot in this lighting and this weather, you'll be more confident shooting during the test."

"What's your best qualifying score?" Pryor asked.

"One fifty."

"That's a perfect score. Where'd you learn to shoot?"

"I did a lot of shooting competitions growing up. It was a family thing. We were judged on speed and accuracy. It's like anything you do; if you want to do it well, you have to work at it. The main thing is a lot of repetition and developing good habits."

Pryor flexed her fingers, then blew into her fist.

"Your hands are sore."

"Little bit."

"Get one of those balloons filled with sand and squeeze it when you're on patrol or sitting at home watching television."

"Hey, Tracy!"

Tracy turned. Though he was partially obscured by the fog, she could see Lazar standing outside his plum-colored Plymouth with the door open. He was backlit by the dome light and waving his arms overhead. The car's headlights illuminated the thickening fog, and the tailpipe spit puffy white clouds of exhaust. "Office is locked. Lock the gate when you leave?"

"No problem, Lazar."

Lazar waved again before getting back into his car and driving off, the engine rumbling like a boat.

Tracy had Pryor continue to shoot until they'd run out of ammo. When they'd finished, Pryor wore a contented smile. She'd need more practice, but her shooting had already improved.

"I'll help you pick up the brass," she said, though the spent practice casings were aluminum.

"I'll do it," Tracy said, feeling a little guilty for keeping Pryor late in miserable weather. "You get home. Let's not push your luck the first night."

"What about you?" Pryor asked.

"Just a cat waiting for me. Go on. Get home to your family."

They retrieved Pryor's target, and Tracy walked her to the gate. Pryor handed Tracy the goggles and ear protection to return to Lazar. "Listen, I can't thank you enough."

"Yes, you can. Pass your qualification test. Then pass along what I've taught you."

As the hum of Pryor's minivan faded, Tracy retrieved a five-gallon bucket from beneath the control tower and worked her way back toward the metal overhang, picking up the casings. They rattled in the bucket like spare change. The dogs in the kennel, quiet since Pryor had stopped shooting, began barking again. Tracy stopped, thinking it unlikely they'd heard the clatter of the shell casings. She thought she detected the sound of a car engine and looked to the road, but no headlights reflected in the fog. A click overhead drew her attention, but not before the stanchion lights shut off, bringing a profound darkness. She checked her cell: 9:00 on the nose. Lazar had the lights on a kill switch.

She heard the rattle of the cyclone fence, and thought she saw someone standing near the open gate but couldn't be certain with the fog. She set down the bucket, put her hand on the butt of her Glock, and shouted over the dogs' barking. "I'm a Seattle police officer, and I'm armed. If anyone is there, call out."

No one did.

She kept her hand on her Glock, picked up the bucket, and carried it to the control tower, where she set it against the wall and retrieved Pryor's eye and ear protection—she'd drop it in the slot in the office door on her way out. She walked toward the exit, eyes scanning the road for any sign of movement.

As she passed through the gate, something prickly brushed the top of her head. She jumped back, swiping at air, Glock raised. When no one came at her, she pulled out her phone and pressed the flashlight icon. The sharp light made it more difficult to see, like high beams illuminating fog at night. She stepped closer to the exit and raised the light.

A hangman's noose dangled from a length of rope caught in the razor wire atop the fence.

She quickly assessed her situation. She was alone and, at the moment, exposed. She killed the light.

The noose had clearly not been there when Pryor had left and the stanchion lights were still on. Tracy had not been hearing or seeing things. She was right when she thought she'd heard a car and seen someone standing at the gate. It was a bold act to leave a noose at a police shooting range. Did the person know she was still there or think the range deserted? The fog would have made it difficult for anyone to see her. She dismissed that thought. It was too big a coincidence for someone to leave the noose on a night Tracy was shooting. That meant someone had followed her. The act had been intentional. The question was whether it was personal. The department had come under media fire recently because women's groups were upset about the investigation of a North Seattle erotic dancer strangled with a noose in a motel room. The Nicole Hansen investigation had been Tracy's until her abrupt departure to Cedar Grove for the hearing that had led to the release of her sister's convicted killer. While she was gone, Nolasco sent the Hansen investigation to the Cold Case Unit, sparking an uproar from Hansen's parents and the women's rights groups.

Tracy punched in numbers on her cell. When dispatch answered, she provided her name, badge number, and location, then asked for backup and a team from the CSI Unit.

Disconnecting, she continued to assess her situation. She didn't like being out in the open. Her truck was parked just to the left of the gate. If she could get to it, she could drive back to the entrance of the shooting range to wait for backup.

Tracy shuffled forward, Glock raised. She avoided the noose and stepped through the gate, keeping her back pressed to the fence. Gravel crunched under her boots as she worked her way from the hood down the side of her truck to the driver's door. She retrieved her car key, dropped her gaze to fit the teeth into the lock, and turned the key. The door lock popped. She didn't rush, waiting a beat before pulling the door open. About to get in, she noticed something protruding from the back of the truck bed and realized it was the corner of the spring-loaded window to the truck canopy.

She slid to the rear bumper, paused, then spun and swept the bed. Empty. She spun again and swept the area behind her but saw only the outlines of telephone poles shrouded in fog.

She lowered the canopy window and turned the handle, hearing it latch.

As she made her way back to the truck cab, the dogs in the kennel began to bark again.

CHAPTER 2

Tracy drove back to the street in front of the alley leading to the Seattle Police Athletic Association. She didn't have to wait long for a patrol unit to arrive. She instructed the uniformed officer to string yellow-and-black crime scene tape across the entrance to the alley. Shortly thereafter, she was glad she had. The news vans and reporters arrived, followed by her sergeant, Billy Williams.

"Thought you called it in on your cell," Williams said, eyeing the media.

"I did," Tracy said.

Using a cell phone should have skirted the media, but SPD had long been a sieve. The brass liked to cull favors with reporters by feeding them information, and it was suspected among the detectives in the Violent Crimes Section that they had a leak. Tracy also remained relevant news after what had happened in Cedar Grove.

Williams adjusted a black knit driving cap that had become a fixture since he'd conceded the inevitable and shaved his head. He said the cap provided warmth in the fall and winter and protected his scalp from the sun during the summer. Tracy suspected Billy just liked the look. He'd also grown a pencil-thin mustache and soul patch, which made him look a lot like the actor Samuel L. Jackson.

Kinsington Rowe, Tracy's partner, arrived ten minutes later. Kins got out of an older-model BMW, slipping into a leather car coat. "Sorry," he said. "We were at Shannah's parents' for dinner. What do we got?"

"I'll show you," Tracy said. Kins climbed in the truck cab with her. Billy followed in his Jeep.

"You all right?" Kins asked.

"Me?"

"You seem a little freaked."

"I'm fine." Wanting to change the topic, she said, "Shannah's parents?"

Kins made a face. "We're trying to have Sunday night dinners together to see if it helps. I got caught in a discussion with her father on gun control."

"How'd that go?"

"About as you'd expect."

Tracy swung the truck wide and parked well clear of the entrance to the range. She turned on the wipers to clear the mist from the windshield. The truck's headlights spotlighted the hangman's noose.

"What do you make of it?" Kins asked.

"Not sure. Someone put it up right after the lights went out."

"He wanted you to find it."

"Appears that way."

"Got to be."

They got out of the cab and approached the spot where Williams now stood. "Looks like the same rope," Kins said. "Same color. Can't see the knot."

Nicole Hansen hadn't just been strangled. She'd been hog-tied, with an elaborate system intended to torture the victim. If Hansen straightened her legs, it pulled the rope and tightened the noose.

Eventually, she tired trying to hold the pose and strangled herself. Tracy and Kins had treated it as a homicide, though they didn't immediately rule out the possibility that Hansen had died during a sex act gone horribly wrong. Hard as it was for some to imagine a woman agreeing to such torture, Tracy had seen worse when she'd been assigned to the Sexual Assault Unit. When Hansen's toxicology report revealed Rohypnol, a well-known date rape drug, they scratched that theory.

"So door number one, it's the same guy who killed Nicole Hansen," Kins said. "Door number two, it's somebody angry about the Hansen investigation being sent to cold cases who wants to make a point."

"Could be a copycat," Billy said.

"Door number three," Kins said.

During the Hansen investigation, Maria Vanpelt, a local television reporter, had leaked an expert's opinion that the rope used to strangle Hansen was polypropylene with a Z twist. SPD had loudly protested to the station manager, who'd apologized profusely and said it would never happen again. No one at SPD was holding their breath.

"Whatever the choice," Billy said, "he left it where you couldn't miss it. It means he followed you. I'm going to have a detail keep an eye on you."

"I don't need a babysitter, Billy."

"Just until we figure out what this guy intended."

"I'll put a hole in him before he can get within ten feet of me," Tracy said.

"One problem," Kins said. "You don't have a clue who he is."

CHAPTER 3

A patrol car from the Southwest Precinct parked at the curb in front of Tracy's house in West Seattle's Admiral District as she pulled into the driveway. She gave the officer a wave and drove into a garage far too neat and organized. Furniture and cardboard boxes containing most of her belongings from her Capitol Hill apartment remained neatly stacked on the other half of the two-car space. She'd rented the house fully furnished from an FBI agent who'd moved with his wife to Hawaii but didn't want to sell until certain they'd enjoy living in paradise.

Tracy stepped through the door leading into a small hall off the kitchen, retrieved an open bottle of chardonnay from the refrigerator, and poured herself a glass. Roger, her black tabby, trotted into the room and jumped onto the counter, pacing and mewing. It wasn't love. He wanted to be fed. She had an automatic dispenser for his dry food, but she'd spoiled him by giving him canned food at night. By the time she'd returned home from the shooting range, it was well past the appointed dinner hour. "Typical man," she said, scratching Roger's head and stroking his back. "Now you expect it every night."

She pulled a can of food from the cupboard and dumped it in a bowl. She stood reconsidering her evening, until the intercom buzzed. She crossed the living room with Roger at her heels and pressed the button to activate the intercom at the gate to the nine-foot wrought-iron fence surrounding the front courtyard.

"It's me," Dan said.

Tracy pushed a second button to free the gate's lock, and picked up Roger. He'd become an escape artist, and at this late hour he was also potentially a coyote's meal. She pulled open the front door and gave an "it's okay" wave to the patrol officer as Dan held the gate open for Rex and Sherlock. The dogs, both from a Rhodesian-mastiff mix, weighed more than 280 pounds combined. They shoved through, separated at the fountain in the center of the patio, and converged on Tracy. Wanting nothing to do with them, Roger wriggled free and rushed back inside, likely to high ground. Tracy grabbed the dogs about their snouts and rubbed their fur. "How are my guys, huh? How are my boys?"

Dan set down an overnight bag on the marble entry. "Why is there an officer sitting in a police car outside your front door?"

"I told you, you don't have to ring the buzzer," she said. "You can use the code." The lock on the gate and the front door each had a keypad activated by a four-digit code. Though Tracy and Dan had been dating seriously for three months, Dan had never let himself in, nor had he given her a key to his home in Cedar Grove.

She closed the door. The dogs raced in search of Roger, who stood atop a bookcase, back arched, hissing.

"What's going on?" Dan said.

She held up her glass as she made her way to the kitchen. "You want one?"

"Sure, but I better let them out first." Cedar Grove, the small town where Dan and Tracy were raised and where Dan had recently moved back, was an hour and a half to the north.

She heard him descend the staircase to the lower level, the dogs' paws thundering after him. The house was built on piers. The top story, at street level, consisted of a kitchen, open dining room/living room area, and a master bedroom and bath. It was twice the square footage of Tracy's apartment on Capitol Hill. She never used the lower floor—a family room with a fully stocked bar, L-shaped leather couch, projection television, two bedrooms, and another bathroom. She kept the door at the bottom of the staircase deadbolted. The only time it was opened was when Dan took Rex and Sherlock down to conduct their business in the tiny backyard.

Tracy stepped onto the deck off the dining room. The fog hovered gray and somber over Elliott Bay, obscuring much of the Seattle skyline. On clear nights she had a spectacular panoramic view of the lights in the buildings of downtown Seattle shimmering off the bay's blackened surface, the water taxis skidding like water bugs from Pier 50 to West Seattle, and the illuminated ferries making their way from Colman Dock to Bainbridge Island and Bremerton. The view, and the security, had been what convinced Tracy to rent the home.

Below her, Rex and Sherlock burst out the back door, triggering the motion detector on the floodlights Dan had installed during his last visit. Their bodies cast elongated shadows as they sniffed along the edges of the small patch of lawn abutting a hillside that descended another two hundred feet to Harbor Way, the road along Elliott Bay.

After they'd finished, Dan called to them and they followed him inside. When Dan joined Tracy on the deck, he was slightly out of breath. "The lights are working," he said, accepting his glass of wine.

"I saw."

"Okay, so quit stalling and tell me what happened. Why is there a police car parked outside?"

Tracy told him about the noose.

Dan set his glass down on the table. "And you think it could be the same guy who killed the dancer?"

"I don't know. It could just be a copycat. It could be someone upset about the investigation being sent to cold cases."

"What are the chances it could be a copycat?"

"Greater since Maria Vanpelt reported that Hansen was strangled with a noose and disclosed the type of rope."

"Well, I agree with your sergeant. Whoever it is, the guy followed you. And people don't ordinarily follow cops. This isn't somebody to be taken lightly."

"I know that," she said. "It's why I asked you to come down."

Dan looked momentarily stunned, likely because Tracy wasn't one to often admit feeling vulnerable. The realization that someone had followed her had made her think again of two similar occasions in Cedar Grove. The first time was at the veterinary clinic when Rex got shot. She'd thought someone was watching her from a car. Unfortunately, because of heavy snow she'd been unable to determine the make of car or see anyone inside, so she'd dismissed it. She didn't dismiss it when she saw a car parked outside her motel room late at night with its windshield cleared, though it was snowing heavily. But by the time she'd gone back into the room and retrieved her gun, the car was gone.

"Okay," Dan said finally. "Well, I'm glad you did."

She stepped to him and pressed her face to his chest. His cashmere sweater felt soft and warm against her cheek. He embraced her and kissed the top of her head. She heard the low moan of a foghorn, and thought again of the noose.

CHAPTER 4

He had time to kill.

He shifted his chair—the cheap variety found in banquet halls—so he had a better view of the television mounted to the ceiling in the corner of the room. It was a dinosaur, with a built-in VCR and DVD player. He'd been about to start the videocassette but had become intrigued when the newscaster issued a tease just before going to commercial, a trick that really annoyed him. Apparently, there was breaking news involving a Seattle homicide detective, but first, he'd have to suffer through an inane commercial for Cialis, watching an older man and woman dive into a lake and emerge in a loving embrace.

"Are you watching this crap?" he asked the woman. "They're actors. You know they're actors, right? They pay these people money to announce to the world they can't get it up or they have hemorrhoids." He shook his head. "What some people won't do for a buck, huh?"

The woman mumbled an inaudible response, which was fine, because mercifully, the commercial had ended and the news was starting. "Shh," he said.

A male anchor sat behind a studio desk, a graphic of a hangman's noose over his right shoulder. "Breaking news tonight—a Seattle homicide detective makes a disturbing discovery at the police department's shooting range," he said. "KRIX investigative reporter Maria Vanpelt is live from the Seattle Police Athletic Association in Tukwila."

The blonde reporter stood in the glow of a camera's spotlight, droplets shimmering on her purple-and-black Gore-Tex jacket. "CSI detectives rushed to the shooting range here earlier this evening," she said.

"They try to make everything so dramatic, don't they?" the man said.

The woman did not respond.

"That was after a homicide detective shooting at the police combat range discovered a hangman's noose."

The man sat up.

"You might recall my exclusive report revealing that exotic dancer Nicole Hansen was strangled with a noose in a motel room on Aurora Avenue," Vanpelt said. "Well, tonight we have learned that the homicide detective leading that investigation was the detective who found the noose at the shooting range."

The screen showed uniformed and plainclothes police officers, along with patrol cars and a CSI van. "The family of Nicole Hansen has been critical of the Seattle Police Department's decision to send that murder investigation to the Cold Case Unit after only four weeks, a decision that also resulted in vocal protests by several women's rights organizations. The police department is declining to comment on whether there is any connection between the Hansen case and the noose found this evening, but it certainly appears to have been intended as a pointed message."

The anchor shuffled papers on the desk. "Thank you, Maria. It is, of course, a story we at KRIX will continue to keep a close watch on."

"Not me." The man picked up the remote, pointed it at the television, and pressed "Play." The VCR clicked and whirred. The screen went black, then filled with static. A moment later, the music started and Bugs Bunny and Daffy Duck danced out from behind a red velvet curtain dressed as vaudeville performers with straw hats and canes. The man sang with them, feeling the comforting warmth begin to radiate through his body.

He had time to kill.

He checked his watch. Not that much time. He struck a match, the flame flaring blue and yellow in the darkened room, and lit the tip of the cigarette until it glowed red. Like America's former esteemed president Bill Clinton, he didn't inhale. He expelled the smoke in the direction of the plastic "No Smoking" sign glued to the yellowed wallpaper outside the bathroom door.

"Time for the show." He leaned forward and pressed the glowing red tip to the sole of the woman's foot.

CHAPTER 5

Tracy awoke at just after four in the morning, after what had been a fitful few hours of sleep. Not wanting to wake Dan, she slipped quietly out of bed. Rex and Sherlock sat up from their dog beds, watching her. She retrieved her cell phone and her Glock from atop the nightstand, grabbed her robe from the back of the door, and started out of the room. Rex lowered back down, emitting a tired moan, but Sherlock stretched his legs and arched his back, then followed Tracy out of the room as if compelled by some sense of chivalry.

Tracy shut the bedroom door and rubbed the bony knob of his head. "You're a good dog, you know that?"

In the kitchen she made tea and rewarded Sherlock with a synthetic dog bone. With Dan staying over regularly, she kept a bag in her pantry. Sherlock followed Tracy into the dining room and dropped at her feet when she sat at the table. Tracy continued to stroke his head and sip her tea, giving her body and mind time to wake. A foghorn moaned again, causing Sherlock's ears to momentarily perk before he resumed chewing on his bone. Outside the sliding glass doors, the fog continued to obscure much of the view.

Except for Sherlock's gnawing, and the occasional creak and tick of the house, it was quiet.

Tracy opened her laptop and hit the keyboard. The screen emitted a soft blue light. With a few keystrokes, she pulled up the website for the Washington State Office of the Attorney General, typed her username and password, and entered the Homicide Investigation Tracking System database. HITS contained information on more than 22,000 homicides and sexual assaults across Washington, Idaho, and Oregon. Detectives could use search words like "rope" and "noose" to search for cases similar to their own. Tracy had reduced the universe of cases to 2,240, then narrowed it to a much more manageable 43 cases when she restricted the search to victims who had not been sexually assaulted.

She and Kins had been surprised when the medical examiner's report revealed no semen in Nicole Hansen's body cavities and no indication of spermicide or lubricants to suggest the use of a condom. Hansen had not been sexually assaulted by the person who had killed her. Tracy had been sifting through the forty-three cases at night, but the process had been slow and laborious. The HITS form required the investigating detective to answer more than two hundred questions on topics that included the manner of death; identifying characteristics of the victim, such as tattoos or birthmarks; and specific details on each person of interest. Paperwork was the bane of every detective's existence, and Tracy had not been surprised to find some of the questionnaires less than complete.

"What do you think, Sherlock?"

The big dog lifted his head from his bone, watching her.

"Do you have any insight?"

His eyebrows arched as if in question.

"Never mind. Eat your bone."

An hour into her review, she'd eliminated three more cases, refreshed her tea, and eaten two pieces of toast. Sherlock lay flopped on his side, gently snoring. Tracy envied him. Out the plate-glass windows, the buildings of downtown Seattle had emerged from the fog—dark silhouettes against a rust morning sky that made Tracy instinctively recite the proverb she'd memorized as a child: "Red sky at night, sailor's delight. Red sky in morning, sailor's warning." She hoped that wasn't the case.

She considered the clock on her computer and decided she had time to review one more HITS file before she needed to wake Dan. She also wanted to take the officer sitting in his cruiser a cup of coffee. She'd done stakeouts. It wasn't much fun, especially when you had to pee. Male officers could bring pee bottles. That wasn't so simple for her.

She began scrolling through the next form. Beth Stinson had been living alone when she'd been murdered in her North Seattle home. Tracy scrolled to the description of how Stinson died, and her interest piqued when she read the words "rope" and "noose." Stinson had been found naked on her bedroom floor with a noose around her neck, her wrists tied behind her back and bound to her ankles. Tracy's pulse quickened. The investigating detective noted that Stinson's bed remained made, likely a detail that struck him as odd given that Stinson had died early in the morning. Tracy and Kins had the same reaction to the neatly made bed in Nicole Hansen's motel room.

"No indication of forced entry into the home," she read aloud, eyes scanning faster. "No indication the killer had searched or disturbed the home." Stinson's purse had been found on the kitchen counter, her wallet flush with $350. Jewelry in her bedroom had also not been stolen. "Not a robbery."

Tracy quickly scrolled to the section asking questions about Stinson's lifestyle. Twenty-one years old, Stinson worked in North Seattle as a bookkeeper for a big-box store. Nothing on the form indicated she partied, brought home men, or was into bondage or rough sex.

She scrolled to the box for question 102, whether the crime had been "sex-related." The "yes" box was checked. She scrolled to question 105:

Was semen found in body cavities of the victim?
☒ *No*
☐ *Yes*

"What?" she said aloud. She reread the two questions. The answers seemed incongruous. It was possible the killer had worn a condom, but Tracy wouldn't know that unless it was in the medical examiner's report. Given the date of the murder, nine years earlier, she wouldn't have access to that information online.

She scrolled to the section on the offender. Wayne Gerhardt, a twenty-eight-year-old Roto-Rooter technician, had made a house call to Stinson's home the previous afternoon. Except for an arrest for driving under the influence, he had no known criminal history. Detectives found a dirty bootprint on Stinson's bedroom carpet that matched the sole of a pair of boots found in Gerhardt's apartment closet. Gerhardt's fingerprints were lifted from surfaces in the bathroom and the bedroom, and from the kitchen counter. Tracy scrolled to question 135, which asked whether Gerhardt's blood, semen, or other forensic evidence, such as hair, had been found on Stinson's body. The "no" box had been checked.

Tracy sat back thinking that also odd. Why would a killer take no apparent precaution to prevent leaving behind fingerprints, yet somehow not leave behind any other forensic evidence? It didn't make sense.

Deciding the similarities to the details of Nicole Hansen's death were enough to warrant pulling the file and talking to the detectives who'd worked the case, she scrolled back to the top of the form.

4. Officer/Detective Last Name: Nolasco 5. First Name: Johnny

"Damn," she said. No way Johnny Nolasco would want her, of all people, digging around in one of his old files.

Her cell phone vibrated on the dining room table. Sherlock sat up as if he'd been shocked. The number on the screen puzzled her. She and Kins were not the homicide team on call.

So why was the on-call sergeant calling her?

CHAPTER 6

Tracy had patrolled the Aurora strip the first year after she graduated from the Academy, when she was assigned to the North Precinct. She'd become even more familiar with it over the past seven years, when she'd investigated several homicides on the strip, including Nicole Hansen's.

Once the main artery in and out of Seattle, Aurora Avenue, also known as State Route 99, was now a multilane thoroughfare with a cluttered skyline of tangled wires strung between telephone poles and traffic lights, and billboards advertising massage and tanning parlors, tobacco shops, and adults-only establishments. A string of motels also lined the strip, some quickly built to house the throng of visitors to the 1962 Seattle World's Fair. Fifty-plus years later, those structures that had not already been razed and replaced by more modern accommodations were showing their age, but they continued on life support, catering to those who now frequented the strip with cold hard cash looking to buy drugs or hire a prostitute.

Tracy slowed her truck as she approached the turn for the Aurora Motor Inn, badged a patrol officer on traffic duty, and drove down a sloped driveway into the parking lot. The Aurora

Motor Inn was typical of the older motels on the strip, a U-shaped two-story auto court with rooms accessed from exterior landings. Kins stood in the parking lot, his hands thrust in his jacket pockets, his chin tucked in the lining of his upturned collar. Billy Williams, who would serve as the scene sergeant, stood beside him. They both squinted at the glare from the truck's headlights.

Tracy zipped up her down jacket and stepped out into the chilled morning air.

"Déjà vu all over again," Kins said.

Williams gave her a "here we go" nod and lifted the glasses dangling from a chain around his neck onto the tip of his nose. His hands shook from the cold as he read from a spiral notepad. "Decedent is Angela Schreiber, a dancer at the Pink Palace." Tracy looked to Kins, who arched his eyebrows. Williams pointed to a glass door beneath a porte cochere. "Manager lives in a unit behind the office. Says Schreiber came in just after one this morning, paid cash."

"Anyone come in with her?" Tracy asked.

"Claims he didn't see anyone with her, didn't pay attention. Didn't care until her time was up and she failed to return the room key."

"He familiar with her?" Tracy asked.

"Says she started coming in a couple months ago. Always alone. Always cash. Always returns the key. Very polite and prompt. Until tonight. When she didn't bring the key back, he went to the room and knocked. When he got no answer, he let himself in. Didn't get far. Went back to his office and called 911. Patrol secured the room. CSI and the ME are on the way. Likely someone from MDOP."

Whenever there was a violent crime in King County, one of the county's most experienced prosecutors was dispatched to the scene as part of the Most Dangerous Offender Project. The prosecutor was assigned to the case from beginning to end, and available to detectives for legal questions or concerns, with the intent to make the investigations more efficient and collaborative. Some of the older detectives resented having prosecutors underfoot at crime scenes, but it had never bothered Tracy.

"You had a look?" Tracy asked Kins.

Kins nodded. "In this instance, a picture is truly worth a thousand words."

Tracy walked to the last door beneath a narrow overhang. Williams had set the interior perimeter with red tape, and a patrol officer stood outside the door holding the scene log. Anyone crossing that line had to sign the log and file a written statement. The brass liked to make appearances at high-profile crime scenes, but they really hated writing statements.

"Were you the responding officer?" Tracy asked, signing the log.

"Yeah."

"Fire department been in?"

"Left about ten minutes ago."

"You note the engine number?"

The officer pulled out a small notepad. "Engine 24."

Tracy would follow up and get the crew's report. It was ludicrous, but the fire department always responded to homicides, ostensibly in case the victim was still alive, and if not, to declare the victim dead. That was more often than not the case, and in many instances easily discernible, but the firefighters stormed the crime scene anyway, screwing up forensic evidence by leaving multiple bootprints that had to be considered and eliminated, stepping on shell casings, and sometimes repositioning the body.

Tracy looked to the edge of the parking lot where the patrol sergeant had set the exterior perimeter with yellow-and-black crime scene tape. "Let's run that tape across the driveway entrance," she said.

"Owner's going to squawk about it."

She wasn't in the mood. "Arrest him if he gets in your way."

The officer departed.

"Bad night?" Kins asked, giving her a look.

"Bad month," she said. "Got a feeling it's about to get a whole lot worse."

She stepped inside the room. Angela Schreiber had toppled onto her side at the foot of the bed, her naked body bound and contorted, head back, neck craning, eyes open. A rope extended through a slipknot and ran down her spine, binding her wrists and ankles. Her legs were bent so severely her heels nearly touched her buttocks.

"Hog-tied," Kins said, standing at the threshold, "like an animal at some sadistic rodeo."

"They don't kill the animals at the rodeo, Kins," Tracy said.

Kins ran a hand through his hair and let out a sigh. "Yeah, well, looks like we got ourselves a cowboy."

—

Angela Schreiber's pupils had turned gray, and her corneas had filmed over. Petechiae, tiny red dots from burst blood vessels caused by excess pressure, spotted her face, a telltale indication of strangulation, though the noose had pretty much ended that debate. As with Nicole Hansen, Tracy estimated Schreiber to be early- to mid-twenties. She was an attractive young woman with a blonde ponytail and a petite figure.

"Was she on her side?" Tracy asked the patrol officer who'd returned. "Or did Fire move her?"

"She was like that," the officer said.

Tracy bent to a knee to look more closely at the soles of Schreiber's feet. "What are those? Are those cigarette burns?"

Kins stepped closer, snapping photographs with his cell phone. CSI would photograph the crap out of the room, but he liked to have his own. Sometimes the camera captured things the eyes didn't see. "I don't recall those on Hansen."

"They weren't there," Tracy said. She looked again to the noose and the rope running down Schreiber's back, then considered the room, typical of the motels on the strip—a double bed with a thin floral bedspread, pressboard furniture, and wallpaper yellowed from cigarette smoke that fouled the air. She did not see any cigarette butts or spent matches.

"Guess we'll be getting Hansen back," Kins said.

Nolasco's decision to send the Hansen investigation to the Cold Case Unit just a month into the investigation was rare, but it was exactly the type of passive-aggressive move Tracy had come to expect from him. It meant that Tracy had an unsolved homicide on her record and indicated that her boss had no confidence she'd solve it. The move backfired, however, when the family protested and the women's rights groups went ballistic. What had been a strangulation of an erotic dancer in a motel room became a lightning rod for activists to push an agenda asserting that the SPD was insensitive to women. The timing could not have been worse. The SPD was already reeling from a Department of Justice investigation that concluded Seattle police officers employed excessive force, and a subsequent federal court decision that found that the department was dragging its feet implementing reforms. The brass wasn't exactly in the mood to have groups of women screaming to the news media.

Tracy considered the worn gray carpet and contemplated the amount of hair, blood, semen, and God-knew-what-else CSI would vacuum up. She didn't envy them. "Forensics is going to be a bitch," she said.

"Maybe this is what they mean by fifty shades of gray."

She gave Kins an eye roll and looked again at the dancer. Tracy wanted to cut the rope, but Stuart Funk, the King County medical examiner, had jurisdiction over the body. She and Kins couldn't touch it. Funk would transport Schreiber back to the ME's office downtown, still naked, bound, and contorted.

A final indignity.

CHAPTER 7

A computer check through the Office of the Secretary of State revealed that a limited liability company, Pink Palace LLC, operated three strip clubs of the same name in Seattle. The president was one Darrell Nash, whose address was a pricey Victorian in the pricey Queen Anne neighborhood.

"Who says sleaze doesn't pay," Kins said, climbing an impressive flight of stone steps.

They'd done a drive-by of the Pink Palace club located just off Aurora a couple of miles from the Aurora Motor Inn. Tracy wanted to get a feel for the magnitude of the operation. As with most things in life, not all strip clubs were created equal, or catered to the same clientele. The Pink Palace looked like one of the more high-end clubs, resembling a modern Cineplex with a glowing neon marquee. A Jumbotron television alternately flashed images of scantily clad, writhing women, and advertised special attractions and discounts. The posted hours revealed the club had closed at two and wouldn't reopen until eleven.

Tracy knocked hard on the front door of Nash's house, sending dogs inside into a barking frenzy. The shirtless man who answered had a serious scowl and some even more serious bedhead. He wore baggy pajama pants. A silver ring pierced his left nipple on an impressive chest above a washboard stomach. A purple-and-gold tiger adorned his right pectoral muscle. He looked like a frat boy roused after a night of partying.

"Do you know what time it is?" he asked.

Already tired and not in the mood for crap, Tracy flashed her shield and ID. "Yes, we do. And I'm guessing it's a lot earlier for us than you." She noticed a woman standing in the entryway. Two young girls in nightgowns clutched her legs. Tracy softened her tone. "We're sorry to disturb you," she said. "Are you Darrell Nash?"

"Yes." Nash winced each time the dogs barked, as if he was nursing a hangover. He yelled over his shoulder, "Can you please go shut them up? And bring me a shirt." He looked back to Tracy. "What's this about?"

"One of your employees," Kins said.

"Which one?"

"One of your dancers."

"I don't employ any dancers," he said. "They're independent contractors, and I have more than ninety. If one of them has done anything illegal, I can't be held liable. I've talked to my lawyer about it."

Tracy sensed Kins's gaze shift to her. She kept her focus on Nash. "May we come in?"

"Do we need to do this now?" Nash asked. He instinctively looked at his wrist, though he wasn't wearing a watch.

"Yes, we do," Tracy said.

Nash led Kins and Tracy to the back of the house, into what he called his "office," though Tracy didn't notice a scrap of paper anywhere in the room. They stood on a purple-and-gold throw rug with a tiger that matched Nash's tattoo. Subtle lighting in glass cases illuminated signed footballs, trophies, and photographs, some of Nash wearing a Louisiana State University uniform.

"Linebacker?" Kins asked, considering a photograph of Nash in football pads.

"Safety," Nash said. "I wasn't fast, but I hit like a truck. I hurt my hammy my senior year or I would have gone pro."

Kins nodded. He almost never spoke about his own abbreviated NFL career, which had ended after a year with a hip injury.

Nash stepped to the door and yelled down the hall, "I'm freezing my tits off here."

Nash's wife—*and what a treat that job must be,* Tracy thought— handed Nash what Tracy referred to as a "meathead sweatshirt," sleeves cut off at the biceps. Nash picked up a football from an expansive desk and sat in a high-back leather chair.

Tracy and Kins stood across the desk from him. "You own the Pink Palace?" Tracy asked.

"A limited liability company owns all three. Which one are you talking about?"

"The one just off Aurora."

"That's the flagship club."

"The flagship club?"

"First one."

"You're the president of the company?"

"That's right."

"You employ a dancer named Angela Schreiber?"

"Independent contractor," Nash said.

"Did you know her?"

"I don't get involved with the dancers."

"I didn't ask if you got involved with them. I asked if you knew her."

Nash put the ball in his lap. "Name doesn't ring a bell."

Tracy placed Angela Schreiber's dance card—the Seattle Municipal Code required erotic dancers to be licensed—now sealed inside a plastic evidence bag, on the desk. Nash leaned forward to consider it. "That's Angel."

"Angel?"

"Her stage name. The dancers all have stage names. Look, Detectives, I'm running legitimate gentlemen's clubs. We don't condone any extracurricular stuff in the club. I have no control over what the girls do after they leave, so if she was giving some guy a blow job in the parking lot, it's not my problem."

"Did you see Angela Schreiber giving someone a blow job in the parking lot last night?" Tracy asked.

"No, I was just . . . Look, I don't remember even seeing her last night."

"But you were at the club?"

"Yeah, I was there. My club."

"And you don't recall seeing Angela Schreiber all night?"

Nash shook his head. "I'm mostly up front working the booth or in my office in back. Like I said, I don't pay much attention to the dancers."

"Independent contractors," Tracy said.

"What?"

"Did you see *anyone* paying attention to Angela Schreiber last night?"

Nash shrugged. "No. But it wouldn't be unusual. I mean, that is how they make their money. They get a guy interested, ask if he wants a lap dance or a private show. Making men pay attention is what they do."

"Who else pays attention to the dancers and customers?"

"Floor manager."

"What's his name?"

"Why do you need that? What did Angel do?"

"She died," Kins said.

Nash looked to Tracy, then to Kins. "Do I need my lawyer here?"

"Why don't we start with the name of your floor manager," Kins said.

"Nabil."

"That a first or last name?" Kins took out a small spiral notebook and scribbled the name.

"First. Last name is Kotar." Nash spelled both names. "I think he's Egyptian or something. How did she die?"

"Someone killed her," Tracy said.

"You have an address or phone number for Nabil?" Kins asked.

"I'll have to ask my director of human resources," Nash said. He looked to Tracy. "Killed how?"

"We're going to need the name of every employee and independent contractor working last night." Kins held out a business card.

Nash hesitated, took the card, and set it on the desk. "So how did she die?"

"That's still under investigation," Tracy said.

"When can you get us that information?" Kins said.

"But she was murdered, right? I mean that's why you're here."

"What about security cameras at the club?" Kins asked.

"Yeah. One mounted in the front office and two covering the exterior of the building and parking lot."

"What about the dance floor?" Tracy said.

Nash shook his head.

"You don't have a camera on the dance floor?"

"No. We want our customers to feel comfortable."

"Having sex with the independent contractors?" Tracy asked.

"I told you that's not allowed."

"But it does happen—that's why you asked if Angel was giving some guy a blow job in the parking lot."

"I said *a* parking lot. I didn't mean our parking lot. Look, I'm not at every club twenty-four–seven. All I can say is it isn't supposed to happen. We find anyone engaging in that sort of activity, we kick them out and fire the dancer."

"Independent contractor," Tracy said.

"Look, Detective, you get a few peep-show freaks, but they learn pretty quick that isn't the kind of club we're running."

Tracy was enjoying getting under Nash's skin. "What kind *are* you running?"

"I told you that already. It's a gentlemen's club. They're big in the South. Guys can relax, have a drink, and watch some beautiful women dance."

"Do you have regulars?"

"Of course. We get some of the athletes coming through—mostly the baseball guys in for a series. But our bread and butter is the business suits downtown. You'd be surprised who shows up."

"I doubt it," Tracy said. "We'll need the names of regulars."

"I don't keep a list of our customers."

"You have an e-mail list, newsletter, anything like that?" she asked.

"Nah, word of mouth is our best advertising."

"What about a website?"

"Sure."

"What's the website for?"

"Advertising. And the men can go online and reserve a lap dance with their favorite dancer."

"We'll need that list," Kins said.

"I'm going to have to talk to my attorney. Don't you need a warrant?"

Tracy handed Nash a card. "I can get a search warrant by the time we're finished talking, or you can agree to cooperate in a murder investigation. What time did you close last night?"

Nash looked like his headache was back. He considered Tracy's card for a moment. Then he said, "Two. It's a city ordinance."

"Do the dancers leave right away?"

"No reason for them to stick around."

"Did you see Angela Schreiber leave?"

"No."

"How about you?" Kins asked. "What time did you leave the club?"

"I counted the registers and prepared the deposits. I'd say I got out of there around two thirty, two forty-five."

"Where'd you go?" Tracy asked.

"Why are you asking me that?"

Tracy didn't answer. Neither did Kins. Silence could be unnerving.

"I came home and went to bed."

"Anyone that can verify that?"

"My wife."

Tracy gave Kins a look to continue without her and stepped to the glass trophy cases.

"Are the cameras on a loop?" Kins asked.

Nash kept an eye on Tracy. "I think it's twenty-four hours," he said.

"We're going to need the tapes from last night. Make a call and make sure they're not erased. You said the cameras cover the parking lot. Do the dancers park in the lot?"

"At that club they do, yeah."

Tracy considered a framed photograph. The shrine wasn't just about football. Nash sat atop a horse, a mustang from the look of it. He wore a felt cowboy hat pushed back off his forehead, a collared denim shirt, and blue jeans over cowboy boots. A stalk of hay protruded from between his front teeth. His hands rested atop a saddle horn, from which hung a coil of rope.

Tracy turned. "Do you ride?"

Nash, who had started tossing the football again, caught it and said, "Yeah. My dad owned a cattle ranch outside Laredo. My brothers and I worked it growing up. We sold it after he died."

Which explained the likely source of the funds Nash used to bankroll an expensive house with a shrine devoted to himself, and a string of strip clubs. "You and your brothers ever do any competitive roping?"

"Some."

"You any good?"

"I could hold my own."

"Three-strand?"

"What's that?"

"You prefer three-strand or five?"

Nash tossed the football again. "Whatever. I didn't pay much attention to that."

"We'll send someone by the club later today," Kins said, "to get the surveillance tapes and the names of the people working last night."

"I'm going to have to consult my lawyer," Nash said. "This is a disruption to my business."

If she'd been carrying a Taser, Tracy might have used it. She and Kins started for the door. Kins turned back and held up his hands. Nash threw him a tight spiral. "Maybe you should have played quarterback," Kins said, returning the toss.

"Nah," Nash said. "Quarterbacks take a beating. I like hitting people."

CHAPTER 8

Tracy sat back from her computer when Kins handed her a fresh cup of coffee.

"That the interview?" Kins asked.

Tracy looked at the screen. "Is 'shithead' one word or two?"

"In his case I don't think spelling matters. Did you make a note of which hand he used to throw the football?"

"Could it be that easy?"

Darrell Nash had tossed Kins the football with his left hand. An expert in the Hansen case said the rope was three-strand polypropylene with a Z, or a "right" twist, and that the knot had been tied by someone left-handed. Polypropylene stretched less than natural fiber and slid more freely through the knot to tighten a noose. Unfortunately, it was also generic and could be bought at any hardware, marine, or big-box store.

"The rope on the saddle horn in the photograph was a five-strand," Tracy said.

"Meaning what?"

"Meaning it's only used by experienced ropers. Nash could be smarter than he looks and could have played dumb when I asked him about it, but I don't think he knew the difference. I don't think he's a cowboy."

"Maybe not," Kins said, "but he's still at the top of the shithead list."

CHAPTER 9

Tracy and Kins spent much of the rest of the day looking into Hansen's and Schreiber's backgrounds to determine what, if anything, the two women had in common, other than the obvious. When CSI e-mailed its initial fingerprint report of Schreiber's motel room, it was as bad as Tracy and Kins had predicted. They had processed more than three dozen prints and had to call in examiners from SPD's Latent Print Unit to help individually compare each print with possible matches generated by the King County Automated Fingerprint Identification System. Referred to as "AFIS," the system stored hundreds of thousands of fingerprints, from people charged and convicted of crimes, people seeking gun permits, federal workers, military personnel, and certain professionals who worked with children.

Vic Fazzio and Delmo Castigliano—the self-proclaimed "Italian Dynamic Duo" of the Violent Crimes Section's five-detective A Team—walked into the bull pen looking spent. As the "next up" homicide team, they had been responsible for canvassing the crime scene—gathering witness statements from the motel owner, guests, and the businesses across the street.

"Nothing, Professor. Nobody saw nobody." Faz topped 250 pounds and favored slacks and loose-fitting bowling shirts that somehow seemed to accentuate his New Jersey accent. Del was bigger, with a face he was fond of saying was one "only a mother could love."

Tracy handed Faz half of the list generated by the Latent Print Unit. "Sorry to do this to you."

"The wife made meatballs," Faz said, sounding seriously disappointed.

"So you have a meatball sandwich to look forward to tomorrow," Del said, taking their half of the list.

—

Tracy and Kins had checked off two names before leaving the Justice Center—two druggies dead more than a month. They'd quickly eliminated two more when the men didn't deny having been in that motel room, just not the previous night, or previous week for that matter, and each could account for his whereabouts.

"Apparently, the staff is not big on dusting," Kins said.

Sitting in the passenger seat of the Ford they'd pulled from the motor pool, Tracy held up the driver's license photograph of the next positive hit on the list. "Walter Gipson," she said. Gipson's photo revealed a man with narrow-set eyes and a hairline receding in a horseshoe pattern, likely the reason he'd cut what remained nub-short.

"Shaving your head—the balding man's solution to hair loss," Kins said, glancing at the photograph from the driver's seat. "How does that make any sense?"

"Why fight the inevitable, I guess," Tracy said.

"That's like complaining you're getting a gut, so you go on an all-Twinkie diet."

"Twenty-six-year-old white male, a special-education teacher," Tracy said.

"And apparently," Kins said, imitating an English accent, "aficionado of prostitutes and fine motels. Does he have a prior?"

"Nope. He applied for a permit for a semiautomatic handgun," Tracy said.

Kins glanced across the car. "Always good to know."

—

Kins pulled into a spot reserved for visitors to the Willowbrook apartment complex in Redmond as Tracy disconnected her call with the chief dispatcher. She'd provided their location and advised of their intent to speak to a suspect. When she stepped from the car, she noticed the air was heavy, with the earthy smell indicative of an impending downpour.

"Which one?" Kins asked, eyeing the two-story wood-framed buildings, typical of the suburban complexes developed on the Eastside in the 1980s.

"Building E," Tracy said, pointing. "That one."

They stepped between covered carports and made their way up a staircase and down the second-story landing. Tracy heard televisions inside the apartments. They stopped outside unit 4, and Kins gave a polite knock. The door emitted a hollow thud and shook in the jamb. "Quality construction," he said.

A woman inside shouted in Spanish. Kins shrugged. "I flunked Spanish in high school."

"Knock again," Tracy said.

Kins did, and they received the same response. "Is she yelling at us or telling someone in the apartment to get the door?" he asked.

"Don't know. I took French."

"Use that a lot, do you?"

"Oui. About as much as you use your Spanish."

Kins reached to knock a third time when the door pulled open. A heavyset Hispanic woman held a young girl wrapped in a canary-yellow bath towel on her hip.

"Sorry," Tracy said. "You look like you have your hands full."

When the woman responded with a blank stare, Tracy held up her badge. "Do you speak English?"

The woman's eyes widened. "Yes."

Tracy introduced herself and Kins, then said, "We're looking for Walter Gipson. Is he home?"

"He is not here." Her accent was thick.

Tracy felt a drop of rain on her neck. "Are you his wife?"

The woman blew a strand of black hair out of her face. "Yes."

"Where is he now?"

"He is working."

Kins checked his watch. Tracy didn't need a watch to know it was late for a high school teacher to be teaching. "Where does your husband work?" she asked.

"At the school."

"Does he always teach this late?"

"Tonight, yes, at the community college." She looked up at the sky. "Please, my little girl, she is cold."

"What time do you expect him home?" Tracy asked.

The woman's gaze drifted past them to the parking lot. A man in a ball cap carrying a backpack on his shoulder stood looking up at them, then veered suddenly toward the carport.

Kins moved to the walkway railing. "Walter Gipson?" he yelled.

The man bolted.

Kins ran for the staircase they'd ascended. Tracy hurried to the staircase at the opposite end of the landing, losing sight of Gipson behind a carport. She descended the stairs and crossed the parking lot. When she reached the carport, she stopped and removed her

Glock. Kins was slowed by his bad hip. They stepped around the corner. Tracy crouched to look beneath the cars. Kins moved to the back of the carport and pulled on doors, likely storage units, though most were padlocked shut.

"Hey," he whispered and held up a black backpack.

Tracy heard what sounded like the rattle of a chain-link fence and hurried across the parking lot. A fence separated the apartment complex from what looked to be an undeveloped piece of property full of thick brush and trees.

"We're going to need the dogs," Kins said. "I'll radio it in and follow the fence line in case he doubles back."

Tracy found a toehold in the chain link and dropped on the other side. She kicked free of blackberry vines snagging the cuffs of her jeans and pushed through the foliage to a horse trail of matted grass. The trail lead to a grove of trees—Douglas fir, cedars, and maples. The tops swayed in gusts of wind.

"Walter Gipson?" she yelled, wiping rain from her face. "You're making this more difficult than it needs to be. We just want to talk."

She looked for movement and unnatural colors in the underbrush, but the fading light and increasing rain made it difficult to see. A hundred yards in, the brush and trees thinned to rolling pasture. In the near distance, horses had lifted their heads, ears perked, watching her. About to walk back out and wait for the dogs, she heard a branch snap behind her. She spun and raised her Glock. Horses crashed through the brush, veering at the last moment, hooves pounding the ground as they sped past her.

Tracy's heart hammered, and she had to take a moment to catch her breath and realized that the snapping branch had spooked the horses, not the other way around. She looked at the brush the horses had come through and took a blade stance but kept the barrel of the Glock pointed at the ground. "Walter Gipson?"

No answer.

"Mr. Gipson, you need to think of your wife and your daughter. I'm armed, and in about five minutes this place is going to be crawling with dogs and police officers. We don't want an accident here, Mr. Gipson. We just need to talk. Walter?"

"Okay. Okay." Gipson stood suddenly from his hiding place.

"Freeze," Tracy yelled, taking aim. "Do not move! Do not move!"

Gipson continued forward.

"Freeze!" she yelled, louder. "I said, do not move!"

Gipson froze. "Okay. Okay."

"Keep your hands where I can see them."

Gipson's hands shook. His arms started to drop.

"Keep your hands up!" she said.

"All right. All right."

"Where's your gun?"

"It's . . . it's in the apartment."

"Do you have any weapons on you?"

"No."

"Just keep your hands where I can see them." Tracy removed her handcuffs, stepped behind Gipson, and quickly cuffed him.

"I didn't do it," Gipson said. "I swear to God I didn't kill her."

CHAPTER 10

They placed Walter Gipson in one of the hard interrogation rooms on the seventh floor of the Justice Center. A windowless box, the room seemed to radiate beneath white fluorescent lights. They'd let Gipson "cook" for twenty to thirty minutes. With the door shut, the walls closed in quickly, as did the thought of spending years in a room just like it.

Rick Cerrabone, a senior prosecuting attorney and member of MDOP, joined Tracy and Kins, all of them watching Gipson from behind one-way glass. The teacher sat hunched over the nicked and scarred table. He looked older without the baseball cap.

"How'd he know her?" Cerrabone asked. Faz had once pointed out that Cerrabone was the spitting image of former Yankees manager Joe Torre—balding, with a hangdog look about him, dark bags beneath tired eyes, and a heavy five-o'clock shadow.

"She was a student in his writing class at the community college," Tracy said. "He admitted taking her to the motel on Aurora last night, but he swears to God he didn't kill her."

"They always swear to God, don't they?" Kins said. He sat in a chair near the blinking colored lights of one of the recording devices.

"Why'd he run?" Cerrabone asked.

"Says he got scared and panicked," Tracy said. "He'd seen a news report."

"Any DNA?" Cerrabone said.

"None on file."

"So no priors," Cerrabone said. In Washington State everyone *convicted* of a crime was required to provide a DNA sample.

"Not even a parking ticket," Kins said. "The guy teaches handicapped kids."

Cerrabone ran a hand over the stubble of his chin. "Any DNA on the rope?"

"Melton says he's making it a priority," Tracy said, referring to Michael Melton at the Washington State Patrol Crime Lab.

"What about Nicole Hansen? Does he have any known connection to her?"

"He says he's never heard of her," Tracy said. "I've got Faz and Del running his photo over to the Dancing Bare to see if anyone picks him out of a montage."

"How long before we get the search warrants for his house and office?" Kins asked.

"And the storage shed," Tracy added.

Cerrabone checked his cell phone. "Probably have them by the time you're finished. Make sure he waives his right to counsel on the tape."

Kins stood. Tracy said, "I'll take this alone."

"You sure?" They almost always interviewed a suspect with another detective, for safety.

"He started talking the minute I put the cuffs on him and didn't shut up the entire ride here. Let's see if he'll keep talking to me."

Tracy removed Gipson's handcuffs, sat across the table from him, and confirmed that he understood his Miranda rights and agreed to waive them. "Let's go over some things again, Walter. How did you know Angela Schreiber?"

"She was taking a course in English at Seattle Community College. I teach there a couple nights a week."

"Okay. So what happened?"

"She submitted an essay on being a dancer. It was really well written, detailed. After class I asked her about it, and she told me it was true and invited me to come see her."

"And you went to watch her dance?"

"Not at first. Not for a while actually. She kept asking when I was going to go, so I decided to go see, you know, just one time. I only went a couple times."

"So how long before you started having sex?"

Gipson sighed. "I don't recall. She asked for a ride to the club one night after class. She said her car had broken down and she didn't have the money to fix it."

"You had intercourse in your car?"

"No."

"She gave you a blow job?"

Gipson lowered his focus to the table, embarrassed. "Yeah."

"And you paid her for it."

He closed his eyes. "It wasn't like that."

"Tell me what it was like."

He looked up. His eyes were watering. "She said she was having a hard time making ends meet. She'd come to Seattle for a job, but it didn't work out and she hadn't been able to find another one, and living here was more expensive than she thought, and then her car broke down. She said she started dancing to pay the bills."

It sounded like a sob story to separate Gipson from his money. "So, what, you were just helping her out?"

"I know how it sounds now."

"How much would you give her?"

"Fifty. Sometimes a hundred."

"It had nothing to do with the sex?"

Gipson frowned. "I guess it did."

"And you went to the motel last night?" Tracy asked.

"Yeah."

"What about your wife?"

"She went to her sister's to have dinner, then called and said she was going to spend the night in Tacoma."

"So you didn't have to rush home."

"Right."

"Who chose the motel?"

"She did."

"Did you ask her why you didn't just go to her apartment?"

"She said she had a roommate who worked early and she didn't want to wake her." According to Ron Mayweather, the A Team's fifth wheel, Schreiber lived alone in a rented studio apartment on Capitol Hill.

"Who paid for the room?"

"I did. But she got it."

"You didn't want to be seen."

Gipson shrugged. "No."

"What time did you get there?"

"It was after her shift; I think around one or one thirty."

"And you had sex?"

"Yes."

"How much did you pay her?"

"I gave her two hundred." They'd found $343 in Schreiber's purse. Nicole Hansen's purse contained $94.

"Did you wear a condom?"

"Yes."

"Then what?"

"I left."

"Slam, bam, thank you, ma'am?"

Gipson closed his eyes and shook his head. "I had to teach in the morning."

"And were you worried your wife might call the apartment?"

"I guess so, yeah."

Tracy studied him. "Were you having any second thoughts, Walter, like maybe Angela wasn't telling you the truth?"

Gipson sat back and exhaled. "She knew the motel. She knew where the office was, how much the rooms cost."

"You thought maybe she might be playing you?"

"I just knew it had to stop. I knew it was wrong."

"Did you get angry when you figured out she was playing you?"

"A little, I guess. But, you know, it wasn't like she forced me."

"What time did you leave?"

"I don't recall."

"Anyone see you leave?"

"I don't know; I don't think so."

"So you just left her in the motel room."

"I offered to drive her home, but she said she'd take a cab."

"You ever go to a strip club called the Dancing Bare?"

"I've never been to a strip club in my life, not before this, except maybe once for a bachelor party."

"You have any hobbies, Walter?"

"Hobbies?"

"Yeah. You know—golf, beer pong?"

"I fly-fish."

Tracy shifted her gaze to the one-way glass. "Do you tie your own flies?"

"Since I was a kid; my dad taught me."

"Are you right-handed or left-handed?"

"Right-handed."

"Things ever get a little kinky with Angela?"

"What?"

"You know, role-playing, toys. Did she ever ask to be tied up?"

"No. I'm not into that."

"Into what?"

"Bondage. Sadomasochism. That stuff."

"How much money did you give her for the room that night?"

"Forty."

"How much was the room for the hour?"

"I don't know."

"Did she give you back any change?"

"No," he said.

"Where'd you get the money to be dropping on a stripper every week?"

Gipson shrugged. "I took the job at the community college; we needed the money with the baby."

"How old is your daughter?"

"Two."

A thought came to her. "How long have you been married, Walter?"

"A year and a half." Gipson sat back again. After a moment, he gave a resigned "what was I going to do" shrug. "She's my daughter."

Tracy nodded. "Angela Schreiber was somebody's daughter too."

—

Two corrections officers escorted Walter Gipson back to King County Jail. For now they'd hold him on solicitation, and suspicion of murder. Tracy and Kins returned to their bull pen. Cubicle walls divided the Violent Crimes Section into four bull pens, each with four desks and a table in the center. Along the perimeter of the cubicles were the sergeants' and lieutenants' offices. Each team was also assigned a fifth detective, called a "fifth wheel," to take up slack. A flat-screen television hung over the B Team's bull pen. Tonight it aired an NBA game.

Kins's phone rang before he'd reached his desk. He answered, listened a moment, then said, "We'll be right there," and hung up. "Nolasco."

It was a Nolasco power play to make everyone go to his office. They walked around the corner and down the hall. The captain's office had a view west, toward Elliott Bay, or it would have, if Nolasco ever raised the blinds.

Nolasco was seated at his desk with his back to the framed commendations on the wall. On a credenza were stacks of paper and photographs of his two children, a son in a hockey uniform and a daughter holding a soccer ball. Nolasco displayed no pictures of either of his ex-wives, who he frequently complained were stealing him blind.

He did not look happy, but Nolasco rarely looked happy unless he was busting somebody's chops. "Did Mayweather tell you I wanted to see you as soon as you got in?"

"We were with a suspect in the dancer murders," Kins said.

"And?"

"Says he didn't do it."

"Tell me what you got."

Tracy and Kins remained standing. "Angela Schreiber was a stripper at the Pink Palace," Tracy started.

Nolasco leaned back in his chair. "I've read some of the witness statements. I want to know if it's the same guy."

"Appears to be," Tracy said.

"Don't give me 'appears to be.' The mayor and city council are riding the Chief hard, and shit flows downhill."

Which explained why Nolasco was still at the office this late. Despite the similarities in the manner of death between the two dancers, the brass and city hall would be reluctant to acknowledge a "serial killer." Each was well versed in the media frenzy those two words stirred in a population that had experienced more than its fair share of infamous murderers, not to mention the economic impact a task force could have on an already taxed police budget. Serial killers could get away with killing for years, sometimes decades, while task forces devoured man hours, budgets, and often careers.

"Same method to strangle both victims," Kins said. "In both instances the bed was made, the victim's clothes neatly folded."

Tracy watched Nolasco to see if any of the information triggered a recollection of Beth Stinson, but Nolasco didn't flinch.

"What about the ropes?"

"Preliminarily? Looks like same type, same knot. Melton's got it at the lab."

"Who you got working it from here?"

"Faz and Del were next up. They're running down fingerprints. Ron is running down the license plates at the motel and last phone calls and text messages on Schreiber's cell."

"Too many similarities to not be the same guy," Kins concluded.

Nolasco put up a finger. "That's why we're talking in my office, Sparrow," he said using Kins's other nickname. "We don't know that."

"Seriously?" Tracy said.

"The mayor and the Chief don't want to be answering those questions right now. What about this guy you pulled in?"

"Walter Gipson," Tracy said. "He admits being with the victim at the motel last night. Denies killing her."

"Sounds like bullshit."

"It may be," Tracy said.

"How good is the evidence?"

"His fingerprints are all over the motel room. We're waiting on the DNA. The only DNA on the rope that strangled Hansen was hers."

"How does that happen?"

"Don't know," Tracy said.

Kins's phone buzzed. He read the text message. "Cerrabone sent over the warrants. Maybe we find a coil of rope and we all go home."

Tracy didn't think so.

CHAPTER 11

Margarita Gipson answered the door looking tired and scared. Inside the modest but clean apartment, a woman who bore a strong family resemblance, likely the sister from Tacoma, held the little girl, who had her head tucked to the woman's chest, thumb stuck in her mouth.

She's my daughter, Walter Gipson had said, and it seemed to somehow make him more human. Then again, Gary Ridgway, the Green River Killer, had killed at least forty-nine women in Seattle, and he told the detectives who arrested him that he'd lured victims into his car while his young son was in the backseat.

Crosswhite served the warrant to search Walter Gipson's home and storage shed, and the CSI team accompanying them went to work, first retrieving Gipson's handgun from a locked safe in the bedroom closet. The four-digit code to open the safe was Margarita's birthday. "So I don't forget," she said.

As the CSI team continued, Margarita sat in a living room chair, fidgeting with the beads of a rosary and wiping tears with a tissue, her eyes bloodshot and puffy. Tracy sat on a cloth couch across from her. Kins and the sister remained standing. Tracy explained that Walter was in custody at King County Jail and would not be home that night.

"But he say it is no problem," Margarita said. "He say he would not get caught, that it is not the thing the police devote their . . ." She looked to her sister, but the woman shrugged and shook her head.

"Their resources?" Tracy asked.

"Attention . . . He say it is not the thing the police devote their attention." The final words shuddered in her chest, and she covered a sob with her hand.

Tracy and Kins exchanged a glance. Tracy was wondering if maybe they needed a translator. "What did your husband mean about the police not devoting their attention? What was he talking about?"

"The taxes."

"The taxes?"

"He say the police, they no care."

"Your husband was not paying his taxes?" Tracy found it hard to believe Gipson's taxes were not automatically deducted by the school district, then thought of his part-time job at the community college. "Do you mean on the money he makes teaching?"

"No, the fishing flies," Margarita said.

Kins nodded to Tracy. "He sells the fishing flies he makes."

Margarita looked up at him. "With the baby, we need the money."

"And he doesn't pay taxes on what he sells," Tracy said, understanding.

"He say the police no care."

"Where does your husband make these flies?" Tracy asked.

—

They stepped around a Toyota Prius parked in the carport. Margarita turned the dials on a padlock. "He makes the flies at night," she said. She tugged on the lock, but the clasp didn't open.

After Margarita checked the four numbers and pulled again, without success, Tracy said, "Let me try. What's the combination?"

"My birthday," Margarita said. "So I don't forget. 0-4-1-7."

It was the same combination to open the gun safe. Tracy tried without success.

"I've got a bolt cutter in the truck," one of the CSI detectives said.

"Get it."

Minutes later, he'd snapped the lock. Tracy removed it, opened the latch, and pulled open the door.

"There is a light," Margarita said. "A string."

Tracy reached into darkness, felt the string brush across the back of her hand, and tugged. A clear bulb emitted a sharp light above a crude workbench built in a narrow space. A corkboard of intricately tied fishing flies lined the back wall, but the flies were not what immediately caught Tracy's attention. When Margarita Gipson stuck her head inside the space, she quickly covered a sob with her hand and started to cry again.

Walter Gipson was brought back to the interrogation room, this time wearing a red King County Jail jumpsuit, white socks, and flip-flops. Tracy and Kins didn't wait to let him cook. They entered the room together. Tracy did not remove Gipson's handcuffs.

"We've been in the storage shed, Walter," she said.

Gipson's Adam's apple bobbed.

Kins slid a photograph encased in clear plastic across the table.

Margarita's birthday had not worked because her husband had either changed the combination or changed the padlock. Amid the hundreds of flies Walter Gipson had tied, he'd also tacked a half dozen naked photographs of Angela Schreiber to the corkboard. In several, Tracy recognized the worn and stained gray carpet from the Aurora Motor Inn. Walter Gipson had been a little more infatuated with Angela Schreiber than he'd led Tracy to believe. And people who lied usually had something to hide.

Gipson bowed his head and began to weep. "I think I'd like to talk to that attorney now."

CHAPTER 12

Tracy popped a can of cat food and left it on the counter, too tired to take out a dish from the cupboard. Roger didn't seem to mind. For herself she dumped a can of tuna on the remainder of a salad she hadn't had time to finish at lunch and carried it with her. As she crossed through the dining room, she noticed her laptop on the table and thought again of the murder of Beth Stinson. Johnny Nolasco's case.

Nolasco had been partners with a racist bigot named Floyd Hattie for more than a decade. When Nolasco got bumped to sergeant, Hattie was assigned Tracy as his new partner. Hattie took one look at her, said, "I ain't working with no Dickless Tracy," and promptly retired. Faz had told Tracy to count her blessings. Hattie and Nolasco had a perfect conviction record, something they liked to rub in the other detectives' faces, but it was well-known that neither was above the use of questionable police tactics—unknown street sources suddenly showing up as witnesses, well-worn ruses to "encourage" confessions, and even one or two instances of suspects falling and hurting themselves.

Tracy set the salad down next to her laptop and hit the space bar. The screen popped to life, still displaying the attorney general's website. She logged back into HITS and pulled up the Beth Stinson file. She suspected Nolasco had completed the form. She doubted Hattie, with one foot already out the door, would have bothered. She remained puzzled by the inconsistencies: the positive answer to the question about whether Stinson had been sexually assaulted, yet the lack of forensic evidence to substantiate that conclusion. She was also bothered by the similarity in the details of Stinson's bedroom and the motel rooms where they'd found Hansen and Schreiber. She wasn't about to talk to Nolasco about it, and she certainly wouldn't be hunting down Hattie. She doubted he'd improved much in his retirement.

She made a mental note to call the State Archives and have Stinson's file pulled from storage, though she'd have to tread quietly. Nolasco was vindictive, and if he got word she was looking into one of his old files, he'd flip his lid, especially if she found any of the kind of improprieties Faz had hinted at. She thought about whether to say anything to Kins. Married with three kids, he couldn't afford a suspension, if it came to that. She decided she'd take a look at the file on her own, and if nothing came of the similarities to Hansen and Schreiber, she'd send it back. If something did, she'd cross that bridge when she came to it.

She shut down the machine and took her salad to the bedroom. As she entered the room, the floodlight in the backyard triggered and backlit the curtains drawn across the sliding glass doors. She pulled back the curtain and looked down into the yard. The rain continued to fall, but there was little wind and no sign of any furry four-legged creatures that could have triggered the motion detector.

She'd told Billy she didn't need the patrol car, but that had been bravado talking. Any sign of weakness was too easily attributed to her gender. It was a double standard, but it was also reality. In truth, she was glad to have an officer parked at the curb.

She changed into a long T-shirt and climbed into bed, channel surfing while picking at her salad. Though physically exhausted, she continued to go over her interrogation of Walter Gipson, the two crime scenes, and about a thousand questions. She needed to slow her thoughts or she'd never fall asleep. She activated the DVR and pulled up the latest *Downton Abbey*. The curtains lit up again.

She turned off the television to kill the light in the room, slipped from bed, and eased back the curtain. The lawn remained empty, the trees still. So why did she have that sensation like at the shooting range that she was being watched? The floodlights went out. When they did not trigger again, she told herself it was probably the rain, that Dan had likely set the motion detector on too sensitive a setting. She climbed back into bed with her Glock, setting it on the pillow beside her.

—

Tracy Crosswhite had made some changes since his initial visit. The floodlights and motion detector were new, as was the police car parked in front of the house, likely because of the present he'd left for her at the shooting range, which he was starting to think had been a mistake.

The lights had come on unexpectedly as he approached the rear of her house, and he'd had to quickly retreat into the brush, where he crouched, with water dripping from the brim of his camouflage hat.

Ordinarily the rain didn't bother him, but tonight it had managed to find the gaps and seams in his protective gear and he could feel his shirt sticking to his back and moisture seeping through his socks, a Pacific Northwest dampness that made his bones ache. He'd suspected that, with the murder of Angela Schreiber, Tracy would be late getting home. Her schedule fluctuated, depending on whether she was the detective on call. When there was a murder, she had no schedule. Some nights she didn't even make it home.

So it had been a calculated risk to visit her on a night she was investigating a murder, but tonight the urge to see her had been too strong for him to ignore and looking at photographs he'd taken of her simply didn't satisfy him. The need to be close to her, to feel her presence, to feel that connection he'd first felt when he'd seen her on the news at the Nicole Hansen crime scene was overwhelming. Though it had only been through the television, that first moment had been unlike anything he'd ever experienced. Love at first sight. What wasn't to love? Tracy was tall and blonde and beautiful. He had started waiting outside her apartment and following her, keeping a safe distance. Once, he'd even sat not far from her in a coffee shop, but he couldn't bring himself to speak to her. Still, as he'd gotten to know her better, he'd realized the attraction was more than physical. It was spiritual. He wondered if—no, he knew—she was his soul mate, that person he was destined to spend the rest of his life with.

When she'd left for Cedar Grove, he'd felt a gaping hole in his being, like he was missing half of himself. He couldn't feel whole without her. He had to be near her. Not for the whole time—he couldn't do that with work and a family—but he'd managed to get away for a few days. He'd even sat in court one day for the hearing of Edmund House. He snapped photographs of her. His favorite was the one he took while she was standing on the porch outside the veterinary hospital in Pine Flat. He'd managed to get a close-up of her face. It was an incredible shot, breathtaking. The cold had turned her cheeks ruddy, giving her an almost girlish appearance. Snowflakes encircled her like a halo, and her eyes, a dazzling blue, appeared to be looking directly at him. The power of her gaze was so strong he'd lowered the camera to stare back at her. She had that kind of power. Then he'd realized she was staring not at him but at his car. He'd cleared the windshield of snow to take the pictures, making the car stand out among all the others.

Luckily she'd gone inside the clinic, giving him a chance to leave.

He looked up at the back of the house when the kitchen light illuminated. She'd come home. His gamble had paid off. He quickly raised his binoculars, focusing them on the window to the far left and saw the refrigerator door open. He caught a glimpse of her when she shut it and another when she passed the window. Then the window went dark. He redirected the binoculars to the sliding glass door on the far right, her bedroom. When the light did not immediately come on, he panned left, to the sliding glass door that led to the balcony. Tracy always kept the blinds open, no doubt to enjoy the view, but it was too dark for him to see inside and the chances she would step onto the patio were not good, given the late hour and rain.

He could just make out a faint bluish glow. Her laptop. She often worked at the dining room table, sometimes for hours. On those nights he was content just to sit and be in her presence. But tonight he craved more. He craved her.

When five minutes passed and his joints began to ache, he told himself he could wait another five. Five minutes became twenty. The blue light extinguished. His pulse quickened. He shifted the binoculars to her bedroom. The light snapped on. The drapes were drawn.

He swore, profoundly disappointed that he wouldn't see her, not a glimpse.

The light went out. Blue-gray shadows danced across the curtains. She was watching television in bed. Reluctantly, he gathered his belongings, about to leave when an idea struck him. It was a risk, like leaving the noose. The jury was still out on whether that was a good idea or not. It was all about the potential payoff.

He stepped from the brush before he changed his mind. His boots squished and formed small puddles in the saturated lawn. When the light did not come on, he raised his arms and waved them over his head. Nothing. He took another step and repeated the motion.

The floodlights lit up the yard.

He retreated quickly into the brush and raised the binoculars, feeling the rush of anticipation.

And then she was there, standing at the glass door, like an apparition but so very real. She wore a long white T-shirt that stopped midthigh. He'd never seen her legs before, never seen her in a dress, always in blue jeans or slacks. Her legs were as he'd imagined them, long and lean, and toned. He inched forward, as if pulled by that magnetic attraction, and had to fight the urge to walk to her. He couldn't do that. Not yet. She didn't know him yet. She'd think he was a nut job. She had to see him in a different setting, a setting in which he could show her how much he loved her. Until then, he needed to be patient. Until then, images like this would have to be enough.

CHAPTER 13

Early the following morning, Tracy and Kins sat with Rick Cerrabone in a conference room at the King County Courthouse, drinking black coffee and going over the forensics from the room at the Aurora Motor Inn. Tracy felt dull from a lack of sleep. The floodlights had gone on twice more in the night. She'd ignored them. Now a dull headache throbbed at her temples and across the top of her head, and the ibuprofen she'd taken to dull the pain was upsetting her empty stomach. From Kins's haggard appearance, she deduced he wasn't feeling much better.

"Maybe he was careless," Kins said. He sat hunched over a paper cup. They were discussing how Walter Gipson's fingerprints could be at the motel but not his DNA. "He couldn't very well show up wearing gloves, right? So he puts them on in the bathroom and then he wipes down surfaces after he kills her, but this time he's careless."

"I don't see a guy that careful leaving a fingerprint," Tracy said.

"He burned the bottoms of her feet. If he did it to speed up the process, maybe he was in a hurry and got careless."

"Or maybe he just wanted to see her suffer more," Tracy said.

Cerrabone had removed his suit jacket, draping it carefully over an adjacent chair. There wasn't a wrinkle to be found in his heavily starched white shirt, and his red tie screamed government authority. He was starting a trial that morning. "What *do* we know for sure?" he said.

They had less than forty-eight hours before the law accorded Walter Gipson a probable cause hearing, at which Cerrabone would have to convince a judge there was sufficient evidence to hold Gipson for the murder of Angela Schreiber.

"Dancers at the Pink Palace confirmed he's been hanging around," Kins said, reading from one of the witness statements Faz and Del had obtained. "Schreiber apparently brought him into the dressing room one time."

"He's not denying that," Tracy said.

"And the video of the Pink Palace parking lot shows Schreiber leaving with him at just after one in the morning," Kins said.

"Which he also admitted," Tracy said.

Kins flipped through the pages of their report. "Cell phone records indicate frequent calls to Schreiber during the last two months—"

"Which he isn't denying."

"Cell tower hits for his phone match the hits on Schreiber's phone for that evening."

"But also confirm a hit on a tower on the east side of Lake Washington right about the time Gipson said he returned home."

Kins lowered the report. "I hate it when you do that."

Tracy shrugged. "Better me than a defense attorney."

"What about the Dancing Bare?" Cerrabone asked.

"Faz and Del ran his photo over there. Nobody's seen him," Tracy said.

"What else?" Cerrabone said.

"He can tie a knot like nobody's business," Kins said.

"He says he's right-handed," Tracy said.

"Maybe. We don't know that for sure yet. We know he was more infatuated with her than he admitted." Kins slid copies of the photographs they'd found in the storage shed across the table, talking as Cerrabone considered them. "These were taken in that motel room, and in at least one of them Schreiber is on her hands and knees."

"But not with a rope around her neck," Cerrabone said.

"No, not with a rope around her neck," Kins agreed.

"Anything else?"

"She rented the room for longer than an hour," Tracy said.

"He said his wife was away. He didn't have to rush home." Kins gave her a "two can play devil's advocate" smile.

"Why is that significant?" Cerrabone said.

"Tracy thinks she might have rented the room for longer than an hour because she was meeting someone after Gipson," Kins said.

"That's what prostitutes do, Kins," Tracy said. "It's not a stretch she did it."

"I'm sorry, but I'm not buying it," Kins said. "Really, what are the odds? Gipson takes her to the motel and has sex with her, and it's the next guy who comes along and kills her? That makes Gipson the most unlucky son of a bitch on the planet."

"What did the motel owner say?" Cerrabone said.

"Says he has a two-hour minimum," Kins said, "but he doesn't keep records of cash payments."

Cerrabone looked to Tracy. "You don't think he did it?"

Her head was pounding. She wanted food and sleep. She wasn't going to get the latter for a while. "I don't know."

"Something else?"

"I don't know. I mean . . . he gets his girlfriend pregnant and marries her. I could tell talking to him it wasn't his first choice, but he did the right thing."

Kins grimaced. "Ridgway was married twice, and he was still a sick dung heap. He used his kid to attract women. These guys do things for reasons we'll never understand."

"I'm just saying it's something to weigh, along with everything else. I'm not saying it makes him a Boy Scout," Tracy said.

Cerrabone beat a rhythm on the table with his index and middle fingers. "We *might* get past the probable cause hearing, but we won't get past an arraignment or a motion to dismiss. And if I file a complaint, we'll have played our hand and the media will know about the similarities to Nicole Hansen."

"And then it's Katy bar the freaking door," Kins said.

Cerrabone looked at his watch, stood and slipped on his jacket. "Anything comes up, let my office know." He did not sound optimistic. At the door he turned back. "We have *no* evidence to link him to Hansen?"

"Nothing yet," Tracy said.

Given the lack of evidence, Tracy was not surprised when Cerrabone called late that afternoon as she and Kins left a fly-fishing shop. They'd presented samples of Gipson's flies to the proprietor and asked if he could tell whether the person who tied them was right- or left-handed.

"Something that intricate," the man had said, "he'd have to be able to tie equally well with both hands."

Great, Tracy had thought.

Cerrabone said what Tracy had already deduced. "We're not going forward."

She respected him. Unlike some prosecutors who cherry-picked which cases to try to preserve their win-loss percentage, Cerrabone wasn't afraid to try a case he might lose. But this was a reasoned decision. They did not have enough evidence, and the last thing they wanted to do was to move forward with an evidentiary hearing and give the media another reason to criticize them when a judge ended up setting Gipson free and the murder of another young woman remained unsolved.

After hanging up with Cerrabone, Tracy walked around the corner to Nolasco's office to make a request. She suspected she knew the answer, but she wanted to note in the file that she had tried.

"We want to put a tail on Gipson," she said.

"Do your job and I don't have to authorize an unnecessary expenditure of funds," Nolasco said.

Early that evening, Walter Gipson, aficionado of prostitutes and fine motels, and skilled creator of intricate fishing flies, walked free from King County Jail.

CHAPTER 14

Tracy returned to her desk to go through crime scene photographs, hoping she'd see something she'd missed. From across the bull pen, Faz muttered one of his famous sayings, breaking her concentration.

"Kick me in the nuts—hey, Professor?"

"Rather not, Faz. A few other people I can think of that I'd like to, however."

Faz frequently called Tracy by the nickname given to her at the police academy.

"I think you might want to come see this."

Tracy rotated her chair. It was just the two of them. Kins had left for the day to have dinner with the family. He'd already missed too many, which wasn't helping the strained relations at home. Del, too, had departed, leaving a pile of papers, food wrappers, and coffee mugs on his desk.

She pushed away from her desk and walked to Faz's cubicle, looking over his shoulder. Faz was peering over the top of half-lens reading glasses at his computer screen. Tracy recognized the dark and blurred image of the Pink Palace parking lot captured by one of the two surveillance cameras. She'd also reviewed the surveillance video from inside the club, but it had been focused on the cash register and, more specifically, on Nash's employees handling the money. It didn't record the patrons.

"Tell me what you see," Faz said, tapping his keyboard.

She leaned closer to the screen but pulled back when she detected garlic, a lot of it. Whatever gum Faz was chewing wasn't close to conquering the smell. She waived at the air. "You expecting an attack by vampires, Faz?"

"It ain't Italian food if you don't reek," he said.

"Mission accomplished."

Faz vacated his chair. "You sit. I'll stand and try not to breathe on you."

Tracy took his seat and hit "Play." The video was poor quality, largely because the lights working in the parking lot were sporadic, creating patches of dark shadows. The club's pink stucco walls looked pale gray, and when the neon marquee and Jumbotron flashed, everything on the video washed out. Nash had no doubt skimped on the security cameras when running the budget for his "gentlemen's club."

After thirteen static seconds ticked off the timer in the lower right corner, a man in a cap and a woman with a red handbag slung over her shoulder walked out from behind the building. "Gipson and Schreiber," Tracy said, feeling slightly unnerved watching the final moments of Schreiber's life, like some sort of deity peering down from the heavens, knowing what was about to happen. The couple held hands, swinging their arms like high school sweethearts strolling on a warm summer evening and reveling in the feel of each other's intertwined fingers. Gipson pulled Schreiber to him to sneak a kiss. He looked like he wanted more, but Schreiber leaned away, putting a hand to his chest. She glanced back to the Pink Palace. Did she know there were surveillance cameras and was worried Nash might fire her, or was she just concerned about someone coming out the door?

They separated and quickly slid in opposite sides of the car. The headlights did not immediately illuminate, and it was too dark to see what was happening inside the car, though easy enough for Tracy to venture a good guess. Gipson was probably trying to get some of what Schreiber wouldn't give him in the parking lot. Thirty-eight seconds ticked off the timer before the headlights turned on and two elongated beams of light shot across the asphalt. Gipson drove to the driveway, briefly paused, then turned onto the street fronting the Pink Palace, departing the camera's coverage in the direction of Aurora.

Tracy looked back at Faz, who was grinning like somebody just invited him to dinner. "Nothing, right?"

"Nothing," she agreed.

Faz stepped forward and hit the "Play" button again. "This time, don't watch Gipson and Schreiber; watch the upper left corner of the screen." Gipson and Schreiber reappeared, but Tracy kept her eyes on the corner. When Gipson's car pulled to the driveway entrance, another car appeared, a dark-colored sedan.

Faz said out loud what Tracy immediately noticed. "Headlights are off."

The building blocked the camera's coverage, and the car disappeared from view. Gipson's Toyota pulled out of the lot. Seconds later, the other car, just a blur, flashed past the Pink Palace.

"Remember you said maybe Gipson wasn't the last one with Schreiber?" Faz said.

Tracy went back to the beginning of the video and pointed to the corner. "Watch where the car enters the frame."

"Thinking the same thing," Faz said. "If it was parked, it was parked just out of the camera's coverage."

She played the video again, trying to time the car's reappearance. She hit "Stop," but too late, the blurred image was no longer on the screen. She tried several more times before she'd captured the frame she wanted, the dark-colored sedan just in front of the

Pink Palace. The clarity of the picture, already poor, was made worse by the Jumbotron, which at that moment had flashed a brilliant white.

"Not going to get the license plate," Faz said.

Tracy leaned closer, but she couldn't see inside the car or make out anything definitive about its make or model.

"Let's get it over to the lab," she said. "See if Mike can do anything with it."

"Hey, it ain't nothing, right?" Faz said.

Sometimes it was the little pieces of evidence that, when put together, led to an arrest.

"It ain't nothing," she agreed.

—

Tracy picked up Chinese food on the way home and sat at the dining room table picking at a carton of orange chicken. In the kitchen Roger pushed a tin can across the tile counter. The door intercom buzzed. She knew it wasn't Dan. He'd called earlier to check in and tell her about his arbitration, which he felt was going well, though slow. Tracy set down her chopsticks and made her way to the front door, thinking it could be the officer assigned to watch the house in need of the bathroom.

"Yes?" she said, pushing the button.

"Detective Crosswhite? It's Katie Pryor from the shooting range."

It took a moment for Tracy to register the young female officer she'd trained for her qualifying test. Though it had only been a few days, it felt like weeks. "I'll buzz you in," she said.

Pryor shut the gate behind her and crossed the courtyard carrying a card and a potted plant. She was in uniform. There were now two patrol cars parked in front of the house.

"I hope I'm not disturbing you," she said, reaching the front door.

"Just got home."

"I was going to leave this for you, but the gate . . ." She handed Tracy the plant—a cactus—and a card. "I thought it best to get you something that didn't require a lot of care."

Tracy smiled. "Good call, but you didn't have to do this."

As she took the plant, Roger shot past her. Tracy lunged to stop him, but too late. He bolted into the courtyard and around the side of the house.

"I'm sorry," Pryor said. "Do you want me to help you get him back inside?"

"Easier said than done," Tracy said. "I'll get him in a bit. He doesn't like the cold for long, and he's a sucker for a can of food. Are you heading to work?"

Pryor shook her head. "Finishing up, actually. We live over by the school. I didn't realize you were this close."

Tracy had no idea what school Pryor was referring to. "You want to come in for a minute?"

Pryor surprised Tracy when she accepted. "Maybe for a minute," she said.

Tracy shut the door, and they stepped inside.

"I interrupted your dinner," Pryor said, eyeing the cartons of Chinese food.

"Have you eaten?"

"I don't want to impose."

"No imposition. I have more than I can eat, and I'd enjoy the company."

Tracy went to the kitchen and returned with two plates, another set of chopsticks, two glasses, and a bottle of wine. She poured Pryor a glass, and they sat scooping out rice and exchanging the cartons of orange chicken and garlic beef.

"Do you always work at night?" Pryor said, looking at the laptop.

"We've had a couple homicides."

"The two dancers over in North Seattle? Those are your cases?"

"They're mine."

"Is it the same guy?"

Tracy sipped her wine. "Appears to be."

Pryor worked a piece of beef into her mouth. "Thanks for this."

"How's your husband?"

Pryor smiled. "Surprisingly okay. I've been to the range twice since we met."

"How are you shooting?"

"Really well." Pryor set down her chopsticks. She looked to have something on her mind. "Can I ask you something?"

"Sure?"

"It's just you here?"

"Me and the escape artist."

"Is it the job? I mean, is that why you're not married? Working late? If this is too personal . . ."

Tracy raised a hand. "It's fine. I understand what you're asking. My situation is a lot more complicated than that. I was married, briefly, and a long time ago, before I became a cop." Tracy set down her chopsticks. "Look, I'm not a good role model, Katie. Twenty years ago if you'd asked me where I saw my life in five years, I would have said I would be married with two kids, living in a small town and teaching at the high school."

"What happened?"

"Someone murdered my sister."

"I'm sorry," Pryor said.

"The thing is, her murder was why I became a cop. It isn't why I've remained one."

"Why have you?"

"I love what I do. I love the mental and the physical challenge, and I love to shoot, always have. The thing is, you can make all kinds of plans for your future and then stumble ass-backward into what you were meant to do. Do you like being a cop?"

Pryor smiled. "I was a criminal justice major. I thought I'd become a prosecutor or a defense attorney."

"So what happened?"

"I got married young, got pregnant, the housing market went in the toilet, and we needed the income."

"And now?"

"I enjoy it. I do."

"But . . ."

"I worry about the strain on my marriage and being away from my daughters at night. I've met a lot of divorced cops."

"How old are your daughters?"

Pryor pulled out a photograph from her shirt pocket and handed it to her. "Four and two. This is how I take them to work with me every day."

The little girls, wearing matching floral dresses and black Mary Janes, had their arms around each other's necks in a loving embrace. Tracy had a dozen photographs just like it, of herself and Sarah as young girls. The framed pictures had once adorned their family home in Cedar Grove but were now packed in one of the boxes in the garage. She handed back the photograph. "They're beautiful."

"You have any advice?" Pryor asked.

Tracy found herself suddenly thinking not only of Sarah, but also of Nicole Hansen and Angela Schreiber. "Love them every chance you get," she said.

CHAPTER 15

The 911 call was made at 11:25 the following morning. Tracy and Kins arrived at Joon's Motel half an hour later. They walked across a parking lot littered with uniformed officers and patrol cars. News vans lined Aurora Avenue, and a pack of photographers and reporters jockeyed for position on the sidewalk with a crowd of onlookers attracted to the motel by the two news helicopters hovering overhead, blades thumping. It didn't help that the morning had dawned crisp and clear, and now, near noon, the sun burned bright in a cloudless blue sky. People in the Northwest got outdoors when the sun came out, and nothing piqued curiosity more than a crime scene.

"This is going to get ugly," Kins said, eyeing the crowd.

"It already is."

Two officers stood sentry at the foot of a staircase leading to the second level. "Room 14," the younger-looking officer said. "In the corner."

His hands were empty. So were the other officer's. "Who's keeping the crime scene log?" Tracy asked.

"Responding officer." He pointed.

The stairs vibrated beneath their feet as they climbed to the second floor. At the end of a landing blistered and worn bare, red crime scene tape had been tied from a door handle to the railing. A third uniformed officer stepped from an alcove holding a clipboard.

"Tell us what you did," Tracy said, signing the log and handing the clipboard to Kins.

The officer pointed over the railing to the porte cochere. "The owner met me outside the office. He said the maid found her when she went in to clean the room."

"Where's the maid now?" Kins asked.

"My sergeant's got her in the office with the manager. She's pretty shook up."

"What did she say?"

"She said she knocked, got no answer, and used her passkey to enter. Said she walked in, saw the body, and ran out. The only thing she recalls touching was the door handle." He cleared his throat. "She keeps praying in Spanish, making the sign of the cross, and kissing her crucifix." His voice faded. He was shaken up too, though he was trying hard to hide it.

Kins nodded toward the open door. "Did you go in?"

"No, but I saw her when the fire department went in."

"String another piece of red tape at the foot of the stairs," Tracy said, "and give the log to one of the two officers down there. Tell them I said no one comes up the stairs without signing and providing a shield number. Tell them to tell anyone who tries to cross that line that they're going to have to file a report."

Kins opened his go bag and handed Tracy latex gloves and booties. Slipping them on, they stepped inside. The room smelled of fresh cigarette smoke and urine. As with the rooms where Nicole Hansen and Angela Schreiber were found, the thin bed cover had not been disturbed and the woman's clothes had been neatly folded and left on the edge. The woman lay hog-tied at the foot of the bed.

Unlike Hansen and Schreiber, she hadn't toppled onto her side, nor was she blonde. Her dark-brown hair was pulled back in a ponytail. She was also bigger-boned, stockier. Her breasts pressed flat against the brown shag carpet. Cellulite dimples pocked her buttocks and the back of her thighs. A dark spot stained the carpet beneath her pelvis. Like Schreiber, the soles of her feet were red and blistered. Tracy let out a held breath and closed her eyes.

"You all right?" Kins asked.

"What's his point, Kins? What's he trying to tell us? Is he just humiliating them, or is there something more to it?"

"Don't know. I'll tell Faz to have screens set up outside the alcove and at the foot of the stairs. Funk can back the van up to the landing to block the view."

The King County medical examiner would not be able to straighten the young woman's limbs for several more hours. Even covered with a sheet, it wouldn't be difficult for the media and the growing crowd of civilians to discern that the woman's body was grotesquely contorted.

Tracy looked about the room, taking it all in. She walked to the desk and pointed to a purple purse, a long gold chain dangling over the side. The purse matched the color of the dress folded on the corner of the bed. "You got it?"

Kins photographed the purse. "We're good."

Tracy carefully extracted a thin wallet, the kind with the plastic slip for the driver's license on the outside. "Veronica Watson," she said. She did the math. "Nineteen." She removed several credit cards before she found what she was looking for—Watson's license as an adult entertainer.

"She dances at the Pink Palace," she said.

"Danced," Kins said.

CHAPTER 16

Johnny Nolasco made his way back to his office through the A Team's bull pen, the cubicles empty. He'd just come from a meeting with the brass on the dreaded eighth floor to discuss forming a task force following the murder of a third dancer. He shut the door to his office and unlocked his desk drawer, pulling out the burner phone. A thirty-day prepaid disposable, the burner was a favorite of drug dealers and pimps.

She answered on the first ring. "You have yourself a serial killer," he said. "We're calling him the Cowboy."

"Great name," Maria Vanpelt said. "That will get the national networks interested."

"SPD will be acknowledging it. And I'll be requesting a task force with Tracy Crosswhite as the lead detective."

Vanpelt paused. "When can I run it?"

"It hasn't gone through the proper channels yet. But when it clears, you'll be first. You might want to run a story about this being the third killing by the same man Crosswhite was supposed to be looking for when she left for Cedar Grove trying to get her sister's killer a new trial."

"I don't have a hard-on for Tracy Crosswhite the way you do, Johnny."

"You don't have a story without Tracy Crosswhite . . . or me. We both know that."

Another pause. She was debating it. "I might be able to mention it in a recap."

"Then the news just became a lot more interesting."

CHAPTER 17

Tracy ate a sandwich in the car with Kins, a late lunch—or early dinner. She'd lost track of the hours of the day and the days of the week. They were driving across the 520 floating bridge after paying Walter Gipson a visit to see if he could account for his whereabouts the prior evening.

As they dropped down from the span on the west side of the bridge, a bald eagle sat perched on the arm of a light pole, head cocked to the side looking out over the glass-still blue-gray surface of Lake Washington. With the University of Washington football stadium behind him and the distant snowcapped Olympic Mountains serving as a backdrop, it was the type of iconic image that won contests in magazines, and the type of beauty Tracy had to occasionally make herself acknowledge.

Her cell phone rang. She put Faz on speaker so Kins could hear.

"What did Gipson have to say?" Faz asked.

"Says he was at home," Tracy said.

"Wife verify that?"

"Wife isn't there. Moved to Tacoma with the sister. Gipson says he went running late, came back, and worked in the storage shed tying flies. None of the neighbors can verify it though."

"What do you got, Faz?" Kins said. "You solve the case for us?"

"I wish. Make the wife happy."

"Get in line."

"Mr. Joon was not exactly a wealth of information," Faz said, referring to the motel owner. "But he did say Veronica Watson arrived at the motel in the back of an Orange Cab."

"Alone?" Tracy asked.

"Didn't know, but nobody else came in the office with her—at least not this time. Said he's seen her with a tall guy in a suit with a full head of light-brown hair. Thought you might want to know when you talk to the dancers." Gipson, nearly bald, definitely did not fit that description, nor did Darrell Nash, who wore his dark hair short and spiked in the front with a liberal amount of gel. "Hey, it ain't nothing, right?"

Tracy's phone buzzed, indicating another incoming call. "It ain't nothing, Faz. You and Del taking a drive over to Orange Cab?"

"On our way," Faz said.

She accepted the second call.

"It's Earl Keen." His voice was as deep as a bass drum. "You left a message about Veronica Watson. I heard she's dead."

A black man with a shaved head and a serious scowl, Keen had been Veronica Watson's probation officer. Watson had multiple arrests for solicitation and possession of narcotics, and one petty theft charge to which she'd pled no contest.

"You heard right," Tracy said. "Trying to get some information on her."

Keen's voice poured into the car like rich syrup. "Nothing you haven't heard before. She left home at fifteen when the stepfather moved in and started sneaking down the hall and climbing into her bed. The mother chose to believe her new husband. Veronica got tired of it and took off. She lived on the street then moved in with a dirtbag named Bradley Taggart. Taggart's ten years older. Got a long record for being an all-American shithead. He liked to knock her around. Every so often they'd get loud enough that the neighbors would call, but Veronica wouldn't ever press charges. Girl fell down more staircases than a blind man."

"Was he working her?"

"She was pulling tricks, and he was getting a slice of that pie, but if you're asking whether Taggart is a pimp, forget it. He talks a good game, a real tough guy, but he's a punk. He doesn't have the balls or the brains to be running women. Last I knew, he was working in a marine shop in SoDo to meet the conditions of his parole on a meth charge."

Tracy's initial thought was that if Taggart was working Watson, he might know the names of some of her regulars, or where Watson kept that information. "When did she start dancing?"

"Not long after moving in with Taggart. She was underage, but with her figure I don't think her employers delved too deep into her resume. Girl was a cash cow—pardon the term. Danced under the name Velvet."

"Earl, it's Kinsington Rowe. You said Taggart beat her. Any indication he liked to tie her up?"

"Don't know. Like I said, she wouldn't say much. He was her Prince Charming."

"Sounds more like the toad," Kins said.

"That's an insult to toads."

—

They parked at a meter on First Avenue just north of the entrance to the Pink Palace club at the southern edge of Seattle's iconic Pike Place Market, arguably the city's most popular tourist attraction. The market had overlooked the Seattle waterfront and Elliott Bay for more than a hundred years. Tracy had no doubt the heavy foot traffic was what had attracted Darrell Nash to the location for what he called a "satellite club."

Unlike the club just off Aurora, there was no marquee or Jumbotron, just an understated pink neon sign mounted on the wall. Late afternoon, a young man stood outside the entrance in a tuxedo, looking like a high school senior dressed for a prom he didn't want to attend.

Neither Kins nor Tracy bothered to take out their shields as they stepped past him. "Just looking for some lingerie ideas for the spring," Tracy said.

They pushed aside a black curtain draped across the entrance to keep people on the street from getting a free peek. Tracy nearly gagged on the smell of body odor, talcum powder, and perfume. Flashing neon lights and pulsing techno music made her quickly long for real bands playing real instruments, like Bruce Springsteen, Aerosmith, and the Rolling Stones.

Just inside the drape, a petite Asian woman, hair bleached blonde but for a streak of black running down the middle of her scalp like a reverse skunk, stood on four-inch pumps in a purple bra and matching thong. Tracy had Band-Aids that covered more skin. The ticket booth was just to the woman's right; she was apparently the teaser to get men to commit to paying the cover charge.

Kins bent down and spoke into the woman's ear over the sound of the music. The woman pointed in the direction of the bar at the back of the club, then gave him a flirtatious smile and a "you interested?" look. Kins was a good-looking, well-built man, with boyish features that made him look younger than his forty years. He smiled, gave the woman a wink, and stepped past the ticket booth into the club. Tracy followed.

The Pink Palace near Aurora had multiple dance stages and bars, and several leather booths and interior rooms for the private lap dances and sex acts Darrell Nash swore were frowned upon by the management. This club was considerably smaller, just a single stage with chairs and tables arranged in cabaret-style seating. At the moment, a brunette in a white G-string hung from a pole by her leg, her skin glistening beneath overhead lights, music speakers, and a spinning disco ball. She arched her body backward, breasts seeming to defy gravity, and fit her lips over a long-neck Budweiser bottle placed on the edge of the stage by an animated group of Japanese businessmen. They cheered as she lifted herself back up—an impressive feat of core strength.

Kins circled the stage to the place where a bartender in a tuxedo shirt and bow tie leaned on his forearms while talking with a petite redhead and a solidly built African American woman. Both women wore modified tuxedo attire: the shirt just a bib, fishnet leggings, and four-inch pumps.

The bartender straightened. "What can I get you?"

Tracy thought the man had to have the IQ of a rock not to have made them as cops. The dancers clearly had, stepping away.

"Can you make a floor manager appear?" Kins asked.

"A what?"

Kins held up his shield.

The bartender nodded. "Be right back," he said and pushed through a black curtain draped behind the bar.

Tracy looked around. The group of businessmen stuffed the woman's G-string with dollar bills. The redhead had walked to a man sitting alone at a table. Tracy eyed him. He was white, with dark hair, probably midforties. His eyes shifted to Tracy and gave her a disinterested glance before fixating again on the woman onstage.

The bartender returned with a man who looked to be of Middle Eastern descent.

"You the floor manager?" Kins asked.

"Nabil," he said shaking hands. "What can I do for you?"

Tracy recalled Nash telling them that Nabil Kotar had been the floor manager at the Aurora club the night Angela Schreiber was murdered and that the regular floor manager had called in sick that night. That meant Kotar had been one of the employees Ron Mayweather had run a Triple I security check on, using the National Crime Information Center's Interstate Identification Index. Those checks had come back clean.

Like Nash, Kotar had a weightlifter's upper body and favored tight T-shirts, this one black with the sleeves short enough to display a portion of a serpent tattoo slithering on his right biceps. A thick gold cross hung from one of several chains around his neck. By the smell of him, he used a liberal amount of cologne or body spray.

Tracy raised her voice to be heard over the increasingly annoying music. "Is there a place we can talk?"

Kotar led them between two crescent-shaped leather booths and down a short hall to a room with a sheer pink curtain. The room was awash in red and the pungent smell of the club, but at least the music was less offensive.

"How do you not get a headache working here?" Tracy asked.

Kotar shrugged. "You get used to it after a while. Do you want to sit?"

Tracy felt the need to scratch just looking at the booth in front of her. She could only imagine what likely occurred on the table. "We'll stand."

"Is this about Angel?"

"Were you working the floor here last night?"

"Yeah," Kotar said. "I'm fluctuating between here and the Aurora club at the moment."

"You worked this club last night?"

"Manager called in sick. Pain in the ass."

"Why's that?"

"Commute's terrible. Traffic sucks down here, and parking's a bitch."

"So your regular club is the one near Aurora?" Kins asked.

"Yeah."

"What time did you leave the club Tuesday night?" Kins asked.

"I closed it down. So around two thirty or two forty-five."

"You closed it down, not Nash?" Tracy asked. Nash had told them he'd closed down the club that night.

Kotar shrugged. "My job as the manager. I was managing that night."

"Nash say where he was going?"

"I assume home."

"Did he say he was going home?"

"No."

"Where'd you go after you closed it down?" Kins asked.

"Home."

"Anyone verify that?" he asked.

"My wife."

"She was home?"

"Yeah, we got a two-year-old daughter."

"What does your wife think of you working here?" Tracy asked.

Kotar shrugged. "Pay's okay. I get full medical and dental, and I'm home mornings to take my daughter to nursery school. So it works. People think it's a big deal working here, you know? But really, you get anesthetized to it all."

"What does your wife do?"

"She works mornings at a health club. Starts at five thirty."

"Did Veronica Watson work this club last night?" Tracy said.

"Velvet? Yeah," Kotar said, then stopped, his forehead wrinkling in thought. "I think she was here last night. Sometimes the nights blend."

"Tell me about it," Tracy said.

"I can verify it for you." Kotar's eyes narrowed. "Why are you asking about Velvet? Something happen to her?"

"How many women work a schedule at a time?" Tracy asked.

"Depends on the night of the week; weekends we're busier. It's also the preferred shift, because the tips are better. We have ninety-something dancers floating between the three clubs. Not always easy to know who's working where."

"How many last night?"

"I think there were ten, but don't quote me."

"We'll need that schedule," Kins said.

Kotar looked uncertain. "I'll have to ask Darrell about that."

"Why's that?"

"Darrell controls everything. His club." Kotar's gaze shifted between the two of them. "Is Velvet dead? Is that why you're asking about her?"

"Yeah, she's dead," Kins said.

Kotar swore and closed his eyes. He let out a breath before looking back up at them. "Wow. Same guy?"

"What can you tell us about her?" Tracy asked.

Kotar shrugged. "No problems with her. She seemed to get along with everyone all right, but, like I said, this isn't my primary club. Killer body, though I'd heard she'd put on a few pounds so she wasn't as popular as she once was, but I think she did okay."

"Who told you that?"

"That she'd put on a few? Darrell."

It only further confirmed Tracy's impression that Nash considered the dancers nothing more than commodities, fungible goods that could be replaced if they got too fat or too old, or died.

"Did you notice any particular customer paying attention to her last night?" Tracy asked.

"I think I saw her working one of the booths, but nothing specific."

"How about a tall guy in a suit? Light-brown hair," she said, using the description Mr. Joon had provided to Faz.

Kotar shrugged. "I don't know. Dancers might know. She tipped out, I know that."

"What does that mean?"

"Tipped out? The dancers pay a percentage of what they earn in tips from private tables and lap dances to the house."

"You don't pay them?" Tracy said.

"That's how they get paid—table dances and lap dances. At the end of the night, they pay a tip-out fee to the house and keep the rest."

Tracy thought of the woman onstage performing acrobatics. "What about when they dance onstage? They don't get paid for that?"

"That's called marketing and promotion. The dollar bills are tips."

"So you keep records of how much every dancer tips out at the end of the evening?" Kins said.

"Have to. IRS would shut us down if we didn't."

"We're going to need the names of everyone working last night—the bartenders, cocktail waitresses, security, everybody," Kins said.

"Like I said, I'll have to run it by Darrell. He's going to be pissed."

"Yeah, why's that?" Tracy asked.

Kotar looked sheepish. "He'll say it's bad for business. This is going to freak out some of the girls."

But not enough to get them to stop taking strange men to motels, Tracy thought. Even when Ridgway was at the height of his killing, prostitution continued unabated. A girl had to make a living, even if it might kill her. "Was Velvet close to any of the other dancers?"

Another shrug. "I can find out, set up a meeting with the girls she danced with last night. Better to do it later tonight, though.

Can I ask what happened to her? I read in the paper the guy strangled Angel."

"Was Velvet supplementing her income, Nabil?" Tracy said.

"I wouldn't know that."

"Come on, Nabil," Tracy said. "Now is not the time to try and protect her or the club."

He put up his hands. "That's the truth. Not my business. The girls might know. You can ask them."

"What about Darrell Nash, was he at this club last night?"

"He came in."

"What for?"

"Take a look around, check the gate, ask what kind of night we were having."

"Does he do that often?"

"He owns the place."

"Does he do it often?"

"Every so often. Not every night."

"What time did he come by last night?"

"When he comes, it's usually near the end of the evening."

"How about last night, how long did he stay?"

"Last night? Not long." Kotar raised his hands. "I shouldn't say that. I don't know. I was trying to get things shut down and get home. I really didn't pay attention."

"Did you see him talking with any of the dancers?"

"Darrell?" Kotar looked away, as if considering the question. Tracy thought he was stalling. Then he said, "No. Not that I can remember."

Tracy caught Kins's glance. He'd noticed also. She handed Kotar a card. "We'll be back tonight to talk to the girls who worked with Veronica."

CHAPTER 18

The King County Medical Examiner's Office had moved from a dreary, antiquated bunker to Harborview Medical Center, a modern high-rise with wide hallways and spacious rooms bathed in light streaming through the building's tinted-glass exterior walls. Tracy and Kins found Stuart Funk peering into a microscope in one of the labs. Funk had called them as they left the Pink Palace and drove to the Justice Center. He had Angela Schreiber's preliminary toxicology report back, and Veronica Watson's next of kin were coming in to identify her body.

Others in the criminal justice system considered Funk a bit of an odd duck, but Tracy liked him. His unkempt appearance reminded her of a favorite college chemistry professor. Tufts of graying brown hair stuck out over his ears on a head seemingly too large for his narrow shoulders. Bushy eyebrows Kins had once described as needing "a good mowing" sprouted over the top of silver eyeglass frames. When testifying in court, Funk favored bow ties and a tweed jacket with elbow patches. Jurors loved him.

Funk was filling them in on Angela Schreiber. "As with Nicole Hansen, her blood work indicates the presence of flunitrazepam."

"Rohypnol," Tracy said.

The killer's use of Rohypnol was the type of specific detail that would help when they started interviewing suspects.

Funk continued. "Once tied up, the victim can only hold her position for so long before muscle fatigue and cramping. The only way to relieve the pain is to straighten her limbs, tightening the noose and cutting off the supply of oxygen. Eventually, she passes out."

"How long could she last?"

"Hard to say, considering the victims are under considerable stress."

"What about the burn marks on her feet?" Kins asked.

"Definitely from a cigarette," Funk said.

"But no marks on Nicole Hansen?"

"No."

"So something's changed," Tracy said. "Any other scars or healed bruises to indicate she was into this kind of thing?"

"No. Couple bruises but nothing dramatic," Funk said.

"How long before we get the rest of the toxicology report?"

"Lab promised to rush it, along with the vaginal swabs and cultures. But I don't believe it will reveal she was sexually assaulted." Funk exhaled a long sigh. A serial killer changed every aspect of the investigation. The stakes were higher, the pressure for an arrest were exponentially greater, and the consequences of a mistake that allowed a killer to stay at large were fatal.

Tracy checked her watch. "We better meet Veronica Watson's family."

Funk rolled his chair away from the desk. "Shirley and Lawrence Berkman. They live out in Duvall."

"You meet with them yet?" Tracy asked.

Funk shook his head. "I spoke to the mother over the phone."

"How'd she take the news?" Tracy asked.

"She sounded pretty shaken up. I didn't talk to the father."

"Stepfather," Kins said. "Some indication he's the reason she left home."

Funk led them down a pristine hall and pushed open the door to the family room. Comfortably furnished and softly lit, the room was a dramatic improvement from the cold and drab waiting area in the old facility. A middle-aged couple facing the windows turned from the view when the door opened. Tracy assessed Shirley Berkman to be midfifties trying to look midthirties. Her blue jeans were too tight and tucked into knee-high black boots. A white blouse displayed a freckled chest. She wore heavy makeup and an assortment of rings and bracelets, and Tracy wondered if she'd been so adorned when she received the news of her daughter's murder or had taken the time to put on makeup and jewelry before coming downtown.

Lawrence Berkman had a full head of white hair and a neatly trimmed beard. He wore a black leather jacket covered with colorful patches and blue jeans creased like neatly pressed slacks, which flared over cowboy boots. He, too, favored silver rings and bracelets—and, according to Earl Keen, his young stepdaughter.

Funk introduced himself and then Tracy and Kins. Shirley Berkman extended a limp hand. Lawrence kept a hand pressed against his wife's back, as if steadying her.

"Is it Veronica?" Lawrence asked Kins.

"We think so," he said.

"I'm going to need you to positively identify her," Funk said.

Shirley asked Kins, "Did you find her?"

"We did," Kins said.

"What happened to her?" Lawrence asked. Tracy detected a Texas accent, a subtle twang—and an underlying tone of anger or irritation.

"We'll have time for that later," Kins said.

Funk gave the Berkmans his rehearsed spiel about the shock of seeing a loved one and the possibility they could feel faint. He explained that Veronica was in the processing room, her body covered with a sheet. "I'll wait until you say you're ready. It will only be the face."

When the Berkmans nodded their understanding, Funk led them into the room. Tracy and Kins kept back a respectful distance. No amount of soft lighting or interior decorating could camouflage the cold and harsh reality of the stainless steel tables and sinks. The polished linoleum floors reflected the overhead fluorescent lights, creating a kind of mirage that could be momentarily disorienting.

Funk's staff had placed Veronica's body on the table farthest from the door. Even with Veronica beneath a sheet, Tracy could tell her muscles had relaxed sufficiently for Funk to straighten her limbs, and she was glad Shirley wouldn't have to see her daughter's body twisted and contorted.

Shirley Berkman stepped to the edge of the table with her arms crossed, hugging herself. Lawrence kept an arm around her shoulders. Funk stood on the opposite side, hand on the sheet. When Shirley gave a subtle nod, Funk lowered the sheet. Shirley's hand shot to her mouth, and silent tears leaked from her eyes and rolled down her cheeks, but she did not turn away or collapse. She did not cry out, disbelieving. Shirley had a look of tortured resignation, and Tracy could not help but think she had envisioned this moment, or one like it.

"That's Veronica," Lawrence said, brow furrowed, eyes dry.

Funk began to replace the sheet, but Shirley reached out and Funk stepped back. Shirley shrugged Lawrence's arm from her shoulder and leaned close to her daughter.

"Shirls," Lawrence said.

His wife ignored him. She gently caressed Veronica's forehead and cheeks and lightly stroked her hair. Shirley Berkman looked wistful, as if reliving memories she and her daughter once shared, and now her own regrets. The tableau hit Tracy like a blow to the chest and she felt herself flush. She was having difficulty swallowing. Her eyes watered. It was a moment neither she nor her parents had ever shared with Sarah, a moment to say good-bye. Tracy blamed herself for that. She blamed herself for not being with Sarah when she'd been abducted. And now she found herself feeling guilty for not having captured the Cowboy before he'd had the chance to kill again, inflicting pain and grief on another family. Kins noticed her becoming emotional and gave her a reproachful look. Tracy willed herself to regain her composure.

Shirley kissed her daughter's cheek a final time, wiped her tears, and stepped back. Funk replaced the sheet.

"What happens now?" Lawrence asked.

"There'll be an autopsy," Funk said.

"Why?" he said. "What's the point?"

"We need to understand why she's dead," Funk said.

"It's important to determine the cause of death, time of death, and whether there is any forensic evidence we are unable to see but that may have contributed to her death," Kins said.

"Or that may lead us to the person who did this," Tracy said.

"It's that asshole boyfriend of hers," Lawrence said, pupils small and fixed on Tracy. "He got her into that crap, that lifestyle. Hell, just go arrest him. What's that piece of shit's name?"

"Taggart. Bradley Taggart," Shirley said, sounding tired. She dabbed at the corner of her eyes with a tissue.

"He was sleeping with her when she was fifteen, but you people never did anything about that. He used to beat her up too," Lawrence said. "There's your suspect. Go talk to him."

"We intend to," Tracy said. She took a step to get out of Lawrence's line of fire. "Mrs. Berkman, are you aware of your daughter seeing anyone other than Mr. Taggart? Did she ever talk to you about anyone?"

Shirley shook her head. "We didn't communicate too often."

"The boyfriend kept her from us," Lawrence said. "We couldn't even call."

"Any former boyfriends who might have had an ax to grind?" Kins asked.

"She was fifteen when she moved in with him," Lawrence said. "She didn't have any boyfriends."

"Any enemies you're aware of?" Tracy persisted. "Did she ever mention anyone following her, harassing her at work?"

"No," Shirley said. "No one." Her chest shuddered, but she controlled it. "Veronica was a good girl. She was in a bad situation, but she wasn't a bad person."

"I'm sure she wasn't," Tracy said.

"Where did you find her?"

"A motel room on Aurora Avenue," Tracy said.

Tears streamed down Shirley Berkman's cheeks, leaving trails in her makeup. When Lawrence went to comfort her, she stepped away and hurried from the room, leaving him alone and looking uncertain. He hesitated. Then he lowered his eyes and stepped out, cowboy boots clicking on the linoleum.

CHAPTER 19

The cool air off Elliott Bay felt refreshing, and Tracy sucked it in, still feeling flushed as she and Kins crossed Jefferson Street to their car.

Kins opened the driver's side door but did not get in. "What was that all about in there?"

"Was I wrong to leave, Kins?"

"Don't do that to yourself."

"Maybe I should have stayed. Maybe if I had, we would have caught this guy by now."

"This isn't your fault. Don't make it personal. Nolasco chose to send Hansen to cold cases. He took it from us to make you look bad. You had to go to Cedar Grove, and there's not a single cop on this entire force who wouldn't have done exactly what you did. You had every right to find out what happened to your sister."

She nodded, but Kins's reassurance didn't take away the pain she'd felt watching Shirley Berkman's final moments with her daughter, or the harsh reality that while an arrest of the Cowboy might bring the families of his victims justice, it would never bring them closure.

Tracy knew that firsthand.

—

The Washington State Patrol Crime Lab was located in a block-long squat cement structure in Seattle's SoDo neighborhood, an industrial area south of downtown. As Tracy and Kins maneuvered through the halls and neared Michael Melton's office, they heard the soothing melody of Melton's guitar and equally soothing voice.

"'Country Roads,'" Kins said.

Melton had his office door open but didn't flinch or miss a chord when Tracy and Kins reached the threshold. He ended the song with an impressive guitar riff. "How's my favorite detective?" Melton said.

"I know you're not talking to me," Kins said.

Tracy forced a smile. "Getting ready for your next gig?"

Melton sang in a country-western band called the Fourensics with three other crime lab scientists. They played local bars, small gigs, and at an annual fund-raiser for victims of crime. Melton told Tracy playing guitar and singing kept him sane in an insane world. He looked like a lumberjack, with a mane of graying hair tied in a ponytail, a bushy beard, and a flannel shirt rolled up to reveal forearms that looked like he'd grown up splitting cords of wood.

"Nothing on the calendar," he said. "But you know me. If there's beer, I'll be near."

Melton hung the guitar on a prong protruding from the wall amid an eclectic collection of odd mementos from the various cases he had worked—baseball bats, ball-peen hammers, knives, guns, even a slingshot.

"Might be a while though; we're so backed up here my eyes are brown."

Melton handed them his reports on the rope found at the shooting range and the rope used to strangle Veronica Watson. "Which do you want first?"

"How about the shooting range," Kins said.

"Generic three-strand. Polypropylene with a right twist."

"So same type of rope as the ropes used to strangle Hansen and Schreiber," Kins said.

"Same type."

"Can you tell if it came from the same length of rope?"

"Not definitively. The ends were too frayed."

"If you had to guess?"

"I'd say no."

"What about a manufacturer?"

"Too common. You can buy it pretty much anywhere."

"And the knot?" Tracy asked.

"Different. Definitely different from Hansen or Schreiber. Not nearly as intricate." Melton handed them photos.

"What do you make of it?" Tracy asked.

"Thankfully, that's not my job."

"What about the person who tied it, right- or left-handed?"

Melton shook his head. "Too rudimentary to draw any conclusions."

"So no skill required," Tracy said.

"No skill required," Melton agreed.

Tracy addressed Kins. "Maybe on purpose, to throw us off?"

"Maybe. What about Veronica Watson?" Kins asked Melton.

"Also generic three-strand polypropylene with a right twist. If I had to give an opinion, I'd say it comes from the same length of rope as Schreiber's, but again, that's an educated guess. The knot, however, is identical to Nicole Hansen's and to Angela Schreiber's."

"No question?" Tracy asked.

"None."

"So left-handed," Kins said.

"Definitely," Melton said.

"How long before we get the DNA analysis?" Tracy asked.

"At least twenty-four hours, and that's with me making it a priority."

Tracy sighed. "So tell me, how're we going to get this guy, Mike?"

"Again, thankfully, not in my job description. Hopefully he makes a mistake. They all do. Just a matter of when."

CHAPTER 20

Billy Williams called to give them a heads-up—Maria Vanpelt had filed a special news report confirming that Seattle officially had another serial killer, nicknamed the Cowboy, and that SPD was forming a task force to catch him.

"Nice of her to let us know," Tracy said, unable to hide the disgust in her voice.

"The brass is convening," Billy said. "All the big boys are going to be there, and your presence has been requested."

"Does *request* mean we can say no?" Kins asked.

"No," Billy said.

—

At the Justice Center, Tracy and Kins made a beeline for the kitchen, having not eaten since breakfast. Kins slid two bucks into the community fund and grabbed a bag of Doritos and a bag of Famous Amos cookies. "You want the high fat content or the high fat content?"

"You know me better than to ask." Tracy grabbed the cookies. "Chocolate."

They made their way to the eighth floor and stepped into a bland conference room with walls unadorned by paintings or photographs. Nolasco sat at the far end of the table, his back to tinted windows. He glanced up from a document and peered at them over reading glasses. With his mud-brown hair parted in the middle and a bushy mustache trimmed just below the corners of his mouth, the joke among the women on the force was that Nolasco looked like an aging 1970s porn star. Beside him sat Bennett Lee, a public information officer for SPD; Billy Williams; and Andrew Laub, their lieutenant.

Lee slid two sheets of paper across the table as Kins and Tracy rolled out chairs. "What's this?" Tracy asked.

"Clarridge wants to make a statement," Nolasco said, referring to Chief Sandy Clarridge. Nolasco removed his glasses, twirling them by a stem. "The mayor's going to be with him. Neither is happy with the latest news reports."

"Which are what?" Tracy asked, sitting.

"That we have another serial killer . . . and skepticism about whether we are competent to catch him."

"Manpelt?" Tracy said, using the nickname the detectives had bestowed on Maria Vanpelt.

"That's irrelevant," Nolasco said.

"Not exactly the fountain of truth." Tracy popped a cookie into her mouth.

"She'd turn a convention of Buddhists into a clandestine terrorist gathering," Kins said.

"Either of you want to explain that to the Chief?" Nolasco said.

"Is that why we're here?" Tracy asked.

"You're here because I want to know where we're at with the latest murder and how it ties in with the other two," Nolasco said. "And give me the *Reader's Digest* version. I don't have much time."

"Same type of rope as the rope used to kill Hansen and Schreiber," Tracy said. "Can't tell if it comes from the same coil, but no doubt about the knot. Same guy tied it. Likely left-handed. Room was straightened. Bed made. Clothes folded. Don't know about DNA yet; can't get fingerprints off a rope, but Melton says they lifted enough prints from the motel room to start a small village. It's going to take time."

"So we have a serial killer," Nolasco said.

"We already had a serial killer."

"Maybe we should focus on the statement," Lee said, lifting a sheet of paper from the table, "since we're pressed for time."

Whoever had written the statement described the three murders vaguely, omitting any reference to a noose or rope. "This won't pacify the media," Tracy said.

"We're not in the business of pacifying the media," Nolasco said.

"They already know Hansen and Schreiber were strangled with a noose," she said. "They'll deduce Watson died the same way."

"I want to keep the details vague," Nolasco said.

"You've succeeded."

"You got a problem with that?"

"I don't, but Clarridge reads this and the media will think he's holding back something important. They'll ask for specifics he can't answer, which will put him on the spot." She shrugged. "Your call."

Nolasco reconsidered the statement while rubbing his index finger over his mustache, a habit when he was stalling. After less than a minute, he set the statement down and pressed his fingertips together, forming a pyramid just beneath his lips. "What do you suggest?"

"There's no reason to hide the fact that Watson was strangled or the type of rope," Tracy said.

"I agree," Kins said. "That ship has sailed, thanks to Manpelt."

"But hold back any details about the knot, the method of strangulation, and the condition of the room," Tracy said.

She took a moment to read the second paragraph, which stated that Clarridge would form a task force. "Are you handling the media, Bennett?"

"I am," he said. He didn't sound or look happy about it. Being the PIO in a serial killer investigation was like being a tightrope walker in a windstorm, a delicate balancing act, with each step another chance to make a fatal mistake. Release too much information and Lee would be educating not only the media, but also the killer. Too little information and the press would assume the task force was making no progress or withholding information. Tracy considered Lee a smart choice. He'd stick to an agreed-upon script, and he was good at keeping his facial features bland and his voice under control, revealing little beyond the prepared statement.

The final paragraph was the obligatory assurance to the general public that every available resource was being utilized in the investigation . . . including the local division of the FBI.

"What the hell," Kins said. "Whose idea was it to bring in the Famous But Incompetent?"

Before anyone could answer, Clarridge entered the room with Stephen Martinez, the assistant chief of criminal investigations. Both wore the department's standard French-blue short-sleeve shirts, Clarridge's with four collar stars and his gold "Chief" badge pinned to his left breast pocket. Clarridge always made a point of being in uniform when he stepped to the podium. It was his way of saying, "I'm still a cop"—though maybe not chief for too much longer. Rumor was the recently elected mayor, who had not appointed Clarridge, was losing patience.

After greetings, Clarridge said, "Is that the statement?"

Lee stood and handed copies to Clarridge and Martinez. Clarridge tapped the desk with his middle finger as he read. Tracy glanced at Kins, who sat stewing over Nolasco's insertion of the FBI into their investigation.

When Clarridge set down the statement, Nolasco said, "Chief, it's my suggestion that we not hide the fact that the killer uses a noose to strangle his victims. That cat is already out of the bag. If we withhold it, the media will pepper you for details we don't want to provide at this time."

Clarridge looked across the table at Tracy. "Detective Crosswhite, this is your investigation. Do you agree?"

"I think it's a brilliant suggestion," she said. Lee lowered his head but couldn't suppress a smile. "I also wouldn't use the words 'stripper' or 'prostitute.' The women were dancers. Better yet, call them victims."

"Tell me about them."

—

For the next twenty minutes, Clarridge listened intently, asked intelligent questions, and took notes on the back of the press release as Tracy provided details about the crime scenes, the forensic evidence, leads, and possible suspects. With the building mostly shut down for the night, the air in the room soon became warm and stale. Clarridge's cheeks had flushed, in contrast to his pale Slavic complexion.

"So, little doubt we're dealing with one man," Clarridge said.

"Correct."

"Someone who has a problem with dancers?"

"Maybe. They could simply be victims of opportunity. But yes, all three were dancers."

"So who are we looking at? Employees? Customers?"

"Definitely," Tracy said. "We're running Triple I checks on the male employees and running down anyone with any priors," she said. "But there are close to a hundred dancers working at the clubs, and there's a website for customers to make online reservations with their favorites. The killer might not even be going to one of the clubs. He could be setting up his meetings with the dancers online."

Clarridge gave this some thought, no doubt considering the expense they could anticipate if they had to hire Internet experts. He spoke directly to Tracy and Kins. "Other than the crime scene markers, any definitive characteristics?"

"Forensics believes the person tying the knots is left-handed."

"That could reduce the pool of suspects significantly," Clarridge said.

"It could," Tracy said. "Unfortunately, at the moment that pool is already very small."

"We need to change that. I'm going to shift some funds to put together a task force."

Tracy felt mixed emotions. She was glad they'd form a team dedicated to catching the Cowboy, but she knew it would mean a lot of late nights, long days, and frustrating dead ends. She also knew the assignment could last years, without success, and could exact a significant mental toll on her well-being.

"Detective Crosswhite," Clarridge said. "I'm concerned you might be too close to this situation given your family history and the recent incident involving the noose. I wonder if perhaps it might not be best to let Detective Rowe act as the lead. How you divide up your responsibilities will be between the two of you."

Tracy bristled at the suggestion and was about to say that while Kins was a great choice, she wanted to lead the investigation. She was also concerned Kins's marriage would not take the additional strain of his being the lead on a task force. Before she could respond, however, Nolasco sat forward in his chair.

"With all due respect," Nolasco said, "I disagree."

Stunned, Tracy looked to Kins, whose quizzical facial expression revealed he too was surprised.

"I think having a female detective lead a task force trying to catch a man killing women will be favorably perceived by the media and the public. We might avoid the kind of criticism directed at the King County Sheriff's Office during the Ridgway investigation." Nolasco failed to mention the criticism following his ill-fated and premature decision to send the Nicole Hansen investigation to the Cold Case Unit.

Clarridge pinched his lower lip. "What about it, Detective Crosswhite?"

"I want this case, Chief."

Clarridge nodded. "All right. Then it's your task force. I don't have to tell you that's a double-edged sword."

"Understood," Tracy said.

"Chief," Kins said, "can we address the issue of bringing in the FBI? We all know it gives the public and the politicians a warm and fuzzy, but these guys don't deal in murder, and the only time they've ever caught a serial killer was in novels and movies. Honestly, I'd prefer to work with a Boy Scout troop."

"There are other factors at play here," Nolasco said. "A task force will be expensive, and the FBI can provide additional manpower and federal funds. And it's good for PR. It lets the public know we're using every available resource."

Again, Clarridge was deliberate. "When I announce the task force, I'll announce that the FBI will be *assisting* in *our* investigation. You and Detective Crosswhite can keep them at arm's length, or bring them in to whatever extent you determine necessary."

Clarridge checked his watch. "I have a news conference to prepare for."

After Clarridge and Martinez departed, Nolasco addressed Tracy. "I want a list of names for the task force on my desk before you go home. And don't submit fifty. I want fifteen, at most. This is not going to be another Ridgway. Get on it. We're behind the eight ball, and I don't want to fall behind any further. Find this asshole."

After Nolasco left, Kins said, "He really has a way of motivating, doesn't he? Winston Churchill has nothing on that guy."

"Unfortunately, he's right," Tracy said. "We're way behind this guy, and something seems to have triggered his desire to kill. We don't catch him soon, this *could* be another Ridgway."

CHAPTER 21

Grease-stained hamburger wrappers littered the car. Kins had stopped at Dick's, a drive-in hamburger joint on Capitol Hill that attracted a steady flow of college and high school students looking to stretch a buck. The only appeal it had to Tracy was they used real ice cream in their milk shakes and were still open at one in the morning.

Dan called just as Tracy sucked a hunk of strawberry into her straw. For him to be calling this late, it meant he'd likely seen Clarridge's announcement of a task force and Maria Vanpelt's interview of Shirley and Lawrence Berkman criticizing SPD for not having formed the task force earlier, and he wanted to make sure Tracy was doing all right.

"I could drive down and spend the night," Dan said.

"Are you offering me pity sex?"

Kins, in the driver's seat, snickered and smiled.

"Not at all," Dan said. "My arbitration doesn't get started until ten. These guys keep bankers' hours. Unless you're *into* pity sex. Then absolutely."

Tracy laughed, and it felt good after a long and frustrating day. "Unfortunately, we're still at it."

"As your attorney, I hope they're paying you overtime."

"How's the arbitration going?"

"Slow. The defense attorney is fighting everything. I really have to look into this whole notion of getting paid by the hour instead of on a contingency."

"And sell your soul?"

"I could afford to buy a new one at some of the hourly rates these guys charge. We still on for Friday night?"

"Only if you're still in the pitying mood."

"You kidding? I majored in pity. Any thoughts about what you might want to do?'

"Several."

"You're killing me. You know that don't you?"

"I'll see you Friday." She disconnected and slipped her cell back into her jacket pocket.

Kins lowered his chocolate shake. "Pity sex? How does that work?"

She couldn't keep from grinning. "I'll let you know."

"I thought I could mention it to Shannah," Kins said.

"Things still not going well?"

"It's just ships passing in the night, you know. It's been a rough patch. This isn't going to help."

"You'll get through it."

"She's talking about taking the kids to San Diego to visit her sister."

"That doesn't sound like a bad thing."

"They're in school, Tracy."

"Oh."

"I've been missing too much lately—the kids' games, dinners with friends. She feels like a single parent."

"So sneak out when you can. We'll have people now to take some of the burden."

"Yeah, I guess. What about you? You like this guy?"

She shrugged but found herself smiling again. "I'm taking it slow."

"Pity sex is slow? Damn, I really need to find out how that works."

"We haven't had a lot of free time together since Cedar Grove. I'm worried that when he spends more time with me, he'll see through this façade of charm."

"You have a façade?'

"Fuck you."

"How could he not love you?"

—

Scraps of paper twisted and turned in the wind blowing down the cobblestone street in the shuttered Pike Place Market. Outside the Pink Palace, a new barker, older and harder-looking than the bored young man who'd stood out front that afternoon, stepped from the curb as Kins pulled up to the entrance. The man slapped the hood with the palm of his hand. "You can't park here."

Kins badged him. "Bang on it again and you'll be handcuffed to the bumper." The barker stepped back, hands raised. "Keep an eye on it for me," Kins said, "and there'll be a big tip in it for you."

The Pink Palace was at full throttle, lights flashing and music pulsing the same eardrum-splitting Euro electronic trash that had been playing that afternoon. Two women now stalked the stage— the Asian with the bad dye job and the larger black woman who'd been standing at the bar that afternoon. They strutted, dipped, and shimmied. The Asian woman spun around the pole, clinging to it with one leg while men held out dollar bills and cheered. Other dancers sauntered through the tables in high heels and lingerie.

Tracy scanned the faces of the men, ignoring the more animated and boisterous, and focused on those sitting at tables in the back, nursing beers and hard drinks. She looked to see if anyone was holding a glass in his left hand. She was looking for a tall man with light-brown hair in a suit. One man wore a baseball cap pressed so low it nearly obscured his eyes and, despite the heat, a wool-lined jean jacket. In the corner two men in a booth were giving their rapt attention to a woman slithering nearly naked on the table.

Nabil Kotar met them at the bar, looking anxious. "Okay, come on," he said. He led them through the curtain to a cramped and crowded backstage. They stepped around portable metal clothing racks of skimpy lingerie; spools of black electrical cable; and spare light fixtures and speaker equipment. Kotar spoke to them while looking over his shoulder. "Three dancers called in sick. Another one is so freaked-out she says she's quitting and moving to Colorado. She won't come out of the greenroom."

"Nash been around tonight?" Tracy asked.

"Haven't seen him," Kotar said. "You'll have to ask them your questions in between sets working the stage and floor."

"These girls worked with Veronica?"

"Three of them," Kotar said. "Another one is onstage."

They followed Kotar into an equally cramped and cluttered dressing room. A redhead sat topless at a cluttered makeup station, holding a mascara applicator and making no effort to cover herself. A blonde seated in a metal folding chair at the second station pulled closed a red silk dressing gown. The third woman, a brunette in a sheer robe that left little to the imagination, sifted through a portable rack of lingerie.

"These are the detectives," Kotar announced. Then to Tracy and Kins, "I'll get you a couple of chairs."

"We saw the news," the brunette said as Kotar departed. Chinese symbols ran up her neck to an ear adorned with multiple silver rings. Another ring pierced her right nipple. "I was like, 'Oh shit, not Veronica.' I liked Angela, but she danced mostly at the other club and she was new. I didn't know her as well. Veronica's been here a long time." She slipped lace panties over her three-inch platform shoes, shimmying them up her long legs. "They said it's a serial killer; why do all the crazies have to live here?"

"It's all the rain," the redhead said. "The gray makes people depressed." She had a high-pitched voice and didn't even look old enough to have her learner's permit.

Kotar returned and handed Kins two folding chairs. "Keep it short," he said, almost apologetically. Then he left again.

"Everybody's scared," the redhead said. "I mean, I danced with V last night. She was like, happy and everything. I couldn't believe it. I'm moving back to Colorado."

Tracy and Kins sat near the door. Both knew it best not to interrupt witnesses freely talking.

"I thought you caught the guy," the blonde said. She looked older than the other two, but it was difficult to tell through a healthy dose of pancake makeup. "I thought he was a school-teacher or something."

"He came in with Angela one time," the redhead said. "Not here. At the Aurora club."

"Why don't you arrest him?" the blonde said.

"There isn't enough evidence to prove he did it," Tracy said.

The blonde rolled her eyes and turned to the makeup station.

"Did you notice anyone paying special attention to Veronica last night?" Tracy asked.

"I didn't notice anyone," the redhead said.

Tracy looked to the blonde, who shook her head in the mirror while applying powder to her chest. "I wouldn't even know what *special* attention is."

"Anyone see Darrell Nash here last night?" Tracy asked.

"I saw him." The brunette had slipped on stockings and was snapping them to a garter belt. "Did you see him talking to Veronica?" Tracy asked.

"No."

"I did," the blonde said, using the mirror to watch them. "I was onstage. V had just finished working one of the booths."

"How long did they talk?" Kins asked.

"Not long."

"Did Veronica say anything to you about it?" Tracy said.

"Like what?"

"Anything."

She shook her head.

"Does Nash come in often?" Kins asked.

"He's the boss," the blonde said, and Tracy was definitely detecting an attitude. "V had a boyfriend. You talked to him yet?"

"That guy is a creep." The brunette slipped on a red teddy and unrolled long lace gloves.

"Why do you say that?" Tracy asked.

"V danced here, so he thought he could touch us. Asshole."

"What's the club's policy on that?" Tracy asked.

"You set your own boundaries," the blonde said. "You don't want to be touched, that's up to you. Guys will always try. You just get up and walk away."

"Does that make them mad?"

"It can."

"Especially if they're drunk," the redhead said.

"You ever see a customer get mad at Veronica or Angela?"

"Not that I can remember," the blonde said. The other two shrugged.

"Veronica's parents said the boyfriend knocked her around," Tracy said.

The redhead nodded. "She came in with some bruises once, but she wouldn't talk about it."

The brunette stepped to where Kins sat blocking the door. "I got a set," she said.

Kins started to get up, but the brunette put her hands on his shoulders and deftly lifted a long leg, straddling him momentarily before stepping across his lap. She smiled and winked. "That one was on the house."

As she departed, the African American woman who'd been onstage stepped into the room breathing hard and dabbing a paper towel to her forehead and chest. She was more voluptuous than the others.

"They're the detectives for Angela and Velvet," the redhead said.

"I figured you as cops when you came in this afternoon. I asked Nabil what it was about."

"What did he tell you?" Tracy asked.

"Veronica was dead. You think it's the same guy. Is it?"

"We're working on it."

Kins offered the woman his chair, since there was no place for her to sit.

She smiled. "Are you for real? Thanks. My back's killing me. I'm Shereece."

"They want to know if anyone was bothering V last night or paying special attention to her," the blonde said.

Shereece slid off a wig revealing a peach-colored skullcap. Tracy estimated she was in her early thirties. "It was pretty slow last night."

"No one stood out?" Kins asked.

"What about Mr. Attorney?" the blonde asked.

"He likes big tits," the redhead said. "He doesn't ask for me."

"I didn't see him," Shereece said.

"You know his name?" Tracy asked.

She shook her head. "No."

"But he's an attorney?"

"That's just what we call him," the blonde said, "because he comes in wearing a suit and tie."

"What do you know about him?"

"Likes to talk," the blonde said. "Nothing weird or anything."

"How old?"

"Maybe early forties?" She looked to Shereece. "They asked about V's boyfriend."

"He was here," Shereece said. "Came in looking for money."

"How do you know he came in looking for money?" Tracy said.

"Because that boy's always looking for money. He treated Veronica like an ATM."

"Can you think of any regulars that Angela and Veronica might have had in common?

Shereece shook her head again. "Not really."

"What the hell?"

The women startled. Darrell Nash stood in the doorway red-faced and scowling. Nabil Kotar stood behind him looking sheepish. Nash turned on him. "What the hell, Nabil? Is this why there's only one dancer on my dance floor?"

Kins was on his feet. "We're asking them questions."

"Ask them on their own time."

"They're on break." Kins stepped closer, causing Nash to take a step back and stumble into Kotar.

"This is a private club. You have no right to talk to my employees during business hours."

"Independent contractors," Tracy said. She was also standing now. "And the club is open to the public."

"You're backstage. The public area is out there."

"Fine, we'll finish asking our questions in a booth. How's that?" Tracy said.

"I'm calling my lawyer. You have no right to disrupt my business!"

"While you're at it, ask your lawyer the penalty for hiring underage dancers."

"That doesn't happen here."

"No? Veronica Watson was nineteen. How long was she dancing here?"

"I don't know anything about that. What I know is that when they're here, they dance, or I find others who will."

The women filed out the door, all except Shereece, who took a vacated seat at one of the makeup stations.

"What are you doing?" Nash said.

"What does it look like I'm doing? I'm resting my feet."

"Don't give me lip, Shereece."

"You'll know when I'm giving you lip. I just got done with a set. I'm on break."

Kins said to Nash, "Why'd you come in tonight, Darrell?"

"I came in because I heard we're three girls short, so I brought a couple dancers from the Aurora club."

"Why'd you come in last night?"

"I own the clubs, Detective. I don't need any reason to come into my own club."

"Did you talk to Veronica Watson last night?" Tracy asked.

Nash gave a disgusted laugh. "Are you serious?"

"Is that a yes?" Kins said.

"I don't recall speaking to Veronica."

"What time did you leave?" Tracy asked.

"Am I a suspect?"

"You'll know when you're a suspect," Kins said. "It's a lot of fun. We get to read you your rights."

Nash shook his head. "I came in to check the gate and left just before closing. I went back to the Aurora club, helped shut it down, and went home. You can ask my wife. Now, are we finished?"

"Someone is killing your independent contractors, Darrell," Tracy said. "We're a long way from finished."

Tracy stepped into her kitchen at just after three in the morning. Roger sounded like a litter of cats. She fed him, then walked through the darkened living room to her bedroom, not bothering to turn on the lights. She dropped her briefcase and jacket on the bed along with her badge, keys, and Glock. After leaving the Pink Palace, she and Kins had made a trip to Pioneer Square to wake up Bradley Taggart, but if Veronica Watson's boyfriend was still residing at their last known address, he wasn't home, or chose not to come to the door.

In the bathroom she removed her blouse and pants, tossed them in the dirty-clothes pile in the corner, and gave her teeth a perfunctory brushing before turning to use the toilet.

The seat was up.

She felt her stomach drop. She tried to recall when Dan had last been at her home; the days had become a blur. Unable to remember for certain, she retrieved her Glock and checked the bedroom closet and under the bed. The sliding glass door remained locked. She made her way through the living room and dining room turning on the lights. She looked down the stairs to the door. The deadbolt was flipped to the right, engaged. She checked the closet near the front door and peered out the sidelights to ensure that the patrol officer was present, then crossed the room and rattled the sliding glass door to the patio. Also locked.

Having cleared the upper level, she returned to the bathroom. The water in the toilet bowl was clear. She told herself it was probably just Dan. She lived in a fortress. But when she climbed into bed, she again set the Glock on the pillow.

CHAPTER 22

The following morning, Tracy and Kins stepped into the elevator together and rode it to the seventh floor. "You feel like I look," Kins said, bastardizing the usual phrase.

"You look like crap."

"I know."

They made their way to the A Team's bull pen. Faz, always an early riser, gave them a huge grin. "Look what the cat dragged in," he said. "Are we having fun yet?"

"More like what the cat left in the litter box," Kins said.

Tracy hadn't even taken off her coat before Johnny Nolasco stepped into the bull pen. Nolasco handed Kins the list of names he and Tracy had compiled for the task force. They had left it on Nolasco's desk before leaving to talk to the Pink Palace dancers. And from the amount of red ink she could see, Nolasco had struck at least half the names.

"I told you, I have funding for a *limited* task force," he said. "This is not going to be another Ridgway with fifty detectives running around on wild-goose chases."

"We didn't pick fifty," Tracy said, taking the list and scanning it. "How are we supposed to catch this guy?"

"By doing your jobs. The names on that list are your respon-sibility. Someone screws up, the shit runs downhill and stops with you."

When Nolasco departed, Faz, who was sitting quiet at his desk, stood and hitched up the waist of his slacks. "Am I on that list?"

"You got a resume for us to consider?" Kins said.

"You and the horse you rode in on, Sparrow."

"Your name's on the list," Tracy said.

Faz smiled. "Good."

"You might be the only one happy about it," Kins said.

They'd consulted a detective who'd worked the Green River Task force, which had lingered for years before ultimately being disbanded. He'd instructed them to choose detectives who could handle the psychological strain of pursuing a killer no matter how cold the leads became, and suggested they avoid new detectives and detectives with small children, since a single assignment could stall a career and the department bean counters still cared about production. He also cautioned them not to deplete one unit, since the job of picking up active investigations would fall to those who remained, which could cause friction and animosity.

"I got ADD," Faz said. "I can't focus if I have more than one thing to do."

"Yeah, well, you may have a lot more than one thing to do," Tracy said, shaking the list of names. "This is not enough people."

"You can check one thing off the list," Faz said. "Del and I spoke to Orange Cab about Veronica Watson. The driver is a Russian named Oliver Azarov. Just got off the boat eighteen months ago with a wife and two daughters. I ran him through the system. He's clean. Del and I will take a drive later and see what he knows."

"Any of the local businesses know anything?" Kins asked.

"Nobody saw nobody," Faz said. "The convenience store connected to the gas station across the street has a camera, but it only covers the door. Camera outside is on the pumps. Can't see the motel entrance." Faz checked his watch. "I'll make a call to Wash-DOT to find out what traffic cameras they've got around the motels and put in requests for the days Hansen, Schreiber, and Watson died."

Tracy nodded, but the Wash-DOT cameras wouldn't do them any good unless they had a specific car or license plate to look for, and even that would be like searching for the proverbial needle in the haystack.

—

Tracy and Kins spent much of the day educating the members of their task force on the three victims, the evidence, and a list of possible suspects that included Walter Gipson, Darrell Nash, Bradley Taggart, and every male employee and customer of the Pink Palace.

"That narrows it down," Faz said.

They parceled out assignments, and the men and women went to work. Mike Melton called Tracy's cell late in the afternoon.

"The DNA on the rope belongs to Veronica Watson. No other hits."

"As we suspected," she said.

"But the rope from the shooting range produced three different DNA profiles and one positive hit," Melton said.

"What's the nature of the hit?" Tracy said.

"Don't know."

"You got a name?"

"David Bankston."

Tracy thanked him, hung up, and swiveled her chair to where Kins sat at his desk. "Mike got a positive DNA hit on the rope at the shooting range," she said.

Kins turned to his keyboard. "You got a name?"

Tracy and Faz peered over his shoulder as Kins ran the name David Bankston through the system. Bankston had no criminal record and no outstanding warrants. The DNA hit was the result of a tour in the National Guard. "He served in Desert Storm," he said. He scrolled to another hit in the system and pulled it up. "Looks like he also attended the police academy."

"What happened to him?" Tracy asked.

"Doesn't say," Kins said, reaching for his desk phone.

Five minutes later, he had an answer. "Bankston washed out," he said. "He was unable to complete the fitness training."

"Shit, I hope they don't test me," Faz said.

According to the clerk Kins had spoken with, Bankston's Academy paperwork listed him as five eleven and 245 pounds—big, but not obese.

"So he washes out of the Academy and joins the Army," Kins said. "And becomes a lean, mean fighting machine."

"*Stripes*," Faz said.

"*Stripes*?" Tracy asked.

"Please don't tell me you've never seen the movie *Stripes*," Kins said.

"I'm sure I haven't. But let me guess, it's a 'classic.'" With three boys, Kins could, and often did, recite lines from movies and television shows, most of them sophomoric. He proudly proclaimed he'd seen every *Seinfeld* and *Cheers* episode.

"Isn't every Bill Murray movie a classic?" Faz said.

"Spare me," Tracy said.

"Murray's a cabdriver," Kins said to Tracy. "His life is going down the toilet, so he joins the Army. One of the men in his platoon is John Candy. You do know who John Candy is, don't you?"

"Didn't he die of obesity?"

"How are we partners?"

"Sometimes I wonder."

"Candy explains that the local weight-loss clinic costs four hundred bucks, so instead he joins the Army to become a . . ."

Kins and Faz finished the line together. "Lean, mean fighting machine!"

"Classic," Tracy said.

"Hey, it ain't nothing, Professor. You want me and Del to go talk to this guy?"

"No. We'll handle this. Where're we at on trying to enhance that video from the Pink Palace parking lot?"

"Melton's working on it," Faz said. "The lighting is the shits, and it's tough with the car moving. He said getting any detail is going to be next to impossible. I'm hoping he's just setting himself up to look good."

—

David Bankston worked at a Home Depot warehouse in Kent, where Kins correctly noted he'd have convenient access to a lot of rope. For the first time since they walked into the motel room and found Nicole Hansen, Tracy felt a twinge of optimism.

The warehouse manager escorted them through a large open-air structure filled with home improvement materials to an area at the back of the building with offices, a lunchroom, an employee lounge, and bathrooms. He led them into a generic office of oak veneer furniture and watercolor prints and introduced them to Bankston's supervisor, Haari Rajput, who stood and greeted them formally, offering a soft hand but firm handshake. The manager left.

"How may I be of assistance?" Rajput asked in heavily accented English. Thin, with narrow shoulders, Rajput wore black-framed glasses that, along with a thick mustache and broad nose, brought to mind the classic dime-store Groucho Marx disguise.

"We're interested in speaking to one of your employees," Tracy said. "David Bankston. We understand he's working today."

Rajput reached for a radiophone on his desk. "David? Yes. I will get him."

"Before you do," Tracy said, raising a hand, "we'd like to ask you a few questions."

Rajput slid back his hand. He looked concerned.

"You're Mr. Bankston's supervisor?" Tracy asked, starting slowly to get Rajput to relax.

"Yes."

"How long has Mr. Bankston worked here?"

"I do not know. He started before my employment. I will have to pull his file." Rajput rose from his chair and started for a file cabinet behind the desk.

"Just an estimate is fine," Tracy said.

"Several years," Rajput said, retaking his seat.

"You're open twenty-four hours a day?" Tracy asked.

"Yes."

"So the employees work shifts?"

"Three shifts—day, swing, and night."

"What shift does Mr. Bankston work?" Tracy asked.

Rajput adjusted his glasses. "It varies. Sometimes day. Sometimes swing. Sometimes night."

Tracy pointed to a punch clock on the wall inside the door, the slots filled with beige time cards. "How far back do you keep those cards?"

"Many months. We are required to do so."

"Are those cards for this week?"

"Yes."

"May I see Mr. Bankston's card?"

Rajput rose again and moved to the bank of cards. He lifted his eyeglasses, resting them just above his eyebrows, and bent for a closer look. He plucked a card from its slot and handed it to Tracy.

"When does the swing shift start and end?" Kins asked, taking over the questioning while Tracy reviewed the time card.

Rajput retreated behind the desk and sat. "Four to midnight."

"What kind of guy is David?"

"Good employee. Very good. No problems."

"I mean, what kind of person is he? Is he loud, quiet? What's his demeanor?"

Rajput had a habit of raising his palms, as if under arrest. "Good person. Quiet. He gets his work done with no problems."

"Is he single, married?" Kins continued.

"He is married. Two dependents."

"He has a child," Kins said.

Rajput nodded.

Tracy handed Kins the card. Bankston had checked out just after midnight the nights Angela Schreiber and Veronica Watson were murdered. As Faz would have said, it wasn't nothing.

"Does Mr. Bankston work in any particular department?" she asked.

"No. No department. The employees work all over."

"So electrical, plumbing, construction supplies? He could be loading and unloading materials in any of those departments? Whatever is coming in or going out that day?"

"Yes, exactly."

"And this warehouse delivers to which Home Depot stores?"

"All of the stores in the Puget Sound."

"How many stores is that?"

"Twenty-four."

A lot of stores. A lot of invoices for someone to look through for sales of polypropylene rope with a Z twist.

"Can the employees make purchases here?"

"Yes. They get an employee discount."

"How does that work? How do they get the discount?"

"The computer keeps track of employee numbers. To get the discount, the number must be entered with each purchase."

"So there would be a record if an employee paid cash?"

"If they wanted the employee discount, yes."

Tracy looked to Kins, who nodded. "May we use your office to talk to Mr. Bankston?" Tracy asked.

"Yes. Please." Rajput started for the door. "I will get him."

"No," Tracy said, not wanting Rajput to have time alone to talk to Bankston. She pointed to the radiophone. "Please call him. But please don't tell him why you want to see him."

Rajput's brow furrowed again, but he picked up the phone and pressed a button. It emitted a short musical melody. "David?"

After a moment of silence, a male voice answered. "Yeah?"

"Can you come to my office, please?"

"I'm in the middle of unloading a pallet. Can it wait?"

Tracy shook her head.

"Please come now," Rajput said. "You can finish the pallet after."

Tracy thought she heard a sigh. "Yeah, okay."

Kins put Bankston's time card back in the slot, and they stood waiting for Bankston in an uncomfortable silence. "May I offer you some coffee, or tea?" Rajput asked. Tracy and Kins declined.

David Bankston knocked on the open door. His gaze quickly shifted from Rajput to Tracy and Kins, and his expression changed from bored indifference to concern.

"Yes, David. Come in," Rajput said. "No worries."

Bankston stepped in, looking far from certain. He adjusted his sturdy black-framed glasses, which gave him a studious appearance despite unruly reddish-brown hair and an equally unkempt beard.

"David, these are detectives from the Seattle Police Department, Detective Crosswhite and Detective Rowe. They would like to ask you some questions."

"What about?"

"Should I leave?" Rajput asked.

"Please," Tracy said. They thanked Rajput on his way out. Kins shut the door behind him.

Bankston's Academy paperwork had listed him at five eleven, but in thick-soled work boots he stood almost eye to eye with Kins, who was six two. His blue jeans rode below a pronounced belly, and he wore an orange-and-black back brace that resembled a harness.

"Have a seat," Tracy said, gesturing to one of the two chairs on their side of the desk.

Bankston hesitated, then lowered into a chair. Tracy turned the second chair to face him, and Kins wheeled the chair out from behind the desk and positioned it beside hers.

"Can I call you David?" Tracy asked.

"Okay." Bankston fidgeted, as if unable to get comfortable. He gave them a sheepish smile. "So what's this about?"

"We're investigating the recent deaths of three women in Seattle, David. Have you heard anything about them?"

Bankston's brow wrinkled. "Um, I think I read something in the newspaper or maybe saw it on the news?"

"You sound uncertain," Tracy said.

"No, I mean, I heard about it. Just not sure where."

"What did you read or hear?" Tracy asked. "Just so I'm not repeating anything and wasting your time."

Bankston looked to be studying a spot on the carpet. "Just, you know, that these women got killed."

"Anything else?"

He gave an uncertain shrug. "I don't think so. Not that I really remember. I think they were prostitutes, right?"

Kins reached into his jacket and set photographs of Nicole Hansen, Angela Schreiber, and Veronica Watson on the edge of the desk. Bankston leaned forward and raised his glasses to consider them. Tracy watched intently for any sign that Bankston recognized them, but she saw nothing in his demeanor that raised a red flag.

"Do you recognize any of the women in these photographs?" Kins asked.

"No."

"What about their names—Nicole Hansen, Angela Schreiber, Veronica Watson—do you recognize any of those names?"

Bankston shook his head. "No," he said, voice soft. "I didn't really pay that much attention to it, you know?"

Kins took back the photographs. "Okay, thanks. Can we ask you a few questions about your job?"

"Yeah, sure."

"The materials that you load and unload, I'm assuming that's everything I would find in my neighborhood Home Depot?"

"Pretty much." Bankston picked at the cuticles of his fingernails, which Tracy noticed were nub-short.

"I notice you're not wearing gloves," Kins said.

Bankston shifted to reach behind himself and produced a pair of black-and-yellow work gloves. "I took them off."

"You normally wear gloves?" Kins asked.

"Normally. Not all the time."

"When do you take them off?"

Bankston blew out a breath. "Breaks, lunch. Sometimes I'll forget to put them back on, and then I'm like, 'Oh yeah, my gloves.'" He gave another nervous smile.

"You worked the swing shift Sunday night and last night?" Tracy said.

Bankston fidgeted and leaned back, gazing up at the ceiling. "Uh, yeah I think so. Sometimes it blurs. It varies." Another nervous smile.

"What time does the swing shift end?"

"Midnight."

"What did you do after your shift?"

A shrug. "Went home."

"Are you married, David?" Tracy asked.

Bankston's mood seemed to instantly change. He sat up, looking and sounding defensive. "Why do you want to know if I'm married?"

"I'm just wondering if there was anyone home when you got there."

"Oh. Um, no."

"So you don't live with anyone?"

"She was working."

"Your wife?"

"Right."

"What does she do?" Tracy asked.

"She works for a janitorial company; they clean the buildings downtown."

"She works nights?" Kins said.

"Yeah."

"Do you have kids?" Tracy asked.

"A daughter."

"Who watches your daughter when you and your wife are working nights?"

"My mother-in-law."

"Does she stay at your house?" Tracy said.

"No, my wife drops her off on her way to work."

"So nobody was at home when you got there Sunday night?"

Bankston shook his head. "No." He sat up again. "Can I ask a question?"

"Sure."

"Why are you asking me these questions?"

"That's fair," Kins said, looking to Tracy before answering. "One of our labs found your DNA on a piece of rope left at a crime scene."

"My DNA?"

"It came up in the computer database because of your military service. The computer generated it, so we have to follow up and try to get to the bottom of it. "

"Any thoughts on that?" Tracy said.

Bankston squinted. "I guess I could have touched it when I wasn't wearing my gloves."

Tracy looked to Kins, and they both nodded as if to say, "That's plausible," which was for Bankston's benefit. Her instincts were telling her otherwise. She said, "We were hoping there's a way we could determine where that rope was delivered, to which Home Depot."

"I wouldn't know that," Bankston said.

"Do they keep records of where things are shipped? I mean, is there a way we could match a piece of rope to a particular shipment from this warehouse?"

"I don't know. I wouldn't know how to do that. That's computer stuff, and I'm strictly the labor, you know?"

"What did you do in the Army?" Kins asked.

"Advance detail."

"What does advance detail do?"

"We set up the bases."

"What did that entail?"

"Pouring concrete and putting up the tilt-up buildings and tents."

"So no combat?" Kins asked.

"No."

"Are those tents like those big circus tents?" Tracy asked.

"Sort of like that."

"They still hold them up with stakes and rope?"

"Still do."

"That part of your job?"

"Yeah, sure."

"Okay, listen, David," Tracy said. "I know you were in the police academy."

"You do?"

"It came up on our computer system. So I'm guessing you know that our job is to eliminate suspects just as much as it is to find them."

"Sure."

"And we got your DNA on a piece of rope found at a crime scene."

"Right."

"So I have to ask if you would you be willing to come in and help us clear you."

"Now?"

"No. When you get off work; when it's convenient."

Bankston gave it some thought. "I suppose I could come in after work. I get off around four. I'd have to call my wife."

"Four o'clock works," Tracy said. She was still trying to figure Bankston out. He seemed nervous, which wasn't unexpected when two homicide detectives came to your place of work to ask you questions, but he also seemed to almost be enjoying the interaction, an indication that he might still be a cop wannabe, someone who listened to police and fire scanners and got off on cop shows. But it was more than his demeanor giving her pause. There was the fact that Bankston had handled the rope, that his time card showed he'd had the opportunity to have killed at least Schreiber and Watson, and that he had no alibi for those nights, not with his wife working and his daughter with his mother-in-law. Tracy would have Faz and Del take Bankston's photo to the Dancing Bare and the Pink Palace, to see if anyone recognized him. She'd also run his name through the Department of Licensing to determine what type of car he drove.

"What would I have to do . . . to clear me?"

"We'd like you to take a lie detector test. They'd ask you questions like the ones we just asked you—where you work, details about your job, those sorts of things."

"Would you be the one administering the test?"

"No," Tracy said. "We'd have someone trained to do that give you the test, but both Detective Rowe and I would be there to help get you set up."

"Okay," Bankston said. "But like I said, I have to call my wife."

"Clear it with the boss," Kins said grinning. "I know that drill."

David Bankston gave them a blank stare.

CHAPTER 23

Tracy and Kins met Faz and Del, each carrying two boxes of materials, on the second floor of the King County Courthouse. They descended an interior staircase to a little-used floor, referred to as 1-A, and Tracy led them down a hall to a locked door, which she opened with a key. It led to a shorter metal staircase that ended at a landing and a metal door. Their footsteps echoed as if they were in the bowels of a ship.

"Feel like I'm in a submarine," Faz said, looking up at the pipes traversing the ceiling and running vertically up the walls.

Tracy pulled the metal door open, stepped in, and turned on the light. The room, roughly twenty feet by twenty feet, had the feel of a concrete bunker. Fluorescent tubes on a low ceiling flickered above half a dozen battered desks. Holes pocked the walls where maps and charts and the photos of victims and suspects had hung in the '70s during the search for the Pacific Northwest's first notorious serial killer, Ted Bundy.

"Charming," Del said from the stair landing.

Kins stepped in. "So this is the infamous Bundy Room."

Tracy was told of the room when she said she wanted someplace private that would limit the chance of a leak on the progress, or lack of progress, in the investigation. It was as small and dreary as rumored, though two wood-framed windows at least provided some ambient light.

Kins checked his cell phone. "We got reception, so we can let the world know we're still alive."

"Come on, Fazzio, move your ass," Del said. "These boxes aren't getting lighter, standing here."

Faz lingered on the landing outside the door, looking pale and uncertain. "There's bad karma in this room," he said.

"You afraid of ghosts, Faz?" Del stepped past him and dropped his two boxes on a desk. His head seemed precariously close to the overhead lights. "You want us to leave the light on for you?"

Faz took an uncertain step into the room, and Tracy recalled him once confiding that he suffered from claustrophobia. "Let's just say I have a healthy respect for the dead. This place has seen too much evil."

"Why don't you take one of the desks by the window, Faz," Tracy said.

"Roger that, Professor."

Kins shut the door. "Home sweet home. At least it's quiet."

Maybe Faz's comment about the room having seen too much evil was making Tracy edgy, or maybe she also suffered low levels of claustrophobia, but when Kins closed the door the hairs on her arms twitched and stood on end. The room was eerily silent but for the buzz and tick of the fluorescent tubes, and the stale air smelled of damp concrete dust.

"Let's leave the door open," she said, propping it with a chair.

They used one of the walls to tack and tape photos of the victims, suspects, and crime scenes, along with aerial photographs showing the locations of the motels in relation to the Pink Palace clubs. Since it was their first day, Tracy sent out for pizza and salad, which immediately improved Faz's mood. They ate at one of the desks while a technician worked to set up phones and computers.

"The cabbie says he picked up Veronica Watson alone at the Pink Palace and dropped her off just outside the motel office," Faz said. "Doesn't recall seeing anyone hanging around waiting for her, but he also didn't stay long. Dispatch confirms he got another call and picked up a fare two blocks from the motel. Receipts confirm he was busy most of the rest of the night."

"Has he ever picked her up before?" Tracy speared a piece of lettuce with a plastic fork.

"Couldn't recall her," Faz said. "But his English ain't too good."

"Neither is yours, apparently," Del said.

"Yeah, like you speak the Queen's English."

"Bankston's coming in late this afternoon to take a polygraph," Tracy said. "When he leaves, I want to put a light tail on him. Stay on him a couple nights and see where he goes."

"Why the tail?" Faz asked.

"His time cards indicate he punched out at midnight the nights Schreiber and Watson were killed. We're working to get his cards to check the night Hansen was murdered. Run his photo over in a montage to the Dancing Bare and the Pink Palace and find out if anyone recalls seeing him."

Faz scribbled in a spiral notebook before snaring another piece of pizza. They heard footsteps descending the metal stairs. Ron Mayweather stuck his head in the room, looking uncertain he was in the correct place, or wanted to be.

"Charming," he said. "I take it the morgue wasn't available?"

"Welcome back, Kotter," Faz said. "Your dreams were your ticket out." Nicknames in the department were hard to shake, particularly the good ones. Somebody had watched a late-night rerun of the television show *Welcome Back, Kotter* and thought Mayweather, with his curly black hair and thick mustache, was a dead ringer for Gabe Kaplan, the actor who'd played the lead role. Mayweather hated it.

"Barney Miller called, Faz. He wants his slacks and loafers back."

Del howled.

Mayweather dropped his backpack and snagged a slice of pizza.

"Any luck?" Tracy asked. She had asked Mayweather to find out if there was any way to track a shipment of rope from the Kent warehouse to a particular Home Depot store.

"Maybe," Mayweather said. "I'm still working on it. Everything that goes in and out of that warehouse is tracked by a bar code."

"Can they distinguish between the different types of rope?" Tracy asked.

"I don't know yet. I'm waiting for a guy to call me back. We got phones?"

"Working on it," Kins said. "Use your cell for now. We got reception."

"Supervisor says they can track purchases through employee numbers," Tracy said. "See if you can get records of any purchases made in the last six months by an employee named David Bankston."

Mayweather wrote down the name, then picked up his backpack and took his slice of pizza to one of the remaining open desks.

Kins stood and dumped his paper plate in the trash. "I'm going to call Taggart's employer and see if he's been around."

Tracy's desk phone rang. "We have phones," she said, answering it. "Detective Crosswhite."

"Detective, this is David Bankston."

Tracy checked her watch. "Yes, David. Thank you for calling."

Kins gave her a look, and she nodded.

"Yeah, um, I'm not going to be able to come in today after all."

"No?" She shook her head to let Kins know Bankston was backing out.

"My mother-in-law is sick, so she can't watch my daughter. I have to get home."

"Won't your wife be home?"

Bankston paused. "She got called in early, so that's why she called her mother, to cover until I could get home."

"What about tomorrow?"

"I can't tomorrow. I got to watch my daughter, and I'm working the night shift."

"Tell me what day works for you? We'd really like to get you cleared."

"I'll have to call you back after I find out my schedule and talk with my wife."

"Will you call me tomorrow?"

"Yeah. I mean, I'll try. I have to go now. I'm still at work. We're not supposed to be making personal calls." Bankston disconnected.

Tracy looked to Kins. "Says he can't come in; he has to watch his daughter."

"Maybe he figured out we're not just looking to clear him."

CHAPTER 24

Bradley Taggart's last known employer told Kins that Taggart had called to quit and asked for his last paycheck. "Employer offered to mail it, but Taggart said he would come in and get it," Kins told Tracy.

"Did he say when?" Tracy said.

"This afternoon. We just missed him. Employer said Taggart was amped up on something and was glad to get rid of him. Called him 'dark.'"

"Did he have any idea where he was going?"

"He didn't, but one of the guys in the marine shop said on paydays Taggart likes to drink at a place in Pioneer Square called The Last Shot."

"Might be ours."

—

The Last Shot, in one of the low-rise brick buildings on First Avenue, was already displaying signs that it would have a decent crowd for a midweek evening. People sat in booths nursing beers and shot pool in the long and narrow space at the back of the bar.

Tracy recognized Taggart from his driver's license photograph. He was seated on a barstool, sipping an amber-colored drink, with a bottle of Budweiser on the bar. Taggart's attention was directed up, at a motorcycle race on one of the overhead televisions, watching the competitors skid and slide dirt bikes around a track. He had a small frame, but Taggart's tough-guy attitude came through loud and clear in his clothing choice—black leather vest, black biker boots, and black jeans with a prominent wear mark in his rear left pocket, indicating he liked to chew tobacco. Tracy noted a knife sheath attached to his belt.

She went back outside and discussed the situation with Kins, who'd double-parked, while they waited for backup. Within minutes two patrol units arrived. Tracy directed one to the alley at the back of the building and the other to the corner, where it wouldn't be seen by someone looking out The Last Shot's plate-glass windows.

She and Kins entered the bar together. Tracy took the barstool one removed from Taggart on his right. The stools on Taggart's left were occupied by a couple, so Kins sat at the end of the bar, near the back door.

"Bradley Taggart," Tracy said.

Taggart gave her a cool glance and picked up the bottle of beer. His eyes were glassy, but his knee was bouncing beneath the bar. Taggart either needed a fix or was coming down off one. "Who wants to know?" He tilted the bottle to his lips. Tattoos of colorful flames ran down each of his forearms. A dagger tattoo dripping drops of blood adorned his right biceps.

Tracy showed Taggart her badge and ID. Taggart smirked and went back to watching motocross, but Tracy sensed by the way he'd slid forward on the stool to lower his boots to the floor that he was considering bolting. "There's an officer at the end of the bar and two more at the front door," she said.

Taggart looked to where Kins now stood. "So?"

"So I'm going to ask you to put both hands on the bar where I can see them."

"Why? I'm not doing anything."

"You have an outstanding warrant."

"Bullshit."

Taggart had a habit of running his hand through his hair. "You missed a court date on a possession charge."

"My attorney handled that."

"Apparently not very well. You also broke one of the conditions of your parole when you quit your job."

"Maybe I got a better job."

"You should share that with your probation officer. You still have that warrant."

Taggart tipped the bottle to his lips. "I'd like a lawyer."

"I thought you said you had one."

"I'd like a different one."

"You'll have to make those arrangements after you're booked. Where've you been the last couple days?"

"Grieving."

This was going nowhere fast. "So what's it going to be, Mr. Taggart?"

He exchanged the bottle for the glass. "I haven't finished my drink yet."

"That's not going to happen today."

Taggart slammed back the liquid and gave her a defiant smirk. "Any other predictions?"

"One. You'll walk out that door in handcuffs. You can do it standing, or with me dragging your ass across the floor."

"Ain't you under some federal indictment for police brutality?"

"I'm asking you again to place your hands on the bar. You have an outstanding warrant. I have the legal right to bring you in."

"You gonna frisk me, Officer?" He winked. "'Cause I'm packing heat down the front of my pants."

She nodded to Kins, who approached. Taggart glanced over his left shoulder, sighed, and put down the bottle. He raised his hands in an exaggerated motion of surrender and slapped them on the bar loud enough to draw attention. The couple on the barstools to Taggart's left quickly moved out of the way. Tracy walked behind Taggart and reached around his right side. She slipped a handcuff just below a silver bracelet shaped like a snake with two red stones for eyes. When she pulled Taggart's hand behind his back, the stool rotated. Taggart's left hand shot up and grabbed her crotch.

Startled, Tracy instinctively swung her elbow across Taggart's face and heard bone on bone. She grabbed the back of his head and shoved it hard against the bar. Kins moved in quickly, using his body weight to help pin Taggart, who had started to struggle and to swear a blue streak.

"You're all witnesses! I didn't do nothing! Police brutality!" Blood ran from Taggart's nostrils, coloring his teeth.

"Hey!" The bartender had stepped back behind the bar from wherever he'd been. "Is that necessary?"

Tracy managed to get Taggart's left arm behind his back and finished cuffing him. She removed the knife from his belt and handed it to one of the patrol officers who'd joined them, then patted down Taggart for any other weapons.

Finding none, she said, "Get up."

She yanked Taggart from the seat, but he continued to resist and his foot slipped on the blood and spilled beer. Before Tracy and Kins could right him, Taggart fell, smacking the back of his head hard against the tile floor.

"There's no need for that," the bartender said.

"I want a lawyer," Taggart yelled from the ground. "You're all witnesses. Police brutality!"

The crowd had become interested, never a good thing, and was rapidly becoming animated, voicing its disapproval and hurling profanities. Sensing a bad situation about to get worse, Tracy and Kins lifted Taggart and slid him out the back door, kicking and screaming, to the waiting patrol car.

CHAPTER 25

They decided to let Taggart cool down in a cell at King County Jail. The way he'd continued to carry on in the back of the patrol car and throughout booking, Tracy figured that could take a week. It took much less time for word about the confrontation in the bar to spread through the Violent Crimes Section. Billy called to give her a heads-up that Nolasco wanted to see her in his office and that he didn't sound happy. Tracy had little hope she was going to get any sympathy from the man who'd once grabbed her breast to demonstrate a pat-down to a room full of recruits. Kins accompanied her, though he hadn't actually seen Taggart grab Tracy because Taggart had rotated his stool. He'd only witnessed her response.

The venetian blinds were down, but Nolasco's office door was open. He sat talking on the phone. When he looked up at them, his face was crimson and his jaw clenched. He pointed emphatically to the two chairs. Tracy and Kins sat.

"Yes, sir. I understand. Yes, I will," Nolasco said before replacing the receiver. He took a moment to run a hand over his face, then spoke with his eyes shut. "Please tell me you did not just break a man's nose in front of a bar full of witnesses."

"A suspect," Tracy said

Nolasco lowered his hands. "What?"

"I broke a suspect's nose in front of a bar full of witnesses."

"Are you freaking kidding me, Crosswhite? The guy is scream-ing he's going to sue everyone."

"We know. We were there."

"Yeah, well, did you know we've got five calls already and not one of them is going to bat for you? They say you slammed his face into the bar, then cut out his legs and let his head hit the floor."

"That's not what happened, Captain," Kins said. "The guy grabbed her."

"I want to hear it from her, Sparrow. You'll get your chance to fill out a report. And, trust me, you will be filling out a report, because I guaran-fucking-tee you OPA is going to be crawling up my ass on this. In fact, get out of here."

"Excuse me, Captain," Kins said, "but I believe I can corroborate—"

"That's my problem, Sparrow. I don't want you corroborating shit. If there is an inquiry, they'll claim you just parroted whatever she says here. So get the hell out of here and fill out a report."

Kins stood, gave Tracy a look, and started out of the room.

"And shut the door," Nolasco said. When the door closed, he said, "Do you know who that was on the phone?"

"No, Captain."

"That was Martinez. He called to let me know that with the Justice Department's report still hanging over our heads, this is just about the worst possible time to have something like this hap-pen. What am I supposed to tell him?"

"Tell him Taggart resisted arrest."

"Who's Taggart?"

"Veronica Watson's boyfriend. His employer called and gave us a lead that Taggart drinks at a bar in Pioneer Square. We ran him and found out he has an outstanding warrant and violated his parole when he quit his job. I asked him three times to place his hands on the bar. I told him I intended to leave the bar with him and that he could either walk out in handcuffs or be dragged out. He put his hands on the bar."

"So he complied."

"No."

"You just said he put his hands on the bar."

"He did, and I got the cuff on his right wrist. Then he rotated the stool and grabbed me."

"Grabbed you where?"

"My crotch."

"Did he have a weapon?"

"A knife."

"In his hand?"

"No."

"Do you have any physical injuries?"

"No, Captain."

"And nobody saw it."

"You'll have to ask them."

"The bartender said he saw you slam the guy's face into the bar."

"The bartender walked over after Taggart grabbed me."

"So you did slam his face against the bar."

"I applied an armlock to immobilize him."

"How'd his head hit the floor?"

"When we pulled him from the barstool, his boots slipped."

"And no one was in a position to catch him?"

"Apparently not."

Nolasco ran a hand through his hair. "With everything going on, you couldn't find the ability to control your temper?"

"My temper had nothing to do with it. He provoked the confrontation. He had a knife on his belt, and he told me he had a gun down the front of his pants."

Nolasco leaned forward. "Did he?"

"No."

"Anything else?"

"No, Captain."

Nolasco stared at her. "I know what you're thinking."

"I'm not thinking anything, Captain."

"You're thinking I'm not going to go to bat for you."

"The thought never crossed my mind."

"Well, I'm not going to make it that easy on you."

"Sir?"

"You wanted to be the lead on the Cowboy Task Force. You're not getting off."

"I didn't ask off."

"Because when you screw that up, you're not going to be able to blame me and say I had it out for you because of what happened twenty years ago."

So that was it. That was why Nolasco had backed her as the lead detective, why he'd given them a bare-bones task force. He wanted her to fail. He wanted every Cowboy murder to be another mark on her record. "Are we done?" Tracy asked.

"I'll let OPA know where they can find you."

—

As Tracy passed through the bull pen, she noticed a brown Bekins box on her desk, which momentarily puzzled her until she saw the name below the case number—"Beth Stinson." She picked it up, took the stairs to the garage, and dropped the box in her truck cab. Then she returned to the Bundy Room.

Kins was on his desk phone but ended the conversation when she entered. "I'll call you back," he said. "Yes, I'll talk to him when I get home. I don't know. Hopefully not too late."

"Everything all right?" Tracy asked when Kins disconnected. She could tell from the tone of his voice that he'd been talking with Shannah.

"What?"

"At home. Everything okay?"

"Eric's flunking algebra."

"I thought he was good at math."

"He is. We don't know what it is. We think maybe he's got a girlfriend. What happened with Nolasco?"

She set her purse in the bottom drawer of her desk. "He chewed my ass and said I was on thin ice. Can you get him a tutor?"

"That's what we were debating, but tutors aren't cheap. Are you going to call the Guild?"

"I don't know."

"If there's going to be an investigation, you should be represented."

"We have computers yet?" She played with the mouse, and a generic screensaver of flying windows appeared on her monitor.

"Tracy?"

Maybe it was misguided pride, but Tracy didn't want to tell Kins she'd been appointed the task force lead only because Nolasco wanted her to fail and derail her career. She wanted Kins, and everyone else, to believe it was because she'd earned it. "Nolasco says he's going to back me."

Kins thrust his hands into his pants pockets, studying her. "He said that?"

"That's what he said." She shrugged. "Surprised me too."

"Did he say anything else?"

"Yeah, he asked when we were going to catch this asshole."

CHAPTER 26

A light drizzle splattered the truck's windshield as Tracy left the parking garage just after seven. She'd decided to get home at a decent hour, anxious to review the Beth Stinson files in private. As she crossed the West Seattle Bridge, the drizzle became a steady rain and the wind churned the waters of Elliott Bay. Gusts caused her truck to shudder. By the time she took the off-ramp onto Admiral Way, the rain had become a downpour that her wiper blades struggled to clear.

She gave a wave to the officer in the patrol car parked in front of her home and drove into her garage. When the door rolled shut, Tracy retrieved the cardboard box containing Beth Stinson's files. Juggling it on a knee, she freed a hand to unlock and open the door to the house, and stepped through. She immediately sensed someone inside. She heard approaching footsteps, dropped the box, drew her Glock, and took aim.

"Surpri—!" Dan swallowed the end of the word, and dropped the glasses of wine he'd been holding. They shattered on impact, red wine spraying.

Tracy lowered the gun. Her heart was jackhammering, and the backs of her knees felt weak.

Dan's face had drained of color, and he looked to be having trouble catching his breath. "Surprise," he said, though it came out an almost unintelligible croak.

Tracy fell back against the wall. "What are you doing here?"

"My arbitration settled, so I came over early to make you dinner. I thought I'd surprise you. I guess I succeeded."

She felt like she'd been kicked in the gut. "Why didn't you call?"

"Kind of spoils the surprise."

"Where's your car?"

"I parked across the street. I didn't want to block the driveway and, again, it kind of spoils the surprise if I park in the driveway."

Tracy shut her eyes, still feeling light-headed from the rush of adrenaline.

Dan touched her shoulder. "Hey, are you all right? I'm the one who should be—"

She fell into him, burying her face in his chest, fighting back tears of anger and frustration and fatigue.

Dan wrapped his arms around her. "Hey. Hey, take it easy. I'm fine."

She pulled back, took a breath, and composed herself. "I'm sorry, Dan."

"Don't be sorry; I should have thought this through better, with everything you have going on. I should have called."

"No. No, it was a nice gesture. I'm just on edge, and I'm tired and . . ." She wiped her cheeks. "It's fine, really. I'm glad to see you." She forced a smile and looked around the room. "Where are the boys?"

"I came straight from the arbitration. My neighbor said he'd look in on them to make sure they don't tear the furniture apart. "You sure you're okay?" he said.

"It's been a rough few days. That's all." She stepped into the kitchen, grabbed a paper towel, and blew her nose. She'd spent twenty years burying her emotions. It had been easier than acknowledging that her entire family was gone, easier than acknowledging that, despite all her efforts to find justice for Sarah, she remained a long way from finding closure.

"Are you hungry?" Dan asked.

"Actually," she said, stepping close and wrapping her arms around him, "I'm in the mood to be pitied."

—

Unable to sleep, Tracy slid from bed without waking Dan. She retrieved the box containing Beth Stinson's files from where she'd dropped it in the hallway, and set it on the dining room table. She didn't immediately open it. She traced her finger through a layer of dust on the lid and thought of the moment when she'd pulled the box containing the files she'd compiled on Sarah's murder from the closet in her bedroom.

Years earlier she'd conceded that the investigation had hit a dead end, and stored the files, determined to move on with her life. She recalled how hopeless she'd felt, and how profound her sense of loss. She never expected to open the box again. Then two hunters had stumbled across human remains in the hills above Cedar Grove, and Tracy's hope had flared. When the medical examiner identified the remains as Sarah's, Tracy got the box back out and renewed her investigation.

She knew if she lifted the lid on Beth Stinson's box, there might be no going back, and she doubted Stinson's family, who believed their daughter's killer had been brought to justice, would want to go through those horrible days again.

Still, she set the lid aside, pulled out one of the files, and started reading.

An hour into the task, she heard Dan come up behind her. He draped himself around her, nuzzling his chin into the side of her neck. "Didn't hear you get up." He sounded tired, his voice hoarse.

"I didn't want to wake you."

He yawned, sat in the chair beside her, and looked at the files spread across the table. "So what's all this?"

"An old file. It came up when I was searching for cases similar to Nicole Hansen's."

"Similar how?"

"You don't want to hear this now. You should go back to bed. You can sleep in."

"I'm awake."

"Then let me make some tea."

Back at the table, Tracy grasped her mug of tea and explained what she'd learned about Beth Stinson and Wayne Gerhardt. "Gerhardt made a service call the prior afternoon to Stinson's home in North Seattle. Otherwise, he had no connection to her, at least not one I can tell from the file."

"And the theory is he came back that night and killed her," Dan said.

"They had a witness—JoAnne Anderson, a neighbor across the street—who said she saw a man fitting Gerhardt's description leaving Stinson's home early in the morning."

"But . . ."

"It was still dark, and in her statement she said she couldn't be certain she'd even put on her glasses."

"You think she made it up?"

She heard the doubt in Dan's tone. "No. But she told the officers she got up to get a drink of water and was standing at the sink when she saw the man out the window and across the street. She was sixty-two, nearsighted, and may not have been wearing her glasses."

"Then how'd she ID him?"

"According to the file, she picked him out of a police montage, then picked him out of a lineup." Tracy handed Dan a typed witness statement. "Stinson's credit card records had revealed the service call by Roto-Rooter, and they matched Gerhardt's finger-prints to those found in Stinson's bathroom and on the kitchen counter."

"Gerhardt had no alibi?"

"He lived alone. He said he was sleeping."

"So what's the connection to the guy killing the dancers?"

Tracy handed Dan a couple of crime scene photographs. He considered them briefly and set them aside. "No wonder you can't sleep."

Tracy adjusted in her chair. "It's not just the fact that Stinson was tied up. Look at the room."

Dan reconsidered the photos. "It's neat. No sign of a struggle."

"Look at Stinson's bed."

"It's made."

"The beds in the motel rooms were still made, with the vic-tims' clothes neatly folded and placed on a corner. Stinson was killed early in the morning. Why would her bed be made?"

"What about DNA?"

"This is where it gets interesting; they obtained DNA from Stinson's clothing and beneath her fingernails, but it was never tested."

"Why not?"

"I don't know. Maybe the prosecutor didn't see the need. They had an eyewitness. Fingerprints. Gerhardt had been at the home that afternoon. He had no alibi. We're a lot more adept with DNA now than we were back then."

"What about the defense attorney? Why didn't he ask to have it tested?"

"Again, don't know. He was court-appointed. He must have convinced Gerhardt to plead after JoAnne Anderson testified. That was the end of the trial."

"So the prosecution decides they have enough evidence to convict," Dan said, "and testing might only raise reasonable doubt if the DNA comes back as not being Gerhardt."

"That's my thinking."

"And the defense attorney is lazy, stupid, or both, and he convinces Gerhardt to take the deal."

"Maybe not so stupid. Gerhardt was facing the death penalty or life. He got twenty-five years. He'll be early fifties when he gets out."

"But if he was innocent, why not at least get the DNA tested?"

She shook her head. "Because it may not have exonerated him."

"How could it not exonerate him?"

She handed Dan the HITS form. "The detective who filled this out checked the box indicating that Beth Stinson was sexually assaulted, which is probably why the case didn't come up when I first ran the profile. None of the Cowboy's three victims were sexually assaulted, which is unusual in these cases." She handed Dan the medical examiner's report for Beth Stinson. He squinted to read it without his glasses. "I'll give you the highlights," Tracy said. "They swabbed her body cavities for semen and didn't find anything."

"Condom?"

"Swabs were also clean for lubricants and spermicide."

Dan sat back. Tracy knew what he was thinking even before he said it. "You know what's going to happen if you pursue this? The media is going to crucify you. They'll say you're trying to free another murderer."

"I know. And Nolasco would never allow it," she said.

"What's he got to do with it?"

"He and his partner were the investigating detectives."

Dan set down the report. "Which is why you have the file here at home and not at work."

"Faz once told me that Nolasco and Hattie liked to flaunt their perfect case record," Tracy said, "but word around the unit was they didn't always do everything exactly by the book."

"All the more reason he won't want you looking into this."

"But what if I'm right, Dan? What if Gerhardt is innocent and the guy who killed Beth Stinson is still out there killing?"

After a moment of silence, Dan asked, "What would you need to know? What would you do?"

"Talk to the witness and clarify what she saw and didn't see. Ask her why she was so certain it was Gerhardt. Talk to the other witnesses in the file. There's no indication Nolasco or Hattie ever followed up with them."

"Because they had their guy?"

"That's my assumption. Ultimately, I'd want to get the DNA tested. Though I'm not sure how I could do it with Nolasco watching and waiting for me to screw up."

"What if I did it?"

She smiled. "I can't ask you to do that, Dan. You have your own career. This is my job."

"My client just received a seven-figure settlement, and I pocketed thirty-three percent. I can find time. Let me sniff around the edges. I'll talk to this eyewitness and probe a little bit. Whatever I learn, I'll let you know."

"Ordinarily, I'd say no," Tracy said, and a part of her was thinking just that. *Tell him no. Don't drag him into your professional life.* That was a recipe certain to kill a relationship. Still, the sky outside the sliding glass doors had begun to lighten on a new day, and the only thing Tracy could think about was her cell phone buzzing and a call saying they'd found another body.

CHAPTER 27

The following morning, Tracy and Kins watched Bradley Taggart from behind the one-way glass. In a red King County Jail jumpsuit, he looked like a rooster, with his head swiveling from side to side and his knees bouncing uncontrollably.

"Coming down from something," Kins said. "Meth?"

"That'd be my guess," Tracy said.

"You really did a number on him," Kins said, smiling. Taggart had raccoon eyes, and his nose was swollen and bent slightly to the left, with a small cut across the bridge. "How do you want to play it?"

"He's been around," Tracy said. "He knows we aren't going to be able to hold him on a failure to appear. If we don't find anything in the apartment, he walks."

With an affidavit from Kins, Cerrabone had obtained a search warrant of Veronica Watson's apartment and car. Faz and Del were coordinating the search with a CSI team.

"I think Keen's got him pegged," Tracy said, referring to Taggart's probation officer. "I think he'll puff up his chest and act like a tough guy, but he's just a punk. He's not going to be too happy with me. Why don't you take a crack at him?"

—

Taggart started spewing threats the instant Tracy pulled open the door to the interrogation room. He lifted up off his chair, but the chain from his handcuffs to the eyehook in the floor kept him from standing. "I'm going to sue this entire department for harassment and police brutality."

Tracy moved to one of the two chairs on the opposite side of the metal table as Kins forced Taggart back onto his seat with a firm grip on his shoulder. "My partner wanted to remove your handcuffs, but I told her not to. I told her I was afraid you'd do something stupid again and then she'd have to kick your ass a second time."

"She didn't kick my ass." Taggart looked to Tracy. "It was a cheap shot. My attorney's going to carve you up on the stand."

Kins leaned closer. "Is this the same attorney who couldn't get a possession charge dismissed? How do you think he's going to do with a felony warrant for you not showing for a hearing, a violation of your parole, *and* assault on a police officer? Get comfortable, Bradley. You're going to be sitting in a cell for a while. Maybe you should use that time to find yourself a better attorney."

"I told you the hearing was a misunderstanding. My lawyer will get that sorted out, and I'll make bail in an hour."

"No bail for murder," Kins said.

Taggart scoffed. "That's a joke."

"Is it?" Kins said. "Veronica is dead. She lived with you. We have witnesses who say you were working her. We have a neighbor who says you two were yelling and screaming at all hours of the day and night, that you used to knock her around. And the dancers at the Pink Palace say they saw you in the club Sunday night talking to her. We have sworn statements. You know what impresses a judge? Sworn statements. More than one. So maybe you should shut your mouth and stop talking stupid."

Taggart dropped his gaze to a corner of the room. He looked like a kid pouting.

"Why were you at the Pink Palace on Sunday night?" Kins said.

Taggart reengaged. "Here's what I'll tell you. I want a lawyer."

"Okay." Kins stood and opened the door, speaking to the two corrections officers waiting in the hall. "Take him back. Place him on a seventy-two-hour hold while I go talk to the prosecutor about filing a murder charge."

Taggart had raised his chin in defiance, another tough-guy pose, but Tracy could see the uncertainty in his eyes even before he spoke. "Fine. I'll talk to *him*. I'm not talking to you."

"Lucky you," Tracy said to Kins, who remained in the doorway.

"Here's the deal, Bradley. Procedure requires two detectives in the room. So if she isn't here, I'm not here, and you go back to your cell and wait for your arraignment." Kins paused. "What's it going to be?"

Taggart stewed, eyes shut as if fighting a headache. His knees pistoned beneath the table.

"Got things to do, Bradley. You agree to talk to us or not?"

"Fine."

"Fine what?"

"Fine, I'll talk to *you*."

"You're waiving your right to a lawyer?"

"Whatever."

"No, not 'whatever.' You need to say it. I don't want some lawyer saying we took advantage of you."

"Fine. I agree to talk to you without a lawyer."

Kins retook his seat next to Tracy. "Then let's start with why you were at the Pink Palace on Sunday night."

"I needed money. So what? It's open to the public."

"How long did you stay?"

"Five minutes. Not even that. V said she wouldn't have any money until she tipped out, so I left."

"Where'd you go when you left?" Kins said.

"Around."

"No place in particular?"

"No."

"So no one can confirm they saw you?" Kins said. He looked to Tracy and said, "No alibi."

"When did you expect Veronica home?" Tracy asked.

Taggart scowled. "I said I'm not talking to you." He addressed Kins. "I didn't."

"You had no expectation she was coming home?" Kins asked.

"I didn't keep tabs on her."

"Because you knew she had dates after her shift. You get a piece of that action?"

"We lived together."

"What does that mean?"

"It means I wasn't paying the rent myself."

"Did you ever arrange any dates for Veronica?" Kins asked.

Taggart was shaking his head before Kins finished his question. "No need. She did fine by herself, except when she put on the weight."

"You have any idea who Veronica met Sunday night?"

"Nope. Like I said, I don't keep tabs on her."

"Did she have any regulars?" Kins asked.

"A few." Taggart looked at Tracy. "She gave a hell of a blow job. I'm going to miss that the most."

Taggart was a dirtbag, but after twenty years of dealing with his type, Tracy knew the city had a way of eventually spitting out its trash on its own terms. She had little doubt she'd find out in later years that Taggart had died of an overdose or been stabbed or shot and left in an alley to die. Justice came in all different forms.

"Did she ever tell you the names of any of those regulars?" Kins asked.

"No. And she didn't keep any little black book, if that's your next question."

"How'd you know how much money she was making, that she wasn't holding back on you?"

Taggart chuckled. "'Cause she wasn't stupid."

"Meaning what?" Tracy asked.

"Meaning she knew better."

"You'd knock her around a bit," Tracy said.

"I didn't say that."

"Dancers at the Pink Palace said you did. So did her mother and father," Tracy said.

Taggart scoffed and leaned forward, chin directed at Tracy. "Her stepfather going to be your big witness, is he? He was banging her when she was fifteen. That's why she left. The guy is a shitbag."

"*You* were doing her when she was fifteen," Kins said.

"I'm not her stepfather."

"You talk to her again that night, after you left the Pink Palace?" Tracy asked.

Taggart shook his head. "Nope."

"So when we check your cell phone records, we're not going to find any voice mails or text messages," Kins said.

"What cell phone?"

Kins took out the photographs of Nicole Hansen and Angela Schreiber and set them side by side on the table. "You know these women, Bradley?"

Taggart nodded to Angela Schreiber. "I know her." He looked again at Tracy and grinned, displaying the decaying teeth of a meth-head. "I think she gave me a lap dance one time."

"You ever meet her at a motel on Aurora?" Kins said.

"Wouldn't need to with V coming home every night, now would I?"

"Thought you said you didn't keep tabs on her."

"I didn't."

"Why'd you quit your job?" Kins asked.

"The guy was an asshole."

"It's a violation of your parole."

"I'm going to get another job."

"Any leads?"

"I was just getting started when you violated my civil rights."

"Yeah? You thinking about becoming a bartender?" Kins asked.

"So you didn't see or hear from Veronica after you left the Pink Palace Sunday evening?" Tracy asked.

"That's what I said."

They went back over the same ground for another forty-five minutes to test Taggart's story. After two hours, Kins said, "Last question, Bradley. You right- or left-handed?"

"What the hell you want to know that for?"

"For when you write out your statement—I need to know whether to get you a right-handed or left-handed pen."

Taggart looked momentarily stumped but said, "Right."

Kins and Tracy stood. "Okay. We'll have the corrections officers escort you back to jail."

"What? Why?"

"You got to take care of that outstanding warrant, Bradley."

"You said you didn't care about that."

"We don't," Kins said. "But we're not the prosecutor."

CHAPTER 28

Back in the Bundy Room, Tracy hung up her desk phone and spoke to Kins. "Cerrabone says we don't have enough to hold Taggart. He'll be gone after the nine o'clock arraignments tomorrow morning."

"Well, we knew that was going to happen," Kins said, reaching to answer his phone when it rang.

Tracy approached Faz and Del. "Sorry to do this to you, but I'm going to need you to tail Taggart tomorrow morning after he's released. Ask the jail to let us know when."

"I'll bring my pee bottle," Del said.

Tracy considered her watch. "Why don't you both get out of here, get home early? You might be looking at a couple long nights."

"This guy a vampire?" Faz asked.

"Worse," she said.

Kins joined them. "That was Bennett. Called to give us a heads-up. Manpelt is fishing for a comment on a story running tonight."

"What's the story?" Tracy asked.

"She wouldn't tell Bennett. She said she wanted to talk to you."

"I can only imagine." She looked at her watch again. "Almost six. Guess we'll find out."

The technician had wired a flat-screen television and set it up on an unused desk so they could follow the news. Kins picked up the remote and input Channel 8. Those still at the office—Tracy, Kins, Faz, and Del, and a couple of detectives they'd pulled from the Sexual Assault Unit—gathered close to the television. For a change, the Cowboy was not the lead story. Still, it didn't take long to get to Vanpelt.

"A new allegation of police brutality is facing the Seattle Police Department tonight," the anchor said.

"Here we go," Faz said.

"We go live to KRIX investigative reporter Maria Vanpelt, in Pioneer Square."

Vanpelt stood in the glow of the camera's spotlight, dressed in a long camel-colored coat. "This bar in Pioneer Square is where an altercation took place early yesterday evening as homicide detectives sought to question the boyfriend of Veronica Watson, the third victim in the string of grisly murders of Seattle dancers. Witnesses say when the confrontation was over, the boyfriend was taken to Swedish Hospital with a broken nose and possible concussion before being transported to King County Jail. And they say a detective is responsible for beating up the man.

"A Seattle Police spokesman would not say whether charges have been filed against Veronica Watson's boyfriend and would give no other comment except to say that the Office of Professional Accountability is reviewing the incident. But the allegation comes at a bad time for the department—and for its embattled police chief, Sandy Clarridge, who has been trying to address a US Justice Department report criticizing the department for excessive use of force, along with a federal court judge's admonishment of the department for failure to implement changes."

Vanpelt ended her report and tossed back to the studio.

"Well, as Manpelt stories go, that wasn't too bad," Kins said.

Faz said. "She might have even got a fact right."

"Shh," Tracy said.

The news anchor continued. "You may recall that KRIX Channel 8 teamed with the King County Sheriff's Office in the hunt for the Green River Killer. Tonight I am pleased to report that Channel 8 is once again leading the effort to find—and stop—a serial killer. KRIX is offering a reward of one hundred thousand dollars for information leading to the arrest and conviction of the Cowboy, the person responsible for the recent murders of three Seattle dancers. The phone number for the Cowboy Task Force tip line is at the bottom of your screen, and SPD is urging anyone with information to call that number."

"No, we're not," Faz said. "That's the last Goddamned thing we want."

Tracy felt her stomach clench.

Behind them, the phones on the desks started ringing.

CHAPTER 29

The tip line rang nonstop for nearly three hours. As she fielded her own calls, Tracy heard members of the task force struggling to move callers though their stories while trying to quickly determine if they had anything of value to offer. Most who called wanted to know how to collect the reward. One caller was certain the killer was a man who frequented a local tavern and had "a suspicious way about him." Prostitutes called, convinced the killer was one of their johns. Ex-wives called to implicate ex-husbands. The task force took calls from snitches, neighbors, and people certain the killer was a work colleague. It seemed everyone was willing to rat out someone for the chance to win the serial-killer lottery. It was the task force's worst nightmare; for each call, they had to complete a tip sheet, and they'd have to follow up on every one. It would keep them running around in circles for weeks.

As the night wore on and the calls became less frequent, Faz took a call on his cell, then stood. "Be right back," he said. Minutes later he returned with his wife, Vera, and their son, Antonio, who was nearly as big as Faz. Antonio carried a brown cardboard box, and whatever was inside quickly filled the room with the aroma of garlic, Italian spices, and melted cheese. Vera unloaded two large casserole dishes, paper plates, forks and knives, a salad, and several bottles of red wine on one of the desks.

"If I couldn't make it home for cannelloni, cannelloni was going to make it here," Faz said. Tracy had never seen him look so happy. "Is she the best or what?" He reached to hug his wife, but Vera pulled away.

"It'll get cold," she said.

Del wasted no time ending his call. "Take it home or get a plate, Faz, before I trample you." Had Del been on the *Titanic* and food on the lifeboats, women and children would have drowned.

They took shifts answering the phones while the others ate. When the food was gone and the phone calls had become a trickle, Faz stood, Vera and Antonio at his side. "We Italians, when we eat, it's tradition to salute the chef and to pay respects to the most important person in the room." He looked to Vera. "So here's to the best cook in Seattle."

"Amen," Del said.

Vera waived him off, looking embarrassed but pleased by the attention. Everyone followed Faz's lead and raised a glass. *"Salute."*

"I also want to say that I don't like this place much," Faz said. "It gives me the heebie-jeebies, but we all know we got a job to do." He looked to Tracy. "This is our room now, Professor. Nobody calls it 'the Bundy Room' no more. This is the Cowboy Room." He raised the glass again. "So here's to you, Professor. Whatever it takes. We're all in."

This time, the others stood, raised their wineglasses, and said, *"Salute."*

Tracy smiled and raised a glass of water.

As with Nolasco's decision to send the Nicole Hansen investigation to the Cold Case Unit, whatever he'd hoped to accomplish by leaking the OPA investigation, or by convincing someone higher up that the tip line was a good idea—and Tracy had no doubt he'd been behind those decisions—it had backfired. The men and women in the room were experienced detectives. Tracy didn't have to say a word to them. They knew what they were up against. Unwritten rules had been broken. And every cop knew that when the rules were broken, you did what you had to do to protect your back, and the backs of those you worked with.

CHAPTER 30

The day had dawned clear and cold, with billowing brilliant-white clouds drifting across an otherwise sun-drenched sky. Beth Stinson's North Seattle neighborhood had a different feel in daylight, tranquil and inviting, peaceful. It was an older neighborhood. Dan noticed a few two-story remodels, but most of the homes were one-story ramblers, likely built in the 1960s. The cherry trees and the foliage in the front yards were mature, and there were no street lamps or sidewalks. The lawns simply sloped to the edge of the road.

The prior night, when Dan had driven here to simulate the conditions an eyewitness would have encountered trying to identify Wayne Gerhardt the night of Beth Stinson's murder, the neighborhood had not seemed as inviting. The only light came from a few lawns and porches. JoAnne Anderson claimed in her witness statement that she awoke around two thirty in the morning and got out of bed to get a drink of water. She did not recall what, if anything, woke her, but said at her age she got up twice a night to use the bathroom. She said she retrieved a glass from the kitchen cupboard and, while filling it with tap water, looked out her window and "thought" she saw "someone" outside Beth Stinson's home.

Dan had arrived just after midnight and parked across the street from Beth Stinson's home. He assumed Anderson's kitchen to be the rectangular window to the far right. From it, Anderson had an unobstructed view of Stinson's home, but that view was across her own yard, the two-lane street, and Stinson's front yard. In addition, Stinson's driveway, where Anderson claimed she saw Gerhardt, was located at the far south of that property, as far from the kitchen window as possible.

Sitting in his truck, it was difficult for Dan to estimate the distance, but he found it hard to believe Anderson could have positively identified anyone, even wearing glasses, on a night which she'd testified had been overcast with a light rain.

Nevertheless, after reading Anderson's trial testimony, Dan had a better understanding of why Gerhardt's public defender may have convinced Gerhardt to accept the State's plea deal. At trial, Anderson had testified with much more confidence than her witness statement would have otherwise indicated. She had been much more certain she'd seen a man with light-colored hair, whom she described as the height of a tree just to the south of Stinson's garage. That tree, an immature evergreen, had measured six feet three. Gerhardt was six feet two and a half. On cross-examination Gerhardt's counsel had gotten Anderson to admit she could not "specifically recall" if she'd put on glasses before she went to get a drink of water. Unfortunately, Anderson had also testified that she "must have." It was one of those answers trial attorneys dreaded, because you couldn't anticipate what a witness might say to any follow-up question asking her to explain why she "must have." Chances were it would only reinforce to the jury what she claimed to have seen. Gerhardt's attorney had chosen not to take that risk.

For Tracy's sake, a part of Dan had hoped his nighttime drive to the site would confirm JoAnne Anderson's testimony that she got a good look at Wayne Gerhardt and had no doubt he had been the killer.

Dan sighed. "Damn," he said and pushed out of his car. He made his way up the cement walk. The yard looked to be emerging from winter—green shoots sprouted in the planter boxes and the trees were showing the first buds of cherry blossoms.

The woman who answered the front door fit the description in the file. Nine years older, Anderson looked matronly in a white V-neck sweater, blue jeans, and tennis shoes. She appeared to be of Asian heritage. Dan took immediate note of her glasses—plastic-framed and turquoise in color. He gave her his most disarming smile.

"JoAnne Anderson?"

"Yes," she said.

"My name is Dan O'Leary. I'm sorry to be knocking on your door without the courtesy of a phone call." Most people found it easier to hang up a phone than to slam a door. "I was hoping I might ask you a few questions about something that happened here almost ten years ago."

"Beth Stinson's murder," she said. "And it happened nine years ago. It won't be ten years until this April 20. You don't forget something like that."

"I'm sure you don't," Dan said.

"Who did you say you were?"

"Dan O'Leary. I'm from Cedar Grove."

"Cedar Grove?" she asked.

"It's up north, in the Cascades."

"I know where it is. We used to take the kids up every summer. Do you know Ross Lake?"

"I've fished it many times."

"We had a floating cabin on the water."

"You must have gotten in early. I hear they want your next of kin just to get on the wait list."

Anderson smiled. "Forty years ago it wasn't so difficult. Who did you say you worked for?"

"I'm an attorney. I take an interest in these cases," he said, straddling the line between truth and misrepresentation.

"What kind of interest?"

"I look at the evidence and determine if it was sufficient to convict the person."

"But Wayne Gerhardt confessed."

"Yes, I know."

"Has he recanted?"

"Mr. Gerhardt was facing a death sentence. I'm reviewing the evidence."

"You mean like the Innocence Project?"

"You've heard of it?" he asked, still straddling the line.

"Oh, yes," she said.

"May I ask a few questions?"

Anderson shrugged. "I suppose." She did not invite him in.

"You told the detectives that you got up in the middle of the night and went to the kitchen to get a glass of water."

"Yes, that's right."

"You said you couldn't be certain whether you'd put on your glasses."

"No, I wasn't."

"But at trial you said, 'I must have.' Why did you believe you must have?"

"Well, that's a long time ago to try to remember a detail like that."

"I realize it's been many years. Only if you remember."

"I suppose I said it because I couldn't have seen him without them. I couldn't see you clearly without them."

"Do you recall what your vision was nine years ago?"

"No different than it is today, fortunately."

"And what is that, do you know?"

"Not a clue." She looked past him to the street. "Is that your car?"

"Yes, that's mine."

"I can read the license plate just fine." She removed her glasses. "Now it's just a blur."

"So because you were able to see Wayne Gerhardt," Dan said as he turned and pointed, "who I believe you said you saw standing near that far corner of Beth Stinson's home—"

"That's right."

"You concluded you 'must have' put on your glasses. Is that right?"

"That's where I saw him."

"So you assumed you had your glasses on."

"Not an assumption. I had to have had them on in order to see him."

They were going in circles, which would have likely been the outcome had the defense attorney pursued this line of questioning.

"Did the detective who came to speak with you show you any photographs and ask if you recognized the person you saw that night?"

"Detectives," she said. "There were two of them."

"Did they show you photographs?"

"Not the first time. The first time I told them I couldn't be sure I saw Mr. Gerhardt. I didn't want to be responsible for convicting an innocent man unless I was certain. A person doesn't want that on her conscience."

"And did they come back and show you photographs?"

"The younger detective, he had an unusual name . . . I can't recall it now. Anyway, he asked if I would come to the police station for a police lineup."

"And you did that?"

"At first I wasn't going to."

"Why not?"

"I just didn't feel comfortable."

"What changed your mind?"

"The man I saw looked just like the man in the photograph the detective showed me."

"How many photographs did the detective show you?"

"Just the one," she said.

"And they showed it to you before you went to the police station and identified Wayne Gerhardt in the police lineup?"

"Yes, that's right."

"So you were convinced you saw Mr. Gerhardt."

"I didn't know his name."

"But you identified him."

"I was pretty sure."

Dan tried to keep his voice even. "Still not a hundred percent?"

"I don't think we can ever be a hundred percent about something. I felt better about it when I found out that Mr. Gerhardt had no alibi and that he'd been at Beth's house that afternoon."

"Did the detectives tell you that?"

"That's right. And then I remembered I'd seen the Roto-Rooter truck in Beth's driveway earlier that day."

"Did you see Mr. Gerhardt that day also, or just the truck?"

"I saw him." She pointed in the general direction of her yard. "I was weeding that planter, and I'd sat back to take a break and he walked out the front door. He was putting his tools and equipment in the back of the van."

"You had your glasses on?"

"Oh, yes. The only time I take them off is to go to bed."

"So you got a good look at him."

"Yes."

"What was he wearing?"

"What did I say in my statement?"

Dan feigned ignorance. "You know, I don't remember what you said."

"I think I said he was wearing blue coveralls with a white-and-red logo on the back."

"Are you talking about when you saw Mr. Gerhardt that afternoon?"

"Aren't you?"

"And the man you saw that night, what was he wearing?"

"It was the same man."

"Right. What was he wearing?"

"I don't remember that. It was too dark."

JoAnne Anderson had testified at trial she saw Wayne Gerhardt wearing the same blue coveralls. Dan didn't doubt that she had, but he was convinced it was that afternoon, and not that night.

"Thank you, Mrs. Anderson. I won't take up anymore of your time."

"I hope I've been helpful. I'd hate to think I sent an innocent man to jail."

"We all would," Dan said.

CHAPTER 31

Tracy and Kins sat in a lobby that had all the charm one would expect in a federal office building—functional furniture and off-white walls with black-and-white prints of other Seattle government buildings. Nolasco had set up a morning meeting with an FBI profiler. Tracy was certain he'd done it just to spite them, after what he had to know had been a very long night. Neither of them had bothered to go home. To add insult to injury, the profiler was now keeping them waiting.

"This is crap," Tracy said to Kins. She had worn the same clothes for twenty-four hours, hadn't showered, felt tired and gross, and was otherwise in no mood to be kept waiting.

"Let's just hear her out," Kins said, sounding as tired as Tracy felt. "Then we can get out of here before stupid rubs off on us, and get something to eat."

"Screw it," she said, standing. "I'm not waiting any longer."

Tracy was about to tell the receptionist they were leaving when a fit-looking young woman with short hair, hoop earrings, and skin the color of rich milk chocolate walked into the lobby.

"Detective Crosswhite? I'm Amanda Santos. I'm sorry to have kept you waiting. I couldn't get off a phone call with DC." Santos's handshake was firm but not the bone crunching variety some of Tracy's female colleagues employed.

"Not a problem," Kins said, suddenly attentive.

Santos wore a conservatively cut but formfitting black suit, making Tracy even more self-conscious about her own haggard appearance. She adjusted the collar of the blouse beneath her corduroy jacket as Santos led them down the hall.

"Can I offer you coffee?" she asked.

"You can," Kins said. "Unless you have a means to intravenously inject the caffeine."

When Kins glanced in Tracy's direction, she gave him her best "Please, she is so out of your league and you're married anyway" look.

Kins's smile widened.

Armed with cups of coffee, they stepped into a conference room of fluorescent lights, ceiling tiles, and the same generic black-and-white photographs of government buildings. Santos sat behind three file folders. Tracy and Kins sat across the table from her.

"So do you have a name for us?" Tracy asked. "Can I tell the prosecutor to swear out a warrant and we all go out for breakfast?"

"I wish I did," Santos said, displaying perfect white teeth.

Of course they are, Tracy thought.

"Unfortunately I'm not optimistic that's going to happen anytime soon. I don't envy you."

"I don't envy us," Kins said.

"What makes you say that?" Tracy asked.

"You have an organized killer. A disorganized killer is much more impulsive and haphazard. Disorganized killers make mistakes, leave fingerprints, fail to keep from being seen. Organized killers consider murder to be an art that they are trying to perfect. They don't make mistakes."

Tracy thought of Beth Stinson. "What do you mean by 'trying to perfect'?"

"I mean they practice. Let's start with the mechanism your killer uses to strangle his victims, which is elaborate and well thought out. It's doubtful your killer perfected it the first time he employed it, especially since he'd have to move quickly before his victim regained her ability to struggle."

Tracy sat forward, ignoring her coffee. "So there could be other victims out there but possibly not killed with the exact same signature? Slight variations?"

"There could be," Santos said. "Organized killers try very hard to blend in, to lead seemingly stable lives. They don't kill out of passion or anger. They're methodical and they're intelligent. Some have a working knowledge of police work and forensics, and, unlike other killers, they don't tell anyone what they're doing. They don't want to be caught."

"Is that why he's not having sex with his victims?" Kins asked. "He doesn't want to leave behind physical evidence?"

"It could be, but I don't believe this is about sexual gratification."

"What is it about?" Kins asked.

"It's about power and control and dominance. It could be he believes the women he's targeting are beneath him and he *wants* you to know this is not a sexual act."

"Or he could be impotent," Tracy said.

"I don't think so," Santos said.

"Why not?"

"Because I would expect to see some other type of sexual act, penetration of the victims, something."

"Maybe he gets off on the torture," Tracy said.

"I'm sure to an extent he does, but unlike other serial killers I've studied, he isn't trying to hide his victims' bodies. He's not taking their dance cards or IDs. He wants people to know who the 'victims' are and how they died. That speaks much more to someone trying to make a statement, and I think the statement is—this isn't about sex, and he doesn't consider them victims; he considers them bad people deserving of punishment."

"Is that his motivation?" Kins asked.

"He could have multiple motives," Santos said. "Or his motive may be evolving with each murder."

"If you had to offer an opinion," Tracy said, "what would you say his motivation is?"

"He's hog-tying them," Santos said. "That word originated from the hog-tying of pigs. My opinion is he's angry and hostile toward this subgroup of women. It might also be part of a psychological ritualism or internal psychodrama directly related to some perverted fantasy. Your guy could be acting out a script in his head. When Ted Bundy was interviewed, he told the detectives every detail of his crime until the final moments of his victims' lives. He considered those moments to be intimate between him and the victim."

"In what way?" Tracy asked.

"We'll never know," Santos said. Bundy had been executed.

"All right then, so what's this guy's script?" Tracy asked.

"He's interesting," Santos said. "Despite the hostility, he uses Rohypnol to subdue his victims rather than physically assaulting them, which fits with the rope pulley system and the use of cigarettes to burn the bottoms of their feet."

"How so?" Tracy asked.

"He doesn't touch them. He isn't killing them. They're killing themselves. I think it's his way of divorcing himself from, and justifying, the murders."

Kins put down his coffee mug. "What about the fact that the bed is made and the clothes are folded?"

"Definitely a ritualistic act," Santos said. "Those are common chores many children are required to perform."

Kins frowned. "So, what, this guy thinks he's killing his mother because she made him make his bed?"

Santos shook her head. "I'm not a fan of the Freudian crap that every boy wants to sleep with his mother. I wouldn't get too wrapped around the wheel about why he's killing these women. What we've learned is that these guys kill for one common reason. They enjoy it."

Despite her reluctance to meet with a profiler, Tracy was starting to like Santos.

"Is he crazy?" Kins asked.

Santos shook her head. "I think he's very sane, and by that I mean he definitely knows right from wrong. Look, Detectives, I could give you some psychobabble bullshit explanation about why someone chooses to kill being a complex process based on biological, social, and environmental factors, but that's not going to help you. And frankly, it's why profilers have gotten such a bad rap. We try too hard to figure out *why* these guys kill when it's really not possible to identify all of the factors that cause an individual to become a serial murderer. Think of the billions of things that have gone into developing who you are. I'm not just talking genetics and upbringing—think of all the things you've experienced every day of your life that have shaped who you are. That's why there's no template for these guys. The best we can do is to try to identify certain common traits."

"What would those traits be?" Tracy said.

"Antisocial behavior in early childhood."

"Skinning the neighbor's cat or lighting the dog's tail on fire," Kins said.

"Getting in fights at school," Santos said. "A seeming lack of remorse for bad acts, a callousness toward physical pain or torture. Then, usually by late twenties, the urge to control and to kill becomes too powerful to resist, and once they begin to kill, to act out their fantasies, the delusion, whatever it is, takes over."

"But there are instances of serial killers who have stopped killing, some for decades," Kins said. "Ridgway killed most of his victims between 1982 and 1984, and he wasn't caught for two decades."

"Ridgway claimed to have killed as many as eighty women," Santos said. "Who knows when he stopped? He was also married multiple times and could have fulfilled some of his sexual fantasies and impulses with his wives. The same might be true of the BTK Killer in Kansas. My point is, the impulse to kill never left, and the longer the period of time in between killings, the harder that impulse became to suppress. Once they started, they couldn't stop."

"So we can expect this guy to keep killing," Tracy said.

"I'm afraid so."

Kins sat forward. "Let me ask you something. How likely is it, if this guy is all about getting away with killing these women, that he would stalk a police officer?"

Santos looked across the table to Tracy. "If it is the same guy, it would be unusual, but not unprecedented. Detective Crosswhite has been in the news. Serial killers have big egos. They want to be the center of attention. He could see you as stepping into his spotlight." Santos paused. "Or he could see you as his ultimate prize."

CHAPTER 32

The man who greeted Dan in the small reception area did not look much like the profile picture on the firm website. James Tomey had aged and put on weight since the photographer's visit. He wasn't fat, but he had the bloated appearance Dan associated with someone who drank too much. It showed mostly in a broad and puffy face accentuated by thick lips and a full mane of blond hair.

Tomey extended a hand. "You O'Leary?"

"I am." Dan looked up at Tomey. He guessed the attorney was six four.

Tomey shouted down a hallway. "Tara, the conference room open?"

"Garth has it booked."

"For what?"

"The Unger deposition at one."

Tomey tugged up a shirtsleeve, revealing an expensive wristwatch. "Put me in there until then."

"He's got crap all over the table."

"Just put me in there." He rolled his eyes. "Sometimes I wonder who's working for whom."

Dan had run a quick Google search on Tomey. The attorney shared the suite with four other defense lawyers: three former public defenders and one prosecutor. The firm specialized in DUI defense, police misconduct, civil rights violations, sexual deviancy and felony, and misdemeanor defense. They offered payment plans and took plastic.

"You want coffee?" Tomey asked, pouring himself a cup.

"No, thanks," Dan said.

Tomey had the trial lawyers' swagger. He hadn't hesitated when Dan called and asked for an hour of his time to discuss Wayne Gerhardt, and now Tomey's body language as he led Dan into a conference room revealed no concern. In Dan's experience, attorneys like Tomey were usually more gunslinger than technical practitioner. They shot from the hip, which meant they could be sloppy, and unpredictable.

Tomey pushed a stack of papers down the freshly waxed dark wood table and sat back sipping his coffee. "So, Wayne Gerhardt?"

"I was hoping you could tell me a bit about his case."

"He's hired you?"

Dan had not told Tomey he was a lawyer. "I'm just looking into some things for a friend."

"Who's that?"

"I'm not at liberty to divulge my client's identity."

"The sister, right? She never wanted him to plead. He almost didn't."

"Why did he?"

Tomey pursed his lips. "Had to. Prosecutor had him by the short hairs."

"Did Wayne Gerhardt confess?"

"I can't tell you what he said and didn't say—that's a privileged communication—but I'll tell you he claimed he was innocent. That doesn't matter though."

"Why not?"

"Because the evidence is what matters, and they had it in spades. Gerhardt had been at the house that day; his fingerprints were all over the place. He had no alibi. And the neighbor made him. Plus, I didn't like the jury. You get a feel for these things. They were gonna hang him."

"He pled after the neighbor testified."

"Had to. Like I said, she'd made him. Dead certain."

"She didn't seem dead certain in her police statement."

Tomey gave a condescending smile and set down his coffee mug. "Mr. O'Leary, I've been doing this a while now, and let me tell you, what the witness says to the police doesn't mean squat. What matters is what she tells the twelve idiots seated in the idiot box, and what she told them was she saw Gerhardt at the house. You try to impeach a nice old lady like that too much and the jury just ends up disliking you and your client even more."

Tomey's condescending tone confirmed he thought Dan was a private investigator, and Dan was content to let him keep thinking it. "I can appreciate that," Dan said. "What about the DNA evidence? Why not get it tested?"

Tomey showed Dan his palms. "You get the DNA tested and it proves it's your client, the prosecutor isn't going to swing a deal. He can't. He's got to go for the jugular. What's he gonna tell the victim's family if he doesn't? You see the problem? You guess wrong and you just signed your client's death certificate, because they're gonna hang him."

"And what if the DNA proved it wasn't Gerhardt?"

"See, this is what the general public doesn't understand. The DNA was on her clothes. It wasn't inside her. He drops his seed inside her and it isn't your guy, now you got something to argue. But the medical examiner's report said no sex. So even if the DNA hadn't been a hit, it doesn't mean he didn't do it. It just means she picked up DNA from some other guy—a boyfriend or somebody else who'd been in the house. It isn't definitive. It isn't exonerating.

So you're gambling. You're gambling on the death penalty or life without parole versus twenty-five years. Gerhardt was young. With good behavior, time served, maybe he gets out in fifteen."

"No sex in seventy-two hours?" Dan asked. "So what was your guy's motivation?"

Tomey shrugged. "Who knows, right?"

"What was the prosecutor's theory?"

"Didn't get the chance to rape her because she died."

"Did she have a boyfriend?"

"Who?"

"Beth Stinson. You said the DNA could have belonged to a boyfriend. Did she have one?"

"I don't remember whether she did or didn't; what I'm saying is you're gambling with the house's money you go down that road."

Dan didn't fully understand the mixed metaphor, but he got the gist. "What about the other witnesses?"

"What other witnesses?"

"The ones listed in the police file; did you speak to them?"

"Probably. Nothing that rocked my world that I can remember." Tomey checked that expensive watch again. "Okay, we good?"

Dan nodded. "Yeah, we're good." He wasn't, but he knew Tomey wasn't going to give him any more time. In Tomey's world, time was money, and he wasn't making any sitting and talking to Dan about a client from a decade ago sitting in prison. Besides, Dan had figured out what he needed to know.

Tomey had done a horseshit job defending Gerhardt.

—

When he got back to Tracy's, Dan took a long run, showered, and spent the rest of the afternoon going through the remainder of the materials in the Beth Stinson file. Tracy called at five in the afternoon to tell him she was coming home early, then called again at five thirty and said she'd been delayed.

Dan managed to scrape together a salad to serve with frozen chicken breasts he'd marinated in soy sauce, which was about all he could find in Tracy's refrigerator. He put the chicken in the oven when he heard the garage door roll open. The oven clock said 6:33. When he heard the door to the house open, he stood behind the wall and reached out waving a white towel. "Is it safe to come out?"

She laughed. He poked his head around the corner. Despite her smile, she looked as tired and beat as she'd sounded on the phone. She set her briefcase down and tossed her coat over the back of a chair. Dan gave her a kiss. "You want a glass of wine?"

"I better not," she said. "I'm liable to fall asleep."

"Dinner will be ready in twenty minutes. I thought you might want time for a shower."

"Thanks. I'm a bit ripe. What did you do with your day off?"

"Day off? I wish. It can wait. Take your shower."

She eyed him. "You want to tell me something. I can tell."

"Actually, I'm debating how much I should tell you."

"Beth Stinson?"

"I talked to JoAnne Anderson this morning."

"Yeah?"

"Then I spoke to Wayne Gerhardt's public defender."

"And?"

"What if they start asking you questions—Nolasco or someone else? Maybe it's best if you don't know the details."

She leaned back against the counter. She appreciated Dan's concern, but at the moment the investigation was going nowhere fast. And if finding some evidence to change that meant risking getting in trouble for working an old file, then so be it. "I talked to an FBI profiler today," Tracy said. "She said this kind of serial killer practices killing the way the rest of us practice golf swings, that he doesn't necessarily get it right the first time. It could explain the difference between the way Stinson was tied and the other dancers."

Dan appeared to be giving that some thought. Then he said, "Anderson's nearsighted. She can't see to the sidewalk without her glasses. I asked her if she was wearing them that night. She said she couldn't be certain. She *thinks* she put them on because she *thinks* she saw Gerhardt. I don't think she did, and I'm not certain she could have seen him even if she had. I drove out to her house late last night to get a perspective similar to the one she would have had. It was pitch-black—no street lamps, just a few lawn lights. No lights on the exterior of Beth Stinson's home."

"Could have been different nine years ago."

Dan shook his head. "There are some photos of the exterior of the home in the file. Besides, people usually add exterior lights, not take them down."

"So how'd Anderson ID Gerhardt?" Tracy asked.

"Initially, she didn't. She told Nolasco and his partner she couldn't be certain about what she had seen, that she thought she saw a man but she didn't want to be responsible for convicting an innocent man and have that on her conscience."

"But she testified she saw Gerhardt."

"Only after she picked him out of a police lineup, which was after Nolasco showed her a photograph of Gerhardt."

"She picked him out of a montage?"

Dan shook his head. "She said they showed her just Gerhardt's photograph."

"But there are photographs of four other men in the file," Tracy said.

"I know. But Anderson was certain."

"I think I need that glass of wine," Tracy said.

Dan poured a glass and handed it to her. Tracy took a sip. Then she said, "So they show her Gerhardt's picture, she sees the same guy in the lineup, and now she's convinced she was wearing her glasses and saw Gerhardt."

"She also said she was outside gardening the afternoon Gerhardt was working to clear the clog in Stinson's bathroom, and she saw him walk out of the house to the back of the van."

"She could be remembering him from that afternoon and not that night."

"She testified Gerhardt was wearing coveralls." Dan shook his head. "No way, even wearing glasses, she could make out that much detail. It was overcast and raining. I'm betting she saw him in coveralls that afternoon."

"None of this is in the file."

"No," Dan said. "But I'm not sure it would have come out at trial even if it had been in the police reports after meeting Gerhardt's attorney. He told me he didn't go at Anderson too hard because he was afraid of pissing off the jury. His client was looking at prison, and he didn't want to piss off the jury?"

For a minute they stood not speaking. Then Tracy asked, "So what next?"

"The next logical step would be for me to speak to Gerhardt, but we need to think this through first, Tracy."

"Nothing to think through, Dan. Not now."

"If someone finds out I'm talking to Gerhardt, how long do you think it's going to take the media, and your boss, to tie me to you? And if he and his partner did railroad Gerhardt, he's really not going to want you looking into this. He'll paint you as a crusader trying to free another convicted murderer instead of catching a serial killer. I'm not sure how you survive, especially if someone starts asking how I got a police file."

Tracy looked out the sliding glass door. The final light of day reflected in bursts of gold off the glass exteriors of the downtown Seattle office buildings. "Do you remember Walter Gipson?"

"The schoolteacher?"

"He admitted being in the motel with Schreiber the night she was killed, but he says he didn't kill her. If he's telling the truth, it means someone went to that motel room after him. Had to have, right?"

"That would make sense."

"The profiler I spoke with today said the killer is very intelligent, careful, deliberate. So what if he knew Schreiber was going to be with Gipson and used Gipson as a cover?"

"Knew how?"

"Schreiber brought Gipson into the greenroom at least once, and Faz found something on the surveillance video of the Pink Palace parking lot the night Schreiber and Gipson left together."

"What did he find?"

"A car parked on a side street pulls from the curb and appears to follow Gipson and Schreiber as they drive off."

"So you're thinking that if Gerhardt didn't kill Stinson, then the killer might have known Gerhardt performed a service call at Stinson's house earlier that afternoon and used it as a cover."

"That would be the logical deduction, right?"

"What about the other two dancers?"

"I don't know yet. I'm still fleshing this out. But if there's something to it, it could mean I'm going about this all wrong. If this guy had prior contact with his victims, then maybe I need to reassess whether this really is a stranger-to-stranger killer."

Dan recognized the look in her eye—the look Tracy got at the shooting range when she was zeroing in on a target. "I thought you said you ran every employee through the system, and nothing suspicious came up."

"We did, but that doesn't mean a lot. The profiler said these guys fly under the radar, lead seemingly normal lives with no prior criminal records. They're one and done. They get caught and it's life or the death penalty."

"There's something else," Dan said. Tracy followed him from the kitchen to the dining room table. He picked up the HITS form for Beth Stinson and handed it to her. "Look at question 102. It says there's evidence of a sexual assault, but they didn't check the box indicating they found semen in the body cavities of the victim."

"I noticed that also."

Tracy was about to say something more, but Dan said, "Hold that thought." He picked up a copy of the medical examiner's report, this one with his yellow highlights and sticky notes. He flipped a few stapled pages and read from the report. "No evidence of redness, soreness, or other signs of physical trauma to corroborate that sexual contact occurred. Swabs collected of the body cavities did not reveal seminal fluid. A colposcopy was performed but did not indicate any genital microtrauma indicating recent sexual contact and penetration. No seminal fluid, no spermatozoa or acid phosphatase."

Tracy had spent a year on the Sexual Assault Unit. "Cases negative for sperm but positive for ACP typically indicate the assailant had a vasectomy or wore a condom."

"And that's probably what Nolasco and his partner assumed when they checked the box," Dan said, "except the medical examiner ruled out a condom." Dan read again from the report. "No exchangeable traces of particulates, lubricants, or spermicides." He lowered the report. "Whoever killed Beth Stinson didn't have sex with her. Nolasco or his partner checked box 102 prematurely because—"

"They needed a motive."

Dan nodded. "Just like they needed a suspect. And because the defense attorney got Gerhardt to plead, none of this ever came out and they never bothered to go back and correct the form."

Tracy said, "So you have to talk to Gerhardt and find out who else knew he'd made a service call that afternoon and follow up on those other witness leads."

"Beth Stinson's family is not going to want to relive this."

"I know, and I don't blame them. But if we're right, we're not just talking about an innocent man in prison for a crime he didn't commit, we're talking about someone who might have been killing for nearly a decade, maybe longer, someone who might have killed a lot more than three or four women. And if the profiler is right, something has triggered him to kill again, and this time he's not going to stop on his own."

CHAPTER 33

He pressed the "Eject" button and looked again at the woman on the floor. Still upright, she had her eyes open, staring at him with her mouth hanging agape. She'd been more work than the others. Each time he'd thought she was dead, she'd flinch, then gasp, and come back to life. It was like one of those zombie horror movies where the zombies wouldn't die unless they had their heads blown off. At first it had been intoxicating, but it soon got old. He just wanted her to die so he could leave. Her perfume and body odor disgusted him, and the smell of cigarettes was nauseating.

The VCR continued to whir. Then it stopped. He reached for the cassette tape, but it didn't come out. He pressed "Eject" again and heard a click, indicating that the tape had rewound, but again the cassette did not come out. He pressed the button repeatedly. "Come on. Come on. Come on, you piece of crap!"

He banged his fist on the top of the machine, which caused the dresser to bump hard against the wall. He froze. He'd heard people in the room next door earlier, though it had been quiet the last hour. He lifted the flap on the VCR and peered inside. The tape was there, but it hadn't popped up. A cold sweat broke out across his forehead and the back of his neck. Rivulets of perspiration dribbled down the side of his face from his temples.

He looked again at the woman. She continued to stare up at him.

"Stop looking at me," he said. He stood and kicked her with his foot. She wobbled but didn't topple over.

He gripped the machine, but it was bolted to the top of the wood laminate dresser. "Like someone would steal a decades-old piece-of-shit VCR you couldn't get ten bucks for in a pawnshop," he said.

He pressed the "Eject" button again, then opened and closed the dresser drawers, frantically searching for something to pry up the tape. The drawers were empty. He swore under his breath. *What kind of motel doesn't provide a pen?* He removed his keys from his pocket and tried to work a key beneath the tape. This wasn't just about sentimentality; he'd had the tape since he was a child, but he was more practical. The tape had his fingerprints all over it.

He checked his watch. How long had she rented the room? He always gave them money for the night but found they were cheap. They'd pay for an hour or two and pocket the change. It was why he'd started to use cigarettes to burn the bottoms of their feet. They were taking too long to die, and he feared a manager would come to the room, looking for the rest of his money. He could use the tip of the cigarette without having to touch them. They disgusted him, but again there were the practicalities to consider. Any contact meant a potential transfer of evidence, a piece of hair, flakes of skin, something.

He looked to the door. The security latch remained in place, the chain lock in its slot.

The woman continued to stare up at him.

He turned his back to her to focus on the problem at hand. He just needed to remain calm. He practiced his breathing exercises the way he'd been taught to center himself before a performance. Within a minute the solution came to him, and its simplicity made him laugh. He hadn't rented the room. It wasn't like they had his credit card or driver's license. What did he care if he damaged the damn VCR.

He followed the electrical cord protruding from the back, wiping at dust balls that had trapped dead bugs down behind the dresser, and pulled it from the outlet. Then he gripped the VCR by its edges and applied steady pressure until he heard the cheap laminate crack and the machine pop free.

Time to go.

He slid the VCR inside his gym bag, but one end stuck out. He tried a different angle, turned the machine on its side, and tried to stretch the bag, all to no avail. There was no way to fit it. He'd have to improvise. He'd always been good on his feet. His teachers had said it was one of his best talents. He tugged his sweatshirt over his head and covered the end of the VCR. It wasn't perfect, but if he gripped the handles a certain way it looked natural. Besides, he had no other options. It would have to do. He took a final look around the room. The bed was pristine, the clothes folded neatly.

His performance was finished.

He pulled the ball cap low on his head, slid the leather gloves over the latex ones, and made his way to the door. He unlatched the security prong and slid free the chain, careful not to make a noise. Slowly he pulled open the door, waiting again before looking out. No one lingered on the walkway. No one stood in the parking lot. Stepping out, he quickly turned his back and closed the door, ensuring that it locked. He lifted the strap of his gym bag onto his shoulder, feeling the extra weight of the VCR but trying not to show it, and quietly walked around the side of the building.

The back of the property abutted the adjacent street. He headed south one block, walking deliberately, though not rushing. He was a man coming from a workout. He took a left, then his first right. He'd parked in front of a chain-link fence enclosing a vacant dirt lot. Signs on the fence indicated the lot was for sale and zoned commercial. It was the perfect place to leave his car, far from night-owl nosy neighbors. With distance from the motel, he started to relax, though he continued to perspire. The cool air felt good on his skin and when he sucked it deep into his chest.

He unlocked the car door with the key, purposefully avoiding using the remote, which chirped, and slid his gym bag onto the backseat. Inside, he started the car, not that you could hear it—the hybrid was silent—and pulled from the curb. Halfway down the block, he turned on the headlights and made a full stop at the stop sign before turning right. "Home free," he said and checked his rearview mirror.

A car turned right off of Aurora and came down the block. He checked his speedometer: 25 miles per hour. He made another full stop at the corner, checked the mirror again, and saw swirling blue and red lights.

His heart rate spiked. His pulse began to beat at his temples. He couldn't do anything to stop perspiring. He tried to center himself. "Calm down," he told himself. "You're prepared for this. You've rehearsed it. You've memorized your lines. Just stay in character and stick to the script."

He eased the car to the curb and watched the side mirror. A single officer exited the patrol car quickly, a good sign. He hadn't likely run the license plate.

He lowered the window. "Is there a problem, Officer?"

"You got a brake light out." The officer looked like a kid, with a military haircut and an immature face. Likely a newbie, hopefully not a do-it-by-the-book type.

"I do? Which side?"

"Passenger side."

"Could I get out of the car and take a look?" *Always ask permission. Be polite.*

"Sure."

He unbuckled his seat belt and stepped out, eyeing his gym bag as he stepped to the rear bumper.

"You want me to press down on the brake so you can see?" the officer said.

"That would be great."

The officer held on to the car door and stuck his right leg inside the car, depressing the pedal.

"Well, you're right. It's out."

"Looks like a relatively new car."

"Haven't had it that long, but I bought it used. I'll take it in today at lunch and get it fixed." He wiped the continued flow of perspiration rolling down his temples.

"You're perspiring an awful lot."

"I take a long time to cool down after a workout."

He saw the officer glance at the rear seat. "Where do you work out around here?"

"24 Hour Fitness. They have one just around the corner." He pointed to the backseat. "I keep my gym bag in the car." The officer shone a flashlight through the window. "Had to cut it short this morning, though. I'm on cat patrol before work."

"Cat patrol?"

He stepped to the driver's side and leaned inside the car, retrieving a small stack of fliers from the passenger seat. He handed one to the officer. "My daughter lost her cat, Angus, three days ago. She really loved that cat. He slept right on the bed beside her. I'm putting up fliers all over the neighborhood, though I'm not optimistic we'll find him. Probably roadkill, I'm afraid, but you never know. Stranger things have happened."

The officer considered the flier, then handed it back. "Get that taillight fixed."

"I will. Thank you, Officer." He turned and bent to put the fliers back inside the car, then exhaled.

"Hey?"

He rose up, turning. The officer was walking back, and he was certain it was to ask to see his license and registration. "Yes, Officer?"

"Let me have one of those fliers. I got two kids. They'd be heartbroken if they lost their cat. I'll keep my eye out for Angus."

CHAPTER 34

Kins stood when Tracy entered the Cowboy Room the following morning. "OPA called, asking me for my statement.
They're opening a file for Taggart. I thought you said Nolasco was
going to back you?"

"He did. I guess they still have to do an inquiry."

"Tracy?"

Bennett Lee was entering the room cautiously, as if worried
he'd get cement dust on his blue pin-striped suit. "You're not
returning my calls."

"Been a little busy here, Bennett."

"Yeah, well, the Chief wants me to provide the press an update
this afternoon."

"I don't have an update for you."

"Nolasco says you have a profile; said you met with the FBI."

"You got to be freaking kidding me," Kins said.

Tracy shut her eyes. She'd known there had to be a reason
Nolasco had sent them to talk to Amanda Santos, though she
was glad he had. If Nolasco wanted the task force to fail, releas-
ing an incomplete or erroneous profile was the next logical step. It
would be misinterpreted by the media and the public to mean an

arrest was imminent. When that didn't happen, it gave the media the chance to skewer the task force. Worse, a profile would bury them under another flood of mostly useless tips, and they'd already received more than a thousand.

Lee raised his hands. "Don't shoot the messenger, Sparrow. You know how it goes. When we don't issue a profile, it makes us look like we don't have a clue."

"We don't have a clue," Kins said.

"The national networks are calling Seattle 'the Killing Ground.' I'm getting a lot of pressure here, Tracy. Nolasco says it's making us look bad."

"You know what will make us look worse, Bennett?" Kins said. "A profile that says the killer is possibly a white male between the ages of twenty-five and forty-five, possibly married, possibly divorced, possibly a father, possibly raised by an overly protective mother who sexually stimulated him, possibly a bed wetter, who possibly tortured small animals."

Lee looked to Tracy. "Can you give me anything?"

Tracy was sympathetic, and she was about to tell Lee she would sit down and pen something out when her desk phone rang. "Hold on," she said, answering. She listened for a moment. Her stomach gripped, and she felt her adrenaline spike. "We're on our way." She hung up. Kins was already grabbing his jacket. She looked to Lee. "You're not going to have to worry about a profile today, Bennett."

———

The last time Dan had been inside the walls of the Walla Walla State Penitentiary he'd been sitting next to Tracy at a cafeteria-style table, speaking with Edmund House, a hardened prisoner with ropy muscles and bulging veins. The man who stepped into the phone booth–sized room on the other side of scratched plexiglass this time was a sharp contrast to House. Wayne Gerhardt's prison-issued khaki pullover and pants hung from narrow shoulders and almost nonexistent hips. A thin face, prominent chin and nose, and hair the color of sunburned straw brought to mind the image of a midwestern scarecrow.

Gerhardt pulled out a chair and sat, looking through the partition at Dan with prison-washed dull-blue eyes.

"Mr. Gerhardt. I'm Dan—"

"I know who you are." Gerhardt's voice was soft, nonconfrontational. "Everyone in here knows who you are. You represented Edmund House."

"That's right."

"What do you want with me?"

"I'd like to ask you a few questions."

"Why?"

"I'm curious about some of the details of Beth Stinson's murder."

"You writing a book?"

"No, I'm a lawyer."

"So? You writing a book? Isn't that what every lawyer does now?" The corners of his mouth rose.

"I'm not writing a book," Dan said, returning a passive smile.

"Who told you about my case?"

"I can't tell you that at this moment."

Gerhardt's gaze narrowed. If he was considering leaving, now was the likely moment. But Dan didn't think he would. He was betting from the man's appearance—nothing like the mug shots in his police file—that having someone to talk to, anyone other than rapists and murderers and crazies, was probably a welcome distraction. "I'm an attorney, Mr. Gerhardt, but technically I'm not *your* attorney. Therefore what we say here isn't considered protected unless you intend for it to have been a communication with me in my capacity as an attorney. So I can't reveal everything to you, because it isn't protected. So for now, you're going to have to trust me."

Gerhardt smiled again, but this time it was more of a smirk. "The last time I trusted a lawyer I ended up in here with a twenty-five-year sentence."

"Will you answer my questions?"

Gerhardt straightened and moved closer to the partition. "Only one question and one answer that matters." His eyebrows arched, nearly touching his blond bangs. "Did I kill her? No, I did not."

Dan took the opening and pressed forward. "Had you ever met Beth Stinson before the day you made the service call?"

"No."

"What can you tell me about that day?"

"What do you want to know?" Gerhardt said. "I've had ten years to think about it."

"Whatever you can remember."

"She had a clogged toilet. I had another job before hers, and it took me longer than I thought, so I was late getting there."

"What time of day was it?"

"Afternoon, close to four. She was anxious, because she needed to get to work but she was afraid the toilet would back up when she wasn't home and create a real mess. I guess it had happened before."

"Where did you park your van?"

"In the driveway. She'd moved her car onto the street. It was new, and she didn't want to get it scratched. She also didn't want me to block her in."

"So she could get to work."

"Right."

"What else?"

"She walked me through the house to the bathroom—"

"You're talking about the bathroom off the master bedroom at the back?"

"That's right."

"So you had to walk through her bedroom."

"No other way to get to that bathroom."

"Did you touch anything in the bedroom?"

"They said they found my fingerprints on a dresser, so I guess I did."

"And your fingerprints were all over the bathroom."

"No way to prevent that."

"What type of woman was Beth Stinson?"

"What do you mean?"

Dan thought how best to phrase the question. "Was she reserved, standoffish, outgoing, friendly?"

"She seemed all right, you know. I'd say friendly. Nice-looking, I remember that. She had on those tights, spandex, and a sweatshirt cut midstomach. Nice body."

"Were you able to clear the drain?"

"Not right away. I had to go back and forth to my van for tools and the snake. Finally, I had to go at it from a trap outside."

"Where was Beth Stinson while you were doing this?"

"She mostly stayed in the kitchen flipping through magazines, though she'd come in a few times to ask how it was going."

"She was anxious," Dan said.

"Like I said."

"Did you ever go into the kitchen?"

"Only to tell her that the clog was farther down the line and I was going to try to get at it from outside."

They'd found Gerhardt's fingerprints on the kitchen counter and used it as evidence that he'd tried to clean up a dirty bootprint he'd left on Stinson's carpet.

"Where was the trap?"

"Under the house." He looked up for a moment, remembering. "It was the north side."

The side closest to JoAnne Anderson's house. Gerhardt would have been facing Anderson's direction each time he walked out Stinson's front door.

"Was there dirt on that side of the house?"

"Yeah. I tracked in a little bit. She wasn't upset or anything. She just rubbed at it a bit. She wanted to replace the carpet with hardwood floor."

"Did you see anyone when you went outside?"

"The neighbor across the street was gardening. She's the one who testified. She said she saw me that night. She didn't."

"Was she wearing glasses when you saw her?"

"I don't remember that. She testified that she wore glasses, so I suppose she was. I remember she was wearing one of those wide sun hats, you know, the kind that droops down to shield the face."

"Did you wave to her, greet her in any manner?"

"No."

"What were you wearing?"

"Same thing I always wore for work. Gray pants, blue shirt."

"So you weren't wearing coveralls?"

"I slipped them on when I had to go under the house."

Dan scratched two lines beneath his note that JoAnne Anderson had seen Gerhardt in coveralls that afternoon.

"What kind of boots?"

"Timberland."

"How thick were the soles?"

Gerhardt held his fingers two to three inches apart.

"How tall are you, Mr. Gerhardt?"

"Just under six three. Why?"

Dan continued scribbling. "JoAnne Anderson said the man she saw that night was the same height as the tree in the yard.

Nine years ago the tree was six feet. With your work boots on, you would have been closer to six five."

"She'll say it was dark, that she couldn't see all that well."

Dan smiled, and for the first time a light seemed to shine in Wayne Gerhardt's eyes.

"Why'd you plead if you didn't do it, Wayne?"

Gerhardt shrugged. Then he dropped his gaze. When he looked up, his eyes were watering. "Felt like it was stacked against me, you know. The woman picking me out of a lineup and then at trial." His chest shuddered. The man was struggling to hold on. "My attorney said I didn't have a chance. He said if I didn't take the deal, they'd go for the death penalty. He said there was evidence I raped her before I killed her and they'd say that was an aggravating circumstance."

"Did he say what the evidence was?"

"DNA."

"Did he talk to you about getting the DNA evidence tested?"

"He said if they found my DNA, they wouldn't make the deal—that the prosecutor wouldn't be able to justify it to his boss and then the plea deal would be off the table. It was a mistake. I was young and scared." He wiped away an errant tear. Then he sat up and composed himself. "I shouldn't have pled. I've been trying to get someone to take my case for years. I've written to the Innocence Project at UW and back East, just about everywhere."

"What about your attorney?"

"He's the reason I'm in here. I haven't heard from him in years. You got any ideas?"

"A few. We could seek a post-conviction DNA analysis. A judge can order the testing on his own now."

"Why would a judge do that?"

"He wouldn't, not unless I gave him a very good reason."

"You got one?"

"Let me ask you, Wayne. Did you tell anyone you were going to be working at Beth Stinson's home? I mean, who would have known that you were there that afternoon?"

Gerhardt thought a bit. "My supervisor. Some of the other techs. I would have radioed it in that I was making the call. Could have been any number of people at work."

Dan wrote a few more notes.

"Why'd you ask me that?"

"Simple logic, Wayne. If you didn't kill Beth Stinson, someone else did. Maybe someone who knew you were at her house that afternoon."

"Sounds like a long shot."

"Could be."

"You think it's enough to get the DNA tested?"

"Not by itself, but I'm working on it."

Gerhardt didn't smile or otherwise react. He just sat, staring through the plexiglass. After almost ten years, Dan didn't doubt the man's hopes had been crushed too many times.

CHAPTER 35

The crowd of reporters began hurling questions as soon as Tracy and Kins stepped from their car into the motel parking lot.

"Is it the Cowboy, Detectives?"

"Is it another dancer?"

"Detective Crosswhite, do you have a profile of the killer?"

As with the other murders, the room was located far from the motel office. Tracy did not immediately enter the room, in the corner of the one-story L-shaped layout. She stepped past the door to where the walkway continued to the back of the building, which led to a side street off Aurora. Kins joined her. "I don't think he's parking in the parking lot," she said. "That's why we're not getting any hits for the license plates. I think he's parking on adjacent streets and walking." She called over the patrol sergeant and asked that he string crime scene tape around an area at the back of the building. "Maybe CSI can find a shoe impression, cigarette butt. Anything."

She and Kins signed the log and stepped inside the room. "Oh no," Tracy said, seeing the victim. She was small-boned, with red hair. They didn't need to check for her dance card. She had been one of the dancers they'd spoken with in the Pink Palace greenroom.

—

Hours later, back in the Cowboy Room, Tracy found messages stacked up on her desk from Nolasco, Bennett Lee, and Billy Williams. A detective named Ferris had also called, from OPA. She threw that message in the garbage. The tip line was ringing non-stop, and the task force couldn't keep up with the calls. Everyone was expressing frustration at being chained to their desks and not in the field getting things done. It would take weeks to track down all of the leads, and getting more manpower was off the table; Nolasco was carefully managing the budget while waiting for Tracy to fail.

Someone had added a new photograph to the wall. The redhead was Gabrielle Lizotte, stage name, "French Fire." Twenty-two years old, she'd danced for two and a half years at the Pink Palace, mostly the club on First Avenue where Tracy and Kins had interviewed her. Prior to that, to Tracy's surprise, Lizotte had danced at the Dancing Bare, and Tracy was beating herself up that she had not asked the dancers if any of them had known Nicole Hansen. Faz and Del were running Hansen's picture back to the Pink Palace before heading to the Dancing Bare to ask about Lizotte's time there. Ron Mayweather was comparing a list of current Pink Palace employees to current and past Dancing Bare employees and running down the names of anyone who'd made an appointment with Lizotte online through the Pink Palace's website. The Dancing Bare did not have a website.

Tracy walked to Kins's desk. When he'd finished his call, she nodded for him to follow her out of the room. Shutting the door behind themselves, they stood in the sallow light of the stairwell, surrounded by the stale smell of damp concrete. Somewhere below them, footsteps echoed on the metal stairs and a door slammed shut.

"What's up?" Kins asked.

"I think she knew him. I think they all knew him."

"Knew him how? A customer? Nash?"

"He'd certainly have some leverage if they said no, and he's connected to everyone but Nicole Hansen."

"So is Taggart," Kins said. "And maybe Gipson. And all the employees."

She agreed. Her theory only ruled out David Bankston. No one at the Pink Palace or the Dancing Bare had picked his photograph out of a montage.

Ron Mayweather stuck his head out the door. "Tracy? Bennett Lee's on the phone. Says he really needs to speak to you."

"I'll be there in a minute."

Mayweather closed the door.

"What makes you think they all knew him?" Kins said. "That thing with Angela Schreiber renting the room for longer than an hour?"

"That started it," she said, "but now I'm starting to wonder why would Gabrielle Lizotte go? You saw how scared she was the night we talked to her. She didn't want to leave the greenroom."

"It's worth considering," Kins said. "But we ran the employees."

"Could be a regular, somebody online."

"He'd use an alias."

Tracy agreed. "At least we finally have some connection to Nicole Hansen if Gabrielle Lizotte danced there."

Kins exhaled loudly. "I guess it ain't nothing."

They stepped back into the room. Tracy picked up her phone.

"I need a statement for the media," Lee said.

"Not a good time, Bennett. I've got the next-up detectives bringing in all the witness statements now, and the phones are ringing off the hook here."

"Yeah, well, Nolasco says the Chief is pushing him for something. What about that profile?"

"I told you I'm going to need some time to put it together, Bennett, and I'm telling you right now it will be generic."

"When will you have it?"

Kins turned from his desk, phone pressed against his chest. "David Bankston. He says he'll come in."

"When?" Tracy asked Kins.

"I need it yesterday," Lee said.

"Today," Kins said. "After his shift ends. I'll call Ludlow and see if she can do a polygraph."

"What?" Lee asked.

"I have to call you back, Bennett."

"Tracy, when can I—?"

"I'll call you back." She hung up and listened as Kins confirmed the time with David Bankston for late that afternoon.

Kins hung up. "We're doing great aren't we? The one suspect we can't tie to the dancers and he's the one willing to take a polygraph."

"What about reaching out to Santos about her coming to have a look at him, get her suggestions on the type of questions to ask?"

A patrol officer answering phones turned from her desk. "Detective Crosswhite? I got a caller says she'll only speak to you."

"Tell her she'll have to speak to you." Some callers asked to speak to Tracy because they saw her as some type of celebrity and wanted to inject themselves into her investigation. Independent forensic companies and profilers were calling to offer their services. A well-known psychic had called, certain she could assist. One guy had even called just to ask Tracy to dinner.

"I'll handle Bankston," Kins said, checking his watch. "Can you take care of the statement for Lee?"

Tracy's cell rang. Caller ID indicated it was the Washington State Patrol Crime Lab. She answered. "Mike?"

"I've got something for you."

Tracy looked at her watch. "I'm not sure when I can get down there."

"I'm in the building, next door at the AFIS examiner's office."

She turned to Kins, but he was back on the phone.

"I'm on my way."

The patrol officer put the phone to her shoulder as Tracy started for the door. "Detective?"

"Take a message. Tell her I'll call her back. Get as much detail as you can."

Melton met Tracy in the lobby of room W-150, the office of the regional AFIS examiner, and led her to one of the labs in the back. Tracy greeted Sherri Belle, whom she knew from prior cases. Veronica Watson's purple handbag rested on a table, smudged with traces of the gray aluminum powder used to lift fingerprints.

"I ran the victim's purse in the tank," Belle said. "We got five usable prints. Three belong to the victim. Two produced a positive hit for a Bradley Taggart. Mike says you know him."

"Taggart was the victim's boyfriend," Tracy said. She could think of a hundred different reasons why his fingerprints would be on her handbag and recalled Shereece saying Taggart treated Watson like an ATM.

Perhaps sensing that Tracy was not impressed, Melton nodded to Belle. "Tell her."

"The Latent Print Unit was able to match the print to a partial we lifted from the dresser in the motel room."

CHAPTER 36

The detectives still on duty strained their necks trying to get a good look at Amanda Santos as Kins escorted her from the elevator through the seventh floor of the Justice Center.

"Can't promise anything," he said, reaching for the coffee in the tiny kitchenette.

"I work for the federal government," Santos said. "Tar would taste better than some of the coffee I've had."

They took their cups to the A Team's bull pen and sat at the table in the center, reviewing the questions that Santos had recommended the polygraph examiner, Stephanie Ludlow, ask David Bankston.

"Let me ask you," Kins said. "Suppose he's guilty. Why would he agree to do a polygraph? Do these guys really think they can beat it?"

"Some might, but most don't think that way. They don't beat it using schemes or techniques. They beat it because they have no remorse for what they did; they think their actions were perfectly justifiable."

"Then why take the test?"

Santos shrugged. "Hard to know. Bundy couldn't help himself. He fancied himself a lawyer, thought he was smarter than everyone, and didn't think he'd get caught. These guys will keep scrapbooks with newspaper clippings. Some keep trophies."

"Jeffrey Dahmer."

"Exactly. Ridgway went back and had sex with the bodies after he *knew* he was a suspect. He even agreed to have his house searched, because he'd already had the carpet torn out and replaced and knew the detectives wouldn't find anything. He thought it would exonerate him. Personally, I don't think we'll ever figure these guys out."

The phone on Kins's desk rang, and he answered it. "I'll be right down." He hung up. "That's him," he said to Santos.

Kins greeted David Bankston in the lobby and endured an uncomfortable elevator ride. Bankston stared at the metal doors.

"Thanks for coming in," Kins said.

Bankston gave him a quick glance. "Sure. How long will it take?"

"Shouldn't be too long. How old is your daughter?"

"She's two."

"The terrible twos. That's a joyful time for every parent."

"Yeah," Bankston said, keeping his gaze fixed on the doors.

"Did you talk to your wife?"

"What about?"

"Coming in here."

He shook his head. "No."

"Didn't mention it?"

"No."

When Kins walked Bankston to the soft interrogation room, Bankston saw Santos sitting at the table and hesitated. He turned to Kins. "Where's Detective Crosswhite?"

"She's involved in another matter," Kins said.

"They took her off the case?"

"This is Santos," Kins said, deliberately avoiding the use of the term 'agent.'" Santos had come to the door. She offered her hand, but Bankston turned again to Kins. "I thought I was meeting with Detective Crosswhite."

"Was there something in particular you wanted to tell Detective Crosswhite?" Kins asked.

"She asked about the rope, whether we can track the shipments."

"Did you find something out?" Kins asked, though he already knew the answer, because Mayweather had been going through the store's inventory and had been complaining it was like trying to find an honest man in Congress. Mayweather had also gone through Bankston's purchases using his employee discount, which did not reveal polypropylene rope.

When Bankston didn't immediately answer, Kins said, "Why don't we sit down?" For a moment Bankston looked uncertain. Then he walked in, and they sat at a round table.

"What did you find?" Kins asked.

"What?"

"About the shipments, what did you find?"

"They can track the inventory. They use bar codes. They can track where the inventory is shipped, to which store. Once the shipment arrives, it's inventoried at that store, which means they can track sales from that store."

"But only if the person used a credit card," Kins said.

"Not necessarily. They have these rewards programs people can sign up for. They get credits even if they use cash. But they have to provide a phone number."

"Hadn't thought of that," Kins said. They had, but doubted the Cowboy was providing a phone number. "That's a good tip."

Bankston nodded. "And I was thinking, you know, that the stores have cameras all over the place, so you could maybe go through the videos, find out if someone was buying rope on the day that the women were killed."

Kins nodded and looked to Santos. "Another good suggestion. I can tell you were at the Academy. You think like a cop."

"The police academy?" Santos asked.

"David was a recruit before he joined the Army," Kins said, noting that Bankston was rubbing his hands on his thighs.

"Is that right?" Santos said. "Why did you decide not to become a police officer?"

Bankston directed his answer to Kins. "It just didn't work out."

"Why was that?" Santos knew. The answer was in Bankston's file. Kins wondered if she was pushing him to see how quickly Bankston might anger.

"I messed up the physical." He looked to Kins. "So how long before the examiner is ready?"

"The Academy can be rough," Santos said. "How many times did you try?"

Bankston sat back, eyes focused on the floor. "Just once. I figured no point trying again." Again he looked to Kins. "How do we start?"

"The examiner is getting the room ready. It shouldn't be long."

Bankston looked to Santos. "You're not the examiner?"

"No."

"The room's down the hall," Kins said. "Let me go over the procedure while we're waiting, David. Are you nervous?"

"Why?"

"Stressful situation," Kins said. "It would be natural to be a little nervous."

Bankston shrugged. "Maybe a little."

Kins slid Bankston a piece of paper. "These are the questions the examiner will ask you."

Bankston's focus shifted from the paper to Kins, then to Santos. "You're giving me the questions?"

Kins smiled. "Not like high school, right? We give you the questions but not the answers. We're not trying to trick you, David. You can take as much time as you'd like to go over the questions. You'll see the first few are pretty basic—your name, address, age. The examiner calls them control questions. She uses your responses to those questions to get a baseline of your reaction to the other questions. As I said, this is all about clearing you so you can get on with your life."

He handed Bankston a pen and noted that he took it with his right hand.

After further explanation of the procedure, Kins looked to Santos, who subtly shook her head.

"Okay," Kins said. "Unless you have any questions, David, I'll introduce you to the examiner."

He walked Bankston down the hall to Stephanie Ludlow's office. She'd already put a sign in the hall asking for quiet. The anteroom was all about comfort, an open space with leather chairs, a potted plant, and soft colors and lighting. After introducing Bankston to Ludlow, Kins went back to the interrogation room.

"Strange guy," Santos said. "He wouldn't make eye contact with me."

"Yeah, I noticed."

"What about when you and Detective Crosswhite first interviewed him? Did you notice anything like that?"

Kins shook his head. "No, but Tracy took the lead."

"Ask the examiner her impression," Santos said.

"He didn't tell his wife," Kins said. "I asked him in the elevator if he'd told his wife he was coming in. Does that strike you as odd that he wouldn't tell her?"

"Maybe. Or maybe he didn't want to upset her unnecessarily," Santos said.

"Or he's afraid of her reaction," Kins said. "What do you make about him wanting to help with the rope and the video cameras?"

"With all the cop shows now on TV," Santos said, "everyone is an amateur detective. I think a part of him is enjoying being a part of this."

—

Kins wasn't at his desk when Tracy returned to the Cowboy Room, so she'd asked Faz if he wanted to take a drive to find Taggart. They'd struck out at the apartment building in Pioneer Square— the superintendent hadn't seen Bradley Taggart for days. They'd knocked on the neighbor's door, but she also hadn't seen or heard him, nor had the bartender at The Last Shot.

Late on a Friday afternoon, traffic was heavy, and they were inching their way back to the Justice Center garage when Tracy's cell rang. Dispatch had a bead on Taggart's car, and the location instantly improved Tracy's mood. Disconnecting, she said to Faz, "Taggart's parked on Fourth Avenue South."

"Fourth Avenue South," Kins said. "Why does that sound familiar?"

Tracy nodded. "Because he's at the Dancing Bare."

—

Graffiti artists had tagged the bluish-gray stucco, which was nicked and chipped where patrons had misjudged the distance between the one-story building and their cars' bumpers. The Dancing Bare preferred a lower profile than The Pink Palace—the only thing that revealed the nature of the club was the name, hand-painted across the façade, along with the outline of a nude dancer.

Tracy and Faz did a drive-by to confirm that Taggart's car remained parked out front.

"That's our boy," Faz said.

The windows facing the street had been blacked out from the inside with heavy film, but Tracy recalled the club's layout from the Hansen investigation. She also recalled that the building was situated on a V-shaped lot, with the tip of the lot at the intersection of Fourth Avenue South and the BNSF railroad tracks.

They drove around the corner. The back of the building abutted a chain-link fence that separated the lot from the railroad tracks. The alley was too narrow to get a patrol car behind the building, and on the other side of the fence was a gated parking lot, for a warehouse with semitrailers parked in loading bays.

"This dump even have a rear exit?" Faz asked.

Tracy pointed to the only door. "That's it."

A patrol unit pulled up alongside them. Tracy gave the two officers a photograph of Taggart and explained the problems with the layout of the building and the lot. She instructed them to wait on Sixth, where the warehouse parking lot exited.

As the officers departed, Tracy turned to Faz. "He obviously knows me. I go in and he's liable to run. You go in the front. I'll wait out back."

—

Tracy was in position outside the back door when she heard Faz's call on the radio.

"We got a rabbit!"

But Taggart did not burst out the back door. He came around the corner of the building, skidded to a stop when he saw Tracy, then leapt onto a waist-high concrete-block wall and launched himself at the fence. He caught the top rail, but his square-toed boots prevented him from getting a toehold and he started kicking at the fence, unable to pull himself over.

Tracy made the same leap and caught Taggart around the waist, her weight pulling his grip from the rail. She hit the ground, and her right ankle twisted, producing a stabbing pain. Taggart rolled and kicked at her. She avoided a blow to the face, but the heel of his boot struck her hard in the collarbone. She managed to pull herself up Taggart's body and pin him until Faz arrived, wheezing like a man with asthma, dropped a knee, and put all of his considerable weight on Taggart's shoulders and neck.

"Okay, okay," Taggart groaned, going suddenly limp.

Tracy jerked both his arms behind his back, cuffed his wrists, and rolled off, winded and in pain. Her shoulder and ankle felt like they were on fire.

Faz grabbed Taggart by the collar and nearly lifted him off the ground, which triggered more profanity-laced threats. "I'm going to sue all of you. This is harassment. I'll be out in the morning, and I'm going straight to the news station."

"You ain't seen harassment yet, pal," Faz said, "But keep talking and I guarantee you, you will."

CHAPTER 37

Kins sat in Stephanie Ludlow's office, staring in disbelief at her preliminary assessment of David Bankston's polygraph.

"Not all the questions," Ludlow said, "but—"

"What questions did he fail?"

She pointed. "Flip the pages. There. Stop there. See? Whether he knew any of the victims; whether he'd ever been with any of them."

Kins looked up from the report. "What about whether he killed them?"

"No discernible response."

"How can that be, Stephanie? How could he be lying about not knowing them but not be lying that he didn't kill them?"

"I don't know what to tell you, Kins." Ludlow handed him the list of questions and her preliminary conclusions. "He also spiked when I asked him his current place of residence."

"So it's inconclusive."

"That he's lying? No. But *what* he's lying about, that's hard to say. He's skittish and distrusting. He never did fully calm down."

Kins remembered Santos's request. "What about eye contact? Did he make eye contact with you?"

"I sit off to the side when I'm administering the test. He was facing straight ahead. But nothing really struck me as out of the ordinary." She considered her watch. "I told him someone would get in touch with him. I have to be somewhere. Why don't you go over the questions and results and call me tomorrow to discuss it further."

Kins thanked her and made his way back to his desk. He phoned Tracy, but the call went directly to voice mail. When he called Amanda Santos, she answered on the third ring.

"It's Detective Rowe. So, you said that sometimes these guys can beat the test because they feel no remorse, that they don't believe they did anything wrong. What does it mean when they fail?"

—

Tracy limped into the bull pen with Faz's help, surprised to find Kins sitting at his cubicle desk.

Kins stood. "What happened to you?"

"Professor here kicked the crap out of Taggart again," Faz said, helping Tracy drop into her desk chair. "I'll get some ice and a first-aid kit."

Her ankle and back ached, and her right elbow was tender. She wondered if Taggart's kick had broken her collarbone. It hurt to lift her arm overhead. She anticipated the pain would get a whole lot worse before it got better. She pulled open her bottom desk drawer and found a small white bottle of Aleve.

"Why did you pick up Taggart?" Kins asked.

Tracy shook out two of the little blue pills, swallowing them without water, then told Kins about Latent's matching a print in Veronica Watson's motel room to Taggart.

"Patrol spotted his car parked outside the Dancing Bare. When we arrived, he bolted."

HER FINAL BREATH   221

"So he's got a connection to the Dancing Bare."

"Maybe. He said he only went there after he wasn't welcome at the Pink Palace."

Faz reentered carrying an ice pack and the first-aid kit. "Professor here was leaping tall fences in a single bound."

Tracy looked down at a tear in her jeans. Her knee was scraped and bleeding. "These were brand-new jeans."

"I think that's the style now," Faz said. "My son's girlfriend wears them that way."

"That's great," she said, "if I'm ever out looking to pick up fifteen-year-old boys." She took off her shoe and sock and pulled up her pants cuff, examining her ankle. Thankfully, it didn't look swollen or discolored.

"How bad is it?" Kins said.

"Just twisted it." She set the ice pack on her collarbone. The cold felt soothing. "They're bringing Taggart up after he's booked. I told them to call us. I want to go at him before he has time to start thinking things through." She readjusted the ice. "Did Bankston show?"

Kins handed her Ludlow's preliminary findings. "He failed."

Tracy looked up at Kins, then started flipping through the pages. "He failed?"

"Not every question, but Stephanie says it's enough to make his answers suspect. He lied about whether he knew the dancers."

Tracy quickly skimmed that portion of Ludlow's evaluation.

Have you ever met Veronica Watson?
No.

Have you ever met Nicole Hansen?
No.

Have you ever met Angela Schreiber?

No.

In the polygraph recordings, there were significant physiological responses, which are usually indicative of deception, when Mr. Bankston answered the above series of relevant questions. It is the opinion of the polygraph examiner, based on careful evaluation of the physiological responses, which were quality-controlled by computerized statistical evaluation, that Mr. David Bankston was NOT being TRUTHFUL (deception indicated) in his responses to these questions.

"He knew them?" Tracy asked.

"The test would indicate that to be the case."

Tracy continued reading.

Did you kill Veronica Watson?
No.

Did you kill Nicole Hansen?
No.

Did you kill Angela Schreiber?
No.

In the polygraph recordings, there were no significant physiological responses, which are usually indicative of truthfulness. It is the opinion of the polygraph examiner, based on careful evaluation of the physiological responses, which were quality-controlled by computerized statistical evaluation, that Mr.

David Bankston is being TRUTHFUL (no deception indicated) in his responses to these questions.

"This doesn't make any sense."

"I said the same thing."

"How does Stephanie explain it?"

"She didn't. She wants to talk tomorrow. I called Santos and sent her the test."

"Where's Bankston now?"

"Home. I had a car pick him up when he left the parking lot but told them to keep it loose. His car is parked in his driveway, and they're parked in a gravel lot near I-90. If Bankston gets on the freeway to come downtown, we'll know it. If he drives to the grocery store, we won't."

Tracy's desk phone rang. King County Jail advised that Taggart had been booked. "They're bringing him up," she said.

—

Dan had spent the remainder of the afternoon trying to track down witnesses identified in Beth Stinson's murder file. After nine years, some of the telephone numbers were no longer working and the memories of the witnesses had faded dramatically. Two people told him that they remembered calling the police but couldn't remember what information they thought relevant and they hadn't given it much thought in years. A third person said he'd sold Stinson a car earlier in the week and just thought the police might want to know, not that he'd really thought it had any significance. Dan made a note that Tracy might want to check the guy out, given her comment that the killer might have had contact with Stinson. She'd been right about one thing. Nolasco and Hattie had not followed up with any of the witnesses.

Dan's most productive call was to Beth Stinson's former supervisor at the big-box retail store in North Seattle where Stinson had worked as a bookkeeper. Abe Drotzky told him Stinson hadn't lit the world on fire but she was at work every Monday through Friday "earning her keep." He knew little about her personal life but said he got the impression she burned the candle at both ends, often coming to work looking a little bleary-eyed.

As Dan left the interview, he decided to try one more name in the file—Celeste Johnson—before getting something to eat. Her telephone number was no longer in service, but the address provided wasn't far from the big-box store. Dan decided to drive over.

He guessed the woman who answered the door to be mid-seventies. She looked amused when Dan asked for Celeste. "Celeste hasn't lived at home for years."

"She's your daughter?" Dan guessed.

"And who are you?"

Dan told the woman he was an attorney looking into the Beth Stinson matter.

"Is that animal coming up for parole?" the woman said.

"I wasn't able to reach your daughter with the number in the file."

"Celeste's married now. Her last name is Bingham."

"Does she still live in the area?"

"She better," the woman said. "I need my granny fix at least once a week."

The woman wouldn't give out Celeste's address but provided a phone number. When Dan called, he got one of the children.

"Hey, Mom, phone's for you!"

"You don't have to shout. I'm right here."

The kid, being a kid, shouted again. "Phone's for you!"

"Stop it!" Dan heard the phone being exchanged. "Hello?"

"Celeste Bingham?"

"If this is a solicitation, please put me on your no-call list."

"This isn't a sales call," Dan said. "Your mother gave me your phone number. I was calling about Beth Stinson."

The response was silence, and Dan spoke quickly to fill it. "You called the police when Ms. Stinson was murdered and indicated you might have some information relevant to the case."

Another extended silence.

"Ms. Bingham, are you still there?"

"What's this about?" she said.

"I'm trying to follow up on a few things, and I wonder if I could ask you some questions."

"Are you a police officer?"

"I'm an attorney."

Another hesitation. Dan sensed Bingham was about to tell him either that she couldn't recall or didn't want to be bothered. "What is this about?" she asked again, sounding more upset.

"I'm trying to find out if Mr. Gerhardt got a fair trial," Dan said, not feeling like he could avoid her question any longer.

Again, Bingham did not immediately respond, and this time Dan was certain she would tell him she had nothing to offer. He tried once more to fill the silence. "I could meet you at a convenient time if that would be easier. Or I could come to your house."

"No," she said. "Not to my house."

Dan waited, sensing it better not to speak.

"I'm about to take my son to a soccer practice. I'll have an hour while I'm waiting for him to finish. There's a sports bar in North Seattle called the Iron Bone, on Fifteenth Avenue across the street from a strip mall. I'll meet you there."

CHAPTER 38

Tracy nodded to the two corrections officers standing outside the hard interrogation room. "This may not take long," she said.

"Take your time," the male officer said. "Boy needs a serious attitude adjustment."

"I'm going to watch from the other room," Faz said, turning to leave.

About to pull open the door, Tracy recalled Taggart's probation officer saying the tough-guy attitude was a façade and Taggart was just another punk. She grabbed Faz's arm. "You still able to do your Italian gumba act?"

"What do you mean 'act'?" Faz said, his New Jersey accent suddenly pronounced.

To Kins, Tracy said, "I have a hunch about this."

"You want me to sit this one out?"

"Call my cell in five minutes."

Kins departed to watch from behind the glass. Tracy pulled open the door and stepped in with Faz lumbering in behind her like an extra-large bodyguard.

"This is bullshit," Taggart started. The bruises around his eyes had become nasty shades of purple and yellow. "I'm going to sue you, the police department, and the city. My attorney says this case is worth millions."

"Hey, dirtbag," Faz said, dwarfing Taggart. "Shut your freaking pie hole or I'm gonna shut it for you. And I shut it, it's gonna be wired shut."

"You touch me and I'll sue you too."

Faz gripped the edge of the table and leaned into Taggart's personal space. Tracy could only hope his lunch had been laced with garlic. Taggart pulled back, but with his hands cuffed to a chain leading to an eyehook on the floor, he wasn't going far. Faz smiled. "We got people who slip and fall in these rooms all the time. They hit their heads on the table and get all kinds of boo-boos."

Taggart winced. "You can't do that; you got a tape going."

"A tape?" Faz looked over his shoulder at Tracy, who was enjoying the moment but trying not to show it. "Who does this guy think we are—KGB? Who am I—Putin?" He leaned closer. Taggart looked to be holding his breath. Faz pointed at the glass. "We don't tape nothing. That there is a mirror so you can see how ugly you are. Now shut up and listen to the detective." Faz straightened and took his seat beside Tracy.

"Why'd you run, Bradley?" Tracy asked.

Taggart had turned sideways, like a petulant child. "I was getting some exercise. You people are harassing me. You got no reason to keep me here."

Tracy placed a blown-up copy of the print generated by the AFIS computer on the table alongside the latent print CSI had pulled off the dresser in Veronica Watson's motel room. Taggart gave the photographs a disinterested glance, then went back to ignoring her. Tracy sensed that inside he wasn't so calm, and she let the moment linger in silence.

Taggart broke first, looking at her. "What?"

"Anything more you want to tell us about the night Veronica was murdered?"

"I told you everything already."

"Then let's see what we know," Tracy said. "We know you went to the Pink Palace that night. You lied and said you didn't, then changed your statement and said you went to get money but Veronica couldn't give you any until after she'd tipped out for the evening. I wonder what you used for money that night."

Taggart smirked. "I robbed a bank."

"Or maybe you robbed her purse." That comment got another brief glance from Taggart. "Purple, long gold-chain shoulder strap?"

"I don't know anything about that."

Tracy's cell phone started to vibrate. Hearing his cue, Faz slammed his fist down hard on the table, causing it to bounce and Taggart to scurry backward.

Timing was everything.

"I'm tired of this dirtbag's attitude. Let's just take him back to jail and let him rot."

Tracy answered her phone while Faz gave Taggart the death stare. Kins said, "Faz really missed his calling. With all those mafia movies in the nineties, the guy would have been a star."

"Yeah," Tracy said. "Okay, no worries. I'm on my way." She disconnected and turned to Faz. "Can you handle this on your own?"

Faz continued to study Taggart like he was a T-bone steak. "It would be my distinct pleasure."

Tracy stepped past Faz and pushed open the door. "When you're finished with him, have them drop him back in jail. Make sure they book him for assault on a police officer."

"You're going to leave me in here," Taggart said, "with him?"

She shrugged. "You don't want to talk to me. Talk to him."

"Wait," Taggart said.

Tracy sighed. "I have places I need to be, Bradley."

"Fine. I went to the Pink Palace that night, okay? And I asked Veronica for some money, but she said she couldn't give me any because she hadn't tipped out yet."

"We already know that," Tracy said. "Now you're wasting my time."

Taggart began to rock his chair, the front legs lifting off the ground and tapping the floor. "I need a deal."

"A deal?"

"Yeah." He tapped the table with an index finger. "A deal that says what I say can't be used against me in court."

"Who are you—Perry Mason now?" Faz said.

"A deal in exchange for what?" Tracy asked.

"No way; I'm not saying nothing without a deal."

Tracy reached for the copies of the two prints and slid them closer to Taggart's side of the table. He gave them another side-long glance. "Take a close look, Bradley. You know what those are? Those are your fingerprints. That one, that's the print we have on file for you. You know why the computer spit it out? It spit it out because this print was pulled off the dresser in the motel room where we found Veronica's body."

Taggart lowered his gaze but didn't otherwise move.

"So you tell me, Bradley, how did your fingerprint get on a dresser in a motel room when you told me you didn't see Veronica after the Pink Palace?" Tracy paused. Taggart looked to be having difficulty swallowing. "You're in no position to be making any deals, Bradley. Right now you're looking at spending an awfully long time in jail, maybe the rest of your life—unless you get the death penalty."

Taggart rocked faster. The chair legs started banging against the floor, and he was making wheezing noises. Tracy had seen people hyperventilate in this room. He raised his cuffed hands and leaned forward to wipe perspiration from his forehead. "Okay, look. I went to the club to get some money but V didn't have any, so I left."

"Where'd you go?"

"The Last Shot."

"How'd you end up at the motel room?"

"I was shooting pool. Next thing I know, the bartender is saying last call. By the time I got back to the club, they said V had already tipped out and left. I called her cell and told her I needed the money. So she told me to meet her at the motel."

"Why'd you need the money?"

"That's what I can't tell you, not without a deal."

"You were buying drugs," Tracy said.

"I'm just saying . . . you know, yeah, I went to the motel, okay, and I took the money. She didn't need it. She was going to get a couple hundred."

Tracy looked to Faz, who remained statue-still, arms folded across his chest and resting on his stomach. "That sound plausible to you, Faz?"

"Not a freaking of word of it."

"Man, I'm telling you the truth now, okay?" Taggart said. "I didn't tell you before, but now I am."

Tracy leaned closer. Her left shoulder ached where he'd kicked her. The scrape on her knee burned, and her ankle was sore. "Let me tell you my problem, Bradley. I gather the information. The prosecutor? He's the guy who's going to decide whether he believes you or not, and I guarantee you that if I go to him with 'He was lying before, but now he's telling the truth,' he's going to say, 'We have his prints in the room. He admits being there, he's got no alibi, and now we have him patronizing the Dancing Bare. We have more than enough to hold him indefinitely on a murder charge.'" She shrugged and felt pain in her collarbone. "So you're going to have to give me something to go to him with, Bradley. Something to make him think you're not a liar."

"I'll take a lie detector test," he said. "Hook me up."

"You know the problem with lie detectors?" Tracy said. "Defense attorneys start making all kinds of objections and motions at trial, and you just can't be certain the test is going to get in. So it really doesn't do you, or us, any good."

Taggart was biting at his lower lip, and the front legs of the chair steadily pounded the floor.

Tracy made a show of looking at her watch. "It's getting late, Bradley, and Faz here likes to have Friday dinners at home."

"I get irritable when I don't eat. What do they call that, Professor?"

"Hypoglycemic."

"That's it."

"I can't tell you what I was doing without some kind of deal," Taggart said.

"He wants the King's X," Faz said.

"The what?" Taggart asked.

"Didn't you ever play tag?" Faz made an X with his two index fingers. "It means time-out. You're safe."

Taggart looked to Tracy as if Faz was crazy. Then he said, "I was in Belltown, okay. I was at an apartment picking up some product. So the guy there, you know, he can prove I was there, but . . ."

"What kind of product?"

"Meth."

"What's this guy's name?" Tracy asked.

"That's what I can't tell you, man. He'll kill me."

"I need an address."

"Come on, man."

"Let's say the prosecutor agrees," Tracy said. "We still have resisting arrest and assaulting a police officer."

"You could talk to him, though, explain what happened."

She spoke to Faz. "Maybe we could let the prosecutor know he's cooperating in a murder investigation. I suppose that couldn't hurt his cause."

Faz shrugged his big shoulders, and what existed of his neck disappeared. "Not that much. He might be the murderer."

Taggart's eyes shifted between the two of them. "I cared about her, you know. I did. And not just because she gave a good blow job. I didn't mean that; I just said it to piss you off. Yeah, we fought. Who doesn't, right? But it was nice having someone. I never had that before."

"Touching," Faz said. "Just like Romeo and Juliet."

"Look, you asked if I was working her. I wasn't. That's the truth."

"What does that mean?" Tracy asked.

"V got her own clients. I didn't force her to do any of that."

Tracy thought it over. She didn't think Taggart was the Cowboy, but he might have information they could use. "Who saw you talking to Veronica at the club that night?"

"I don't know. But it was right out there at one of the tables, so anyone could have seen us."

"Did you tell anyone you were going to the motel?"

"No."

"What about Darrell Nash. Did you see him that night?"

"Nash? Yeah, he was there."

"Did he see you talking to Veronica or to any of the dancers when you went back?"

"I don't know. I didn't stay long. They wanted me to pay the cover, and I was like, 'No way.'"

"What about at the motel, did Veronica tell you who she was meeting?"

"No."

"Not a name?"

"Nothing. She didn't say nothing."

"And you didn't see anyone hanging around the room or the motel?" Faz asked. "No one in the parking lot, sitting in a car?"

"Nobody."

"Had she been with anyone yet?"

Taggart nodded. "I think so."

"You think so?" Tracy said.

"When I called, she told me to give her an hour. So I think so."

Tracy looked to the one-way glass. "And you didn't see anyone?"

"Not when I went into the room," he said. "It was only V."

"Did she ever talk about any regular customers?"

"Yeah, there was a guy made appointments online. They called him 'Mr. Attorney.' He liked V. Always asked for her."

"But you don't know if that's the guy she was meeting that night."

"No."

Tracy glanced at Faz, then said, "Tell you what, Bradley. I'm going to take you up on that lie-detector offer. You pass, and I won't bust your chops about the name of the dealer. You fail, and I'm going to tell the prosecutor to put you away for a very long time."

CHAPTER 39

Johnny Nolasco slid the reports into the top drawer of his desk and locked it. At the door he slipped on his jacket. His desk phone buzzed.

"Yeah?"

"Got a call for you, Captain," the receptionist said over the speaker. "Woman says she spoke to you several years back about a murder in North Seattle. JoAnne Anderson?"

Nolasco blew out a breath, debating whether to take the call. He checked his watch. "What did she say the victim's name was?"

"Didn't say. She was apparently the witness. Said *her* name was JoAnne Anderson."

Nolasco walked back to his desk. "Put her through." He lifted the receiver on the first ring. "This is Captain Nolasco. How can I help you?"

"Detective, my name is JoAnne Anderson. We spoke more than nine years ago about the murder of my neighbor, Beth Stinson. I lived across the street from Beth. I was the eyewitness."

The name and the murder clicked, though Nolasco hadn't thought about either in years. Beth Stinson was the last homicide he and Floyd Hattie had worked before Hattie retired. He remembered JoAnne Anderson. Her testifying had been like putting Betty Crocker on the witness stand. "Certainly, I remember you, Mrs. Anderson. What can I do for you?"

"I was hoping you could tell me how the investigation is going?"

"I'm sorry?"

"I'm sorry to trouble you, but I couldn't find the card for the attorney who came to see me."

"An attorney came to see you?"

"He said he was looking into some matters and talking to witnesses."

The picture started to clear. "Mrs. Anderson, I'm sure the attorney was hired by Mr. Gerhardt's family. It isn't unusual. He's either coming up for parole and they're looking for something that might help him, or he's getting ready to file another appeal to overturn his conviction. It's nothing to worry about. If Mr. Gerhardt were ever to be released, we would be certain to alert you."

"It's just that I still think about that horrible night," she said.

"There's nothing to worry about," Nolasco said. "And, Mrs. Anderson, you don't have to talk to these people if it upsets you. You're under no legal or moral obligation to speak to them. So if this attorney is pressuring you in any way—"

"Oh, no, he was very nice. I just can't seem to find his card. Maybe he didn't give me one. I'm not certain. I forget things now. I'm sorry to have disturbed you."

"Not a problem." Nolasco was about to hang up, then said, "Mrs. Anderson, if you'd like, I could make a few calls and find out what's going on and get back to you."

"I'd appreciate that."

"Not a problem." He picked up a pen and found a piece of paper, turning it over to the blank side. "Would you happen to remember the attorney's name?"

"I do. It was Dan. Dan O'Leary."

—

The Iron Bone looked to be popular. Men and women shot pool and played at a shuffleboard table. Others chatted and glanced at an NBA game on a television monitor or sat in booths eating pub food. Dan caught the eye of a woman sitting alone in a booth at the back, beneath a wall of license plates from all over the United States.

"Celeste Bingham?" he asked, reaching the table.

The woman nodded but didn't get up. When Dan introduced himself, she reached out and briefly shook his hand. Dan guessed Bingham to be early thirties, about the same age Beth Stinson would have been had she still been alive. She was attractive but in a stressed-out soccer-mom sort of way. Her red hair looked to have been hastily pulled back in a ponytail, and she had pronounced crow's-feet. Dan didn't detect any makeup or, but for a modest wedding ring, jewelry.

As Dan removed his jacket, a waitress approached. He ordered a beer and looked to Bingham, who had both hands wrapped around a glass of water but who looked in dire need of something stronger. "Can I buy you a drink?"

Bingham shook her head. "Just water for me."

The waitress departed. Dan slid into the booth. Music filtered down from overhead speakers, classic '80s rock—Steve Perry from Journey singing "Don't Stop Believin'," which Dan thought might have been the theme to his senior prom. "What time do you need to pick up your son?"

Bingham checked her watch. "I have about forty-five minutes." Her gaze flicked around the bar before again settling on him. "You said this has to do with Beth?"

"You knew her well?"

"We were best friends since high school."

"I'm sorry about what happened to her."

"Who do you work for, Mr. O'Leary?"

"Call me Dan. I'm sorry. I can't reveal my client at the moment," he said. "I can tell you that I'm going back through the file and trying to follow up on a few things. I noticed that, well, it appears that the police detectives never called you back."

Bingham shook her head. Her hands remained wrapped around the glass of ice water, her thumb carving lines in the condensation. "No, they didn't."

"You had something you wanted to share with them?"

Bingham started to answer but stopped when the waitress returned with Dan's beer. She set it on a coaster. "Anything from the kitchen?" the waitress said.

"I think we're good," Dan said, though he was starving and hadn't eaten since breakfast.

Bingham waited until the waitress had departed. "I can't get involved in anything," she said. "I mean, I can't be a witness or testify in court or anything."

"Okay."

"I mean, if this goes further and you go to court for something, I can't . . . I can't testify."

"Okay. Why don't you just tell me what you wanted to tell the police."

Bingham settled back against the leather and dropped her hands onto the table. As she spoke, she picked at her fingernails and cuticles. "My husband and I own a printing and marketing company in town. We do a lot of work here for the schools and the church. My husband's a bishop in the Mormon Church. Are you familiar with the Mormon Church?"

Dan smiled. "I saw the play when it came to town."

Bingham didn't smile. "I was Catholic before I converted. Do you understand what I'm telling you?"

"I think so," Dan said. "You converted to Mormonism when you got married."

"I converted *to get* married. Dale wouldn't marry someone who wasn't a Mormon. His family wouldn't allow it. He doesn't know anything about what I'm about to tell you, and he can't find out. He . . . can't . . . find . . . out." She looked past Dan, as if to be sure the couple in the booth behind them wasn't eavesdropping. Then she took a breath, struggling to calm herself. "Sorry, it's just . . ."

"Take your time," Dan said, understanding now why Bingham had chosen a bar. It was unlikely she'd run into anyone from her church community.

Bingham sipped her ice water and set the glass down. "Like I said, Beth and I were best friends in high school. We partied pretty hard with another friend back then. None of us went to college. I worked as a receptionist, and Beth was doing some bookkeeping. We went out a lot, just about every night."

It confirmed what Beth Stinson's employer had suspected. "That wouldn't have been unusual for people your age back then," Dan said.

Bingham took another sip of water and another deep breath. "One night, we'd been drinking and getting high, and out of the blue, Beth says, 'Let's go to a strip club.'"

Dan felt as if a rock dropped in his stomach.

"At first I thought she was joking," Bingham said, "but she wasn't. She was serious. There was this club that had just opened in Shoreline, and everyone was going crazy about it. It had been in the paper and on the news. Beth wanted to check it out. I was like, 'What?' But she kept saying it would be fun to just see, you know, what it was like. So finally I said, 'What the hell,' right? So we went. We just sat in one of the booths in the back, and when the women came around, Beth started talking to them, asking them all types of questions about how much money they made and how much they worked. Some of them were making a couple hundred bucks a night— more on the weekends. They were making way more than us. Back then minimum wage was nothing. One of the dancers looked us over and said, 'You should dance. With your figures, you'd make a lot of money.' The men apparently preferred women who were well-endowed. Beth fit that mold. Me, not so much."

Dan was furiously working through his conversations with Beth Stinson's former employer and with Wayne Gerhardt, as well as trying to remember the information he'd learned from the police file. Stinson's employer had said Stinson worked Monday through Friday. Wayne Gerhardt had told Dan he'd made the service call on a Saturday, but that Stinson had moved her new car because she had to get to work.

"Beth called me the next day to talk about what the dancers had said, about us being able to make a lot of money," Bingham said. "She wanted to go talk to the manager. I wasn't going to do it, but Beth could be pretty persuasive when she wanted something. She'd thought it all through. She said we could dance under assumed names and that some of the dancers wore wigs. She said no one we knew would likely go there anyway. So finally, just to get her to stop talking about it, I said I'd go with her when she talked to the manager, but only for support. We went the next day. I think it was a Saturday. I remember that we smoked a joint in Beth's car before we went in. The interview was nothing. All the manager wanted to know was our ages and whether we had criminal records. Then he pointed to a pole and said, 'Have at it.' So Beth went over and just started swinging and spinning. She'd done gymnastics in high school and was really good. He hired her on the spot. Then he looked at me and said, 'Your turn.' I told him no, but he said, 'Just give it a shot. What the hell. You're here.' I still wasn't going to, but then Beth started in again and I was pretty high, so I just did what Beth did, being silly, acting stupid, you know?"

"And he offered you a job also," Dan said.

"I'd run up some pretty sizable debt, and I really wanted to get out of my parents' house, you know? And I guess if I'm being honest, the thought of being a dancer was kind of exciting."

"What was the club called?" Dan didn't dare take out a notepad, afraid Bingham might bolt like a skittish horse.

"Dirty Ernie's. Beth and I worked the same shift, you know, to get over our nerves—my nerves, really. Beth didn't seem nervous at all. We went after work and danced until around eleven or twelve, depending on the crowd. It was topless only. Beth was better than me, less inhibited. Men started coming in and asking her for table dances and lap dances. Because the club was new, it was pretty popular and Beth started to make a lot of money. She was talking about quitting her bookkeeping job. I wasn't making that much. I didn't like doing the private dances, and that's really where they make their money."

"What stage name did Beth use?" Dan asked.

"Betty Boobs." Bingham paused and sighed, as if out of breath. Tears trickled down her cheeks. Dan pulled a brown paper napkin from the dispenser and handed it to her. "I have a lot of guilt about this," she said, wiping her eyes, struggling to get the words out. Her chest shuddered. Dan gave her time to compose herself. After another moment, Bingham blew her nose and reached for more napkins. "Beth started bringing some of the men home." The words spilled out of her mouth as if she'd been holding them in for years and no longer could. Dan's mind was churning with questions, but he wanted to let her finish what she'd come to say.

"She'd started renting a house in North Seattle, and she'd bring them there. It wasn't all the time. And it wasn't just anybody." Bingham wiped at her tears. She looked physically exhausted and emotionally drained. "I mean, she knew the men from the club."

Dan prodded gently. "What happened, Celeste?"

"I went to the manager and quit. I told Beth she should quit too, but . . . she liked the money too much. We kind of had a fight about it and fell out of touch for a while."

"So when you heard that Beth had been murdered, you thought it was one of the men she'd brought home with her."

Bingham nodded. "But then no one ever came to talk to me. And I read in the paper they had a suspect and that the guy pled guilty. I figured I'd never have to tell anyone about it. You know, why embarrass our families? I'd moved back home with my parents, and I was attending AA meetings twice a week. I met my husband about six months after Beth died. He doesn't know any of this. He *can't* know any of this."

"Did you know Wayne Gerhardt? Was he one of the men Beth brought home?"

"I didn't know him. I'd never seen him at the club. You get to know the regulars, you know?"

"And he wasn't one of them."

"No."

Sensing there was something else, something more Bingham wanted to say, that she hadn't come to the bar just to tell Dan that she and Beth used to dance, Dan said, "Can I ask you something, Celeste?" She nodded. "Why'd you agree to talk to me? Why not just tell me you didn't remember why you'd called the police and just leave it at that?"

She nodded. "Are you familiar with Alcoholics Anonymous?"

"Somewhat."

"Step nine in the treatment is making amends. You make amends unless it could injure someone. I don't want to hurt my husband or my children, Mr. O'Leary. I have four kids. I have a good life, a good community. But it's always bothered me, the thought that maybe that man didn't do it."

And there was the reason Bingham was sitting in the booth like a penitent in a confessional. Guilt.

"He said he did it," Dan said.

The tears started to roll again. This time, Bingham made no effort to wipe them away.

"What aren't you telling me, Celeste?"

Her chest heaved. She took another sip of her water. "I'd talked to Beth that day. We'd started talking again on the phone, you know, just checking in, trying to get past what we'd said to each other. And I asked about maybe going out later that night, after she got off work. But she said she had a date."

"Maybe her date was with Gerhardt."

She shook her head.

Dan was trying not to rush the conversation. "Why not?"

"Because I was worried about her, you know? And I told her to be careful. I said I wouldn't know what I'd do if anything happened to her, and she told me not to worry. She said that it was okay . . . ," Bingham's chest shuddered. "She said it was okay because . . . because the guy was someone *I* knew, and that he was a nice guy."

CHAPTER 40

Tracy didn't see Dan's Tahoe parked in the driveway or in the street. The police cruiser from the Southwest Precinct arrived as the garage door rattled open. She thought about asking the officer to come inside while she checked the house, then decided against it. She was a cop, with a gun. What was he going to do that she couldn't?

She took out her Glock as she stepped into the house and did a sweep of the entire upstairs before returning to the kitchen. She set the Glock on the counter, retrieved the leftover pasta from the refrigerator, and poked at cold noodles with a fork while her brain continued to mull the seeming inconsistencies in the evidence—from Bankston failing his polygraph, to Taggart's fingerprint showing up in Veronica Watson's motel room, to Beth Stinson's murder nine years earlier.

Exhausted, and her aches and pains crying out for a soothing, warm shower, she put the pasta back in the refrigerator and realized Roger had not greeted her. It was really not like him. She walked through the house calling his name, thought she heard soft mewing, and stopped to listen. She opened the door to the garage but didn't find him. When she called out, she heard him respond, and followed the sound into the dining room but still didn't see him. "Roger?"

She heard him a third time, this time more distinctly, and followed the sound to the top of the stairs leading to the lower level. The deadbolt was turned to the left, in the locked position. "Roger?"

His mewing grew in volume and intensity. A black paw swiped at her from beneath the door.

Tracy stepped back into the kitchen and retrieved her Glock. She was thinking of the raised toilet seat, which she hadn't asked Dan about. He'd been staying at the house; it was possible he'd gone to the lower level or the backyard, but for what? He didn't bring the dogs with him. Then she thought, *Maybe he went down to adjust the light sensor.* It was possible Dan had left the door open and Roger had seen it as an opportunity to explore.

Roger clawed at the bottom of the door again, sounding annoyed. Tracy stepped down to the landing, clicked the dead-bolt straight up, turned the doorknob, and yanked open the door, aiming into the darkened room. Roger darted past her and up the stairs, a black blur. Gun raised, Tracy reached around the wall and slapped at the switch. Recessed lights illuminated the L-shaped leather couch and an older-model projection table that faced a large television screen on the back wall.

Tracy looked across the room to the door leading outside. Like the door at the bottom of the stairs, the deadbolt was engaged. She closed the interior door, reapplied the bolt, and hurried back up the stairs.

Roger paced the kitchen counter, making a fuss about wanting to be fed. "Well, don't go places you shouldn't and this won't be a problem." Tracy picked him up. "Maybe I should have named you Houdini, huh? How did you get down there?"

Roger whined at her, annoyed and in no mood to play. "Okay. Okay." She popped open a can of food, spooned a dollop on a plate, and watched Roger eat while she called Dan's cell. He didn't answer. She ended the call without leaving a message and walked to the bathroom and shut and locked the door. She set the Glock and her phone on the counter and gingerly slid off her clothes. Her knee was red but not swollen. Her ankle hurt, but not as bad as she'd feared it might. It was her collarbone, where Taggart had kicked her, that was bothering her most. The reflection in the mirror showed signs of bruising. About to toss her jeans in the dirty-clothes pile, she checked the pockets for cash and found the message slip the officer staffing the tip line had handed her just before Tracy had left the Cowboy Room to talk with Michael Melton. That reminded her that she'd also failed to call back Bennett Lee, who was likely pitching a hissy fit.

Tracy unfolded the piece of paper and read the name. "Shereece," she said, recalling the name of the African American dancer from the Pink Palace. She called the number.

A woman answered. Tracy said, "Shereece, this is Detective Crosswhite."

"'Bout time you called me back," Shereece said. "We need to talk. Now."

—

Johnny Nolasco chose a table in the corner beside a stone fireplace. The surrounding tables were empty. He nursed a coffee and watched the door while replaying his conversation with JoAnne Anderson in his head, growing angrier each time through it.

Dan O'Leary was the attorney who had represented Edmund House. He was Tracy Crosswhite's childhood friend. If he was looking into the Beth Stinson case, Crosswhite had to be behind it.

The Stinson investigation had been intense. Beth Stinson was not some dead prostitute, drug addict, or runaway. She was the girl next door, living in a middle-class neighborhood, attacked in her own home. Murders didn't happen to the girl next door. They didn't happen to the daughters of the middle class living in safe neighborhoods. The neighbors were scared, the local politicians were outraged, and the politicians downtown were pushing the brass for an arrest. And, since shit flowed downhill, Nolasco and Hattie were getting a steady flow day and night.

They caught a break when a review of Stinson's credit cards revealed a service call from Roto-Rooter the day before she was murdered. A few quick phone calls led to Wayne Gerhardt, a twenty-eight-year-old living alone in an apartment not far from Stinson's rented home. Gerhardt's fingerprints were all over the house, and he'd left a muddy bootprint on the carpet, which he'd unsuccessfully tried to clean up. He had no alibi. Nolasco and Hattie were convinced he was their guy, but although the neighbor initially said she believed she'd seen Gerhardt that night when she got up to get a glass of water, she was the religious type and kept vacillating, concerned about convicting an innocent man. Without the witness's testimony, they didn't have enough to convict.

Back then, it had been a different time and a different administration. Montages could be manipulated. So could police lineups. Witnesses could be encouraged to remember what they saw. There were techniques, subtle but effective, with the sole goal being to put the bad guy in jail, and no homicide team had ever had the success rate Nolasco and Hattie had put together. Hattie hadn't been about to retire with an open case, and Nolasco didn't want that on his record as he worked his way up the ranks. Wayne Gerhardt was their guy. They were certain of it. They just had to give JoAnne Anderson reason to be confident in her ID. They knew that once she got on the witness stand, the trial would be over. Gerhardt would have two choices: take a plea or face the death penalty. Nolasco predicted Gerhardt would see the light.

So they told Anderson they had a suspect and just needed her to confirm he was the guy she'd seen that night. They showed her

Gerhardt's photo, and she ID'd him. Then they asked her to come downtown for a police lineup and she picked Gerhardt without hesitation, dead certain. And when she got on the stand at trial, she didn't equivocate. Gerhardt took the plea, and Hattie put four other suspects' photos in the file along with Gerhardt's mug shot and rode off into retirement with a clean slate. Nolasco left the streets and started to make his way up the ranks to lieutenant, then to captain. He'd never given Beth Stinson or Wayne Gerhardt another moment of thought.

Until now.

After hanging up with Anderson, Nolasco had made a call to Olympia and confirmed that Crosswhite had pulled the Stinson file from storage and had it shipped to the Justice Center. Initially he could think of only one reason why she'd be looking at his old files: she'd heard the rumors circulating among the older detectives questioning his and Hattie's investigation methods, and she was looking for something to embarrass him. When his initial anger had subsided, he began to think more clearly. Tracy Crosswhite was not stupid; she wouldn't be pursuing a decade-old case without good reason, especially not one of his. She had to know any attempt to get another killer a new trial would make her media fodder. So there had to be a reason.

Nolasco reconsidered the details of the old case and recalled that Stinson had been tied up and strangled with a rope. He also remembered that they had noted something odd about the crime scene—that Stinson's bed had been made despite the fact that the murder occurred in the early hours of the morning. That left one possible conclusion. Crosswhite thought there was a connection between Stinson and the Cowboy killings, and she had O'Leary going through the file and talking to the witnesses, who would no doubt tell him that Nolasco and Hattie had never followed through with them. He wondered if JoAnne Anderson recalled that Hattie had only showed her Gerhardt's photograph and not a montage. If she had, O'Leary might argue that Nolasco and Hattie had improperly influenced a witness to convict Gerhardt, and that maybe, because of police misconduct, not only had an innocent man been convicted, but a serial killer had been left free to kill for nearly a decade. Nolasco didn't believe that to be the case. He believed Gerhardt had killed Beth Stinson. But he didn't want Crosswhite poking her nose in his old files.

He'd stewed for several hours, thinking about how best to respond. If he confronted Crosswhite directly, she could go over his head, maybe go to OPA or to one of the prosecutors. She could suggest that not just the Beth Stinson case be reviewed, but all of Nolasco and Hattie's cases.

He couldn't make it look personal.

That's when he'd thought of Maria Vanpelt. Sure, it was a risk saying anything to an investigative reporter, but even he had to admit Vanpelt was a hack. More often than not, she chose the low-hanging fruit, because she was lazy, not interested in doing any real work to uncover facts. She sought out the sensational stories that would get her face front and center on the six and eleven o'clock newscasts.

And Nolasco had something that could do just that—make her career.

Vanpelt walked into the coffee shop looking and sounding annoyed.

"This better not be some ploy to just get me over here, Johnny. I've had a long day."

"Nice to see you too," he said.

She dropped her keys on the table, which drew the barista's attention. "Coffee, decaf. Black."

The young girl stared as if Vanpelt were speaking a foreign language.

"They don't have table service," Nolasco said.

"Just bring me a cup of coffee," Vanpelt said to the girl. "There's a tip in it for you."

The girl went to work. Vanpelt gave Nolasco her everything-has-a-price smile. "So what's so important it couldn't wait until the morning?"

"I may have a big story for you."

"I already have a big story. The Cowboy is getting me the nightly lead, and I'm going live tomorrow with Anderson Cooper about Seattle being a killing ground. Nancy Grace may want me early next week."

"Good for you." Nolasco slowly adjusted his position in his seat, put his forearms on the table, and leaned over his cup. "Tracy Crosswhite's at it again," he said.

The barista approached. Nolasco sat back to clear room. Vanpelt said, "I don't have any cash on me." Nolasco reached into his front pocket, flipped through some bills, and handed the girl a five. "Keep the change," Vanpelt said. She sipped her coffee and set the cup down. "So what is *it*?"

"What if I told you I have information Crosswhite is working to free another convicted murderer—another man who killed a young woman?"

Vanpelt had lifted her cup but set it down without drinking. "How good is your information?"

"Infallible. All you'd need to do is make a few phone calls." He slid a piece of paper across the table. "Start with this one. It's the number for the State Archives."

"What am I supposed to do with that?"

"Tell them you'd like to review a file. I wrote the case number below the telephone number."

"They're not going to give me the file without a FOIA request."

"They're not going to give you the file because it isn't there. Ask who last checked it out and when."

"What's in the file?"

Nolasco sat back. "This is when you might want to get out a notepad and pen."

Vanpelt slowly reached into her purse and retrieved a pen, but she didn't take out a pad. Instead she flipped over a napkin.

"Nine years ago Beth Stinson was a single woman living alone in North Seattle," Nolasco said. "Wayne Gerhardt, a Roto-Rooter man, comes to the house to unclog her drain. He comes back later that night and murders her. An eyewitness saw Gerhardt leaving Stinson's house early in the morning. His prints and DNA were all over the crime scene. He had no alibi, and he pled to the killing and received a twenty-five-year sentence."

"So what's Crosswhite's interest in it?"

"That's your job."

"Why isn't it your job?"

"Because she's keeping it from me, which means she doesn't want me to know what she's doing and isn't likely to give me a straight answer. I can tell you, however, that she's working with the same attorney who represented Edmund House. He's already spoken to the eyewitness and visited Gerhardt in Walla Walla."

"Dan O'Leary," Vanpelt said, smiling, clearly remembering him. She scribbled another note, then stopped, sat back, and studied Nolasco with a hint of a smile. "You're worried about this."

"'Pissed' is a better word."

Vanpelt's grin widened. She looked positively gleeful. "It was your case." When Nolasco didn't answer she said, "What could Crosswhite hope to get out of it?"

"I think it's her way to try and embarrass me, to get back at me for whatever perceived injustice she thinks I've caused her."

"Embarrass you?" Her eyebrows arched. "You said you had an eyewitness, DNA, a confession. How could she embarrass you?" She paused. "Could this guy be innocent?"

"Of course not."

"Then what are you worried about?"

"I told you, I'm not worried. I'm pissed."

"You sound worried."

"Look, I'm throwing you another bone. You don't want it, I'll make another call."

"To whom?"

"Don't you think it would make for interesting television drama?"

Vanpelt smirked. "I don't know, Johnny. If Crosswhite gets booted from the force, I lose my best stories."

"You don't need Crosswhite to make your career for you. I can do that."

"How?"

"There's something else I'm working on," Nolasco said. "Something bigger, but you can't move on it, not yet." If Tracy Crosswhite was determined to embarrass him, Nolasco would be more than happy to reciprocate.

"What is it?" Vanpelt asked.

"One of the prime suspects in the Cowboy case failed a polygraph."

"Which one?"

"Like I said, you can't move on it just yet."

—

Tracy pulled to the curb and gazed up at a house typical of the houses in the Central District. Two stories with a narrow front porch, it sat perched above the sidewalk with a sloping front yard. Tracy ascended wooden steps to the porch and knocked on a red door. A moment later she was staring down at the cherubic face of a young boy in blue pajamas spotted with red basketballs. Tracy guessed he was seven or eight.

"Hello," he said. "Scott residence, may I help you?"

That got a smile. "Yes, you may. Is your mother home?"

Tracy almost didn't recognize the woman who appeared at the door, but she recognized the voice. "What are you doing out of bed, young man? And what have I told you about opening the door to strangers?"

"It's a lady."

"Do you know her?" Shereece asked, hands on hips. "Hmm? Do you know her?"

The boy shook his head.

"Then she's a stranger."

The boy displayed a mischievous grin, and a gap where his two front teeth would have been. Tracy had no doubt he was a handful.

"Were you expecting company?" Shereece asked.

He shook his head again.

"Then get on back up those stairs to bed."

"Good-bye, stranger lady." The boy dipped beneath his mother's arm and scurried up carpeted steps.

Shereece couldn't suppress a smile. "Come on in." Long curls framed her face and softened her appearance. So did a tight-fitting long-sleeve white shirt and black leggings.

"I'll bet he gives you a run for your money," Tracy said.

"That one's my ticket to heaven," Shereece said. "If I can keep him out of trouble, I might make sainthood."

An older woman bearing a strong resemblance to Shereece walked from the back of the house to the edge of the staircase and rested a hand on the banister.

"Hello," Tracy said.

"You're that detective who's been on the television."

"Yes."

"When are you going to catch this man?"

"Hopefully soon. We're working hard on it."

The woman gave Tracy a disbelieving look. "I heard that on the television a few days ago."

"TJ's out of bed, Mama," Shereece said. "Can you handle it?"

Dressed in blue jeans and a pullover hooded sweatshirt, Shereece's mother didn't look much older than Tracy. "Can I handle it? Yes, I think I can handle it." She started up the stairs, stopped, and peered down at Tracy. "Nice to have met you."

"Nice to have met you," Tracy said.

Shereece waited until her mother had reached the top of the stairs and disappeared into one of the bedrooms. "Sorry about that."

"Not a problem."

"Come in and sit down."

The front room was tastefully furnished with comfortable-looking furniture on a dark hardwood floor partially covered by a throw rug. Framed family pictures lined the mantel over a tile fireplace. Tracy lowered slowly into a cloth armchair.

"What happened to you?" Shereece asked.

"Just some aches and pains. Your mother lives with you?"

Shereece sat down across from her on a red leather couch and folded one bare foot beneath her. "We built out the basement after we lost my dad. My husband works some nights so we needed Mama to watch the kids."

"You're lucky to have her," Tracy said, wishing her own mother was still alive.

"It gets a little crowded at times," Shereece said, glancing up the stairs. "And she does forget I'm a grown woman. Sometimes I wonder how my husband and I managed to have three kids."

Tracy smiled. Then she said, "You're not working tonight."

"I called in sick. I'm thinking about calling in sick permanently. The money is great, but not enough to die for. We've talked about me going back to school when my husband got settled in his job, but maybe now would be a good time." Shereece sat forward. "But that's not what I called to talk to you about. I called because Mr. Attorney was in last night. He's the guy I was telling you about, the one who likes the girls with big boobs. He liked Veronica, a lot."

"I remember."

"Yeah, well, last night I saw him paying attention to Gabby."

Tracy sat forward. "What kind of attention?"

"You know what kind of attention. I was onstage, and I saw him reach out and touch Gabby's wrist as she walked past his table. Girl looked shocked. He whispered something in her ear, and Gabby was smiling and nodding. Then she took him into the back room. So now I'm thinking, what is he doing with that skinny girl?"

"Did you see them come back out?"

"I made a point of it. Gabby was still grinning from ear to ear. Backstage I asked her what that was all about, and she said he gave her a fifty-dollar tip for a lap dance. *Fifty.* She was so happy about it I didn't have the heart to say anything like, 'Why'd he pick you?' You know? Now I wish I had."

"How long did he stay?"

Shereece looked to be on the verge of tears. "Finished his drink and left. Maybe another ten minutes."

"What time was that?"

"Right around eleven thirty, quarter to twelve."

"Did Gabby leave about the same time?"

"No. She finished her shift." Shereece raised a hand. "Stop asking me questions and let me tell you what I called to tell you. When I saw him getting ready to leave, I took a break and went out to have a smoke. I was watching for him, you know, but off to the side. He had his car keys in his hand and I was just about to follow him when a car parked right out front chirped. A BMW. Nice car."

Tracy felt her pulse quicken as she thought of the dark-colored sedan in the video that had followed Walter Gipson and Angela Schreiber from the Pink Palace parking lot. "What color?"

"Blue. Dark blue."

"Did you get the license plate number?"

Shereece smiled. "Not a number. One of those vanity plates. Defense for you. Spelled D-F-E-N-C-E, the number four, then the letter U."

CHAPTER 41

Tracy looked up from her iPad as Kins jogged out his front door carrying his leather car coat. He pulled open the passenger door and slid into the truck cab. "You have someone run the plate?"

Tracy handed him her iPad and started driving through the narrow streets. She'd pulled up the law firm website. "Believe it or not, it turns out 'Mr. Attorney' is indeed an attorney."

"I figured as much," Kins said, scrolling through the site. "Only a lawyer would have the balls to have that license plate."

"His bio indicates he was a public defender before opening his own practice. I don't recall the name, do you?"

"Not ringing any bells." Kins set down the iPad. "Where does he live?"

"Washington Park."

He whistled. "He must have done all right in private practice."

Tracy wound her way through the Arboretum and crossed Madison. Past the exclusive Bush School, the road twisted and they turned left as they neared the lake. Ancient oaks and maples spread their limbs across large lots with lush lawns and manicured gardens. The absence of streetlights and, in some instances, large hedges surrounding the properties, made it difficult to find addresses.

"Slow down," Kins said, peering out the passenger side window. "I hope nobody ever has a heart attack around here. They'd be dead before anyone found the place." When the GPS announced that they had arrived at the address registered with the license plate, Kins looked down a driveway between two stone pillars. "I don't know. I don't see an address, but GPS says this is it."

Tracy turned between the pillars and drove forward, past a manicured lawn with its own impressive oak. She stopped before three dark wood garage doors illuminated by lamps. A covered walk connected the garage to an English Tudor with a rock façade, a steeply pitched roof, cross gables, and narrow windows of leaded glass emitting fractured light. The house reminded Tracy of her childhood home in Cedar Grove.

Stepping from the truck, they walked a path to an arched door. "You'd think a house this expensive they could afford to put the address someplace, wouldn't you?" Kins said, still whining.

"You're like a dog with a bone, aren't you?" Tracy said.

"It's my OCD."

The porch light hanging over their heads turned on before Tracy could knock. The door pulled open. "May I help you?"

The man fit Shereece's description, tall with broad features on a wide face and Mick Jagger lips. Tracy and Kins flashed their shields. "Are you James Tomey?" Tracy asked.

"What's this about?"

"We'd like to ask you a few questions."

Tomey wore khakis, slippers, and a black cardigan sweater, but he didn't look comfortable. He looked on edge. "It's rather late to be making house calls, Detectives. What is the nature of your questions? Do they relate to one of my clients? If so, I'll have to invoke the attorney-client privilege."

Tracy didn't like the guy's condescending attitude. She also detected a false bravado. "We know how late it is, Mr. Tomey, and we'd like nothing better than to also be at home. So do you want us to ask you questions out here on your porch, or is there someplace private we can speak? If not, I can find a quiet place for us."

Tomey peered at her through round, tortoiseshell glasses. After a moment, he sighed in resignation and stepped back from the door. They entered a wood-paneled foyer, where a woman stood leaning against a doorframe. "These are Seattle detectives," Tomey said. "They'd like to ask me a few questions about one of my clients. I'm going to use the study."

"It's awfully late," the woman said.

"We won't be long," Tomey said.

Tomey led Tracy and Kins through an expensively adorned front room into an equally impressive den with an ornate desk and floor-to-ceiling bookshelves, the books lined up flush with the edges of the shelves. Tomey slid the doors shut and offered them seats. The furniture was masculine leather, and the lighting sub- tle, provided by recessed bulbs in the bookcase and a Tiffany desk lamp with a green shade. Tracy detected the lingering odor of an expensive cigar. The leather chair behind the desk creaked when Tomey lowered into it. "So, what is this about?"

"Gabrielle Lizotte," Tracy said.

"I'm afraid I don't know that name." Tomey pushed a mane of blond hair back off his forehead, still doing his best to look relaxed.

"You may have known her as French Fire," Tracy said, continu- ing to watch Tomey intently.

"I'm afraid I don't," Tomey said.

Tracy wasn't in the mood. "Mr. Tomey, do you drive a blue BMW, license plate DFENCE4U?"

"Yes, I do."

"And that blue BMW was parked on First Avenue last night around eleven o'clock."

"Is that a question, Detective?"

"No. It's a fact."

"Do you have a question?"

"Did you go to the Pink Palace with anyone, or were you alone?"

Tomey took a moment to clear his throat. "I went alone. It's not far from my office. It also isn't illegal."

"Did you ask for and receive a lap dance from a redheaded dancer known as French Fire?"

Tomey maintained a poker face. "I recall a lap dance. I don't recall the name of the dancer."

"Red hair. Petite figure. Ring any bells yet?"

"Yes, it does."

Tracy put a photograph of Gabrielle Lizotte on Tomey's desk. "She approached your table. You reached out and touched her wrist, whispered in her ear, and she led you to the room at the back of the club."

"That's usually how the negotiations are conducted, Detective. And as I said, they are not illegal."

"So tell me about that negotiation."

Tomey again cleared his throat. He sat parallel to the desk, legs crossed, looking at Tracy and Kins over his left shoulder, like a man about to tell a casual story. "I offered thirty-five dollars. She accepted my offer."

"You must have found her services satisfactory. You paid her an additional fifty dollars. That's what, like a hundred and fifty percent tip."

"Again, is there a question, Detective?"

"Were you expecting anything more in return for such a large tip?"

"I resent the insinuation."

"Do you read the newspaper, Mr. Tomey?"

"I'm partial to the *New York Times* and the *Washington Post*."

"Then let me fill you in on local news. Gabrielle Lizotte was found murdered in a motel room on Aurora early this morning. Did that make the *Times* or *Post*?"

Tomey faced them. His eyes lowered to a spot on the desk. His voice softened. "I was aware another dancer had been murdered. You pay attention to those things in my line of work. I don't believe the paper issued the victim's name or identity."

"So you're hearing this for the first time?" Tracy asked.

"The identity of the woman? Yes."

"How about Veronica Watson, did you know her? She danced under the name Velvet."

"Yes."

"You favored her, didn't you?"

"Favored?"

"You favor large-breasted dancers, do you not?"

Tomey's brow furrowed. "Are you questioning me as a witness or a suspect, Detective?"

"You're a criminal defense lawyer, Mr. Tomey. You were seen in the company of two of the victims, including Gabrielle Lizotte last night. You had an intimate conversation and an even more intimate rendezvous. You also paid her an exorbitant tip. Shortly thereafter, you left the club."

"Those facts are correct."

"Where'd you go after you left?"

"I came home to finish up a legal brief I needed to file today."

"What case?" Kins looked up from his notepad. Sometimes his timing was impeccable. Nothing threw off a lying witness quite like a specific question asked by the person with pen and paper in hand.

"What?"

Kins sat forward. "What was the name of the case you filed the legal brief in today?"

"I don't recall."

"I thought you just filed it today."

"My schedule is rather busy. I'd have to look at my calendar."

"What's the name of your client?"

Tomey looked from Kins to Tracy. "I'd like an attorney." He reached for the phone on the desk.

Tracy sat forward and put her hand on the phone. "You certainly have that right. Since you've asked for an attorney, let's make it official. Stand up and put your hands behind your back."

"What?"

"You have the right to remain silent. Anything you say can be used against you in a court of law."

"Are you Mirandizing me?"

"Please don't interrupt me, Mr. Tomey. You know it's important that you hear and understand your full rights."

"You can't do this," he said.

Tracy continued. "You have the right to an attorney. If you cannot afford an attorney, one will be provided for you."

Kins had stood and removed his handcuffs. "Please turn around and put your hands behind your back."

"This is outrageous," Tomey said. "There's no need for handcuffs."

"Do you understand the rights I have just read to you, Mr. Tomey?" Tracy said.

"I want to call my attorney."

"Do you understand your rights?" she asked.

"Yes. I understand them."

"You will have the right to make that call once you are booked," Kins said.

"On what charge? There is nothing illegal about having a drink in a gentlemen's club."

"We're booking you on solicitation," Tracy said. She was certain Mr. Joon would identify Tomey as the man he'd seen at his motel on at least two occasions in the company of Veronica

Watson. Tracy suspected Tomey had been Watson's date the night Taggart showed up at her motel room to get money, and that he had met Lizotte at her motel room. Whether he'd killed them or not was a different question.

"Stand up," Kins said.

Tomey spoke in a hushed tone. "My children are upstairs."

"Mine are at home getting ready for bed," Kins said. "Turn around."

CHAPTER 42

Tracy stood beside Rick Cerrabone, watching Tomey from behind the one-way mirror. They'd brought him straight to the Justice Center rather than King County Jail to be booked. Given Tomey's profession and request for an attorney, Tracy thought it was important to consult someone from the prosecutor's office. Kins was at his desk preparing search warrants for Tomey's home and office, and to obtain samples of his blood, hair, and saliva for DNA analysis. He'd go over the paperwork with Cerrabone, and if Cerrabone found it in order, he would reach the judge on call to get the warrants signed. In the meantime, Tracy had Faz and Del running a photo montage including Tomey's picture over to Joon's Motel. They'd take the same montage to the Dancing Bare. They already knew he frequented the Pink Palace.

With the overhead lights off, the buttons of the recording equipment glowed yellow, green, and red. "I'm certain Mr. Joon will ID him as the man he saw with Veronica Watson on at least two occasions. And I'm betting he was with Gabrielle Lizotte last night."

"Who'd he call?" Cerrabone asked. "Who's his attorney?"

"One of his partners. Former prosecutor. Stan Bustamante."

Cerrabone smiled. "I trained Stan. We worked together for about six years before he went to the dark side."

Tracy's cell phone rang. The officer at the front desk in the building lobby said she had a visitor. "Bring him up."

"Is that him?" Cerrabone asked.

"No, it's a friend of mine."

Dan had called earlier and said they had a lot to talk about. Tracy told him they'd just pulled in a suspect and it would likely be another long night, if she made it home at all. Dan persisted, saying it couldn't wait. With the Justice Center largely deserted and Nolasco nowhere to be found, she decided it was safe to meet him there.

Dan stepped into the room, escorted by a uniformed officer. Tracy made the introductions. After, Dan looked past Cerrabone and stepped to the mirrored glass. "What's James Tomey doing here?"

Tracy and Cerrabone exchanged a glance. "You know him?" Tracy asked.

Dan turned from the window. "He's one of the reasons I needed to talk to you. Tomey was Wayne Gerhardt's public defender."

"I remember that case," Cerrabone said. "Beth Stinson, right?"

Tracy nodded.

Cerrabone's face brightened. "You think the Stinson case is somehow related to the Cowboy killings?"

"Stinson was tied up and strangled with a noose," Tracy said. "There's no evidence she was sexually assaulted, and the bed was made."

"There's a lot more to it than that," Dan said and proceeded to explain what he had learned.

After Dan had finished, Cerrabone looked to Tracy. "I don't think we're going to have a problem convincing Stan his client wants to talk to us."

—

When Bustamante arrived, they moved Tomey to one of the soft interrogation rooms and sat around a circular table. The space was cramped enough that Tracy could smell Tomey's breath, which had a distinct acrid odor. He was using a paper towel to wipe perspiration at his temples and his forehead. Cerrabone had commented that Bustamante had put on weight since he'd left the prosecutor's office; his stomach protruded beneath a Polo shirt. His hairline was receding, and he had combed forward and gently spiked what remained. He and Cerrabone greeted each other by their first names.

"I've advised my client not to speak to you," Bustamante said.

"That's okay," Cerrabone said. "He can listen. So can you. Then you can talk and decide if he wants to speak to us."

Bustamante crossed his arms and sat back as if to say, "Have at it."

Cerrabone nodded to Tracy, and she looked to Tomey. "Nine years ago you represented an individual named Wayne Gerhardt."

"What does that have to do with anything?" Bustamante asked, unfolding his arms and sitting forward. Nothing made an attorney more interested than a question he didn't know the answer to.

"Gerhardt was a Roto-Rooter technician called to the home of a single woman living alone in North Seattle—"

"I don't see how—" Bustamante started.

"Beth Stinson."

Tracy saw the acknowledgement in Tomey's eyes. It was the second time he'd heard those two names in less than forty-eight hours. Bustamante also caught Tomey's expression and scribbled a note on a yellow legal pad.

"Stinson was found murdered in her home, in her bedroom to be more precise. Her wrists and ankles were bound. She was strangled with a noose. The police took one look at the bondage and concluded the murder was sexual in nature. So did you. But the medical examiner's report found no evidence of sexual intercourse during the prior seventy-two hours. No semen was found in any of Stinson's body cavities."

Tomey's brow furrowed.

"Beth Stinson was not sexually assaulted. She was not robbed. Neither were Nicole Hansen, Angela Schreiber, Veronica Watson, or Gabrielle Lizotte. The latter four women all danced at strip clubs in Seattle. We know you fancied at least two of them and knew a third."

"Beth Stinson was a bookkeeper," Tomey said.

Bustamante's hand shot out as if to protect Tomey from a sudden stop at a traffic light. "Just listen, James."

Tracy continued. "You're right. During the day Beth Stinson worked as a bookkeeper. Nights and weekends, however, she danced at a club in Shoreline called Dirty Ernie's Nude Review."

"I didn't know that."

"James, please," Bustamante said.

Tomey looked at his attorney. "I didn't know any of that, Stan."

"Beth Stinson told one of her coworkers at the club she had a date the night she was murdered. She'd gone from dancing at the club to bringing men home. When the friend expressed concern, Beth told her not to worry, that the date was someone she knew."

"A friend? What friend? She's making this up," Tomey said.

"James—"

"She's making it up, Stan."

"We're just here to listen, James."

"The prosecutor never turned over any of this evidence," Tomey said.

"We've determined this on our own," Tracy said, "as part of our current investigation. What I will tell you is that the witness is very real." She addressed Bustamante. "The question is, why did your client convince Wayne Gerhardt not to get DNA evidence from the crime scene tested, when it could have possibly exonerated him?"

"They would have taken the plea off the table," Tomey interjected before Bustamante had a chance to respond. "They had an eyewitness that put him at the scene."

Bustamante dropped his pen in frustration.

"An eyewitness who may or may not have been wearing her glasses," Tracy said. "An eyewitness who was looking across the street and claimed to see a man perhaps as tall as six feet five with light-colored hair. How tall are you, Mr. Tomey?"

"Don't answer that," Bustamante said.

"Why didn't you get the DNA evidence processed?"

"Don't answer that either," Bustamante said.

"Did you ever go to Dirty Ernie's Nude Review?"

"What?" Tomey said.

"Don't," Bustamante said, "answer that."

"Now, nine years later, four women have been murdered in similar fashion to Beth Stinson. Three of the four danced at a club that you are known to frequent. In fact, witnesses will testify they saw you engaged in an intimate conversation with Gabrielle Lizotte last night, just before she escorted you into a private room. They'll testify you gave her a very generous tip just before you quickly departed. They'll also testify that you fancied Veronica Watson." Tracy let those thoughts linger before adding, "And the owner of the motel where Veronica Watson died just picked your face out of a photo montage, confirming he saw you there with Veronica Watson at least twice."

"More than enough to hold him, Stan," Cerrabone said. "More than enough for me to get search warrants for his home and office, and for his DNA. At a minimum I can hold him seventy-two hours. That means through the weekend. The probable cause hearing would be Monday morning at the earliest, and the arraignment sometime after that. Three Strikes is on the arraignment calendar."

Cerrabone was referring to Judge Karen Kerkorian, who had a well-deserved reputation of being pro-prosecution. "She'll find probable cause—you know that—and we'll hold him until I can file the complaint. Then the media circus will begin."

"We'll file for bail."

"On multiple murder charges? Good luck with that."

Bustamante cleared his throat. "May I have a moment to confer with my client?"

Dan stood when Tracy and Cerrabone reentered the observation room. "What did he say?" Dan asked.

"They're considering it," Tracy said.

"How did you get all this information?" Cerrabone asked Tracy.

"The case came up on HITS. I had the file pulled."

"How did you find the witness?"

"I'd rather not say," Tracy said. "If we need to get that far, I'll tell you."

"Dirty Ernie's got shut down by the community," Dan said. "It's now a convenience store. I ran a search with the Secretary of State's Office. Maybe the owner is still around and can ID Tomey."

"Nine years is a long time to remember someone," Cerrabone said.

"I agree," Dan said, "which is why we need a post-conviction DNA analysis of the forensic evidence found at Beth Stinson's home to compare to Tomey."

"I'm going to need the witness's affidavit to justify it," Cerrabone said.

"What happened occurred almost a decade ago," Dan said. "People have moved on with their lives; a lot of people could get hurt if it comes out Beth Stinson was stripping and bringing home men."

"I'm going to need it," Cerrabone said.

"The witness has a new life, a husband, kids, and a church community. And Beth Stinson's parents are still alive. They don't know anything about any of this. These were just young girls being stupid and naïve."

Cerrabone looked to Tracy. "You've got to give me something to go to the judge with, and I'm going to have to justify it with Dunleavy," he said, referring to Cerrabone's boss, King County prosecutor Kevin Dunleavy. "Stinson's murder was high-profile. The people in Shoreline are not going to react well to the possibility of Gerhardt getting out."

"Hang on," Tracy said. "What are the options?"

"I need the affidavit," Cerrabone persisted.

"What if I sign an affidavit saying I spoke to the witness and this is what she told me," Dan said. "I know it's hearsay, but I'm an officer of the court and I could attest to it for the limited purpose of getting the DNA tested. If the test reveals the DNA didn't belong to Gerhardt and does belong to Tomey or some other person, then we can go down that path."

"I'm not sure how that is going to sell," Cerrabone said.

"Come on, Rick," Tracy said. "We're talking about someone who may have gotten started killing women nine years ago. The DNA at that crime scene might very well be his. It might be Tomey's. It could tie him to the other murders. Either way, you want the public to find out this guy continued to go on killing because you didn't want to get the DNA tested? Ask Dunleavy how that's going to look when he comes up for reelection."

"I'm not convinced it's Tomey," Cerrabone said. "It's one hell of a coincidence he ended up defending Gerhardt."

"Maybe not. Maybe it's not a coincidence at all," Tracy said. "The FBI profiler said the Cowboy is extremely bright. We know

Tomey is smart enough to pass the bar exam. He knows the law. We know he fancies strip clubs, and that could very well have included Dirty Ernie's. So he kills Stinson, and the police investigate and arrest Gerhardt. Tomey's a PD. He goes to his boss and asks to defend him."

"I don't know," Cerrabone said, clearly not convinced.

"Hey, I'm not saying it's gospel," Tracy said. "But at the very least I want to know what else Tomey knows, and who might have seen him with Veronica Watson and Gabrielle Lizotte. You know how these cases go. You follow the evidence where it takes you, which is usually one dead end after another. Then you get a break. This may be that break, Rick. Beth Stinson may be the break we need to catch this guy."

Cerrabone considered it a moment, dour-faced and squinting as if fighting a headache. He turned to Dan. "All right, look, you get me your affidavit—but I want it to include the name of the witness and how you located her." Dan started to protest, but Cerrabone said, "That's the best I can offer. I'll file the request and ask the court to seal her identity on the grounds that we're concerned about her safety and her privacy."

"We need to rush the DNA analysis," Tracy said.

"Yeah, well, tell Melton to start playing a little less guitar." Cerrabone looked at his watch. "I'm tired. They've had enough time to make a decision. Let's go see what Bustamante wants to do."

—

Bustamante had regained his swagger. He started defiantly, as Tracy expected any lawyer would, with his client sitting in the room. "First of all, if this exculpating information was not in the file or turned over by the prosecution, then there is no way my client could have known the witness existed and, by extension, that he could have somehow used that to his advantage, as you insinuate."

"I didn't say it wasn't in the file," Tracy said. "And any attorney worth his bar number representing a client on trial for murder would have combed the police file, found the name, and followed up on every lead."

Bustamante tapped the tip of his pen on his notepad. "Regardless. He didn't know about it. He didn't know Stinson danced or that she was a prostitute. He's never been to Dirty Ernie's. Never even heard of it. As for the Pink Palace, going to a strip club isn't illegal."

"Solicitation is."

"Misdemeanor," Bustamante said.

"Not when the dancer dies."

"Hang on," Cerrabone said. "Can he account for his where-abouts the nights the dancers were murdered?"

"He needs his calendar."

Tracy looked to Tomey. "Do you know the owner of the Pink Palace, Darrell Nash?"

Tomey looked to Bustamante, who nodded his consent. "Yeah, we've talked."

"Did you ever mention meeting Veronica at the motel to him?"

"I don't see why I would have."

"What about last night, did you see Nash at the club?" Shereece had told Tracy that Nash showed up late in the evening.

"I don't recall seeing him last night, no."

"Did you tell anyone you'd made a date with Gabrielle?"

Bustamante's hand shot out. "He won't answer that without some sort of agreement."

"Where did you go after you left the Pink Palace?" Tracy asked.

Tomey's eyes shifted from Tracy to Bustamante, who again nodded. "I drove home. My wife, however, will not be able to attest to that fact."

"Your wife won't be able to vouch that you came home?" Tracy said.

Tomey sat back. "My wife is an alcoholic. By the time I get home, she's usually mean or passed out. She'd have no recollection of specific nights when I came home, or even if I came home. I frequently sleep in the guest room, and I'm often out of the house before she gets out of bed."

"Why does she drink?" Tracy asked.

"Irrelevant," Bustamante said. "Don't answer that."

"Maybe she drinks because her husband is out sleeping with prostitutes," Tracy said, trying to get under Tomey's skin and find out how easily he angered.

"Don't answer that either." Bustamante gave Tracy his best death stare.

Tomey looked more tired than upset. "I need to check my calendar. We have season tickets to the Fifth Avenue Theatre and to the symphony. It also could have been one of those rare nights when my wife was relatively sober and we all went out to dinner. It would be on my credit card. I'm also active with my children's sports teams. I could have left work to coach one of them."

"We're willing to voluntarily turn over James's calendars," Bustamante said.

"We want permission to search his home as well as his office and car," Cerrabone said. "And we're going to need a DNA sample. We've prepared search warrants, but it would expedite things if your client cooperated."

"So long as the search of the home can be done when his children are in school and the office search is completed after hours, and only after I've ensured protected attorney-client information is not compromised. We have several active files against your office, Rick."

"I can live with that," Cerrabone said.

"And my client's name stays out of the newspaper," Bustamante said. "If you decide you're going to charge him, you call and give me twenty-four hours' notice for him to turn himself in. No big show with police descending on his home."

"I can assure you I'm not looking for any more press coverage," Tracy said.

CHAPTER 43

He closed the door, crossed quietly to the desk, and unlocked the drawer, removing the videocassette. He'd dismantled the VCR and disposed of the various pieces in Dumpsters around the city. He'd also monitored the news reports for the fourth dancer, but there had been no mention of the VCR, which didn't surprise him. It was the kind of detail the police didn't like to divulge, a piece of evidence they could use to interrogate their suspects. It was why they'd been so upset when the reporter leaked the type of rope he'd used for Nicole Hansen.

He turned on the television, which had DVD and video players built in, and carefully slid the cassette into the slot. His palms were slick and his stomach queasy. The cassette didn't look damaged, but he had no way to know for sure until he played it.

He stepped back, remote in hand, and sat in the armchair, watching. The screen went black, then filled with static. He could hear the cassette spinning, but nothing seemed to be happening. The screen flickered and went black again. Then it flashed a burst of static. His stomach gripped.

The cartoon started. *Scooby-Doo.*

He smiled as the familiar comforting feeling warmed his groin and radiated throughout his body.

The door to the room opened behind him, and he heard them stumble in. He didn't have to turn around to know she wasn't alone. She was never alone. She always brought someone home with her. He could hear them talking in hushed voices, and he smelled the sickening odor of cigarettes and sweat, perfume, and alcohol.

He sat on the floor, legs crossed, concentrating on the television.

"Shit, you didn't tell me you got a kid," the man said.

"Don't worry about him. He doesn't pay attention to anything but his cartoons." She rubbed his head as she walked past. "He's a good boy. He keeps the apartment clean for me. Don't you, baby?"

He shifted and lowered his head so he wouldn't have to feel her touching him. The man walked over and stood in front of him. Beefy legs in gray slacks blocked his view of the television. He slowly raised his gaze. The man's vest was unbuttoned and his shirt stretched tight. Hairs poked through the gaps between the buttons. His stomach protruded over a belt buckle. Folds of skin fell over the collar of his shirt, and he was bald.

He looked like Porky Pig.

"What, what, what are you making?" the man asked.

He even stuttered like Porky Pig.

"He ties knots," the woman said from the small kitchen. "He's obsessed with them. Sits there and ties them all day unless I make him do something. Knots and cartoons."

"Is he retarded?"

He stared at the man's face and continued to tie the knot.

"Why are, are, are you looking at me like that, boy? Why, why is he looking at me like that?"

"You're blocking his view."

The man turned and, off balance, stumbled, nearly falling. "I don't like him look, looking at me like that."

"Stop looking at him," she said, then to the man, "Come on. Let's have that drink."

The man pointed a finger at him. "Don't look at me, boy."

On the television, Foghorn Leghorn, the overgrown rooster, was doing battle with the chicken hawk, getting smashed over the head with a mallet, tied up, and roasted over a fire.

He had to turn up the volume to cover the moans and grunts coming from the other room. The bedsprings creaked and snapped. Their noises grew louder.

Sylvester the Cat had hatched another plan to get to Tweety. He was trying to cross the water to get to the bird's cage, but he wouldn't make it. A big wave would pick up his raft and smash him face-first into the rocks. That was the funniest part of the cartoon, seeing the cat smashed against the rocks.

Their breathing slowed. The bed had gone silent.

He reached under the sofa and pulled out the noose he'd been tying; he'd learned from a book. He held it up, admiring it. He liked it the best, liked the way the rope slid through the knot, making the noose shrink and grow.

He turned and looked to the bedroom but heard no further sounds.

He walked to the door, peering in. The fat man had collapsed on top of her.

He stepped in quietly to her side of the bed and gently touched her shoulder. "Mom?" He touched it again. "Mom?"

She didn't respond. The man did not move.

He slid a loop around her wrist and secured the rope to the bedpost using a simple figure-eight knot. He did the same with her other wrist, tying it to the post on the other side of the bed. His mother's breathing remained deep and rhythmic.

The fat man snored, twitched and coughed, and rolled off her, but he did not awake.

Carefully, he slid the noose over her head and slowly cinched the knot until it was close to her chin. He weaved the other end of rope under the bottom rail of the headboard, then up and over the top rail, watching it slither between the boards like a snake. He left the room and returned with one of the kitchen chairs, positioning it close to the bed. Standing on the seat, he held the length of rope over his shoulder and looked back out the open door to the television. The cartoon was ending. The stupid cat had failed again. He always failed.

The music played. He waited, wanting to time it.

Porky Pig popped onto the screen.

He said the words with him. "Ba-dee, ba-dee, ba-dee . . . That's all, folks."

He jumped.

"Daddy?"

He looked up from the television. His daughter stood in the doorway, holding the doorknob, her pink nightgown dragging on the floor.

"What are you doing out of bed?"

"I had a bad dream."

He held out his arms, and she walked into them. He lifted her, cradling her to his chest, and sat back. She curled into him, sucking her thumb, her other hand twirling a lock of hair as she watched the cartoons. "They're funny, Daddy."

He smiled. "They're my friends," he said.

CHAPTER 44

James Tomey had voluntarily provided a DNA swab and hair samples, but he'd declined to take a polygraph before departing the Justice Center with Bustamante.

The following morning, Tracy and Kins were awaiting a telephone call from Cerrabone, who was talking to his boss about bringing a motion in King County Superior Court for post-conviction DNA analysis in the Beth Stinson case. If Dunleavy provided his consent and the judge granted the motion, Tracy would drive to the evidence warehouse and pick up the DNA evidence from the investigation, assuming it was still there. SPD had a policy of keeping homicide evidence for eighty years, unless the detectives had a reason to approve of its earlier disposal, such as if the person convicted died in prison. Tracy doubted Nolasco or Hattie, long retired, had given Beth Stinson a second thought.

She looked at the bottom right corner of her computer screen. The second the clock showed 8:00, she picked up the phone and called the Evidence Unit, provided the sergeant at the desk with the case number, and listened to his fingers striking keys. The sergeant sighed and cleared his throat. Then he said, "Still here."

Tracy started to ask if the biological evidence was also still there when the sergeant interrupted. "You're the second person to call in two days. Something going on in that case, Detective?"

Tracy felt like she'd been kicked in the gut. Recovering, she said, "Sorry. You know how these things go; they heat up when they come up for parole and appeal. Was it my partner, Kinsington Rowe, who called? Sometimes we don't know if one hand is washing the other."

Fingers again pecked the keyboard. "Nope, wasn't him. It was your captain, Johnny Nolasco, Violent Crimes. Called late yesterday, just before we closed."

She kept her voice even. "Sorry to double up your work. Has Captain Nolasco picked up the evidence?"

"Not yet. Just asked if it was still here."

"I'm close. I'll stop by and take care of it."

"I'm here all day."

Tracy hung up and quickly slipped on her corduroy jacket, which caught Kins's attention. "Where're you going? We have Taggart's polygraph this morning."

For six years they'd worked together under a "total honesty" policy, and she was breaching it. Kins would not be happy she'd kept the information from him, but Nolasco calling to ask about the evidence only confirmed she was doing the right thing. It was possible Nolasco had somehow put together the similarities between the current Cowboy killings and Beth Stinson, but even if he had, it didn't explain why he'd called the Evidence Unit. The only reason for him to do that would be if he was concerned, and the only reason she could think of for why Nolasco would be concerned was that he'd somehow learned Tracy or Dan was looking into the investigation. Now more than ever, she needed to protect Kins and his family from any potential fallout.

"Can you handle it?" Tracy said. "That was Cerrabone. I need to coordinate CSI's inspection of Tomey's house, and we have a short window. Why don't you meet me there after Taggart takes his test."

—

Half an hour later, Tracy hurried from the warehouse to her truck, box in hand. She checked South Stacy Street in both directions, expecting to see Nolasco's red Corvette speeding down the block, but the street was clear. She slid into the cab of her truck, set the box on the seat, and pulled quickly from the parking lot.

Her cell rang. She put the caller on speaker.

"The judge signed the order," Cerrabone said. "You can pick up the evidence and bring it to Melton."

"I'm on my way," she said.

CHAPTER 45

Dan pulled to the curb, looked out the window at a dilapidated A-frame house on a plum-tree-lined street in the city of Everett, and double-checked the address. He'd spent the morning going through the Secretary of State records online. Dirty Ernie's business license had lapsed after a year. The registered agent was an A. Gotchley, but the address provided was no longer correct and the listed phone number had been disconnected. Dan ran further searches for other businesses registered to the same person, and the computer spit out dozens of UBI numbers—for development companies, construction companies, two bars, a pawnshop, a real estate company, a door- and window-repair company. The most recent was a limited liability company called A-Frame Restorations, with an address in Everett, thirty miles north of Seattle.

If the condition of the property were any indication, A. Gotchley had made some poor investments. It looked like a crack house, the wood siding unpainted, the front porch slanted, the concrete front walk crumbling, and the brown lawn overrun by dandelions.

Dan stepped from his Tahoe and walked around the hood to the sidewalk. He noticed a "For Sale" sign staked in front of the house to the immediate left. He noticed two additional signs in front of the two houses further down the block, but those two said "Sold." The three homes were remarkably similar to each other and to the crack house. In fact, all four were identical in terms of their architecture. Maybe A. Gotchley hadn't made bad investments after all.

Dan felt the wooden steps sag under his weight. The porch boards also felt soft, like a plank could give way at any moment. He stepped lightly and knocked on the front door, which had been stripped and sanded to the bare wood. A woman answered, wearing splattered painter's coveralls and a backward painter's cap that covered short gray hair folded behind her ears.

Dan smiled. "Looks like I'm catching you at a bad time. I'm looking for an A. Gotchley."

"You're looking at A. Gotchley. Who might you be?" Gotchley had multiple rings piercing her right earlobe and the tiniest diamond stud in her left nostril to go with her youthful demeanor, but Dan estimated from the dates she first started incorporating her businesses that she had to be early to midfifties.

"I might be Dan O'Leary."

"Ah, Dan O'Leary," she said, imitating a thick Irish brogue. Her blue eyes shimmered. "You're a nice-looking man, Dan O'Leary, and wearing some fine dungarees you are. I don't suppose you've come to bid on me house for sale now, have ya?"

"I'm afraid I haven't," Dan said.

She dropped the accent. "Well, that's a damn shame. Do you paint?"

Dan smiled. "I've been known to slop on a coat or two, but I haven't brought my work clothes."

"Alita," she said, introducing herself. "And you're catching me at a good time. Unless you're a process server."

"Nope. Just a man looking for some information."

"All right then. I just finished applying a coat to the kitchen, and I need to let it dry."

"These are all your houses, Alita?"

She stepped out onto the porch and pointed down the row. "Two sold. That one just went on the market, and one to go."

"Is this one going to make it? It looks like it's on life support."

"Should have seen the other three when I bought them. These houses are nearly a hundred and fifty years old."

"I feel for you. I remodeled my parents' home in Cedar Grove, and it was a lot of work," Dan offered, continuing to try to find common ground.

"Where's Cedar Grove?"

"North Cascades."

Well you're a long way from home," she said. "What can I do for you?"

"I'm looking for information about a business you once owned."

"You're going to have to be more specific. I've started upwards of fifty-two businesses. Secretary of State loves me."

"Dirty Ernie's," Dan said.

Alita smiled. "Ah, yes, Dirty Ernie's Nude Review. That was short-lived but a lot of fun. People say I brought the city council of that town together as never before or since."

"They shut you down."

"Changed the zoning—no nudity. Bunch of prudes. I did a bus-tling business for about a year. Hypocrites, all of them. Everyone talked a good game—too close to schools, attracts the wrong ele-ment, but let me tell you, they came in droves and they weren't coming from far. Nothing sells better than beer and boobs, Dan, remember that. What kind of information you looking for?"

"You know, Alita, it's one of those things that I'll know when I see it."

"That's a mouthful of nothing, isn't it?"

"Here's what I know. You had two dancers work for you. One was Beth Stinson."

"Betty Boobs," Alita said. "Nice kid. Wicked figure. Tragic end. I remember getting the news. So sad—young girl like that. And so random. Would you believe, the politicians used it to close me down. Said it was attracting the wrong kind of people. You a cop?"

"A lawyer. The other dancer was Celeste Bingham."

"Bing Cherry. More reserved. Quieter than Beth. Didn't stay as long. They were high school buddies if I remember correctly."

"You have a good memory."

"For good people, good lovers, and good wine."

"Do you remember all your employees?"

"Fifty-two businesses, Dan O'Leary. Give me a name."

"I don't have one. That's the problem. Like I said, I might know it if I see it."

"I think you better give me a bit more information. I'd invite you in, but you're liable to get paint on those nice dungarees."

They sat on the top step of the porch, and Dan explained the purpose of his visit. Finishing, he said, "So I'm trying to see if there could be any connection, the name of an employee who was working for you at Dirty Ernie's that comes up now."

"I get you."

"Did you know Beth or Celeste outside of work?"

"No."

"So no inkling Beth was taking some of the customers home?"

"None. Too bad. I would have said something to her. Young girl like that probably didn't realize fully what she was getting herself into. Live and let live, I say, but that's a dangerous line to cross."

"Did you keep employment records, W-2s, anything that would help me identify former employees?"

"Wouldn't be in business if I hadn't; the IRS requires I keep certain records for a certain number of years—seven, I think it is, but

I'm a bit of a pack rat. Actually, I'm lazy. I keep everything because it's easier than going through it and deciding what to throw out. But I can't guarantee you what I have and what I don't have."

"How would we find out?"

"By digging through a lot of boxes of crap."

"Where would I find those boxes?"

"Same place you'd find the boxes for the other fifty-two businesses—the storage locker I rent across town. I could look for it after I wrap up here. Have to finish a few touch-ups on the house next door. I have an open house coming up. And I want to get another coat on the kitchen."

"I could meet you at the storage shed and help you go through the boxes."

"The more the merrier, especially if the merrier isn't married." She nodded to Dan's hands. "I noticed you're not wearing a wedding ring, Dan O'Leary. Maybe I'll remember you."

Dan smiled. "I'm seeing someone."

"Are you faithful?"

"I am."

"Good for you," she said.

"Can I ask you a personal question, Alita?"

"Tit for tat."

"Why a strip club?"

"Because the good ones make money, and I like to make money. Never punched a clock in my life. Dirty Ernie's would have been a gold mine." She shrugged. "That's all right. I take my lumps and move on."

"So who was Ernie?"

Alita smiled. "My ex-husband. I name all my businesses after people who've wronged me. Stinky Pete's Café, Stuck-Up Richard's Lube and Oil. I can't tell you the pleasure I got going to work every day and seeing 'Dirty Ernie's' in bright lights atop the building."

"You're a brave woman."

"He threatened to sue me. I begged him to. I'm like Madonna. Any publicity is good publicity. Fighting with the city of Everett to renovate these eyesores had me front-page news. People lined up to buy them when I put them on the market." She stood. "You happy in love, Dan? I'm a wealthy woman and could be a hell of a sugar mama."

"I doubt you're hurting for male companionship," Dan said.

"You meet me here at five and I'll let you go through my things." She winked and headed back inside the house.

—

Tracy and Kins stood beside the CSI truck parked in the driveway of James Tomey's home. Sunlight streamed through the branches of the gnarled oak, casting slatted rays on the ground. "Taggart passed the lie detector," Kins said. "No indication of any deception."

"Of course he did. Taggart passes, Bankston fails. Nothing in this case makes sense. What did you do with him?"

"Sent him to back to jail. I talked to narcotics. Got a name for Taggart's likely meth source in Belltown. They said they'd roust him for us, but I told them to hold off. I think Taggart's telling the truth. The guy in Belltown is well connected. If Taggart was going to lie, this would not be the guy he'd give up." Kins looked around. "What do you got here?"

"No coils of rope yet," she said. She'd dropped the DNA evidence off at the Washington State Patrol Crime Lab. While she was talking to Melton about her hunch, Cerrabone had texted her to advise that they had the green light to search James Tomey's home. He was still working to coordinate a search of Tomey's office.

"Let's go see where they're at," she said, indicating the CSI team.

—

Dan returned to the dilapidated house in Everett just after five but didn't get an answer when he knocked on the door. He put his ear to the freshly sanded wood, heard no sounds inside, and wondered if Alita had stood him up. He had descended from the porch and started down the gravel drive when she came around the corner at the back of the house.

"Thought I heard someone. I was cleaning rollers in the backyard."

She smelled of paint thinner. "I thought maybe you forgot about our date," Dan said.

"Don't tease an older woman, Dan. There's a lot of cougar left in this one."

"You want me to follow you?"

"It's not far," she said. "I'll ride with you if you wouldn't mind dropping me back here when we're done."

"I'd be glad to. Could I buy you dinner for your troubles?"

Alita smiled. "I'm warning you, Dan. You keep talking dates and dinners and I might never let you go."

The storage facility wasn't far. Alita directed him down the aisles to a locker the size of a one-car garage. The rolling metal gate was padlocked to an eyehook in the ground. Alita removed it and raised the gate.

"Ta-da!" she said.

Dan winced. She hadn't exaggerated about being a pack rat. Boxes were stacked from the cement floor to the metal ceiling and appeared to fill the space back to front. The task could take days. "Do you have them organized by year or company?" he asked.

"That would have made sense, wouldn't it?" she said.

"Well," Dan said, rolling up his sleeves, "I guess there's only one way to go about this then."

Alita pulled a stepladder from behind a stack of boxes. "Why don't you hand the top boxes down to me. I can go through them more quickly, and maybe this is a good time to start throwing some of this stuff away."

Dan climbed the ladder. Alita grunted when he lowered her the first box. "You sure you don't want to switch places?" he said.

She smiled, her eyes focusing on his backside. "And miss this fine view?"

CHAPTER 46

They didn't find coils of rope or bottles of Rohypnol at James Tomey's house, and Tracy doubted they'd find any at his office. When Tracy and Kins returned to the Cowboy Room, she gave Ron Mayweather the task of going through Tomey's calendars checking the dates of the four murders.

"We got copies of Bankston's time cards from Home Depot," Mayweather said. "He worked the swing shift the night of all four murders."

Faz pulled open the door and stepped in, Del behind him. "Hey, Sparrow, heard that little shit Taggart passed his polygraph."

"You heard right," Kins said.

"In the good old days, we would have just beat the truth out of him and saved the county the expense."

"When was that, 1920?" Ron Mayweather said.

"Nah," Del said. "Just before the Justice Department report came out."

Everyone laughed.

"The news is starting," Mayweather said. "And there's our favorite reporter. Maybe she'll tell us there's been another murder; seems like she knows more than the rest of us."

Vanpelt wasn't standing outside a motel room or a bar. This time, she sat at the studio desk, which was unusual. "Surprising new developments tonight in the Cowboy investigation," the anchor said as she tossed to Vanpelt.

"That's right. Police have still not caught the so-called Cowboy," Vanpelt said. "But Channel 8 has learned that the Cowboy Task Force is looking into a possible link between the four recent killings and a murder that happened nine years ago."

Tracy felt her blood run cold.

Vanpelt continued, "Embattled Police Chief Sandy Clarridge held a news conference this afternoon to report on the progress of the Cowboy Task Force, and it was there that I asked him about the old case."

The video rolled, and Clarridge appeared, reading from the prepared statement Tracy had written for Bennett, before Clarridge went off-script and said, "The men and women of the task force are devoting one hundred percent of their time to this investigation, and that will remain the case until the killer is found and brought to justice."

Vanpelt, seated in the front row, stood. "Chief Clarridge, why is the task force also investigating a decade-old murder that took place in North Seattle?"

Clarridge froze. Then he looked to Bennett, who looked equally stumped.

"What's she talking about?" Faz said.

"More Vanpelt bullshit," Kins said.

Tracy felt sick.

"I understand that the task force has reopened the investigation into the murder of Beth Stinson," Vanpelt said, "and that they've requestioned the eyewitness in that investigation. Is that true?"

Clarridge's cheeks flushed. "I have no comment on any specifics of the task force's work," he said.

"Are you aware that an attorney named Dan O'Leary recently met with Wayne Gerhardt at the Walla Walla State Penitentiary?"

"Again, I won't comment on any specifics," Clarridge said. He looked over the crowd. "Thank you."

Tracy felt Kins staring at her.

Back live in the studio, Vanpelt was wrapping up her report. "You may recall the gruesome murder of twenty-one-year-old Beth Stinson. A man named Wayne Gerhardt pled guilty to that crime and is serving a twenty-five-year sentence. Despite the fact that the case was closed, Channel 8 has learned that an attorney has been reinterviewing witnesses from the Stinson case. And, according to records at the Walla Walla State Penitentiary, the attorney met with Gerhardt at the prison.

"To make matters even more interesting, it turns out that the attorney is none other than Dan O'Leary, who successfully argued for the release of Edmund House. House had been convicted for the murder of Sarah Crosswhite, the sister of Seattle homicide detective Tracy Crosswhite. And Tracy Crosswhite is the lead detective on the Cowboy Task Force. We have tried to reach Detective Crosswhite and Dan O'Leary, but neither has returned our calls.

"Earlier this evening I spoke to Beth Stinson's mother and father, and they expressed outrage at the prospect of their daughter's killer being freed. Neither had been told that the investigation has been reopened."

"What the hell?" Kins said.

"What's going on, Professor?" Faz asked.

The phone on Tracy's desk started to ring.

———

Sandy Clarridge's cheeks remained as flushed as they'd appeared on camera. Thin maroon veins traversed his nose like a street map.

To his left sat Stephen Martinez, eyes blazing. Johnny Nolasco had also taken a seat on their side of the table, leaving no doubt of his loyalties. Tracy joined Kins; their lieutenant, Andrew Laub; and Billy Williams across the table. She wasn't expecting much support, however. They knew nothing about Beth Stinson.

"Kins had nothing to do with this," Tracy assured. "This was my decision."

"You didn't bother to tell your partner?" Clarridge asked.

"No."

"Because you knew the impropriety of your actions?"

"I understood the potential blowback if I was wrong."

Clarridge squinted as if not understanding. "Then why do it?"

"Because I don't believe I'm wrong. I believe the evidence supports my instincts."

"And what is that evidence?"

Tracy summarized the similarities between Beth Stinson's murder and the deaths of the four dancers.

"Chief, Beth Stinson was my case," Nolasco said. "The witness was certain in her identification of Wayne Gerhardt."

"The witness was not certain until she was shown a photograph of Gerhardt as a person of interest."

"She picked him out of a police lineup, Chief, and Gerhardt pled." Nolasco sounded more tired than irritated.

"She picked him after she was shown his photograph, and he pled because he was told he was facing the death penalty if it went to the jury."

"Or because he was guilty," Nolasco said.

Tracy looked to Clarridge. "There was forensic evidence available that neither the prosecutor nor the defense attorney asked to have analyzed."

"The defense attorney declined because had the test derived a hit for Gerhardt, the plea was off the table," Nolasco said. "The prosecutor won't plead a murder one charge. Gerhardt faced the death penalty—"

"The medical examiner didn't find any evidence of sexual intercourse in the seventy-two hours prior to her death," Tracy said. Nolasco looked like he'd taken a short jab, and she used his stunned silence to push forward. "The HITS form stated that Beth Stinson had been raped, which is in direct conflict with the medical examiner's findings."

Nolasco looked to Clarridge. "Chief, we all know Detective Crosswhite and I have a history."

"This has nothing to do with our history. Beth Stinson was not raped," Tracy said, voice rising.

"Then how would the DNA analysis exonerate Gerhardt?" Clarridge asked.

"Gerhardt was at the house that afternoon attempting to unclog a toilet," Tracy said. "His fingerprints and bootprints were all over the house. One would have expected someone that careless to have left hairs, sweat, bodily fluids, something, on either the victim or on the rope."

"Chief, there was no way to pull fingerprints from a piece of rope then or now," Nolasco said.

"But you can get DNA," Tracy said. "His DNA should have been on the rope or the victim."

"Again, Chief, this is all pure speculation."

"You never followed up with the other witnesses."

Nolasco dismissed the comment with a wave of his hand. "We spoke to the witnesses."

"There are no reports in the file."

"Nothing led us to believe we had the wrong individual."

Tracy countered again. "If you spoke to the witnesses, why didn't you know Beth Stinson was stripping?"

Nolasco remained outwardly calm for the most part, but his Adam's apple bobbed and he paused as if absorbing another blow. "Stinson was a bookkeeper."

"By day. At night she was dancing and bringing men home."

Clarridge raised a hand. "Regardless, how did"—he checked his notes—"Dan O'Leary obtain the information concerning this case?"

"I provided it to him."

Clarridge scowled. "And did you provide him with the file and reveal your concerns?"

"I did. And I would do it again if I believed—and I do—that it might help us catch the son of a bitch who is killing these women."

"Revisionist history," Nolasco said.

"It needed to be pursued."

Clarridge removed his glasses and pinched the bridge of his nose. "Detective Rowe?" Kins looked up from a spot on the table he'd been tracing with his finger. "You had no knowledge of this investigation?"

Kins shook his head, his voice barely audible. "No."

"You're free to go. You will continue in your role on the task force."

Kins pushed back his chair but did not immediately stand, as if he had something he wanted to say. Then he stood, turned his back to Tracy, and left the room.

"Detective Crosswhite," Clarridge said, "I've been a proponent of yours, because I believed, and continue to believe, it is important to have female officers at every level of this department, and because, regardless of your gender, you are an excellent detective. But your actions have not only brought criticism on this department, they have forced me to reevaluate my personal assessment of your priorities, and your abilities. Providing an attorney with access to a police file is an impropriety I cannot ignore. I will ask

OPA to make an official and complete inquiry, and you will partic-
ipate fully in that inquiry. Do I make myself clear?"

"Yes."

"Until they've had a chance to gather the evidence and ren-
der a decision, you'll be assigned to an administrative role in the
department." He turned to Nolasco. "Captain Nolasco, you'll over-
see the Cowboy investigation and report directly to me."

"Yes, sir," Nolasco said.

Clarridge pushed back his chair. So did the others. Tracy
remained seated.

—

Tracy found an empty box at the back of the seventh floor, where
the administrative staff sat, and brought it to her cubicle. Kins sat
at his desk, his back to her. When he didn't turn from his keyboard,
she commenced cleaning out her desk drawers.

"You made me look like an idiot," Kins finally said. "If I'd
known, I might have been able to support you."

"That's exactly what I didn't want. If you'd known, you'd be
packing your desk with me."

"Total honesty," he said. She heard his chair creak, put down a
stapler, and turned. He was facing her.

"I knew that if Nolasco found out, this was likely."

"We're partners," he said, approaching.

"And you have a wife and three boys depending on you. If you
didn't know, no one could blame you and say you should have
come forward."

Hands shoved in his pants pockets, Kins stared at the floor.
Tracy knew him well enough to know he was processing her rea-
soning. He looked up.

"So what happened after I left?"

"I'm off the task force. Nolasco's in charge. And I can't help but think this is how he wanted it."

Kins stifled a sarcastic laugh. "Can't imagine why. We're no closer to catching this guy than we were the first day. This has all the makings of a career-killer." He looked over the tops of the cubicles before lowering his voice. "What about this Beth Stinson case? You don't think Nolasco and Hattie were covering something up, do you?"

"No, nothing that sinister." Tracy also lowered her voice. "Stinson was Hattie's last homicide. He'd put in for retirement. I think he had one foot out the door and didn't want to put in the work. He and Nolasco had a perfect record. According to the witness, they showed her Wayne Gerhardt's photograph before she picked him out of the lineup."

"That's not unusual."

"It wasn't a montage, Kins. She apparently said it was just the one photograph, though you'll find four other photographs in the file."

"She could be mistaken. That's a long time to remember a detail like that."

"Nolasco and Hattie also didn't follow up with any of the other witnesses in the file. If they had, they'd have known Stinson was dancing at a local club and had started to bring men home with her. Stinson's best friend told Dan she spoke to Stinson the night she was murdered and told her to be careful. Stinson told her not to worry about the guy she was bringing home that night because she said they both *knew* him."

"So maybe Nolasco's worried for good reason," Kins said. "Maybe they got the wrong guy. How far did you get with the DNA evidence?"

"Cerrabone got a judge to issue an order. I dropped it off to Mike this morning and asked him to rush the analysis. It may not exonerate Gerhardt, but it may give us—you—another suspect, or confirm one you already have."

"You're not going to let it go, are you?"

"Not a lot more they can do to me, Kins."

"They can fire you."

"They probably will."

Kins's jaw clenched. "Where's the Stinson file?"

"Nolasco will never let you see it. I'm to box it up and get it back here right away."

Kins was mulling this over, his lips pinched tight. "You'll keep me posted?"

"Yeah, I'll keep you posted."

"Okay. And keep your head down."

"I'm not worried about Nolasco."

"That's not what I meant. Remember, while you're out there trying to find out who this guy is, he already knows who you are."

CHAPTER 47

She exited the elevator into the secure garage and made her way toward her truck to drop off her box of belongings. She intended to go to the Cowboy Room to speak to anyone who was there. She owed them an explanation. Though the concrete bunker had indeed started out creepy, as Faz had said, it had begun to feel like home. If nothing else, that told her that she and Kins had chosen their team wisely, dedicated men and women who'd make the sacrifices necessary to catch a killer. She'd miss them. She'd miss working with them. And she'd really miss the rush of the hunt.

The din of the cars on the I-5 freeway, adjacent to the garage, nearly drowned out the cooing of pigeons in the overhead concrete recesses, and everything took on an orange tint beneath the garage's dim lighting. As she neared her truck, Tracy sensed she was not alone. That cold tickle of self-preservation that made the hairs on her neck tingle migrated up her spine as she unlocked the cab door and set the box on the bench seat.

Footsteps behind her.

She drew her Glock as she spun and raised the barrel, dead center on her target.

Nolasco's eyes widened, and he stumbled backward, off balance, into a parked car. "What the hell is wrong with you?" He looked to be having trouble catching his breath. When Tracy didn't answer he said, "You always draw your gun without fully assessing your situation?"

"I'd fully assessed my situation," Tracy said, her weapon still raised. "If I hadn't, you'd be lying on the pavement with a bullet hole in your forehead and two in your chest."

Nolasco raised a hand. "You want to put the gun down?"

She kept it raised a moment longer, then lowered it, but didn't put it back in its holster. Nolasco's eyes appeared glassy, and now she smelled alcohol poorly disguised by a wintergreen fragrance. If Nolasco had been chewing gum, he'd swallowed it. "What do you want?" she said.

"I just wanted to know why you did it."

"I told you why."

"We know that wasn't the reason," Nolasco said. "Did you think I was going to let you embarrass me?"

"Is your ego so fragile you're still trying to recover from something that happened twenty years ago?" Tracy said. "That's just sad."

"And what were you doing, going after one of my closed files?"

"Trying to catch a killer."

Nolasco smirked. "Bullshit. You were trying to embarrass me. Well, now you know the outcome." He turned and started for his car.

"Who told you about Gerhardt?" Tracy said.

"Doesn't matter."

She raised her voice. "Doesn't it bother you that an innocent man may be in prison, and the guy killing women is still out there?"

Nolasco reached his Corvette and turned back to face her. "That's a fantasy. Gerhardt was our guy. We knew it from day one."

"Is that why you made JoAnne Anderson believe she'd seen him?"

"She saw things just fine."

"Then why'd you lie in there today? Why'd you say you spoke to the witnesses when you hadn't?"

"I have a big day tomorrow," Nolasco said, smiling. "I have to tell the media the circumstances of your dismissal from the task force. You might want to get a good night's sleep too. I imagine they're going to have plenty of questions for you, along with OPA."

—

Dan's Tahoe was parked where the police cruiser had been the prior four nights. Likely another move by Nolasco—Tracy was no longer on the task force, so she was no longer in need of protection. She parked her truck in the garage, got out, and retrieved her box of personal belongings.

Dan held the door open for her, and Tracy's expression must have revealed how she felt. "What happened?" he said. "What's wrong?"

She stepped past him and set the box down on the kitchen counter. Roger hopped up to greet her, and she stroked his back and listened to him purr.

"Tracy, what's going on? What's in the box?"

"You didn't see the news?"

"I've been in a storage shed for two hours."

She opened the fridge and pulled out an open can of cat food. "Nolasco found out about Gerhardt and fed it to Vanpelt."

Dan's face went blank. She stepped past him and pulled a plate from the cabinet.

"How bad was it?"

"I just came from a meeting with the brass. I'm off the task force. Assigned to desk duty until OPA conducts an investigation."

"What does that all mean?"

She spooned the food onto a plate, fending off Roger until she could empty the tin can. "It means I'm likely fired."

She dropped the spoon in the sink and the can in the garbage and stepped to the sliding glass doors, but she didn't go out onto the deck when she saw that it had started to rain. Dan came up behind her and put his arms around her.

"Are you all right?"

She considered the view. It was beautiful, no doubt, but she'd spent many nights viewing it alone. "You asked me once if I could be happy again in Cedar Grove." When Dan didn't respond, Tracy continued. "It was the life I once wanted. I think I could want it again."

"Tracy, there's nothing I'd want more than for you to mean what you're saying—"

"I do mean it." She turned to face him.

He smiled, but the expression had a sad quality to it. "This is your life now. This is what makes you happy. And you're good at it. You love it."

"I was a good chemistry teacher too, and I was doing something useful."

"Why don't you take a few days—?"

"I've taken twenty years, Dan. Isn't that long enough?"

"You're serious about this?" He sounded cautious.

She wrapped her arms around his waist and gave him a deep kiss. "Yes, I'm serious."

Roger jumped onto the dining room table and whined at them. "Did you talk this over with him?" Dan said. "Because I don't think he'll be too happy about it."

"He'll get used to it," she said. "How long did it take you, when you moved back?"

He gave it a moment of thought and ran his hands along her back. "Not as long as I thought it might. I mean, I'd been gone as long as you, but it really didn't feel that different. I don't think we ever completely get our hometown out of our system. Cedar Grove is part of our DNA."

"I just wish Sarah was still there," Tracy said. "I still miss her, Dan. I still think about her every day. I don't think I'm ever going to stop."

—

Tracy cranked the water temperature to almost unbearably hot and eased beneath the shower, allowing the beating jets to sting her skin. Her muscles began to slowly relax, and she felt the tension in her neck and shoulders dissipate. Feeling weak, perhaps overwhelmed, she leaned her head against the tile wall and let the water soothe her.

After twenty minutes, she shut off the shower, wrapped herself in a banana-yellow towel, and stepped out onto the marble to her bedroom. Roger lay sprawled on her comforter, and Tracy took a moment to give him some affection, scratching him beneath his neck and about his head and ears. He rolled onto his back, paws raised in submission, gently purring as she stroked his stomach. "It's a good thing you're self-sufficient," she said. "You have a terrible owner."

The lights in the backyard came on.

Annoyed, Tracy wrapped the towel tighter and stepped to the sliding glass door. The wind had picked up and was blowing the rain sideways across the two shafts of light. The lawn was empty.

Dan crossed the room and joined her at the door. "The lights *still* coming on?"

"Apparently," she said, peering down at the empty yard.

"I set the sensors on their lowest setting."

"When?"

"The other day, before I left."

It explained how Roger had gotten himself locked downstairs. "Maybe I should just shut them off. You do live in a fortress."

"No," she said. "They don't bother me." In truth she liked having the lights. They were like having a dog that barked—an early warning system.

Dan embraced her. "Feel better?"

"Much."

"Good. Are you hungry?"

"Actually, I am," she said, surprised.

He smiled. "Then I better get out of here, because you in that towel is a lot more enticing than chicken Alfredo." Their kiss lingered. Dan pulled back. "I can't believe I'm saying this, but I'm leaving the room now."

After he'd left, she pulled a T-shirt from the dresser and was about to put it on when she got an idea. Still wrapped in the towel, she walked to the bedroom door. "How's dinner coming?"

"Getting there." Dan stood at the center island, sliding noodles into a pot of boiling water, steam rising.

"I was hoping for that glass of red wine you promised me."

Dan grabbed the bottle, poured a glass, and looked up at her through fogged lenses. Tracy leaned back against the door frame, leg bent to reveal much of her thigh. Dan pulled off his glasses. "This is so not fair," he said. "I just put in the noodles."

"That gives us twelve minutes, doesn't it?"

Dan picked up the pasta box and turned it over to consider the instructions on the back. "Nine, I think."

Tracy lowered her leg and straightened. "Really?"

Dan laughed, tossed the empty box over his shoulder, and pulled his shirt over his head as he hurried across the living room and embraced her.

"Make love to me, Dan."

He kissed her hard on the mouth, then softly about her neck and shoulders, hands finding the towel. It fell gently to the floor.

Tracy felt herself drifting with his touch, as soothing as the shower's warm water. Her arms and legs weakened, and she became light-headed. She managed to help him remove his pants, but they never made it to the bed. Dan lifted her against the wall, and Tracy wrapped her legs around his waist.

—

Afterward, both of them still breathing heavily, Dan turned his head to see the clock on her nightstand. "I never thought I'd be proud to say that I made love in the time it takes to boil noodles."

"And with three minutes to spare," she said.

They laughed. Dan said, "Unless you like your pasta soggy, I better get out there." He gathered his clothes, slipped on his boxer shorts and T-shirt, gave her another kiss, and left the room.

After jumping back in the shower to rinse off, Tracy slid on sweats and ran a brush through her hair. The rain came in a rush, hard enough that it sounded like the roar of cars on a freeway and triggered the lights in the backyard.

Tracy stepped to the glass doors. This time, the yard was not empty. A hooded figure stood in the spotlight on her lawn, though rain cascaded all around him and a shadow obscured the details of his face. Then the lights shut off.

Pulse racing, Tracy quickly crossed the room, grabbed her Glock, and hurried for the living room stairs.

Dan looked up as she exited the bedroom. "You want that glass—?"

Tracy bounded down the stairs.

"Tracy?"

She unlocked the deadbolt and pulled open the door.

"What's going on?" Dan shouted.

She hurried across the darkened lower floor to the door leading to the backyard, snapped that deadbolt, and rushed out into the pounding rain, Glock raised, head swiveling left and right, eyes searching. The floodlights burst on, illuminating an empty yard. She swung the gun left to right, following the edge of the perimeter of light while moving toward the thick shrubbery. Her bare feet sank into the water-soaked lawn. Rain blurred her vision. She shook her head to clear it. "Where are you?" she said. "Where the hell are you?"

"Tracy?" Dan shouted from the open door. "Tracy?"

At the edge of the brush, she searched for broken branches, a worn path, footprints in the sodden soil.

Dan was suddenly beside her, talking over the rain. "What are you doing?"

"He was here."

"What? Who?"

She continued to search, making her way clockwise around the edge of the lawn, gun aimed at the brush. "Someone was standing on the lawn. He triggered the light."

"Are you sure?"

"Yes, I'm sure. I saw him standing right over there, staring up at me."

"Let's go inside. We can call—"

She spun. "Who, Dan? Who am I going to call? I am the police. Okay? I'm the damn police, and that bastard was standing right there in the middle of my yard! My yard!" She turned back to the bushes and glimpsed something in the brush. She stepped in, the branches pricking her skin through her sweats and scratching her bare arms. She picked up a sodden piece of paper and noticed several more in the dirt and clinging to branches.

"What is it?" Dan asked.

"I don't know." She stepped farther in, careful she wasn't stepping on a footprint or disturbing other potential evidence, and retrieved the pieces of paper. As she collected them, she began to get a better sense of what they had been a part of.

A photograph.

—

Tracy set the pieces of paper on the dining room table, arranging and rearranging them as if putting together a jigsaw puzzle. Her pants and shirt were saturated, puddling on the carpet; her hair was matted. Dan came into the room and handed her a towel. She wiped the water from her face, frantically moving the bits and pieces of paper. The image slowly took shape.

Her stomach dropped, and she stepped back from the table.

"It's you," Dan said.

It was a close-up of her face shot with a telephoto lens. The hood of her jacket framed her face and protected her from the falling snow.

"Where was it taken?" Dan asked.

She remembered the moment. She'd been standing on the porch of the veterinary clinic in Pine Flat while Dan was attending to Rex. She'd been talking on her cell phone and looking out across a snow-covered field at a parked car. Despite the heavy snow, the windshield had been freshly cleared and she'd sensed someone inside, watching her.

"Pine Flat," she said. "The veterinary clinic."

"What?"

She hurried to the hall, where she'd left her purse, and retrieved her cell phone.

Dan followed. "Pine Flat? That was more than a month ago. Six weeks."

"He could have left a shoeprint in the mud. A piece of his clothes or hair could have snagged on one of the bushes. Something." She called dispatch, provided her name and badge number, and asked to be patched through to the CSI Unit.

"You mean when Rex was shot?" Dan asked, sounding as though he was still coming to grips with it. Rex had taken buckshot in the side, and they'd had to rush him to the veterinary clinic.

"I saw a car," she said. "I thought it was abandoned in the snowstorm until I realized the windshield was clear. I saw it again later, at night, parked outside the motel."

"Why didn't you tell me?"

"I wasn't sure it was anything. I thought it was a reporter."

She raised her hand, but Dan continued talking. "So it's him. It's the same guy. The guy who left the noose. He's been following you for weeks?" He walked to the sliding glass door and looked down into the yard.

After hanging up with CSI, Tracy joined him. "He was in camouflage, I think. I couldn't tell, but I think he was wearing one of those wide-brimmed hats. It was raining too hard, and the shadows fell across his face. Then the lights went out."

She stepped back from the window and sat in one of the dining room chairs, feeling a sudden chill. She started to shake. Dan grabbed the towel from her and wrapped it around her shoulders. He started for her bedroom. "You need to get out of those wet clothes," he said, but Tracy wasn't certain wet clothes were the reason she was shaking.

CHAPTER 48

Kaylee Wright was the last of the CSI detectives to leave, and Tracy walked her out to the gray CSI van. The rain had lessened to a light mist. Wright was a "man-tracker" with the Special Operations Section of the King County Sheriff's Office. An expert in crime scene investigation and reconstruction, Wright had been one of the trackers who'd sought out the remains of the victims Gary Ridgway had dumped in woods and marshes, and along the Green River. Wright said she'd found bootprints in the brush several feet from the edge of Tracy's backyard, and broken foliage where the man had made ingress and egress up the steep hill. She also found bootprints in the water-soaked lawn, indicating the path he'd taken to cut across the backyard. The torrent of water had obliterated many of the impressions, and Wright wasn't sure she'd be able to identify the tread to determine the brand of boot, but she was confident in the size, between a twelve and thirteen.

As Wright and the CSI van departed, Kins and Tracy stood together on the sidewalk. "You sure you're going to be okay?" he asked.

"Yeah. I have Dan, and I have my Glock."

"You'll call if you notice anything."

"You know it."

"I'll see about getting a patrol officer put back on watch."

Tracy doubted Nolasco would authorize it. "Go on home. I appreciate you coming out, Kins."

"No problem." He started for his car, then stopped. "Hey, I just wanted you to know. There's no hard feelings. I know you were just trying to protect me."

Tracy nodded.

"So we're good?" Kins said.

"We're good."

Tracy shut the wrought iron gate behind him and shook it to ensure that it was locked. She watched Kins drive off down the street, his BMW disappearing over the small crest in the road. They'd seen each other nearly every day, eight to ten hours a day, for more than six years. She'd miss working with him.

Inside, she closed the front door, hearing the deadbolt engage automatically.

Dan was ascending the stairs from the lower level. "Everything is locked up tight," he said. "I checked every window and door. Did you change the code to the gate and the front door?"

She nodded.

"I'll bring down Rex and Sherlock and leave them here when I can't stay." He looked at his watch, which caused Tracy to check the clock on the kitchen wall. It was just after two. So much for an early night.

"I don't think I can sleep," she said. She went to a cabinet beneath the kitchen counter and pulled out a bottle of Scotch and two glasses. She poured two fingers in each and handed a glass to Dan. They sat at the dining room table.

"So, the noose and the photograph," Dan said, "what's it all supposed to mean?"

She'd been thinking it over as CSI scoured her backyard. "I think the noose was to get my attention, to let me know he was out there. He killed Angela Schreiber later that night."

"Is that why he left the photograph?"

Tracy hesitated. Then she said, "The drapes in the bedroom were open, and the lights were on."

Dan set down his drink. "He saw us."

Tracy nodded. "I noticed it when I was down there with CSI. You can see into the bedroom and the dining room from where the tracker says he was hiding. She said that from the position of his bootprints, the pressure points were more on the balls of his feet than his heels, so he was likely crouching, the way someone might if they were in a duck blind while using binoculars to watch the sky."

CHAPTER 49

The following morning, exhausted and mentally drained, Tracy drove to the Justice Center with the same feeling of trepidation she'd felt the day she reported to the Violent Crimes Section as one of Seattle's first female homicide detectives. Unlike that morning, when the staff and most of the other detectives made a point of welcoming her, this time, only Nolasco's assistant met Tracy as she stepped off the elevator. He advised her that she'd been assigned to be the D Team's fifth wheel and given a desk at the back of the seventh floor with the rest of the administrative staff. If Nolasco wanted Tracy out of sight, he'd succeeded. Her new desk was in a corner and literally surrounded by stacks of boxes.

Tracy avoided the morning news and refrained from reading the *Seattle Times*. She had an afternoon meeting scheduled with OPA to discuss both her assault on Bradley Taggart, which was suddenly an issue again, as well as the impropriety of sharing a police file with a civilian attorney. She'd called her union representative and asked for legal representation. The lawyer was supposed to get back in touch with her about whether the meeting would proceed or be delayed.

She spent the morning combing the Internet, reading articles on the Cowboy killings. Then she Googled the names Wayne Gerhardt and Beth Stinson and was surprised to find several pages of results. She methodically went through each hit. It wasn't until her stomach growled that she checked the clock on her computer. Almost noon. She called Kins on his cell. "Just checking in to see how things are going."

Kins lowered his voice. "Nolasco moved us all back to the Justice Center, and he's using your desk. I get the sense he's keeping an eye on everyone. The mood in here is like a funeral. He's called a noon meeting. What do they have you doing?'

"Twiddling my thumbs," she said.

"Any word from Melton?"

"Nothing yet. Let's get coffee."

"I'll call if I can get away."

As Tracy disconnected, she looked up to see Preston Polanco, a member of the D Team, step around a stack of boxes, carrying a pile of documents. Polanco dropped the documents on her desk. "Nolasco said to give you something to keep you busy," he said, smiling. "I need someone to go through these witness statements and make a timeline. Not nearly as interesting as your Cowboy—just a couple gangbangers shooting each other, but we all got to do the grunt work sometimes, right?"

—

Dan jogged down the hill toward the Don Armeni Boat Ramp. He could feel the impact of the pavement in his shins and knees, and suspected the pounding wasn't great on forty-two-year-old joints. Though the temperature remained cool, low fifties, the sun had come out and the warmth felt good on his face. Once he reached Harbor Way and his lungs warmed, Dan kept up a brisk pace, his ultimate destination the Alki Point Lighthouse.

Running had always been therapeutic for him, a time to think through problems or to just clear his head. Tracy had hit him with a lot to consider, namely the possibility of her moving back to Cedar Grove and the two of them starting a new life together. He knew part of her decision was the disappointment of being pulled from the task force, which was why he initially wanted her to take her time, but after what had transpired later, the killer showing up in her backyard, Dan wanted to get her back to Cedar Grove that day, someplace where he could protect her and keep her safe.

He was worried about her. He'd always been concerned that she'd never fully dealt with Sarah's death. She hadn't had the time to properly do so. The events that unfolded in Cedar Grove had been fast and furious. Then when Tracy returned to Seattle, she was thrown immediately into more insanity with the deaths of the dancers. Dan suspected she saw those victims as she saw her sister—her responsibility—and he was worried about the stress that guilt created.

Forty-four minutes into his run, Dan was back at the foot of the hill leading up to Tracy's house. Round-trip, the run was just over six miles, but the hill made it feel like ten. Sherlock and Rex would have loved the run along the water, but they would have taken one look at that hill, sat their big butts on the concrete, and made it very clear the only way they were going up was in the back of the Tahoe. This morning, his adrenaline pumping, Dan didn't hesitate. He hit the hill hard. When he reached the top, he was breathing heavily and sweating profusely. He intertwined his fingers behind his head as he walked down the block to Tracy's gated entrance, stopping there to take some deep breaths. When he could once again breathe normally, he entered the new code on the keypad and pushed through the gate into the courtyard.

Tracy spent an hour reading the documents Polanco had dropped on her desk, highlighting dates and times and beginning to construct a timeline. Though nearly bored to tears, she was glad to have something to pass the time. Still, she was relieved when her desk phone rang, thinking it Kins.

"Detective Crosswhite, this is Detective Sergeant Rawley with OPA. We had a meeting at one thirty."

Tracy looked at the clock on her computer, surprised to find that it was 1:40. "I was told to wait until my attorney called."

"Your attorney is here."

"News to me. I'll head over."

She hung up, retrieved her jacket and purse and started from her desk when her cell rang. She fished it from her purse and saw the number for the Washington State Patrol Crime Lab. "Mike?" she said, looking around as she headed quickly to the elevator bank.

"There's a place called Hooverville on First Avenue, far enough south and just divey enough that nobody but the cool kids go there. Buy me a beer and I'll spill my guts."

Tracy looked at her watch. "Be there in ten minutes."

Detective Sergeant Rawley was not going to be happy.

—

He maneuvered the van to the curb and looked at the reflection in the side mirror. He could see the spiked fence enclosing the courtyard leading to Tracy Crosswhite's home. A nice security measure, like the motion-activated floodlights in the backyard. It just meant he had to be more resourceful.

He knew the attorney had gone for a run, because he saw him jogging along the water's edge. If he kept to the same route he'd been running, he'd be back in less than an hour, which was more than enough time to get set up.

He stepped from the van, put on an orange reflector vest and yellow hard hat, took out a transit level, and set it on a tripod so that the lens was facing the house at a forty-five-degree angle. The attorney was right-handed.

He went back to the van and removed a can of fluorescent orange spray paint and sprayed a few lines and random numbers on the pavement. Then he waited.

The attorney came down the block a few minutes ahead of schedule, but with his hands clasped behind his head, struggling to catch his breath. Maybe he wasn't in such great shape after all, though there was no doubt he was what Tracy wanted. There was no refuting that. He'd seen it for himself. He felt like such a fool. She'd made him feel like such a damn fool. She'd had a boyfriend the whole time.

He set his eye to the lens and adjusted the focus, scribbled random numbers on a small pad of paper for effect, and acted as if he were adjusting the level. The attorney turned and looked at him as he approached the gated entrance, but it was only a passing glance.

He focused the lens on the keypad for the lock. The attorney made no attempt to conceal it. He pressed four numbers, 5-8-2-9, then the pound sign. Tracy had changed the combination, as he'd suspected she might. She was a smart, well-trained detective after all. The attorney pushed the gate open, shut it behind him, and walked across the courtyard.

He shifted the transit and quickly adjusted the focus to see clearly the keypad to the front door. The attorney entered the same four numbers, wiped his feet, and went inside.

She was smart. He was smarter.

—

Melton hadn't oversold the bar. Hooverville wasn't much to look at from the outside, understated with a green-and-white sign over the door that simply said "Bar." Metal cages covered the two windows facing the sidewalk. Inside, Tracy's boots crunched peanut shells strewn across the floor. Vintage chandeliers hung over retro dinette tables. Melton stood at a pinball machine in the corner, pushing levers and shaking the machine, making lights flash and bells ring. Tracy waited until he mistimed the flippers, and the silver ball rolled down the chute.

"Hate this game," he said. "Let's grab a booth."

He carried a pint of beer to a cracked leather booth and sat shucking peanuts and tossing the shells. A waitress in a white T-shirt, sporting a fair number of tattoos approached.

"Iced tea," Tracy said.

Melton tapped his pint of beer. "Bring her one of these, Kay."

The waitress left, and a different woman brought out a tray of what appeared to be fixings for tacos. She set it on a table against the wall and departed without saying a word to anyone.

"Lunch," Melton said, already sliding from his seat. "Come on, they do this occasionally for the regulars. Grab one. They won't last."

Tracy followed Melton's lead, returning to the table with a shell overflowing with ground beef, cheese, and tomatoes. She was grateful for the taco. She hadn't eaten all day. She crunched the shell and leaned over her plate as some of the filling squirted out the other side.

Melton wiped at his beard with a paper napkin. "Heard you got a scare last night."

Tracy finished swallowing, set down her taco, and wiped her fingers. "Came to my home, Mike."

"Too bad you didn't shoot his ass," Melton said.

"Can you help me with that?"

Melton reached into his coat pocket and slid a folded sheet of paper across the table. "DNA from Beth Stinson."

Tracy picked it up, reading.

"Not a hit for Wayne Gerhardt," Melton said.

Tracy knew it. "And?"

"Sorry. Not a hit for anyone in the system."

She sat back and considered the information. She'd had visions of Melton giving her a name and her driving to the police station to tell Johnny Nolasco to take the job and shove it. "Would have made my job easier, but as Faz likes to say, it ain't nothing."

"I heard it's not your job anymore," Melton said. "Nolasco called. Told me not to do the analysis, not to spend the money."

"But you'd already done it."

"I hadn't," he said, wiping his beard again. "I just needed the right motivation."

CHAPTER 50

Tracy met Kins early the following morning at a coffee shop in the Madison Park neighborhood. She was nursing a hangover. She and Dan had gone out to dinner, and she'd indulged in two martinis. On top of the two beers she'd had with Melton earlier that afternoon, it was more than she'd drunk in months. She didn't mention her evening to Kins, suspecting he'd worked another late night.

"You need to look into Nicole Hansen and Gabrielle Lizotte," she said, her head pounding like it might split. "Find out if they told anyone they had a date that evening, or if they had any service repairs done at their apartments, on their cars, anything at all."

"You really think this guy knows his victims?"

"Melton ran the DNA analysis for Beth Stinson."

"I thought Nolasco told him not to."

"He'd already run it," she lied. "He didn't get a hit for Gerhardt. Think about that. The guy's fingerprints were all over the house, but no DNA?"

"And since he's spent the last nine years in prison, we can be reasonably certain he isn't our Cowboy."

"Exactly."

"Did Melton get *any* positive hits?"

"No one in the system."

"So not Bankston, Gipson, Taggart, or Tomey," Kins said, each of whom had either been convicted of a crime, served in the military, or had voluntarily provided a DNA sample. That leaves Nash."

"My thoughts exactly."

Kins sat back, hands cradling his cup of coffee. "Nolasco's up to something. He's leaving the building but not telling anyone where he's going. Amanda Santos called looking for him yesterday. She said he left her a message to call him ASAP but didn't say what about. She also said he's asked the FBI to become more involved. He's playing things close to the vest, asking us all a lot of questions but not sharing much." Kins looked at his watch. "I better get moving. He called another meeting. If Justice had windows that opened, Faz would have jumped by now."

They stepped outside. The temperature was brisk, but at least it wasn't raining. The cold air felt soothing on Tracy's headache.

"Have you met with OPA?" Kins said.

"I was supposed to yesterday, but I skipped out."

"Be careful. I heard Rawley's a hard-ass. He takes his shit seriously."

"I told him I had some female problems and left work early."

Kins smiled. "And he didn't ask for specifics?"

"Imagine that. I'm taking a sick day today just to be convincing."

"You weren't drinking alone were you?" After six years together, Kins knew her well. "Do I need to worry about you?'

She smiled.

"Well, I'm glad one of us is getting laid."

"I didn't say I got laid."

"You didn't have to," Kins said.

A block from the Justice Center, Johnny Nolasco took out the burner phone. Maria Vanpelt answered on the first ring.

"We're moving this afternoon."

"That fast?"

"The Chief wants a splash. This will be a hell of a splash."

"How certain are you this is our guy?"

"I spoke at length with the profiler. He fits the profile. He's a wannabe cop and ex-military. He knows how to tie knots, and he has ready access to rope. We've done our homework. The rope came through that Home Depot warehouse. And, he failed the polygraph. It certainly warrants a search of his property."

"So how is it going to go down?"

"I have FBI agents ready to go. All I have to do is make the call."

"Why not SPD?"

"Because there's a leak." He smiled at that. "How can I trust Tracy Crosswhite's team if one of them is the leak?"

"And you get full credit."

"I'll call when we're on the move. Timing will be important. Have you thought about how you got the tip?"

"Better. I went to my editor and said with the new task force in place, I wanted to do a 'where are we at' story, including an interview with you. It looks like I just happened to pick the day you were on the move to do the search."

"Stay close to your phone," Nolasco said.

CHAPTER 51

Kins pushed back from his desk, bored and longing for exercise, which lately had been limited to getting up to use the bathroom, or to get coffee. Nolasco had given him grunt work—entering tip sheets into the computer, making charts, reviewing witness statements—anything to keep Kins chained to his desk and, he suspected, make sure he had nothing of substance to talk about with Tracy.

Kins found Faz in the break room draining the remnants of coffee from the stained pot into a coffee cup with the word "Mug" embossed on the front and Faz's face on the back.

"Here." Faz held out the cup. "You look like you could use it more than me, and that's bad."

Kins waved it off. "And give up the precious minutes I can kill making another pot? Not on your life, Fazzio. This is the highlight of my day."

"What the hell is Nolasco up to?" Faz said. "We ain't gonna catch this guy sitting with our thumbs up our asses."

"Don't know," Kins said, "but Santos called looking for him again. Said he asked for her notes on the profile she put together and her assessment of each suspect."

"She didn't know why?"

"Nolasco didn't tell her why, just asked for them ASAP."

"Where's he now?"

"Don't know."

"Well, that's one good thing about him being out of the office. He ain't here."

On the way back to his desk, still in need of a mental break, Kins picked up the remote and turned on the television. It remained tuned to Channel 8 from the previous night when they'd gathered to watch the news. He stood sipping his freshly brewed coffee and noticed a news ticker scrolling along the bottom of the screen.

Breaking News in Cowboy Investigation.

Kins's stomach fluttered. He was watching an aerial shot from a helicopter hovering above a white single-story home on a patch of lush green lawn with what looked like half a dozen fruit trees and a metal shed.

"Hey, Faz?" Kins called out.

"Yeah?"

"I think I know what Nolasco is up to."

—

Tracy's phone woke her from a deep sleep. She lay facedown on her bed, where she'd collapsed fully dressed after getting home from meeting Kins. The screen on her cell glowed just inches from her face, but when she reached for it her right arm felt leaden. She'd slept on it, cutting off the circulation, and her arm and hand had gone numb. She rolled onto her back and felt the tingling sensation shooting needles all over her skin. She and Sarah used to call it a "dead arm," which could also be caused by a well-placed knuckle punch just above the biceps. She tried to sit up, but her head felt as heavy as her arm.

She recognized the incoming number and answered the call still lying on her bed. "Hey," her voice croaked. She cleared her throat and tried again. "Hey."

"Did I wake you?" Dan asked, and she heard the surprise in his voice.

"What time is it?"

"Almost four thirty."

Disbelieving, she turned her head enough to see the clock on her nightstand. "Damn." She'd only intended to sleep an hour.

Dan started to laugh. "How long was your nap?"

"About seven hours."

"You must have needed it."

She yawned and looked down at her feet. "Didn't even take my boots off."

"Everything all right there?"

"Yeah, everything's fine. Are you still at the storage shed?"

"Just about to finish up."

"Any luck?" she asked.

"Nothing yet. I'm about halfway through, but at least now I have a system. It gives me the false hope that I'm actually making progress. I thought since I'm this far north I'd better get home and get the boys, make sure I still have a house standing."

"I'm looking forward to seeing them both."

"Nothing strange? You're sure?"

"I'm fine, Dan, seriously. It's like you said, I live in a fortress."

"I should be there around eight."

"I'll cook dinner."

"You'll cook dinner?"

"Hey, I can cook."

"Knock my socks off then."

Tracy disconnected, dropped the phone on the bed, and took another couple minutes to wake up. Lying there, she realized she was hungry. She also felt gross. Eat or shower?

Definitely food.

She got up slowly and walked to the kitchen, pulling a carton of leftover Chinese from the fridge and poking at it with chopsticks as she walked to the sliding glass door. She did small stretching exercises with her neck and shoulders, letting her mind and body continue to wake, and looked down into the yard where the man had stood the night before.

A black ball was trotting across the lawn toward the bushes.

Roger.

—

Kins stood staring at the television, not quite believing what he was witnessing.

"Who is that?" Faz asked.

"That would be the FBI. That's what Nolasco's been doing. He brought in the Famous But Incompetent to show us up."

They didn't have to wait long to find out who else Nolasco had brought in. Maria Vanpelt held a microphone and pressed a finger to her earpiece. She looked to be the only reporter on the scene. "He tipped her," Faz said.

"Had to have," Kins agreed.

"I'm live on the scene of what we are being told is a significant break in the Cowboy investigation." She pointed down the street to the single-story house. "Moments ago FBI agents rushed the home of David Bankston, who they are describing as a person of interest in the killings."

"Bankston?" Kins said.

Vanpelt continued. "Bankston, who works at a warehouse in Kent, came under suspicion when his DNA turned up on a noose found at one of the crime scenes."

"It wasn't at a crime scene," Kins said.

Faz was swearing a blue streak. "He shut us out. Nolasco shut us out."

"The search is being led by Seattle Police Department captain Johnny Nolasco, who recently took over the Cowboy Task Force."

The front door to the house opened, and Vanpelt continued her narration. "FBI agents are now escorting a woman and a young girl out of the house." The camera cut to a large shed. "Other agents are using what looks to be a bolt cutter to remove a padlock on the shed behind that house."

The camera zoomed in. Men and women in blue jackets with *FBI* in gold across the back were using a pry bar to pop the clasp on the shed. Then they regrouped and entered the shed in tactical gear, guns drawn.

"Idiots," Kins said. "If he was inside the shed, how could he have applied the lock!"

"We're going to cut away for a moment," Vanpelt said, "to talk to Captain Johnny Nolasco." Nolasco, walking across the lawn by the house, wore jeans and a blue jacket, though his said *SPD* in white. Vanpelt shouted, "Captain Nolasco?" He stopped. "Can you tell us what's going on?"

Nolasco raised a hand, like he couldn't be bothered, and kept walking. The camera followed him to the shed, where he looked to be speaking with agents before ducking inside.

"I got to call Tracy," Kins said. He hurried to his desk and retrieved his cell phone, placing the call as he walked back to the bull pen. He got voice mail and left a short message. "Tracy, call me. Turn on your television to Channel 8. You're not going to believe this."

On TV, Nolasco was walking out of the shed with something in his hand.

"It appears that Captain Nolasco has found something of interest in the shed," Vanpelt said as the camera zoomed in. "That's a coil of rope."

Kins felt his blood run cold.

Vanpelt shouted again. "Captain Nolasco?"

This time Nolasco did not wave her away. He stepped closer, holding the coil of yellow rope. Nolasco had his cop face on, stern and determined.

"Can you tell us if that is the same rope used in the Cowboy killings?" Vanpelt said.

"I won't comment on any evidence."

"Then why are you holding it?" Kins asked loudly.

"Is David Bankston the Cowboy?" Vanpelt said.

"I won't comment at this time."

"Can you tell us what led you to search this property?"

"When we made changes in the task force, I revisited the evidence, and based on my assessment of that evidence, I felt it warranted."

"Do you have David Bankston in custody?"

Nolasco paused, just a slight hesitation, but Kins instantly knew why. "They don't have him in custody," Kins said. "They don't know where he is."

"Are you freaking kidding me?" Faz said. "They didn't find him before they went to his home?"

"We expect to have him in custody shortly," Nolasco said.

Kins looked at his phone.

"What is it, Sparrow?" Faz asked.

"Tracy didn't answer. Why wouldn't she answer her phone?"

"Maybe she turned it off," Faz said.

"She never turns her phone off." Kins tried Tracy's number again. The call again went to voice mail. He tried her home phone number, but it rang through to voice mail too. "Screw this," he said and hurried to his desk to grab his wallet and keys.

"I'm going with you," Faz said.

CHAPTER 52

Dan rolled the metal door shut and reapplied the padlock through the eyehook. Going through the boxes had been tedious and slow. He'd found files and documents from one business misplaced in a box labeled for a different business, and other files similarly mismarked. It meant that he had to look through the contents of every single box and file. When he'd called Tracy, he'd gone through approximately half the shed. He'd thought about stopping, but the search had become addicting, the odds of finding the materials increasing with the elimination of each box. Three times Dan had lifted the lid on a box, telling himself it was the last box for the day. Three times he'd opened another lid. And on the third box, he beat the odds. He found folders with "Dirty Ernie's" written on the tabs. A quick look indicated financial records and employment information.

With the light fading, he'd decided to take the whole box, and now he carried it to the back of the Tahoe. As he shoved the box in the back, lights came around the corner of the row of buildings. Alita Gotchley rolled her Jeep to a stop and stepped out, leaving the engine running and the headlights mixing with the murky dusk.

"You found what you were looking for?" she asked, looking at the box.

"I hope so," Dan said. "I haven't had the chance to look too closely. I'm assuming it's all right if I take the box with me?"

"Be my guest and Godspeed," she said. "I came to see if you wanted to get that bite to eat before heading home. Traffic heading south will be a bitch this time of night."

"I appreciate the offer, but since I'm this far north I'm going to sneak home to Cedar Grove and get my dogs. I've been gone so long I'm sure they think I've abandoned them."

"I like to go antiquing up that way, and there's a hot spring to die for. A friend of mine turned me on to it. I don't suppose I could convince you to join me some weekend? You wouldn't need a suit."

Dan smiled. "Alita, I don't think I could keep up with you."

"Story of my life. Your physique, I figured you had a shot." She gave him another wink and slipped back into her Irish brogue. "I guess this is good-bye then, Dan O'Leary. May the road rise up to meet you. May the wind be always at your back. May the sun shine upon your face, the rains fall soft upon your fields. And until we meet again, may God hold you in the palm of his hand."

"Ditto," Dan said and gave her a hug.

—

Johnny Nolasco stepped back inside the shed, stomach and mind churning. The FBI had sent two agents to the Home Depot warehouse to arrest David Bankston. According to his supervisor, Bankston was working there that afternoon, but when the agents went to find him, Bankston was gone. No one had seen him leave, but his van wasn't in the employee parking lot. When Nolasco got word that Bankston wasn't at his job, he had a critical decision to make. He'd already texted Vanpelt, who was en route to Bankston's home. The plan was for her to stumble upon the search and to call in a news helicopter. Timing was critical.

Nolasco made the call to go forward, figuring the odds were Bankston was either at home or they'd pick him up on his way. But that hadn't been the case. And that was a problem.

At the back of the shed, Bankston had built a false wall with an interior door secured by a second padlock. When Nolasco stepped in, the first thing he saw was the nylon rope on the table. He felt elated, certain his instincts had been validated. He'd found the Cowboy. There was also a spiral notebook with handwritten entries, like a diary, and multiple scrapbooks containing articles and photographs meticulously cut out and glued to the pages—seemingly every news story on each of the four killings, with words underlined and paragraphs highlighted. It further confirmed Nolasco's certainty that he had his man. What was troubling him were the dozens of photographs lining a side wall, a collage that seemed to have been meticulously put together—and in every picture a black X had been scratched across Tracy Crosswhite's face.

—

Tracy grabbed a can of cat food from the cabinet and retrieved a spoon to bang on the top. The sound never failed to draw Roger's attention. Daylight was fading fast, and raccoons and an occasional coyote roamed through the brush beneath her yard at night. Roger didn't have the temperament for a fight. He was more likely to roll onto his back at the sight of a predator. And if he ventured down the hill to Harbor Way, he'd be certain roadkill.

She quickly descended the stairs and unlocked the door to the lower landing. With the curtains covering the windows facing east, the room was as dark as night. It wasn't until Tracy had quickly crossed to the back door and reached to unlock it that she realized the deadbolt had been disengaged.

—

Kins bounced his BMW from the parking garage onto Seattle's surface streets, the portable strobe lights flashing blue and red in the dusk. Faz gripped the handle above the passenger door. The other hand pressed his cell phone to his ear as he talked with dispatch.

Kins maneuvered around an SUV that had pulled only partway to the curb, slowed to let additional traffic congestion clear, and continued down the hill to the on-ramp to the Alaskan Way Viaduct.

"Tell them to get ahold of the officer watching her house and have him knock on her door," Faz instructed dispatch.

"No good," Kins said from the driver's seat. "Nolasco removed the patrol. They're not watching the house anymore. Have them send a patrol car out of the Southwest Precinct."

Faz relayed the request.

"And tell them to bring the Ram-It," Kins said.

Faz repeated that request as well. Then he hung up. "How fast can we get there?"

"Going to depend on traffic." Kins merged onto the Viaduct and hit the brakes. A long span of red taillights snaked along the narrow elevated roadway. Faz gave a blast on the siren, but with just three lanes and no shoulders, the cars didn't have a lot of room to move out of the way. Kins had no choice but to wait for cars to creep over.

"Bankston wouldn't look at her," he said.

"Who, Tracy?"

"When Bankston came in for his polygraph, Santos sat in for Tracy. Bankston seemed unhappy about it and kept asking about Tracy, saying he had information for her. He wouldn't even look at Santos."

Faz gave another blast on the siren. His lights lit up the interiors of the cars attempting to pull to the side. Kins weaved slowly forward.

"So he wouldn't look at her. So what?"

"You've never seen Santos; most guys can't take their eyes *off* her. Bankston wouldn't even make eye contact. Then he failed the polygraph."

"But not the questions about whether he killed them."

"Santos says these guys can pass a polygraph because they have no conscience. They don't believe they did anything wrong and feel no remorse. So maybe it fits. Maybe he couldn't hide the fact that he knew the women, but he felt nothing about killing them, or he doesn't believe he *is* killing them."

"You lost me."

Kins had to stop again to wait for an SUV trying to get out of the way without much success. "Santos says that the elaborate strangulation system the Cowboy uses may be a way of divorcing himself from the actual act of killing. *He* isn't killing the dancers. *They're* killing themselves. Move!" Kins yelled, slapping the steering wheel in frustration.

"Sounds like a bunch of pyschobabble shit to me," Faz said.

"Call dispatch back. Find out if they've got Bankston in custody. And try Tracy's cell again. Hopefully this is one giant wild-goose chase."

—

Tracy turned and ran. In her peripheral vision, she saw him burst from the shadows. She grabbed the wooden handrail and took the stairs two at a time. She'd nearly reached the top when she felt him grip her right ankle. She slipped, fell to her knees, and kicked backward, but the intruder hurled himself forward, pinning her to the stairs. He was heavy, and strong. His hand pressed down on the back of her head, smashing her face against the step. She rammed an elbow into his side and heard him groan. She rammed it again, then reached back and grabbed a hunk of hair, yanking hard. He screamed, enraged, but let go of her head to grab her hand. She'd dropped the can but not the spoon, and she used it to stab at him just below his rib cage. When he retreated, she rolled over.

David Bankston. And he was holding a noose.

She kicked at him with both legs, knocking him off balance, but he managed to grab hold of her as he fell backward. They tumbled down the stairs together, rebounding off the walls. Tracy reached for the wooden handrail to stop her descent, then heard it crack and splinter as a piece yanked free of the wall. She tumbled again, heels over head, and landed on her stomach, hard. Bankston landed on top of her, and she heard a pop and felt a sharp pain in her collarbone. The blow had knocked the wind out of her. Trying to gulp in air, she lifted her head.

When she did, David Bankston slipped the noose over her head, cinching it tight.

—

Rex and Sherlock began to bark and howl with delight the instant Dan pulled the Tahoe into the driveway. He could see them side by side inside the plate-glass window, front paws resting on the sill, chests raised, ears perked, tails whipping the air. They became even more frantic when he exited the car.

"Hey, guys. I'm happy to see you too," Dan called out, trying to calm them as he approached the house. The trick was going to be greeting them without getting trampled. Unconditional love was great; he just hoped it didn't get him seriously injured. It was also why he decided to leave the box with the Dirty Ernie documents in the car. As he neared the front door, the dogs began to prance, nails clicking against the window and the sill. His neighbor had taken them out for daily walks and let them run at the park in Cedar Grove. Dan didn't even want to think about what they would have been like if they hadn't exercised. They'd likely come straight through the window.

As Dan unlocked the deadbolt, they dropped their front legs from the sill and bounded toward the door. His attempts to soothe them continued to fail. "Okay. Okay. I'm home. I missed you too. Easy now. Easy."

He struggled to push the door open with 280 pounds of dog on the other side, each fighting to be first to greet him. Their snouts batted the edge of the door, forcing it open, and they burst out. They knocked Dan off balance, but he managed to brace himself and not get sent sprawling to the ground. He rubbed their fur and scratched their heads as they circled him, whining with pure joy. After a minute, Dan stepped onto his front lawn. "Go run. Go run."

The dogs raced around the yard, slamming into and bouncing off one another like bumper cars. Dan encouraged them—any-thing to get them to expend their pent-up energy before going back inside. Luckily they weren't built for endurance, and after a few minutes they came back with their tongues hanging out the sides of their mouths. He gave them another minute of attention before they all went inside.

He shut the door and called Tracy's cell again. He'd tried on his drive, but his calls had gone to voice mail. This one did as well. He checked his watch, wondering if she'd gone for a run, though by this point it would have been a really long run and he doubted she'd have left the house at night alone, given the circumstances. He tried her home phone, but that, too, went to voice mail.

He was concerned, but not overly. He'd spoken to her earlier, and she'd told him she was locked inside and everything was fine.

So then why wasn't she answering the phone?

He set his phone on the marble counter, turned on the television to the local news, and went into the kitchen. He found a lone

Corona at the back of the fridge and a block of Reggiano cheese. He retrieved a box of crackers from the pantry and a knife from a drawer and started snacking and drinking his beer. About to take another sip of his Corona, he turned to the television and noticed a ticker running across the bottom of the screen.

He thought of the lights tripping in Tracy's backyard. Then he thought again about her not answering her phone.

—

Kins took the exit for the West Seattle Bridge, kept left at the fork in the ramp, and blew by the line of cars waiting at the stoplight. The evening commute across the bridge was also heavy, but there were more lanes to work with, so the other cars could more easily move out of his way.

Faz hung up with dispatch, who had called him back to tell him units were on their way to Tracy's home.

"Have they been able to contact her?" Kins asked.

"Not yet."

"At this rate we'll beat them there," Kins said, his frustration peaking.

Admiral Way was the first exit off the bridge. At the bottom of the ramp, he turned right, ascending a steep grade. As they neared the top, he slowed to turn, moved his foot to hit the accelerator, then had to quickly brake hard. The car stopped inches from the back of a UPS truck parked in the narrow road.

—

Tracy lay on her stomach, Bankston atop her, his breath and spittle warm on her neck, the rope strangling her. She had managed to get the fingers of her left hand beneath the rope just before Bankston had cinched the noose tight, and she was now fighting to keep that precious half inch, to keep him from completely cutting off her oxygen.

Something was jabbing into her rib cage. With her right hand, she felt around and found the piece of broken handrail wedged tight beneath her. She gripped it, summoned her core strength, and lifted with her hip and stomach muscles just enough to slide out the piece of wood.

The rope cinched tighter. She started to see bursts of light.

She lifted her hips again, rolled, and swung the piece of wood like a club, striking Bankston hard on the left side of the head, a dull thud. The blow knocked him to his right, and he lost his grip on the rope. Tracy yanked the rope away from her throat and sucked in a deep breath. She swung the club again, then a third time. Bankston rolled off her, trying to ward off the blows. She rolled away from him and struggled to her knees, in pain and still gasping for breath. She yanked the noose over her head and threw it into a corner of the room. She sucked in more air, gagging and wheezing. It felt like someone was burning her shoulder with a branding iron. She felt light-headed and nauseated.

And pissed. Really pissed.

Unsteadily, she got to her feet.

Bankston, blood flowing from a gash on the side of his head, staggered and also stood.

Tracy raised the broken piece of banister. "Come on," she said, teeth clenched. "Come on, you son of a bitch."

Bankston charged.

—

Kins had never seen a UPS driver move so fast. With Faz screaming for him to move his truck, the man ran across the lawn and nearly vaulted behind the steering wheel. Gears ground, and the van lurched forward, front wheels bouncing up onto the sidewalk.

Kins squeezed past, and they shot down the street, tires skidding to a stop in front of Tracy's house. They flung open their doors and jumped out. Kins rushed to the gate and pushed the intercom button, still hopeful Tracy would answer.

She didn't.

"Where is the damn patrol car?" he said, looking back up the street while pressing the buzzer again and again.

Two patrol units screamed down the block, emergency lights flashing. They stopped in the middle of the street behind the BMW, and four officers exited. One carried the Ram-It, a tubular piece of steel with handles that could be wielded like a battering ram.

Kins stepped back from the gate. "Break it down."

The biggest of the officers gripped the handles, swung the steel tube back, and smashed it hard into the gate just above the keypad. The fence rattled and flexed, but the gate didn't open.

"Again," Kins said.

He hit it again, then a third time, and a fourth. With each blow, the gate flexed and shook, but that was it. "Hang on." Kins bent and looked more closely at the lock. The deadbolt, a thick piece of steel, extended at least two inches into the metal plate. With the flex in the fence, they couldn't get the bolt to pop free of the lock.

"No good," Kins said. "Too much movement." He considered the fence, then spoke to two of the other officers. "Cup your hands. Give me a boost."

"You can't go over," Faz said. "What about your hip?"

"You got a better idea?"

"Send one of them," Faz said.

"Cup your hands," Kins said. The two officers did as instructed, and Kins stepped into their hands. "On three. Lift me and hold me up until I tell you to let go. I've had one vasectomy in my life. I don't want another. Ready? Three."

The officers lifted. Kins reached for the horizontal bar running six inches below the spear tips, used his arms to brace himself, and swung his right leg, and good hip, over the bar. He straddled the spear tips, holding himself up like a gymnast on the pommel horse. His arms shook from the exertion. "Okay, let go," he said.

Kins held his breath, clenched his teeth, and swung his left leg over the fence. When it cleared the spear tips, he pushed off, dropped, and rolled to soften the impact. A bolt of white-hot pain shot from his hip down his leg.

"You all right?" Faz asked.

Kins struggled to his feet, the pain taking his breath away. He grimaced and said, "Toss the Ram-It over."

It landed with a bang, cracking one of the patio tiles. Kins picked it up and limped to the front door. He stood back a foot and rammed it just above the keypad. He heard the wood crack, but the door didn't give. He hit it a second time. The wood splintered, but again the deadbolt held. When he hit the lock a third time, the door exploded inward.

He dropped the Ram-It, pulled his Glock, stepped inside, and hit the button on the control panel to the right of the door to release the gate. Then he rushed in calling Tracy's name.

——

Maria Vanpelt's photographer slid the last of the equipment into the news van and turned to her. "Outstanding," he said. "You must have fallen under a lucky star or made a deal with the devil."

She smiled. "Maybe both."

Vanpelt was still feeling the adrenaline rush. She'd just scooped not only all the other local stations, but every national network. The station's assignment editor had called to tell her that all the major affiliates were running their video. Vanpelt's cell phone rang. "Did you see that live shot?" she said, answering. "Has anyone ever been live on the scene when police found the hideout of a serial killer?"

"Where are you?" the assignment editor said, and Vanpelt detected concern in her voice.

"We're just packing up the van. Why? What's wrong?"

"We're getting all kinds of reports of something happening at Tracy Crosswhite's home in West Seattle."

"What?" Vanpelt felt her stomach drop. "What kind of reports?"

"Don't know. But something big is happening. The scanners are going crazy. I'm sending someone—"

"No," Vanpelt said. "I'll take it."

"You're too far."

"It's my story. I'll get there." She hung up and looked across the yard, past the two CSI vans parked on the lawn. Johnny Nolasco stood huddled with the FBI team. Despite what they'd found, no one looked to be celebrating. There were no high fives or hand-shakes, no satisfied smiles.

"Maria?" her photographer said.

"We need to move, now."

—

As David Bankston rushed forward, Tracy timed his approach. She pivoted sideways and swung with her right arm. Bankston absorbed the blow with his forearm and crashed into her, hurling them both backward. The pain in her shoulder exploded upon impact and again when she hit the floor, but she kicked and scratched and beat at Bankston until he yanked the piece of railing from her grasp.

Straddling her, breathing heavily, glasses askew, with blood flowing down the side of his face and beard, Bankston raised the club.

—

Kins rushed through Tracy's bedroom and bathroom, didn't find her, then hurried back to the stairwell, passing Faz and the other officers entering the house. Something crashed below them. Kins limped quickly down the stairs, his hip burning, Faz close behind. In the gray-black light, he saw two silhouettes. A man sat atop Tracy, his back to them, arm raised, something in his hand.

Kins raised his Glock, feet separating naturally into a blade stance, left hand rising up to meet the right, arms forming a triangle with the gun at the tip. He sighted the tiny red dot. "Freeze," he yelled. The man spun. David Bankston. "Drop whatever is in your hand, David."

But David Bankston didn't.

"Don't!" Kins yelled.

Bankston hurled what he'd been holding. Faz raised an arm to deflect the blow, but Kins didn't flinch. He slowly exhaled, and squeezed off three shots.

—

The noise was deafening, and the three shots lit up the room in bursts of silver-white light. The smell of gunpowder quickly permeated the air. "Call it in," Kins told one of the officers. "We're going need an ambulance and the ME. Tell them to send a CSI team."

He moved first to where Bankston lay on his back, eyes open. Bankston had been propelled backward by the impact of the bullets. Kins dropped with effort to a knee and felt for a pulse, but couldn't find one. He turned his attention to Tracy. She sat holding her left arm close to her body. "I think my collarbone is broken." Her voice sounded like someone had rubbed the inside of her throat raw with sandpaper, and even in the dull light he could see a red line on her neck.

"We have an ambulance coming," he said.

Tracy pointed. "You better check on Faz."

Faz remained on one knee, hand pressed to his forehead, bleeding from where the piece of wood had struck. "I'm all right," he said. "I absorbed the blow with my face."

"Can you walk?" Kins asked Tracy.

"I think so. Help me up."

He helped her to her feet. "How'd you know?" she asked.

"We saw the news report. And you weren't answering your phone."

"News report?"

"Let's get you some medical attention, and I'll fill you in."

"I should have told you about Stinson."

"Water under the bridge," he said.

"Can you do something for me?"

"Anything."

"Call Dan. Tell him I'm okay."

"No problem."

She turned to one of the officers still there. "There's a can of cat food and a spoon on the floor somewhere. Take it out back and bang on it. My cat's still out there."

CHAPTER 53

Tracy sat in the back of the ambulance, her left arm in a black sling. Her throat burned when she swallowed, and she was also having trouble taking a full breath; her ribs hurt each time she inhaled.

The CSI and medical examiner vans had further congested her cul-de-sac, drawing her neighbors out of their homes. They mingled on lawns and sidewalks. Someone had set up a police line well down the street. Behind it she saw the glare of television crews' lights.

As a paramedic looked for a vein in Tracy's arm for an IV drip to administer painkillers, she watched two members of the ME's staff carry a gurney out the front door with David Bankston's corpse zipped into a body bag. They dropped the wheels on the patio tiles and guided the gurney out the gate to the back of a blue van. Kins and Faz followed the gurney across the patio, Faz now sporting a large medical patch.

"How's the head?" Tracy asked.

"They say I'll need a couple stitches. Who knows, could be an improvement. How're you doing?"

"Feels like somebody stomped on my throat."

Faz smiled. "You sound like me now, Professor."

"Thank that dumbshit Nolasco when you see him," Kins said. "They moved on Bankston's house without first taking him into custody."

"Why didn't they wait?" Tracy asked and grimaced in pain.

"I suspect because he wanted the arrest to air live. Vanpelt was there. Front and center, Kins said. Some coincidence, huh?"

"He tipped her," Faz said. "He cut us out, and then he tipped her. He's the damn leak."

"Sure as shit," Kins said.

"He brought in the FBI so he can take the credit," Faz said. "He becomes the detective who caught the Cowboy, and we look like assholes."

"What did they find?" Tracy asked. "What did they find at Bankston's house?"

"I don't know," Kins said. "I suspect they're still processing it, but from what I saw on the television and what I've been told, they found a coil of polypropylene rope and every news article on every murder, along with dozens of photographs of you."

"What about the noose?" she asked, knowing the distinct knot would be important.

Kins shook his head. "Not that I know of."

"I meant the one here, downstairs."

"Oh. CSI is processing it, but it looks like the noose left at the shooting range."

"Tracy!" She recognized Dan's voice. He stood behind the barricade, waving to her.

"Can you get him in?" she asked Faz.

"I'm on it."

Tracy looked to Kins. "We need to try to find some connection between Bankston and Beth Stinson."

"Bankston might not have killed her, Tracy. No match on the DNA."

"He had to have, Kins. Too many similarities."

"Maybe that's where he first got the idea," Kins said. "Maybe he read about it, saw it on the news."

"Then why did he wait so long?"

"He was away. He was in Iraq. When he came back, he got married and had a kid. It's like Santos said. These guys can go years without killing. But when they start, they have trouble stopping."

"We need to look into his background anyway."

"We will. Right now you need to get to a hospital and take care of yourself."

Dan hurried to Tracy's side. "Are you all right?"

She nodded. "This is getting to be a bad habit."

"What happened to your voice?"

"This is my sexy voice." She smiled, then grimaced again.

A paramedic stepped forward. "We need to get you to the hospital and get you looked at, Detective."

"I'll follow you," Dan said.

Tracy looked at her house, CSI detectives going in and out the front door. "I'll make sure things get locked up here," Kins said.

"Did they find Roger?" Tracy asked.

"Police officer said he was hiding in the bushes. The cat food worked to get him to come out. I'll lock him inside."

"Feed him and you'll have a friend for life," she said.

"That means he's Italian," Faz said.

CHAPTER 54

Tracy spent the next week recovering in Cedar Grove, her arm immobilized in a sling. She had indeed cracked her collarbone, though it wasn't dislocated. Her ribs were bruised but not broken. The noose had damaged her vocal cords, and the doctors told her to keep her talking to a minimum.

"I kind of like the quiet Tracy," Dan had said.

"Don't get used to it."

Being laid up and having Dan take care of her had given her time to think again about a return to Cedar Grove, and the thought no longer brought up the anxiety she'd felt when she'd gone back to identify Sarah's remains. She could imagine herself living here, getting to know everyone again. She thought of returning to Cedar Grove High, warming to the idea of challenging young minds and making a difference in their lives. She'd have to renew her teaching license and get up to speed, but she could do it. At this point she felt as though she could handle just about anything. And while Cedar Grove might never again be the home she'd known as a young girl, she was developing a sense that it could be home again, with Dan and Rex and Sherlock, and Roger, of course. Maybe it could even be a place to raise a family. She was only forty-two. She

knew women who'd had children later in life. There were disad-
vantages to being older, but also advantages. She was more patient
and had a better sense of her priorities, and she'd have more time
to devote to raising children. Still, she thought it best to wait to
broach that subject with Dan. She sensed that all of this was happening fast for him also.

The following Monday she returned to the Justice Center.
Kins, Faz, and Del—and Mayweather, who'd taken her spot as
Kins's partner—made a fuss over her, but she was still on administrative leave, assigned to a desk at the back of the floor with the
administrative staff. Now, however, she didn't mind. Tucked in her
cubbyhole, she was away from the questions and the looks. She'd
managed to avoid the OPA investigation while she was out, but
her attorney had called bright and early that morning to tell her
that Detective Sergeant Rawley was eager to reschedule her hearing. She told him she was on painkillers and would need at least
another week.

In addition to OPA, the City Budget Office had called. They'd
started an investigation into Tracy's unauthorized inquiry into the
Wayne Gerhardt case and the possible misuse of public funds. She
had no doubt Nolasco had instigated that investigation. It seemed
as if Chief Clarridge would also be hard pressed to retain his job.
Pressure was building on him to resign. Articles in the *Seattle Times*
were critical of him and his administration. Editorials opined that
he'd lost institutional control of the department and the respect of
his officers.

Nolasco, on the other hand, had come out smelling like a rose.
He was saluted and honored for bringing the Cowboy to justice.
He'd been interviewed on local and national news shows, and word
was he'd be featured in a law enforcement magazine. One rumor
circulating was that the mayor would capitalize on Nolasco's notoriety and appoint him interim police chief while a search commit-
tee interviewed other candidates. Faz said Nolasco was so puffed

up and full of himself he wondered how he fit his head in the elevator every morning. That was the only thing truly bothering her now, the knowledge that Nolasco had gotten what he'd wanted. It had taken him twenty years, but she'd finally be gone. She wanted to hate the man, but she saw him as small and petty and sad.

Maria Vanpelt ran an hour-long special report about the Cowboy investigation on *KRIX Undercover*. Tracy didn't watch, but according to Faz, Vanpelt said the investigation had taken a turn for the better when Nolasco took charge. She also hadn't missed an opportunity to promote herself: Faz had counted no less than nine times during the hour-long program that Vanpelt made a direct reference to herself as 'the reporter who broke the story' and 'the reporter at the scene' when the Cowboy's home was searched and the incriminating evidence discovered.

In the aftermath, everyone seemed to want to focus on the positive. Little discussion was given to the fact that Nolasco had screwed up, big-time, by not making sure David Bankston was in custody before moving on his home, or that his mistake had nearly cost Tracy her life.

Kins had remained in Seattle until OPA cleared him for the use of his firearm in David Bankston's death. Then, fed up and frustrated, he'd taken Shannah on a much-needed vacation to Mexico, where he hoped they could rekindle their relationship.

"Send me a postcard with palm trees, white sand beaches, and brilliant sunshine and I'll pull your eyebrows out next time I see you," Tracy said.

Friday of her first week back, Tracy was thinking she'd dodged a bullet, having not run into her boss all week, when his assistant called to tell her that Nolasco wanted to see her in his office. As she made her way through the Violent Crimes Section, she heard the familiar sounds of phones ringing, animated conversations, and Faz's inimitable voice. "Who took my mug? It's got my face on it for a reason, people!"

It brought the first genuine smile to her face in days. She'd miss being a part of it.

Nolasco's door was open. He sat at his desk, considering paperwork. He glanced up, then motioned her in with no show of emotion. "Take a seat."

Tracy sat. Her arm remained in a sling. She cradled it in her lap.

Nolasco seemed in no hurry, continuing to read. After a long minute, he set down the document. "OPA says you're dodging them."

"I'm on painkillers. My doctor advises against attending a hearing until I'm off them. Have them talk to my attorney."

Nolasco sat back. "Someone needs to put the Cowboy file to bed and shut it down. And the Bundy Room needs to be cleaned out, boxed up, and shipped to storage. I figured you had the time."

The task added insult to injury, but if it meant getting out of the Justice Center for a few days, Tracy didn't mind. "Not a problem," she said.

"Good. Get on it right away, will you."

She stood and headed for the door. Just being near Nolasco made her feel like she needed to take a shower.

"You had to know it wouldn't end well," he said.

There it was. She knew he couldn't resist. His ego was just too big, almost as if he were genetically predisposed to be an ass. When she turned around, Nolasco remained seated, leaning back in his chair. He was pathetic, a bully, maybe even a sociopath. Tracy almost felt sorry for him. But at that moment, what she felt most prominently was that twinge of doubt, the one she'd felt occasionally while recuperating at home, the twinge that something wasn't quite right.

She managed a smile. "I'll let you know when it does," she said.

She spent the weekend relaxing with Dan in Cedar Grove. They made gourmet dinners, watched movies on the couch, eating popcorn and candy, and slept in late. Monday morning, when she got up early to make the drive back to Seattle, she felt sad to be leaving. Going to work no longer excited her the way it used to. She felt ready to move on, to leave SPD and return to Cedar Grove fulltime. She contemplated telling Dan, but decided instead to wait, to make the moment special.

She spent Monday and Tuesday in the Cowboy Room boxing up tip sheets, notebooks, and calendars, and clearing out desks. It wasn't easy work with only one good arm, but she also wasn't in a rush to get it done. As the second day came to an end, she'd filled a dozen boxes, labeled them, and left them to be picked up and taken to storage. Fitting the final lid on the last box, she took a moment to consider the room. The walls were once again stripped bare, though now with a few more holes where thumbtacks had held photos and charts. The desks were vacant. The phones and computers would be disconnected again soon. Despite the grim history of the room, she recalled fondly Vera Fazzio's Italian dinner and Faz's toast, promising they'd pull together as a task force. She couldn't help but think she'd let them down. They'd all wanted nothing more than to prove Nolasco wrong and catch the Cowboy.

Tracy turned out the lights, about to shut the door, when her desk phone rang. She almost ignored it, figuring it had to be Nolasco, since no one else knew she was there, but she decided she wouldn't give him the satisfaction of thinking she was dodging him. She turned on the lights and stepped back in, answering.

"Detective Crosswhite," she said. There was no immediate response. "Hello?"

The voice, a man's, stumbled over his words. "Sorry. I didn't expect *you* to answer the phone." It wasn't Nolasco or Faz.

"Who am I speaking to?"

"I'd prefer to not say."

"Okay. Then what's this about?"

"It's about the Cowboy."

"If this is about the reward—"

"It's not about the reward."

"What is it about?"

"I think you might have killed the wrong guy."

—

Tracy sat on the edge of the desk. She'd taken enough of these calls during the investigation from people claiming to know the identity of the killer to remain guarded. This could be just another one of the crazies, the people who thought they'd solved the crime, the psychics who called to say they'd been in communication with the dead. But there was something about the calm tone of the voice on the other end of the line that made her think otherwise. That, and the call had come from a phone inside SPD. "Okay. Tell me why."

"I don't want to talk over the phone."

"Tell me how you got this number?"

"Isn't this the number for the task force?"

It was, though it was not the tip line that had been broadcast by the news media. Only someone within SPD would have access to her desk number, or know how to get it. "Tell me where and when."

"You choose," he said.

"You know a bar on First Avenue called Hooverville?"

"I'll find it."

They arranged a time for that evening. "How will I know you?" she asked.

"I know you," he said.

—

Hooverville was already crowded with Mariners fans. There was a home game, and the bar was located just down the street from the baseball stadium, where, early in the season, hope still sprung eternal. It seemed a little odd for people to be watching the game on TV, given the proximity of the stadium just half a mile away.

Tracy looked around the room for the tipster. Two men worked the pinball machines. The barstools were full, as were most of the tables. When no one waved or acknowledged her, she settled into a booth facing the door and ordered a Diet Coke while continuing to survey faces, looking for someone distracted, disinterested, fidgeting.

After several minutes a lean man with a buzz cut looked in her direction, swiveled from his barstool at the end of the bar, and walked over. Tracy guessed him to be early thirties. He had the build of a rock climber or avid biker, and intense narrow-set eyes, indicating the unrelenting demeanor needed to compete in those sports. She noted a wedding ring on his left hand and a college ring on his right, which held a half-empty pint of beer. "Detective Crosswhite. Thanks for meeting with me."

Tracy gestured for him to take a seat. Beneath the table, her right hand rested on her Glock.

"Interesting place," he said.

"A friend introduced me to it. It's far enough from the city that only the cool kids know about it."

"Maybe a few years ago I would have too," he said.

"Yeah? Not anymore?"

"I have two kids. Those days are behind me." He sat back, then sat forward, seemingly unable to get comfortable. He glanced at the television, at the bar, back to her. He tapped the edge of the table with the fingers of his right hand. "Sorry about the clandestine meeting."

"Why don't you tell me your name?"

"Izak Casterline."

"How long you been a cop, Izak Casterline?"

He let out a puff of air, not quite a chuckle. "You're good."

"Not that good. You called an inside number. Only SPD has it."

"Eighteen months. I work out of the North Precinct."

The North Precinct patrolled the Aurora strip. "Relax," Tracy said. "I'm just here to listen."

Casterline sipped his beer. "My wife is pregnant."

"Congratulations."

Another half smile. "Thanks. She's a preschool teacher. She was. She stopped. It was cheaper to stay home than pay for day care."

"Money's tight. I get it."

"Very," Casterline said.

"So talk to me. Why do you think they got the wrong guy?"

Casterline took another sip of beer. "I was working graveyard the night they found the third dancer, Veronica Watson."

"Okay."

"I'm doing my normal patrol, driving Aurora, right at Eighty-Fifth Street. That's the corner of the motel where you found the third body."

"Right."

"I make the turn, and there's a car in front of me. Its back light is out."

"What time was this?"

"Between two thirty and three. Right around the time the ME says that dancer was killed. I looked up the report online."

"Did you pull the driver over?"

Casterline nodded. "I asked him what he's doing out so late. He said it was actually early for him—that he was heading to work after a morning workout. He was perspiring heavily and had a bag in the back, you know, like a gym bag. Big guy. Anyway, he said he was also on cat patrol."

"Cat patrol?"

"He said his daughter's cat had gone missing and she was heartbroken over it, so he was putting up fliers. He handed me one." Casterline reached into the inside pocket of his jacket and pulled out a piece of paper, unfolded it, and handed it across the table.

Tracy looked at it. There was a black-and-white picture of the cat in the center of the flier. "Angus," she said.

"Like I said, I have two daughters. They'd be heartbroken if they lost their cat. So I asked for one of the fliers and said I'd keep my eyes open." Casterline pointed to the address below the picture. "Two days ago I realized I was driving in that neighborhood. I still had the flier with me. I have a neighbor whose cat just had kittens, so I figured I'd stop and find out if they ever found Angus, you know, and if not, maybe they'd like one of the kittens. I thought maybe it might look good to my sergeant, you know, if they called and told him."

"What happened when you stopped, Izak?"

"The guy comes to the door, and I show him the flier. He's a little surprised, but he tells me they never found their cat. He was appreciative that I would make the effort and asked for my friend's number so they could go take a look at the kittens." Casterline took another sip of beer. "It wasn't him, Detective. It was the right address, but the guy who came to the door wasn't the guy I pulled over that night. And that's when I started putting the pieces together."

"The guy you pulled over could have been leaving a prostitute, a drug dealer," Tracy surmised.

"I don't think so. This guy was smooth and clearly prepared. How many meth-heads and johns have you ever come across who had the foresight to have a flier ready to hand out. I think he did it to distract me, throw me off my routine."

"Good point."

"This guy had taken the flier from somewhere and gone and made copies. And he was calm. I remember that about him. If he'd had drugs in the car, he wouldn't have been so calm, would he?"

"Did you get a license plate?"

Casterline pursed his lips and shook his head. "I didn't run it. Look, I know I should have. But I figured I'd give the guy a break, you know? I just told him to get the light fixed." Casterline started fidgeting. "I should have run it. I know I should have called it in and run it, and, man, I'm sick, because if I'm right . . ."

"Take it easy," she said. "A lot of cops wouldn't have run the plate under those circumstances. What do you remember about the car?"

"It was a hybrid, but not a cheap one, a Lexus."

"What color?"

"Dark blue or black."

Tracy thought about the car in the video as it drove down the street parallel to the Pink Palace. "Can you describe the driver?"

"That's the other thing. This guy didn't look like a meth-head. Big guy. Well built. Dark hair. Spiked in the front."

Tracy's pulse quickened. "If you saw him again, could you pick him out?"

"You mean like out of a lineup?"

"I mean, could you identify him if you saw him?"

"Yeah, I could identify him. Absolutely." Casterline's eyes narrowed. "You think he could be the guy?"

"Who else have you told about this?"

"No one."

"Don't. Do you understand?"

"Absolutely. I can't lose my job, Detective. I don't know what I'd do . . . you know?"

"You're not going to lose your job."

"But if you got the wrong guy . . . it means he's still out there. The Cowboy. And then he killed that other girl . . ." Casterline choked on the words. His eyes watered, and he took another sip of beer.

"That wasn't your fault, okay? Casterline, look at me." Casterline looked up. "That wasn't your fault. If you're right, if this is the guy, he kills because he wants to and he was going to kill again. Running his plate likely wouldn't have turned up anything of interest, and you would have let him go anyway. All right?"

Casterline nodded.

"Now I'm going to need a number to reach you. I need to get a few things put in place, make some calls. I'll protect you to whatever extent I can, Casterline, but you've got to work with me on this."

"I will," he said.

Tracy handed him a napkin and a pen from her purse. Casterline wrote his phone number on the napkin and slid it across the table to her. "What should I do?"

"Go home to your family. Wait until I call."

—

Tracy drove immediately back to her house in West Seattle and hurried to where Dan had left the box of documents from Dirty Ernie's that he'd found in the storage shed. Her heart was pounding, her palms moist. Her mind was swimming with questions. This is what members of the Ridgway task force had told her about how these guys were often caught. Sometimes it was a tip from the most unexpected of places, something little, a small mistake, and you realize the killer has been under your nose the whole time. Because that's what these guys did. They blended in.

"Relax," she said out loud. "Don't get ahead of yourself." The possibility remained that Casterline was wrong and, despite all the screwups in procedure, that David Bankston was the Cowboy. But something told her that wasn't the case.

Tracy slid the box into the dining room and dropped to a knee, fumbling through the pages, pulling out folders, riffling quickly through them. She kept at it, nearly ten minutes, until she'd found the file she was most interested in, the payroll. She pulled out the sheets of paper, scanning the names as she stood and took the file to the table. She set the pages down, continuing until her finger came to rest on one she recognized.

CHAPTER 55

Tracy got up at just after four thirty Wednesday morning and drove to the Justice Center. She parked in the secured lot and took the elevator to the seventh floor, arriving a few minutes after five thirty, early enough that most detectives would not yet be in, except one notorious early riser. She'd been locked out of the computer system when Nolasco put her on administrative leave. When she entered the A Team's bull pen, she found Faz's chair empty but his computer turned on. She sat down, about to type on the keyboard.

"Whoa! Professor," Faz said, stepping into the bull pen carrying a folded sports section. "What are you doing in this early?"

"Didn't know if you were here," she said. "Nolasco's got me cleaning up the Cowboy."

"Yeah, I heard. Sorry about that."

"I was hoping to get a copy of that video shot outside the Pink Palace to send to storage with the rest of the stuff."

Faz eyeballed her. "And you thought you'd do it at five thirty in the morning? What's going on, Professor? You can't bullshit a bullshitter."

She waited for a detective from burglary to walk past. "Is it still in the system somewhere, Faz?"

"I don't know. I heard they sent everything to never-never land and scrubbed everything clean."

"I'm talking about your computer."

"It ain't Bankston, is it?"

"I don't know, but I don't think it is, Faz. Do you still have a copy on your computer?"

"Shit, you know me, Professor. I don't know how to delete anything."

Tracy gave up the chair and looked over the top of the cubicle walls to see who else was around. Faz sat, navigating through several portals.

"Still got it," he said.

"Run it."

"Can't read the plate, Professor. Melton enhanced it but still couldn't read it."

"Run it anyway."

Faz played the video, which Melton's team had lightened and made less grainy. Walter Gipson and Angela Schreiber walked around the corner of the building in the direction of Gipson's car. Tracy kept her focus on the upper left corner of the screen, on the street, waiting for the car to appear. It drove down the street and exited the camera frame. Gipson pulled from the lot into traffic.

"Okay, slow it down," Tracy said.

Faz hit a couple of buttons. The picture proceeded frame by frame. Tracy waited. The car entered the picture. "Freeze it."

They leaned closer to the screen. "No good," Faz said. "Still can't read the license plate."

"Let me." She reached for the mouse and moved it to enlarge the picture.

"Too grainy," Faz said. "No good."

But Tracy wasn't focused on the license plate. She was focused on the front grill just beneath the hood, on the circle with the bent *L*. A Lexus.

CHAPTER 56

Thursday night, Tracy sat in the cab of her truck, sipping coffee that had long since gone cold. The clock on her phone glowed 1:27. Exactly three minutes later, from her position parked down the block and perpendicular to the front of the Pink Palace, she watched Izak Casterline exit the building. Casterline wore a baseball cap pulled low on his head. He walked calmly to his minivan, got in, started the engine, and took a left out of the parking lot. Tracy tossed the coffee remnants out the window, started her truck, and followed, checking the rearview mirror.

Two blocks from the Pink Palace, she pulled into the parking lot of an IHOP restaurant, drove around the back, and parked beside the van. Casterline got out and climbed into the cab of her truck.

"It's him," he said. "That's the guy I pulled over. One hundred percent certain. Absolutely."

CHAPTER 57

Tracy removed the earbuds and massaged her earlobes, which felt warm to the touch—the only part of her body that felt warm. It wasn't particularly cold—she guessed the temperature to be upper forties. Sitting was the hardest part of a stakeout. After a while every part of your body was stiff and uncomfortable. You couldn't very well get out of the car to stretch or pump out a set of jumping jacks or push-ups in the street. You learned to do little things to fight off the cold and the stiffness—flex your fingers and hands, rotate your ankles, isolate and tense and relax certain muscles. It helped. It didn't make the cold go away, especially not when it was damp. That kind of cold chilled to the bone and made her collarbone ache.

She'd downloaded some classic '80s rock—Aerosmith, Van Halen, Springsteen, a little Journey, even some AC/DC—to help pass the time. She didn't need the music to keep her awake, despite not having slept much since meeting with Izak Casterline. Over the three days and nights since, she'd established a routine. She got home just after five—no longer a problem since she was mostly doing a lot of nothing at work, ate an early dinner, watched television for a bit, then tried, mostly unsuccessfully, to sleep a couple of hours. She arrived at the Pink Palace at midnight and located the Lexus. Sometimes he parked on a side street, sometimes in the parking lot. There seemed to be no pattern. She also varied where she parked, which could be difficult, because she needed to be able to see the Cowboy's car. Tonight she'd parked halfway down a tree-lined street running perpendicular to and slightly east of the Pink Palace entrance, with a view of the parking lot. A midsize SUV provided some cover, but it wasn't so tall as to block her view.

Just after one o'clock, the parking lot would start to thin, and customers would start heading home. The dancers would exit the building by the rear door minutes after two. The remaining staff would exit shortly thereafter. The Cowboy was usually one of the last to leave. So far, he'd driven home each night, though not always the same route. Not wanting to draw attention to her truck in case his inconsistency was purposeful, Tracy broke off her tail blocks from his house, then circled back to confirm the Lexus was parked in the driveway. Even then, she'd awake each morning with a pit in her stomach, certain that she'd pick up the newspaper and see a headline that would make her sick.

Still, she had no doubt she was doing the right thing.

The only two detectives she trusted were Kins, who remained in Mexico, and Faz, who knew something was up but for now was content with being on a need-to-know basis. She couldn't go to Nolasco. She'd considered going directly to Clarridge, but under the circumstances—his career in jeopardy, Tracy discredited—he would be reluctant to accept any argument that David Bankston was not the Cowboy without some definitive proof. At the moment all Tracy had was circumstantial evidence and the word of one young police officer scared to death he would get fired, leaving him unable to support a growing family. It wasn't enough. The King County Sheriff's Office had boxes of circumstantial evidence that pointed to Gary Ridgway as the Green River Killer, but it had taken twenty years to confirm his DNA at crime scenes. Ridgway had discarded a piece of gum, the story went, and detectives watching him had picked it up. Only then did they have him. Truth or urban myth, Tracy didn't know. She only knew she needed more.

She also feared that if she went to Clarridge with her doubts about Bankston and they agreed to reopen the investigation, it would leak to the media. That big a story would be too hard to keep quiet. When it ran in the papers or was broadcast on the news, the Cowboy might flee, maybe change his name, making him free to continue killing somewhere else.

That left Dan. Keeping secrets wasn't a great way to build a relationship, especially if she was going to take the next step and move with him to Cedar Grove, but that dilemma had been at least partially solved by logistics. Dan had spent the week in Cedar Grove playing catch-up on his cases after having been away too long. When he called, Tracy didn't lie, not exactly. She just hadn't offered any details about what she had learned, or how she was spending her evenings. She knew Dan would try to talk her out of what she knew to be the best option—to stake out the Pink Palace and wait. For how long Tracy didn't know, but Amanda Santos had said that once the urge to kill started, it was too strong for most serial killers to ignore. The Cowboy would seek to kill again. It was just a matter of when. Tracy was not going to let that happen.

She slid lower in her seat and stuck the earbuds back in her ears. Springsteen was moaning about a little girl whose daddy went away, leaving her home all alone, and another man with a "bad desire."

"Prophetic," she said.

Rain began to splatter her windshield just after one. The weatherman had forecast early morning showers and intense but short-lived wind. Tracy reached for the windshield wipers, then thought of the cleared windshield on the snow-covered car in Cedar Grove, and decided to leave the wipers off.

She shuffled through her playlist on her phone and watched the raindrops run together until they'd formed a sheet of water.

As closing time neared, she felt more on edge than the prior evenings. Maybe it was the accumulation of too much caffeine, or too many days in a row without exercise, but the feeling that something was going to happen was pronounced. She couldn't explain it any more than she could explain why, when she'd been a patrol officer, bad things seemed to always happen on nights with full moons. It was an instinct developed over two decades of being on the street and years working graveyard shifts. She could sense when a routine traffic stop was not going to be routine, when a seemingly in-hand situation was about to escalate, when it was time to trust her intuition and protect herself.

She detected blurred images—dancers filing out the rear door of the building, running to their cars through the steady rain. The staff left shortly after them. Her target was likely counting the money and doing the books for the night.

The rain suddenly intensified, further obscuring her view. It was one of those rushes of water like God had opened the tap to drain a heavenly lake. The back door to the building opened, but no one emerged. She surmised that he was waiting for the deluge to subside. When it didn't, he shot out the door, stepping lightly, trying in vain to avoid the rapidly expanding puddles. He quickly got in the Lexus but again did not immediately depart. Prior nights, he'd left without hesitation.

After several minutes the headlights illuminated, cones of light piercing the sheeting rain. The Lexus pulled to the driveway, paused briefly, and turned left, toward Aurora.

The direction home.

Tracy started the engine and drove to the intersection. She turned right at the corner and settled in a comfortable distance behind the Lexus. The truck's wipers slapped a steady beat. At the intersection, he turned right onto Aurora, southbound, continuing

HER FINAL BREATH   363

toward home. Perched in the cab of her truck, Tracy had a good view over the cars in front of her. He drove another block and switched to the far right lane. A car on Tracy's right prevented her from immediately merging. She slowed to allow the car to pass and settled in two cars behind the Lexus. The Cowboy continued through the next light.

Cars sprayed rooster tails of water, the gutters momentarily overwhelmed, large puddles creeping into the road. Two more blocks and the Cowboy's brake lights lit up. He turned into a service station with a twenty-four-hour convenience store. This was new.

Tracy drove past the station and watched the rearview and side mirrors. The Lexus didn't stop at the pump. It drove around the side of the building, and Tracy feared it might exit onto the side street. Then the brake lights illuminated, and the Lexus parked. Tracy turned right at the intersection, made a U-turn and pulled into a strip mall parking lot kitty-corner to the convenience store, with a view of the Lexus.

She turned off the lights and the wiper blades but left the engine running.

—

He had time to kill.

He just loved that line. He loved the irony of it. He thought he'd heard it in a movie somewhere, like maybe *American Psycho* or some weird Woody Harrelson film. Harrelson did those kind of movies now—*Natural Born Killers* and *Zombieland*. Hard to believe he'd once been just Woody, the dumb-as-a-post bartender on *Cheers*, but that was a testament to Harrelson's acting chops.

He liked to think he could have been the same type of actor, versatile enough to play different roles, if he'd ever been given the chance to seriously pursue it.

He pulled into the gas station with the twenty-four-hour convenience store and parked on the far side of the building, out of
the glow of the lights above the gas pumps, which was where any
camera would be focused. The rain continued to fall, but at least
the torrent he got caught in as he was leaving work had let up. He
could feel moisture seeping through his shoes and socks, and his
shirt sticking to his back. It was annoying, but it didn't take away
from the tingling sensation pulsing through his body, the same
sensation he'd felt backstage before the start of every show, the sensation that made him feel alive.

He pulled the brim of a nondescript Mariners baseball cap low
on his head and hurried from the car into the store, lowering his
chin as he entered through the glass doors to the buzzing of an
electric eye. Jazz music filtered down from speakers in the ceiling.
He nodded to the man behind the counter, polite but indifferent,
unmemorable, and made his way to the refrigerator. He needed a
jolt of caffeine. It had been a long day, and it was going to be an
even longer morning. The girls had calmed since the news of the
capture of the Cowboy, but that didn't mean they were any easier
to deal with. Bunch of divas is what they were—a demanding pack
of bitches.

He set two cans of an energy drink on the counter, along with
a carton of milk and a six-pack of eggs. Staples. Nothing out of the
ordinary.

"Late night?" the store owner asked.

"Early morning," he said. "Pack of Camels. Silvers."

"King Size or 100's?"

"King Size."

"You heading to work?" the clerk asked.

"Unfortunately." He put a twenty on the counter. "Right after I
drop off supplies at the house. Can I get a bag?"

"Where do you work this early?" the clerk asked, bagging his
items.

"Airport," he said. He checked his watch. "And I better get a move on if I don't want to be late."

The clerk handed him his change.

"Can I get a book of matches?"

The clerk grabbed two from under the counter and dropped them into the bag.

"Thanks. It defeats the whole purpose if you can't light them," he said. "Maybe that would be a good thing." About to leave, he heard the perfect line of dialogue pop into his head—something so good he couldn't resist giving it a try. "I should quit," he said, "but tonight the urge is just too strong."

—

Tracy watched the Cowboy exit the store carrying a brown paper bag. He pulled a can from the bag, popped the tab, and tilted it back, taking a long drink. Then he dashed to his car. This time, he didn't wait. He pulled to the driveway. Tracy thought he was looking south, watching the northbound traffic and waiting to cross the double yellow line.

She was right.

The Lexus pulled into the turn lane and waited for a northbound car to pass. Then it merged. The Cowboy was not heading home.

She felt a rush of adrenaline and hit the gas, timing a gap in the traffic and pulling into the northbound lanes. She sat up and exhaled a deep breath. Time to focus on following. Traffic wasn't heavy, but there were enough cars to allow the truck to blend in, or to get in her way if the Cowboy made a sudden turn.

The wind had picked up, causing the streetlights dangling from wires strung across the road to dance and shake in the gusts, and the rain to splatter hard against the windshield. As the Cowboy neared an intersection, the stoplight turned yellow. She figured he'd stop, not wanting to risk a traffic ticket. But instead, he sped up to make the light. Tracy accelerated, then quickly hit the brake when the car in front of her stopped.

"Damn," she said. She kept an eye on the Lexus as it continued north, hoping it would get stuck at the next light. As she waited, a large delivery van drove into the intersection, obstructing her view. The driver was waiting for the traffic to clear so he could complete a left turn.

"Move," she urged. "Make the damn turn."

The truck inched forward when the light turned yellow. Tracy's light changed from red to green, but the truck remained in the intersection. She hit the horn just as the truck lurched forward.

The Lexus was nowhere to be seen.

—

She continued down Aurora, her head swiveling, frantically searching motel parking lots for any sign of the Lexus. Then she remembered that the Cowboy was likely parking on side streets, something Izak Casterline had mentioned when he'd pulled the Lexus over two blocks from the motel.

She made a right turn at the next intersection and continued down the block, slowed at the four-way intersection, and peered down the tree-lined residential streets, considering the parked cars. The rain and darkness made the already-poor lighting worse, and the number of cars was not insignificant. She took a deep breath, trying to remain calm, and fought to slow her mind. What had Amanda Santos told them? The Cowboy was organized. He was smart, careful. He didn't want to be caught. He didn't want to be seen—or heard, likely the reason he drove a hybrid. He'd take precautions.

She took a right, forcing herself to proceed slowly. He wouldn't want to park in front of a house or under a street lamp, or on a

well-lit street. He'd try to blend in, parking his car in an inconspic-
uous but hidden place.

She felt flushed. Trickles of perspiration rolled from her temples and down her sides. A large rock had dropped in her stomach.

At the next intersection, she looked right and left, taking in the
view between the wiper blades. She saw a dark-blue sedan parked
at the left curb halfway down the block, punched the accelerator,
and pulled up beside it.

—

He slipped on the hooded sweatshirt and pulled the ball cap low
on his brow, walking the side street, gym bag in hand, just a guy
on his way to an early morning workout, which wasn't completely
untrue. Acting was all in the presentation. He'd read half a dozen
books and taken another half a dozen classes on method acting—
how to use your body to convince your mind you were the character you sought to portray. The Stanislavski method was one of
his favorites. He also liked Lee Strasberg. He'd once looked into
applying to the Actors Studio in New York. He had the talent. He
didn't have the cash.

He felt the energy drink kicking in, though it could also have
been the thrill of the anticipated performance. The second can was
in his gym bag, along with the cigarettes and matches. "I should
quit," he said, smiling at the thought of it. "But tonight the urge is
just too strong." He liked the line almost as much as "He had time
to kill."

He had told himself that Gabby—that's what he'd called
Gabrielle Lizotte—would be his last for a while. He'd told himself
that maybe it was time to move, as he'd done after Beth Stinson, go
to a new city for a while. The scrutiny by the police had become
intense. When they'd formed a task force, he knew they were serious. That's what they'd done for Bundy and Ridgway, which was

rarefied air. So was his nickname—the Cowboy. It had a certain ring to it. Not as good as Urban Cowboy or Drugstore Cowboy, but not bad. "The Cowboy," he said.

He'd gone nine years in between Beth Stinson and Nicole Hansen, damn near a decade. Stinson had been his first. He'd never forget that experience. It was like opening night of a long-awaited new show. The thrill had been intense. The urge had been present for years, but he hadn't acted on it until then. For one, he wasn't sure how to meet the women. Then he'd read an article about pedophiles hanging out at places where kids went, which disgusted him but gave him the idea of working at a strip club. What better place to meet whores? What better place for them to become comfortable around him, to trust him? What better way to hide in plain sight? So he went to a new club, someplace where no one would know him, Dirty Ernie's Nude Review, and the owner, a woman—and wasn't that a kick in the pants—hired him. Within two months she'd made him the manager. Of course she had. He'd been punctual and hardworking. He used the time to try and determine which dancer would be his first. Then Beth Stinson and her friend started at the club. The friend didn't last long, but Stinson was a natural—danced under the name Betty Boobs, and the name fit. Nasty figure. She packed a lot of punch on a small frame. She was also naïve, barely out of high school.

He took his time getting to know her, befriending her, gaining her confidence. He talked to her in between her sets on the stage and working the VIP rooms. After her friend quit, Stinson was looking for a confidant. Soon she became comfortable enough to tell him the intimate details of her life—like the fact that she was a whore—just as he'd predicted. Just like his mother. She'd said it was to make extra money, pay the bills. He knew better. She was a whore. That's what whores did.

After Stinson confided in him, he had a hard time hiding his disgust, but his acting classes helped. Besides, her revelation had provided his inspiration on how to do it without getting caught. Wait until a night when she'd been with one of the men. The guy's fingerprints would be all over the room, along with all the others she'd brought home. So would his DNA. That's when he'd started to plan. He learned where she lived and scouted out the neighborhood, a quiet residential street with no street lamps. The neighbors seemed to keep mostly to themselves.

The only flaw in his plan was when the owner came in and told him to start looking for another job, that the city council was moving to shut them down and it would be just a matter of time before they succeeded. Not long after that Stinson came in late for a Saturday shift. When he asked her why she was late, she said she had a clogged toilet and had to wait for the Roto-Rooter man. She said the guy was in her house for hours, trying to unclog it, and had tracked dirt on the carpet.

It was now or never. In acting, he'd learned that success was when opportunity met preparation. To succeed you had to be prepared for when the perfect role came up. This was his perfect role. This was his opportunity.

He approached Stinson late in the shift and asked if he could stop by after work; what would she think of that? She gave him a flirtatious smile and said they could both get fired if their boss found out, but there was an inquisitive lilt in her voice. He said she didn't have to worry about that. He needed the job too much to say anything. And besides, they were both going to be looking for other work anyway. And she invited him over.

A gust of wind blew rain in his face as he neared the end of the block. The motel marquee glowed red amid Aurora Avenue's chaotic skyline of street lamps and billboards, the lights reflecting in the sheen of the water-soaked pavement. He approached the back of the motel and followed a concrete walkway through an arch that led to the parking lot.

Stinson hadn't gone exactly as he'd planned. Opening-night performances rarely did. He'd long since perfected the noose, but he had not quite figured out a way to kill without having to actually touch the woman. He hated it when his mother touched him, knowing the disgusting things she did with the men she brought home—the way she'd touched them and they'd touched her.

When he knocked on Stinson's door, it felt like that rush of coming onstage completely in character, a totally different person, the audience having no idea who he really was. It hadn't been a bad performance, just not his best. He desperately wanted another chance to get it right, but he knew he wasn't ready. He knew that a bad performance could quickly kill a career, that he had to study more, improve, especially with the noose.

What had gone exactly as he'd planned was the arrest of the Roto-Rooter guy. Still, he thought it best to leave the area. Why not? When Dirty Ernie's closed its doors, he was in need of a job anyway. And if he really wanted to be an actor, what better place to go than Los Angeles, to ply his acting trade, maybe catch his break.

In LA, fully devoted to his craft, he found it easier to ignore his urges. He went weeks at a time, sometimes months, without even thinking about Beth Stinson. He met his wife in a local performance of *One Flew Over the Cuckoo's Nest*. He'd played McMurphy. The director called him a natural and said he was born to play the role. His wife had played Nurse Ratched. Man, they'd had some fireworks onstage. The first time they rehearsed the scene when McMurphy chokes her, he'd never felt so powerful, so alive. He almost did it, just squeezed the life out of her right there in front of everyone. The director said he'd been amazing, so believable. When the show's run ended three months later, they got married in a civil ceremony at the downtown courthouse, and for a while they had the same kind of fireworks in the bedroom.

He got headshots made, found an agent, even did a toothpaste commercial. But the agent turned out to be a scam, a way to get you to pay to take her acting classes. He was paying her more than he was making, and when he balked at taking any more of her classes, she stopped calling him for auditions. When he pressed her, she said he wasn't right for any roles. He grew angry with the entire scene, all the bullshit sucking-up, the backstabbing that people did to get a role. His wife had started nagging him to get a real job; they needed the money. She'd become pregnant, and she didn't want to live in Los Angeles. So they packed up and moved to Seattle.

Everything was unraveling. Nothing was working out as he'd planned. He began to resent his wife, to feel the same anger toward her he'd felt for his mother. Without the acting to direct his energy, and the thrill of the performances, his urge returned and this time he couldn't ignore it. He didn't want to ignore it.

He rehearsed during the day, studying on S&M websites how to hog-tie a woman, how to tie the slipknot and thread the rope down the spine to her hands and ankles. He researched date rape drugs and settled on Rohypnol. When he felt prepared, he began to look for a whore for his next performance and started to hang out at a club called the Dancing Bare. He wasn't worried about someone remembering him. Most of the people in the club were lowlifes. He settled on Nicole Hansen when one of the club regulars said she was available after hours and he was seeing her that very night. He left early and waited in his car. When the guy came out, he followed him to the motel and waited for the man to leave. Then he knocked on the door, held up a bottle of vodka, and said, "Gary said you liked to party."

And that was all it took.

So many years had passed it felt like his first all over again—opening night, but this time without the mistakes and the kinks. He found he had no problem falling back into character. And when he'd finished, he found that he wasn't satisfied. He wanted to do it again.

The Pink Palace had a lot more women to choose from. Angela Schreiber started bringing her boyfriend to the club. She just made it too easy. Veronica Watson became his choice when her boyfriend mentioned that she was making more money at night after she left the club. That guy had almost ruined the performance, showing up at the motel room unannounced, in need of money. He'd hidden in the bathroom until the guy left. Turned out to be a stroke of luck—the boyfriend became a suspect. Like that little punk could ever be "the Cowboy." Still, the close call had unnerved him, and he left the motel that morning thinking Watson would be his last, at least for a while. He contemplated getting back into theater, maybe trying improv or stand-up comedy. But when could he do that while working nights?

Then the opportunity with Gabby presented itself. The man the dancers called Mr. Attorney had come in and asked her for a lap dance. That was unusual. Gabby was petite. Mr. Attorney went for women with more meat on the bones. When Gabby came out of the private room, she was grinning ear to ear. He asked her if everything was okay, and she just smiled wider. He heard later that Mr. Attorney had given Gabby a fifty-dollar tip, and he suspected he wasn't just throwing his money around. The guy expected something in return. So he played that hunch, and it turned out his instincts were dead-on. Gabby had made a date. All he had to do was get to the motel and wait for Mr. Attorney to leave the room.

After that performance, his best to date, he was no longer considering stopping. He was considering his next victim.

And again, opportunity knocked. Raina came to work. Her name was actually spelled "Rayna," but she thought the unusual spelling would be cute—"You know, because it rains so much in Seattle." She'd moved from a small town in Texas, and quickly became popular with the customers. They liked her small frame, gymnast's body, and surgically enhanced breasts. She dyed her hair blonde, with gold highlights, which looked ridiculous with her dark eyebrows and reminded him of his mother, who'd worn a blonde wig but painted on her eyebrows with a dark pencil. He knew he'd kill *her* the first time he spoke to her.

Raina had told him she had a room at the back of the motel on the first floor—number 17. "It's my lucky number," she said. She had no idea. She'd said she'd text him when her date had left, but he told her instead to place one of the Pink Palace cards, which the dancers were provided to promote the club, in the window. He didn't want any text messages to his phone. Some of the dancers weren't the sharpest tools in the shed, but he figured if he ever knocked and the date was still present he'd simply improvise and abort the mission. No harm, no foul.

When he arrived at room 17, he saw the card in the window. He knocked softly. She answered wearing a sheer pink camisole that did little to hide the shape of her breasts or the darkness of her nipples and patch of hair. "Hi," she said.

He set his duffel bag on the bed.

"What's in the bag?" she asked, with a slight Texas twang.

"Change of clothes," he said. "And a couple of toys."

"Ooh," she cooed. "Can I look?"

She reached for the bag, but he grabbed her hand. He'd have to remember that he'd touched her. He already felt the need to wash his hands. "I'd rather it be a surprise. Don't worry, nothing too kinky, no whips and chains. I'm going to use the head."

Ordinarily he'd ask them to be undressed when he returned. It saved him the time. But she was already practically naked. He looked to the television in the corner with the built-in VCR and DVD player. "Can you turn on the TV? I brought a movie." He unzipped the bag and handed her the tape. "You can put it in, but don't start it yet. I want to be here to watch the whole thing with you."

He pulled out a bottle of wine. "How about a drink?"

She smiled. "I like that idea."

"I'll wash out the glasses while I'm in there. You never know who's been in these rooms."

He brought the bag into the bathroom and set it on the floor, careful not to touch any of the surfaces. He slipped on a pair of latex gloves and removed the bottle of Rohypnol. He slipped a pill into one of the two plastic glasses and poured the wine. Then he checked his reflection in the mirror, shut his eyes, and took several deep breaths, allowing himself to get into character. Just about at that place, he heard voices coming from inside the room. His heart rate spiked. Then he recognized the music—the prelude. The overture. And he felt a rush of adrenaline.

She'd started the tape.

He grabbed the knife from his bag, quickly pulled open the door, and rushed out.

She turned and looked at him with disgust. She was standing near the television, remote in hand. "What the hell is this?" she said. Then her gaze dropped to his hands, and her eyes went wide. She threw the remote control at him and ran for the door, but he ducked the remote and barreled into her, overpowering her. He clasped a hand over her mouth, muting her scream, and put the knife to her throat.

"You're going to do exactly what I say," he said. "It can be a fun night, or the last night of your life. Do we understand each other?"

She nodded.

"Good. I'd hate to have to cut your throat."

The overture had ended.

Time for the show.

CHAPTER 58

Tracy slapped the steering wheel, realizing even before she saw the logo on the grille that the car was not a Lexus. She punched the gas and sped to the intersection, about to cross, when she saw a large yellow sign indicating a dead end. She considered the street more closely. A lone street lamp. Homes on one side of the street. A cyclone fence, the kind with wood slats in the chain link to provide some measure of privacy, on the other. She drove forward, looking between the slats at the back of a stucco strip mall and blue Dumpsters overflowing with cardboard boxes.

And the Lexus.

She'd found the car.

He had to be close; he wouldn't risk walking far, not at that hour.

She made a U-turn, drove back to the intersection, and made a left onto Aurora. The nearest motel was at the corner. She pulled into the lot, jumped down from the cab, and hurried into the office. Her mending collarbone ached from the exertion.

The clerk was behind the counter watching television. An obese man, he had trouble getting up from his chair. "Help you?"

She flashed her shield. "Did a woman come in alone to rent a room in the last hour?"

The man adjusted the bill of a red hat advertising an auto repair shop. "No."

"That woman's life is in danger. If she came in, I need to know."

"No one's come in," the man said, looking suddenly more concerned. "Had a family check in just after midnight, but it's been quiet otherwise. What does she look like?"

Tracy didn't know. She was already looking out the glass doors at the motel across the street. "Thanks," she said, leaving.

She swung the truck around the parking lot and gunned it across the street. A car in the northbound lanes blasted its horn as she shot in front of it, her truck's front left tire bouncing over the curb. Tracy corrected and drove into the motel's parking lot. A sign for the office pointed to the back of the building.

A heavyset woman missing one of her teeth greeted her at the counter. Tracy flashed her shield. "I'm looking for a woman, maybe came in alone about an hour ago. She might have asked for a room at the back of the building—quiet, needed privacy."

"Yeah. A woman came in about forty-five minutes ago." The clerk spoke with an Eastern European accent.

"What room?"

"27."

"I need to get in that room."

The woman grabbed a plastic card key hanging from a hook by a lanyard. "Come, I will show you."

Tracy followed her out of the office. The woman moved well for her size. They quickly climbed the outdoor staircase and turned left at the second-floor landing. Tracy focused on the numbers on the doors: 24, 25, 26. When they reached 27, the woman knocked, probably out of habit, just before Tracy had the chance to stop her.

Tracy took the card and swiped it in the lock. The light glowed red. She flipped the card and tried again. Again the light glowed red.

"Slowly. Slowly." The clerk took the card and swiped it. The sensor glowed green.

"Stand behind the wall," Tracy said. With her one good arm, she shoved the door open, then reached for her gun.

A woman was sitting up in the bed, a sheet tucked under her chin, eyes wide. On the bed beside her was a bag and an assortment of sex toys. "Where is he?"

The woman pointed to the bathroom.

Tracy stood to the side and reached for the door handle. Locked. She banged once on the door. Hollow.

"Police. Open the door."

She heard no movement, so she stepped back and put her boot to the handle, then pulled back behind the wall as the door crashed inward. No shots rang out. There was just a man yelling, "Okay! Okay. Okay."

Tracy spun around the door frame and took aim. The man was cowered in the bathtub, naked, hands raised like a child pleading against an impending beating.

"I'm sorry. I'm sorry."

It wasn't the Cowboy.

———

He'd remade the bed, smoothed the spread of every wrinkle, folded her clothes with care, and placed them on the corner. Then he'd sat down to watch his cartoons.

Do your chores and you can watch your cartoons.

He checked his watch and tapped a cigarette out of a pack. "Do you smoke? It's a disgusting habit. But it does serve certain purposes." Another good line. He'd have to write it down so he wouldn't forget it.

Raina moaned but the gag in her mouth made it unintelligible. Without the Rohpynol, she was more alert, attentive. Now that she was subdued and hog-tied, it certainly had its advantages. It was like ad-libbing during a live performance, and so far, the rush was incredible.

He lit the cigarette, leaned forward, and placed the tip against her upturned sole. She flinched and tensed, tightening the noose. When the rope gripped, her eyes widened. God, he loved it when their eyes widened. It was like seeing deep into a person's soul, exposing them for who they truly were, without the pretenses and the makeup and the costumes—just naked and unadorned. Whores.

She moaned as her skin smoked and reddened. The muscle fibers in her legs twitched. He sensed that this one would be quick. Perhaps too quick. He didn't want that. Maybe he didn't need the cigarettes. He grabbed the rope extending down her spine and pulled it toward her head to provide slack. "Shh," he said. "Relax. Relax. Breathe. There. Better? Now watch the show. This is one of my favorites. You don't want to miss this."

—

Tracy rushed from the room onto the second-floor landing. From here, she had a better view up and down Aurora. The next-closest motel was to the north, halfway down the block, kitty-corner from where she stood. The stairs shook and the iron railing rattled as she hurried down the staircase, vaguely aware of faces staring out from behind curtained windows. She didn't bother getting into her truck but ran straight to the street. She hesitated at the curb to judge the traffic, then darted across, narrowly dodging a truck. The driver looked at her as if she were a lunatic. In the far lane, a car honked loudly and came to an abrupt stop. "Hey, sweetheart," a guy yelled. "Where're you going?" Tracy ran around the hood.

She reached the sidewalk, one arm pumping, the other braced against her body to lessen the pain. She followed the signs for the office and pulled on the glass door. It rattled but didn't open. She swore and banged hard on the glass. Then she noticed a buzzer to the right and a handwritten sign on a three-by-five card.

After 1:00 A.M.
Push Buzzer

She pushed the buzzer and cupped the tinted glass to peer in. A barefoot man in a T-shirt came out from behind a wall, buttoning his shorts. Tracy had her shield pressed to the glass.

He hurried to unlock the door.

Still out of breath, Tracy said, "I'm looking for a woman. She would have come in alone about an hour to an hour and a half ago, and asked to rent a room for an hour or two."

"Hey, I know you; you're that detective that's been on the news. You were hunting for that serial killer, the Cowboy."

"Has a woman been in the last hour or so?"

"I thought they caught that guy."

"You need to listen to me. A woman's life is in danger, and I need to find her. Have you rented a room to a woman—?"

"Yeah. Yeah. A woman came in," the man said, flustered. "Just about an hour ago. Small. Blonde."

"What room?"

"I don't . . . I don't remember the room. I . . . I need to look."

"Do it." Tracy followed him behind a counter cluttered with stacks of paper, sticky notes, and portions of the newspaper. The man fumbled through it. "What room?" Tracy urged.

"I don't . . . I don't . . ." He spun and riffled through more stacks on the counter behind him. "Here. Here it is. 17. She's in 17."

—

The woman's legs had begun to shake. Her muscles looked like taut bowstrings beneath her sweat-slickened, glistening skin as she fought to hold her pose and keep slack in the rope.

It wouldn't be long now.

"Watch this one," he said. "The bird is a chicken hawk, so even though he's not even a tenth of a size of the big rooster, the rooster is still his prey. It's instinct. He can't shut it off. He's programmed to kill the rooster because . . . well, because that's just the way it is."

He lowered the tip of the cigarette to her blistered sole and pressed it firmly to an already-burned area. The woman tensed and groaned, moaning into the gag. Her legs straightened, and this time her body began to spasm. He ground the burning embers deeper, and her spasms became more violent. Gurgling sounds escaped her throat, and a thin red line of blood trickled down her neck from beneath the rope.

She wouldn't make it to the end of the cartoon.

"Do you want to know how it ends?" he asked.

—

Tracy ran back outside as soon as she grabbed the key from the clerk. It was the old-fashioned kind, with teeth. Her gaze followed the doors around the building, coming to rest on a door at the far end, tucked in an alcove beneath an "Exit" sign. That was the room.

She was only vaguely aware of the clerk following her as she ran across the parking lot. From inside the room, the glow of the television flickered behind a curtained window. She pressed an ear to the door and heard music, silently inserted the key, turned the knob, and shoved against the door. It resisted. He'd applied the interior bar lock. Tracy removed her Glock and stepped back. She took aim, fired her Glock, and kicked the door open.

He sat with his back to the wall, a six-inch serrated knife pressed to the young woman's throat. She remained hog-tied, in the process of choking herself.

Tracy took aim. "Drop the knife, Nabil."

The Pink Palace floor manager smiled. "I drop the knife and you'll shoot me."

Tracy's eyes shifted to the clerk, still standing outside, and the man took off running in the direction of the office.

"Let her go, Nabil."

"Can't," he said. "The show's not over. You must always finish the performance."

Tracy's gaze shifted to the television—a Bugs Bunny cartoon. She looked to the woman. Her chest was rising and falling rapidly. Hissing sounds escaped her mouth from behind the gag, which looked to be soaked with saliva. "At least remove the gag and let her breathe."

"How did you find me, Detective? How did you know?" Kotar displayed no hint of concern or panic. His voice was even, calm. He pulled on the rope, providing slack. The woman's breathing slowed.

"A police officer pulled you over. You told him you were putting up posters for a lost cat."

Kotar smiled. "Angus the cat. He said he had a daughter, that she'd be heartbroken if she lost her cat. He even took one of the fliers. What did he do, call the number?"

"He went to the house."

Kotar chuckled. "A Good Samaritan. Wow. Never saw that coming. How come the newspapers and TV stations don't report those kinds of stories? Seems like all they do is criticize the work you do; don't you get tired of it?"

"Yeah, I do," she said, knowing she needed to keep Kotar talking, and calm. She sensed she needed to let him believe this was his show. Glock still on target, she asked, "Can I sit?"

"Not on the bed," he said. "I just made it. Use the chair."

She pulled over the desk chair and placed it in the doorway so she could be seen from the parking lot. Outside, the rain continued to fall.

"It's tough, you know," Kotar said. "You play your part, and the critics just want to pick it apart. That blonde bitch on Channel 8 sure has it out for you."

"Seems that way, doesn't it?"

Tracy flexed her shoulder and grimaced at the pain.

"I read about that," Kotar said. "Your shoulder?"

"Collarbone."

"That's got to hurt."

"More than you'd think for such a small bone." The woman's eyes pleaded with Tracy. "Why don't you let her go, Nabil?"

"I can't. I can't stop."

"You stopped before."

"How do you know that?"

"Because you killed Beth Stinson almost a decade ago."

Kotar smiled. "You're good. You're really good."

"I'm thinking about quitting," she said, wondering why the hell it was taking backup so long to arrive and whether the man had called 911. She looked for an opening to get off a shot.

"Why would you quit?"

"I'm tired of all the bullshit, Nabil. The politics of it all."

"I know the feeling. I quit acting for the same reason. What would you do?"

"Teach school."

"I read that about you. What was it, biology?"

The woman started to choke, gagging. Kotar looked annoyed at the interruption and pulled on the rope again, providing more slack. The woman seemed to catch her breath.

"Chemistry."

"You shouldn't quit. You quit and the assholes win."

"Maybe," she said. "What about you? What would you do if you weren't managing a club?"

"That's easy. I'd be an actor."

"Yeah? Movies?"

"Eventually. I'd do theater again. That's my passion."

"Were you any good?"

"I was. I could really get into character, you know? The directors said I was totally believable."

"What was your favorite role?"

"Too easy again. McMurphy. *One Flew Over the Cuckoo's Nest.*"

"Good role."

"Yeah, I thought that would be the one that really jump-started my career."

"So what happened?" The woman looked to be calming.

"I got screwed. It happens. LA is a toilet. Everything is a scam down there. No money in it unless you make it big. Plus I have to work nights now. Got to pay the bills, right?"

"Right." She glanced out the door but still didn't see her backup. She remembered Santos telling them that some killers played out a scene in their head, and she wondered if Kotar saw this as his big scene. "So now you have to decide something else, Nabil."

"Yeah, what's that?"

"How do you want to be remembered?"

"You placating me, Detective, or just playing to my enormous ego? That's what they say in the books about serial killers. Have you read that? We have enormous egos."

"I wouldn't know anything about that, Nabil. I don't get much time to read. I'm looking at it from a more practical standpoint.

Do you want to walk out of here with a chance to tell your story—maybe become famous, like Bundy?"

Kotar smiled and looked to the television. "How about I tell you when the show's over? It won't be long now."

CHAPTER 59

The police cars and SWAT van finally arrived, swarming the parking lot, officers fanning out across the lot and up to the second level. Other officers were starting to empty the other rooms, whisking frightened-looking guests away from the building. The patrol units' lights painted everything a pulsing blue and red. Tracy stood from the chair and stepped to the door, gun and gaze still fixed on Kotar.

"Tracy Crosswhite, Seattle Homicide," she shouted. "This is my scene. Tell everyone I said to stand down."

"Your big scene, Detective," Kotar said. "I like that."

"I think I'm just the supporting actor, Nabil. You're the lead here." She nodded out the door. "They're all here, or on their way. You'll have all the news media."

As if on cue, she heard the thumping drone of helicopter blades. A spotlight lit up the parking lot. Kotar's eyes shifted to the window. "News helicopter," she said.

Kotar smiled. "Lights. Camera. Action."

"The audience is waiting, Nabil. What kind of performance you going to give them?" She was improvising here, hoping Kotar didn't see a final scene where everyone ended up dead. She didn't think so. She got a sense Kotar wanted the applause and the accolades.

Kotar started to sing under his breath. She didn't recognize the song at first, then it triggered something from her own childhood. Bugs Bunny. He was singing the overture before the cartoons started.

"We know every part by heart," Kotar sang.

"Bugs Bunny," she said.

His eyebrows arched. "You know it?"

"You kidding? Every Saturday morning my sister and I watched together."

"Yeah?" Kotar grew pensive. "I heard about your sister. Sounds like the guy was a real psycho."

"Yeah, he was."

"You shot him."

"He didn't give me a choice, Nabil. This is a whole different situation."

"Is that why you're doing this? Why you care? Because of your sister?"

"Could be," she said. "I've never really stopped to analyze it."

"Too painful?"

"Maybe."

Kotar dropped his gaze, and Tracy had to resist the urge to pull the trigger. She had no doubt she could put a shot in the center of his forehead, but she was worried he would flinch and slice the woman's throat.

Looking up, he said, "You couldn't stop him, you know? What he did. I mean you can't blame yourself for what happened to your sister."

"Easier said than done."

"No," he said, an edge in his voice. "You don't understand."

"Explain it to me, Nabil."

"He had to do it. *We* have to do it. So this isn't your fault either. It's just the way it is. It's the way I am. We're made this way." Kotar looked down at the woman, then back to Tracy. He gestured with his chin. "Your arm getting tired holding up that gun, Detective?"

"My shoulder, actually."

"The lactic acid starts to build in the muscles until eventually they cramp. The only way to relieve the pain is to change positions, to lengthen and stretch the muscles."

"Did you come up with that system yourself?"

"Over time."

"How's your arm?" she asked. "That knife starting to get heavy? What do you say you cut the rope and lower the knife and I'll lower my gun, and we all walk out of here together?"

"And the state sentences me to death."

"What, in twenty years?" She shook her head. "You know how many lawyers will want to represent you just for the notoriety, just for the chance to say their client was the Cowboy?"

"I like that name by the way. Did you come up with that?"

"No, that was my partner. The media ran with it though."

"Kinsington Rowe. Now that's a name." Kotar rested his head back against the wall, suddenly looking spent. "Either way, I'm going to die—now or twenty years from now."

"None of us is getting out of here alive, Nabil."

Kotar chuckled and sat up. "I like that. That's a good line. 'None of us is getting out of here alive.' That's good. Who said that?"

"I don't know," Tracy said.

"Was it in a movie?"

"I don't think so."

"Nobody is getting out of here alive," he repeated, seeming to savor each word.

"But it doesn't have to be today."

"But it doesn't have to be today," he said, his smile broadening. "None of us is getting out of here alive. But it doesn't have to be today." He looked to Tracy, suddenly more animated. "How about you, Detective? You could be a hero. You could get your reputation back—the detective who killed the Cowboy."

"I've had my fifteen minutes of fame, Nabil. It's overrated."

Kotar laughed. "This is like a screenplay, Detective. You're good. You ever do any acting?"

"Me? Scares the crap out of me to get up in front of a bunch of people."

"Oh, no," Kotar said. "That's the rush. That's the thrill of it. It's live. Anything goes. You think someday they'll write a screenplay about us, about this moment?"

"I wouldn't doubt it; writers seem to go for this sort of thing. Hollywood too. Bet they'd want to interview you. Get your recollection."

He was like a kid. "It would be a hell of a scene, wouldn't it? Who do you think would play you in the movie?"

"Me? No idea."

"Charlize Theron," he said.

"I think you're trying to flatter me, Nabil."

"No, really. I can see it. She's tall like you, athletic build. And you're a beautiful woman. You know what Nash used to say about you?"

"I don't think I want to know."

"He said you'd have been a hell of a dancer, that you've got the legs for it."

"That doesn't sound like Nash."

"I left out the crude parts."

"I appreciate that."

"Okay, your turn. Who would play me?"

Tracy had no idea but wanted to play along, still hoping she could get Kotar to see an ending in which they walked out of that room together. "You tell me." She glanced at the woman, eyes now shut, grimacing, legs starting to shake. "It's been a long time since I've been to a movie."

"I'm thinking Rami Malek. He'd have to get in the gym, though, and put on about twenty pounds of muscle."

"I don't know him."

"Really? He was in one of the *Twilight* movies and *Night at the Museum*."

"I missed those."

"You work too hard; you need to find time to relax."

"You've kept me pretty busy. You mind if I sit down again?"

Kotar gestured with his free hand.

Tracy sat. She was running out of things to talk about and sensed, with the cartoon winding down, that she didn't have much time. The blue and red strobes continued to pulse.

"Woody Harrelson would be my first choice, but he's getting too old."

"He'd be good," she agreed. "So what do you say? You ready to walk out of here with me? Live long enough to see your likeness on the big screen?"

CHAPTER 60

Johnny Nolasco pulled his Corvette up onto the sidewalk and quickly got out. News vans lined the curb, photographers shooting. Overhead a news helicopter hovered, the thump of the blades near deafening, the spotlight blinding in its intensity. Chatter spilled from police car radios. Nolasco badged one of several officers on crowd control and shouted over the din of the helicopter, "Whose scene is it?"

The officer pointed to a barrel-chested man barking out orders in the middle of the fray. Nolasco approached and introduced himself.

"Michael Scruggs," the man said. "Seattle SWAT."

"What's the situation, Sergeant?"

"Captain," Scruggs corrected. "And it's one of yours, Tracy Crosswhite. She's got a hostage situation. Man inside the room is holding a woman at knifepoint. She's told us to stand down."

"Get on the radio and tell them to get that news helicopter out of here."

"Already have. Story this big, the TV station will just pay the fine. You want to try, feel free to give it a go."

"What about HNT?" Nolasco asked, referring to the Hostage Negotiation Team.

"They just pulled up. Heading toward the door."

Nolasco made his way through the crowd to the motel room. He stayed well back, but the room was lit up like daytime. Just inside the door, Tracy Crosswhite sat in a chair.

"Detective?" he said.

Tracy did not turn her head. "Yeah, Captain?"

"What do you got?"

"I got a cowboy in here."

Nolasco heard a second voice, a man, shout, "*The* Cowboy."

"I got *the* Cowboy," Tracy said.

Nolasco felt his stomach drop. "HNT is here."

"We're good," she said. "We're just chatting about books and movies."

"You need us to send in anything? Bottled water?"

"Nobody comes in," the man shouted.

"I said we're good, Captain."

—

"Nobody comes in," Kotar repeated, sitting up and adjusting the knife.

The woman moaned.

"Shut up," he said.

"Take it easy," Tracy said. "Nobody's coming in, Nabil. They figure they'll just starve us into submission."

He looked to be calming, though he was sweating profusely. "What's HNT?"

"Hostage Negotiation Team."

"That's some serious shit, huh?"

Tracy looked to the cartoon. She had no idea how much longer the episode would last, but from what she recalled from her childhood and from what she could deduce about the attention span of children, she thought the whole thing was no more than fifteen minutes total.

Kotar caught her gaze. "Just a few more minutes now," he said quietly, perhaps sensing the reality of his predicament. "Don't *you* have training?" he asked.

"For this kind of thing? Not really. I've done crisis intervention, but it's not really the same thing."

"For what it's worth, I think you're doing a pretty good job."

"You know, Nabil, this is one of those things in which the end result really dictates how I did."

"I can see that," he said. Then he got silent again.

"Why do you tie them up?"

"I don't want to talk about that."

"Okay. Why dancers?"

He looked to be contemplating how to answer, or whether to answer at all. Then he said, "She danced."

"Who's that?"

"My mother. She'd leave me alone at night with the cartoons, and if I didn't behave, didn't have the apartment clean, she'd beat me with an electrical cord or tie me to a chair."

"What happened to her?"

Kotar rested his head against the wall. His gaze shifted to the curtain. "Someone strangled her."

"I'm sorry," Tracy said. "Did they ever catch him?"

Kotar nodded. "It was one of the guys she brought home."

Tracy wondered if maybe Beth Stinson hadn't been Kotar's first. "Well, I'm sorry."

"Don't be." Kotar pressed the knife to the woman's throat. Tracy's finger tensed on the trigger, but she made a snap decision not to shoot. Kotar smiled. "Nice self-restraint, Detective."

She was struggling to remain outwardly calm. Her heart raced, and she was getting a strong sense that this was not going to end well. She looked again to the television. "Cut the rope, Nabil. Let's walk out together."

Kotar's gaze also shifted to the TV.

"This is it," Kotar said. "This is the end."

Porky Pig burst through a paper drum onto the television screen. Kotar stuttered with him. "Ba-dee, ba-dee, ba-dee . . . That's all, folks."

And he raised the knife.

CHAPTER 61

Nabil Kotar slashed the rope. The woman's legs dropped as if spring-loaded and hit the floor with a dull thud. Her head fell forward, dangling like she was a rag doll.

Tracy eased the tension on the trigger. A few more millimeters and she'd have put a bullet between Kotar's eyes.

Kotar rolled the woman away from him. She flopped onto her back, ankles and wrists still bound, coughing and wheezing. Kotar set the knife on the carpet and rested his head against the wall, just beneath a "No Smoking" sign. He looked up at Tracy with tired eyes and gave her a smile.

Tracy took her first deep breath since she'd entered the room. "I have to cuff you, Nabil."

He nodded, the smile turning to a resigned frown. "I know."

—

Tracy walked Kotar to the door, his hands cuffed behind his back. The rain had let up, but the darkened pavement retained a sheen that made the parking lot look like the surface of a body of water.

"You ever see *First Blood*?" Kotar asked.

"Sylvester Stallone, right?" It was one of Kins's favorite movies.

"You remember the scene when he walks out with his commander, and all the police cars are there, all the policemen just waiting for a chance to kill him?"

"I'm not going to let that happen, Nabil," she said, suddenly worried this was a suicide scene.

"I was just thinking this is sort of like that."

"Everything is going to go just as we talked about." She shouted out the door. "We're coming out! I need a clear path to a patrol car with the back door open." She looked to Kotar. "Anything else, Nabil? You want me to put the hood of your sweatshirt up?"

He glanced at her, but it was only for a moment before he looked back to the crowd of police officers—uniformed, plainclothes, others dressed in SWAT tactical gear. Kotar grinned. "Are you kidding? I was born to play this scene."

Outside, an officer repeated Tracy's orders. Car engines started, and patrol cars backed up and shot forward, clearing a path across the parking lot to a lone unit, the back door open. Tracy saw SWAT team members lying prone on the second-story landing and the roof, rifles trained on the door. As much as she wanted to believe Nabil Kotar had given up, that he was harmless with his hands cuffed behind his back, a part of her still worried he was living out a movie scene and he didn't have in mind a thought-provoking ending of dramatic irony. She saw him thinking about a dark action-adventure conclusion that didn't end well for either of them.

"Just like we discussed, okay, Nabil? We take it nice and slow. No sudden movements. Let me lead you. We'll walk straight to that car, and I'll help you into the backseat. We good?"

"Yeah, we're good," he said, eyes flicking left and right.

"Coming out," Tracy yelled. She held Kotar by the sleeve of his sweatshirt and guided him out the door.

Nabil took three steps and abruptly stopped. "Wait."

Tracy glanced up at the snipers. "No hurry, Nabil. This is your show."

"How do I look?"

"You look fine. You look good."

The spotlight from the helicopter found them, and she noticed the drops of perspiration trickling down his face. "Nice and steady now," she said. They started again, making their way toward the car. She glanced at him to make sure he wasn't about to panic. Kotar was smiling.

"Hey, what was that line again I liked so much? The one you said in the room."

"None of us is getting out of here alive?"

"Yeah," he said. "That was it." He stopped just short of the patrol unit and looked out over the crowd. Tracy had no doubt that in his mind he was standing on a stage, looking out at the audience. He projected his voice like an actor in a street performance. "None of us is getting out of here alive," he said. "But it doesn't have to be today." Then he turned to her. "How was that?"

"Nailed it," Tracy said. "Fade to black."

She put her hand on the crown of his head and helped him lower into the backseat. When he'd drawn his legs in, she shut the door. Only then did she feel her body relax, the tension start to dissipate. Only then did she realize the magnitude of the response. The parking lot was filled with SPD patrol units and SWAT vans, along with ambulances and a fire truck. Paramedics were hurrying in and out of the motel room, tending to Raina. Overhead, the first news helicopter was joined by two others and a police helicopter. The media was across the street, lights shining brightly.

Johnny Nolasco met Tracy at the police car. "What the hell happened? How did you get yourself in this situation?"

She was in no mood. "By doing my job."

"I put you on desk duty."

Tracy stepped toward him. "Get out of my way, Captain. I have a suspect to book."

"This isn't over," Nolasco said.

They were toe-to-toe, face-to-face. "Yeah," she said. "It is over. Remember you asked me how I thought it was going to end? Not well for you, Captain."

"The evidence I had was solid."

"Tell that to David Bankston's wife and daughter." She pulled open the passenger door, about to slide in, and saw Izak Casterline standing among the other police officers. Casterline gave her a subtle nod. She returned it, slid in, and closed the door. The driver backed up and pulled toward the exit. From the backseat, Nabil Kotar said, "Hey, Detective?"

"Yeah, Nabil."

"I have the first line of the book. You want to hear it?"

"Sure, Nabil."

"'The Cowboy had time to kill.' What do you think?"

Not anymore, she thought. *Thankfully, not anymore.* "I think you'll have plenty of time to work on it."

CHAPTER 62

For days, the capture of Nabil Kotar, the Cowboy, was front-page news, not that Tracy read the stories or watched the reports. As with her ordeal in Cedar Grove, it had been enough that she'd lived it. She had no desire to read about it.

Dan kept her up-to-date, telling her the substance. Reporters couldn't get enough of the story. They were writing about Beth Stinson and the investigation that had led to the wrongful conviction of Wayne Gerhardt; the day Gerhardt stood in a King County courtroom and a judge ordered him set free; and the botched search warrant executed on the home of David Bankston.

Curious about what had motivated Bankston, Tracy had spent an afternoon with Amanda Santos, offering to buy her lunch and give her an apology. She'd been skeptical that a profiler would be of any help, but Santos's profile of the Cowboy had been close to spot-on.

They met downtown, at a hole-in-the-wall Thai restaurant that Tracy and Kins frequented, on Columbia Street beneath the Viaduct. Even dressed down, in jeans and a leather jacket, Santos drew attention. As she sipped green tea from a tiny porcelain cup, she gave her theory on Bankston. "Stalkers want to interact with their love interests. They just don't necessarily know how. In these types of situations, where the person becomes obsessed not with a person they know, but with a fantasy, they're often too intimidated to approach the person or to interact with them. To David Bankston, you were more than Tracy Crosswhite. You were the persona portrayed in the news. So he tried to find a way to be a part of that person's life."

"That's why he had all the newspaper articles and notes on the investigation."

Santos lowered her cup to the retro Formica table. In the open and cramped kitchen behind them, a woman barked orders, and pots and pans clanged as steam wafted up into the faces of two cooks moving as if choreographed. "If I had to venture a guess, I'd say he saw the Cowboy as competition for your attention and thought he could get close to you by solving the crime, or at least becoming a part of it. That's why he went to the crime scenes and stood in the crowd taking pictures. It put him close to you."

"So why leave me the noose at the shooting range?"

"When you didn't reciprocate his attention, at least the attention he believed he was devoting to you, he became more desperate, and more bold. Again, I would suspect he left the noose intending for you to find his DNA. He did, after all, have police training. He had to know it was a distinct possibility. It was a way of drawing you to him. But the evening he saw you and your boyfriend, his obsession changed. In his mind you'd betrayed him, after everything that he was doing for you. Stalkers are largely an annoyance, until obsessive love becomes obsessive hate."

"So he decided to kill me and make it look like I was another of the Cowboy's victims?"

"That appears to be the case."

"What about the polygraph? How do you explain that?"

"I think," she said, "that he was so familiar with all the intimate details of the killings that he had, in effect, convinced himself he knew the women. But don't quote me on that. This isn't an exact science, and this kind of speculation is exactly the type of thing that gives us profilers a bad reputation." Santos smiled and picked up her tea.

Tracy laughed. "Yeah, sorry about that."

"Buy me lunch and we'll call it good."

—

The press had also dug up old articles and the police file on the death of Nabil Kotar's mother in a skid-row apartment in Boston. The man convicted of killing her, a traveling salesman, had died in prison two years after his sentencing. Oddly, despite Nabil Kotar's willingness to talk in great detail about the five dancers, he refused to speak of his mother's death or to admit to killing her. Santos said that in Kotar's mind, he hadn't killed his mother, just as he hadn't killed any of the five women. To him, they'd killed themselves, with the lifestyle choices they'd made. Kotar told Santos that he loved his mother, and he spoke of her with affection, but he also hated the woman who brought men home at night, drunk and smelling of cigarettes. That was the woman he wanted dead, perhaps think-ing in some demented way that her death would somehow free his mother.

There was even a story on Walter Gipson, the hapless teacher Faz called "the unluckiest son of a bitch in the world." Gipson told a reporter that he finally felt vindicated enough to walk out of his apartment without averting his eyes, but he blamed SPD for the breakup of his family and for otherwise ruining his life. Gipson's wife had not returned, and his old school district had not rein-stated his job.

"Hell of a price to pay just to get laid," Kins said.

Tracy didn't have a lot of sympathy for anyone who cheated on their spouse. "That's what you get when you decide to join the idiot club," she said.

The story that had not been told was how Tracy Crosswhite ended up in the motel room with Nabil Kotar. The brass had put a gag order on her—not that she had any intention of speaking to the press about it—and for once the story didn't leak. In a private meeting with Chief Clarridge, she told him she'd never been fully convinced David Bankston was the Cowboy, and that when Izak Casterline brought her his suspicion that a routine traffic stop had not been routine, she agreed to meet him. Turned out, she told Clarridge, Casterline's suspicion was correct. Clarridge, who was on thin ice, wasn't about to look a gift horse in the mouth or draw any negative attention to what was now being feted in the media as dogged police work.

—

Three weeks after the standoff in the motel room, Tracy waited next door to the SPD press conference room with Sandy Clarridge, Stephen Martinez, Andrew Laub, and Billy Williams. They were all decked out in their dress blues. Johnny Nolasco was not among them. He'd been told by Clarridge to sit this one out. Not that Nolasco had a lot of free time to be attending news conferences, not with OPA looking into the Beth Stinson investigation and rumors circulating that they intended to open other Nolasco and Hattie cases. They were also investigating Nolasco's ill-fated raid on David Bankston's home. Tracy had no illusions, however, that she was rid of Johnny Nolasco. The man was like a cat. Not to offend cats everywhere, but she knew he had at least several more lives to torment her.

Clarridge said, "Did anyone discuss the format with you for this morning, Detective Crosswhite?"

"Yes, sir. Billy went over it with me."

"Stick to the format. Be brief with your answers."

Tracy smiled. "That won't be a problem, sir."

Bennett Lee opened the door and leaned in. "We're ready for you." Clarridge led the group out. As Tracy walked past, Lee said, "Packed house."

The stage with the podium was elevated slightly above the standing-room-only crowd. The front rows had been reserved for the families of Nabil Kotar's victims—mothers and fathers, grandparents and siblings. Shirley and Lawrence Berkman were there. Bradley Taggart was not. Dan sat in the second row in his gray pin-striped suit, looking up at Tracy like a high school senior with his secret girlfriend, trying to suppress a smile. Wayne Gerhardt sat beside him.

Media filled the rows behind the families and stood along the back wall. Tracy looked for Maria Vanpelt, but didn't see her. She'd heard through the grapevine that Vanpelt had been replaced on *KRIX Undercover*.

Along the west wall stood the dozen members of the Cowboy Task Force—Kins, Faz, Del, and Ron Mayweather among them. Tracy had insisted on their presence. Kins, looking tan and healthy from two weeks in Mexico, gave her a nod and a smile.

Clarridge stepped to the podium and gestured for Tracy to stand beside him. Cameras whirred and flashed. Clarridge kept his comments brief, applauding Tracy's courage, fortitude, judgment, and negotiation skills. Then he said, "Ordinarily we bestow the Medal of Valor upon deserving officers at our annual awards ceremony in October. In this instance, we saw no reason to wait."

Bennett Lee handed him a jewelry-size box. Clarridge opened it and displayed the medal and ribbon to the media before removing it and pinning it to Tracy's uniform. He gripped Tracy's right hand, and together they turned to the cameras. Tracy tried her best to smile, but the attention made her uncomfortable. After a sufficient time for photographs, Clarridge released his grip and ceded Tracy the podium. This was the moment she'd really not been looking forward to. She cleared her throat, which still bothered her at times, especially in moments like this when her mouth was dry. Her prepared statement rested on the podium, but she didn't look down. She knew what she intended to say. "This medal belongs to all those officers standing along the wall who made up the Cowboy Task Force. I wouldn't be standing here without their dedication and their professionalism." She looked at the victims' families. "Had it not been for their unwavering pursuit of the Cowboy, we would not have found justice for Nicole Hansen, Angela Schreiber, Veronica Watson, and Gabrielle Lizotte, or for Beth Stinson." She looked to the members of the task force and held up the box. "This is your medal."

She stepped back, and Bennett Lee stepped to the podium. "Are there questions for Detective Crosswhite?"

The first question came from a *Seattle Times* reporter. "Detective Crosswhite, there are rumors you might retire. Can you comment on those rumors?"

Tracy gave the question a moment before looking again to the families of Nabil Kotar's victims. She knew what it felt like to have your entire world turned upside down because of one deranged psychopath. She knew the persistent ache and the helpless, nagging guilt that maybe you could have done something to prevent it. She knew the hole they would try to, but never, fill.

And she knew she was not prepared to abandon them.

She looked to Dan, who must have read her mind, because he was grinning. He gave her a simple knowing nod.

"For now, I'm a cop," she said. "This is what I do."

The men and women at the back of the room began to applaud, slow at first, then with greater volume and enthusiasm. Faz raised a hand as if raising a glass, and the others followed his lead.

EPILOGUE

Tracy shot over the top of the wooden station, a twenty-five-yard distance to where her target hung, riddled with holes. She'd been shooting for the better part of an hour. Because of her collarbone, she hadn't been able to shoot for a month, and she'd been itching to get back to the range. She lowered her weapon, slid it back into her holster, and removed the earmuffs, about to retrieve her target, when someone spoke to her.

"Not bad."

Katie Pryor stood off to the side with another female officer, both watching Tracy. They each held boxes of ammunition and targets. Pryor also held a roll of blue tape.

"I heard you passed your qualifying test," Tracy said.

"Thanks to you," Pryor said, then she turned to make introductions. "This is Officer Theresa Goetz. She's having a little bit of trouble with her shot."

"You're in good hands," Tracy said to Goetz.

Pryor smiled. "She asked what the blue tape was for. I told her she'd find out."

Tracy returned the grin. "Yes, you will."

"Can you stay, offer a little advice?" Pryor asked.

"It sounds like you've got it covered," Tracy said. "And I need to get home. My boyfriend called. He's making dinner for me tonight. Pasta, which means we have twelve minutes before the noodles are ready."

ACKNOWLEDGMENTS

A s always, there are many to thank.
I am not a police officer, and I have never served in law
enforcement or worked in the criminal justice system. These Tracy
Crosswhite novels would not exist without the generosity of so
many people who give me their time with the hope I just might get
a few things right. I used their expertise for *Murder One*, for *My
Sister's Grave*, for this novel, and for the third book in this series.
Therefore, I'm going to thank them all again. The people acknowledged are experts in their fields. I am not. Any mistakes or errors
are mine, and mine alone.

So thank you to Kathy Taylor, forensic anthropologist at the
King County Medical Examiner's Office, for all of her insight on
the excavation of a decades-old grave site in wooded, hilly terrain.
Thank you also to Kristopher Kern, forensic scientist and Crime
Scene Response Team manager with the Washington State Patrol,
for his similar but distinct expertise.

Thank you to Jeni Gregory, PhD, LICSW, supervisor of the
Western Regional Medical Command's Care Provider Support
Program at Joint Base Lewis-McChord. Thank you also to David
Embrey, PhD, PT, research program coordinator in the Good

Samaritan Children's Therapy Unit's Movement Laboratory. David approached me at the Pacific Northwest Writers Association conference several years ago when I indicated to an audience a general idea for my next novel. He put me in touch with Jeni Gregory. They provided fascinating insight into the minds of sociopaths and psychopaths, which is truly frightening.

I've also been fortunate to meet many wonderful people in the police community who are always generous with their time and their knowledge. I could not have written this book without the assistance of Detective Jennifer Southworth, Violent Crimes Section, Seattle Police Department. Jennifer first helped me when she was working for the CSI Unit. She was since promoted to Homicide and became an inspiration for this novel. My thanks also to Detective Scott Thompson, King County Sheriff's Office, Major Crimes Unit. Scott's willingness to always help me by sharing his knowledge, or by putting me in touch with others who could provide the information I was looking for, has been invaluable. One of those individuals he put me in touch with was Tom Jensen, who some say was the last man standing on the Green River Task Force, which, after twenty years of dedication, obtained the evidence to convict Gary Ridgway.

Thanks also to Kelly Rosa, supervisor of the Violent Crimes Unit, King County Prosecuting Attorney's Office, and lifelong friend. Kelly has helped me with just about every novel I've written, and she promotes them like crazy.

Thank you also to Sue Rahr, former King County sheriff and now the executive director of the Washington State Criminal Justice Training Commission—the police academy. I didn't know it when I wrote the novel, but Tracy also has a bit of Sue in her—she's tough and determined, with a sense of humor. Thanks for taking the time to give insight into your career in what remains a largely male-dominated profession. I want to thank Detective Dana Duffy, Violent Crimes Section, Seattle Police Department, for the same reason. Years ago Detective Duffy took the time to speak with me candidly, not only about her career and her job but to provide necessary perspective.

I do a lot of written research as well and usually don't list it, but I want to take the time to identify just a few of the books, manuals, and articles I found helpful:

Tracker: Hunting Down Serial Killers, by Dr. Maurice Godwin and Fred Rosen

Chasing the Devil: My Twenty-Year Quest to Capture the Green River Killer, by Sheriff David Reichert

Tracking Serial Killers, by Diane Yancey

The Psychology of Serial Killer Investigations: The Grisly Business Unit, by Robert D. Keppel and William J. Birnes

Serial Murder: Multi-Disciplinary Perspectives for Investigators, Behavioral Analysis Unit, National Center for the Analysis of Violent Crime

Multi-Agency Investigative Team Manual, United States Department of Justice, National Institute of Justice

Thank you to super-agent Meg Ruley, a fellow Aquarian, and her team at the Jane Rotrosen Agency, especially Rebecca Scherer and Michael Conroy, two cold readers who are tough to get any mistakes or inconsistencies past. Ms. Meg, as I like to call her, just keeps working wonders for me. I'm grateful to have been one of her writers for more than a decade, and she always makes me feel like I'm her number-one priority. You are, simply, one of the very best people I have had the pleasure of getting to know. I couldn't do it without you. Now let's learn and play cribbage!

Thanks to Thomas & Mercer! You believed in *My Sister's Grave* and made it an Amazon number-one bestseller. Your enthusiasm for *Her Final Breath* has been just as spectacular. Special thanks to Jeff Belle, vice president of Amazon Publishing; Charlotte

Herscher, editor; Kjersti Egerdahl, acquisitions editor; Jacque Ben-Zekry, marketing manager; Tiffany Pokorny, author relations manager; Sean Baker, production manager; and Gracie Doyle, my fabulous publicist.

A special thanks also to Alan Turkus, editorial director. Your vision for Tracy and your insights have been spot-on, and I am deeply grateful for the time you take to answer my questions and provide guidance. If I missed anyone else at Amazon Publishing, you know you have my thanks.

Thanks to Tami Taylor, who runs my website and does a fantastic job. Thanks to Sean McVeigh at 425 Media, a guru with social media who patiently tutors me. Thanks to the cold readers who labor through my early drafts and help make my manuscripts better. Thanks to Pam Binder and the Pacific Northwest Writers Association for their tremendous support of my work.

Mostly, thank you, loyal readers who e-mail me to tell me how much you enjoy my books and await the next. You are the reason I keep looking for the next great story.

I've dedicated this book to the men and women in law enforcement. I always invite people to step into these police officers' shoes and spend a week dealing with the things they deal with on a daily basis. An interviewer once asked me if writers had an obligation to sanitize crime novels. I don't know if we do or don't. What I can say is that a crime novel, even the most graphic, can never capture the brutality and horror of an actual violent crime, no matter how well written. Yet these men and women see it far too often and willingly immerse themselves in investigations so that the families of crime victims can hopefully find justice, if not closure. The men and women I've met have all been dedicated public servants paid far too little for a job of such importance. We need to be slower to criticize and quicker to thank them for their service. I'm glad you're out there for me and my family.

Finally, I have a new mantra of gratitude I try to express every day: "I have a great wife. I have great kids. I have a great life." Yes, it's corny, but it works. Cristina is my rock, my anchor, my soul mate, and the love of my life. Joe and Catherine—yes, I talk about you a lot, but only because I am so very proud. Wow. You both just keep amazing me.

As my father-in-law, Dr. Bob, likes to say, "When ninety-five percent of your life is good, don't sweat the other five percent." Smart man. Wisdom to live by.

Last but not least, to my mother, Patricia Dugoni: You have always been an inspiration to me and the toughest woman I've ever known, even at eighty-two. God broke the mold for tough Irish ladies after he made you. I think of you and thank you every day for the wonderful childhood you provided for all of us. Did I mention I'm one of ten? Yes, all from the same mother. Yes, she is remarkable.

Say it fast with me now, without any commas: AileenSusie-BillieBonnieBobbyJoAnnTommyLaurenceSeanMichael. Love you guys.

ABOUT THE AUTHOR

Robert Dugoni is the critically acclaimed author of eight bestselling thrillers. His very first novel, *The Jury Master*, made the *New York Times* bestseller list, launching the popular David Sloane series, which includes *Wrongful Death*, *Bodily Harm*, *Murder One*, and *The Conviction*. Dugoni is also the author of the novel *Damage Control*, as well as the nonfiction exposé *The Cyanide Canary*. His books have been likened to those of Scott Turow and Nelson DeMille, and he has been hailed as "the undisputed king of the legal thriller" and the "heir to Grisham's literary throne." The first book in the Tracy Crosswhite series, *My Sister's Grave*, became a number-one bestseller on Amazon, and a *New York Times* and *Wall Street Journal* bestseller, and was named one of the best thrillers of 2014 by both *Library Journal* and *Suspense Magazine*. Visit his website at www.robertdugoni.com, e-mail him at bob@robertdugoni.com, and follow him on Twitter @robertdugoni and on Facebook at www.facebook.com/AuthorRobertDugoni.